Long Ever Ago

By RUPERT HUGHES

AUTHOR OF

"We Can't Have Everything,"
"Clipped Wings," Etc.

WILDSIDE PRESS

www.wildsidepress.com

TO

THE FIGHTING 69TH
NOW THE 165TH INFANTRY
WITH HOMAGE AND WITH ENVY
"THE 69TH IN FRANCE AND I NOT WITH THEM!"

THE MURPHY THAT MADE AMERICA

"IF it werrunt for us Murphys there'd be no United Shtates here whativer."

Mrs. Morahan had a decided leaning toward politeness, but this was too much, especially as she had no Murphy blood in her. She protested:

"Ah, what talk have you now, Mr. Murphy? It's Coloombus you're thinkin' of, belike."

"Coloombus me eye! It's the thruth I'm givin' you, did you but know it when you seen it," the old man howled. "A Murphy saved this counthry once and a Murphy will save it again if need be."

Mrs. Morahan laughed the braggart to scorn.

"A Murphy saved this country! We see ducks!" She brought down on her not only an old man's wrath, but an old man's argument. She was calling on her cousin Ellen, who had married a Murphy and had more children than luck of the match. It was a "long family" and never short of disaster in one place or other. Ellen had a plenty to say to her cousin Delia, but the old man kept breaking in on the pleasant exchange the women were making of their sorrows and the sorry romances of their children.

Mrs. Murphy wanted to discuss especially her boy Thady's infatuation for Minnie O'Fee, a high-headed, cool-souled, laughing, railing thing, and very crool to Thady, who was meek and solemn with hardly a laugh in him, one of those unusual creatures, a frightenable Irishman.

"That O'Fee gerl is what they call the icy Irish," Mrs. Murphy was saying, "and thinks herself too good for my poor Thady, who has a heart cookin' in him that's that warrum you would think it was a sod of turf was under it."

It was this that had started the old man from his apparent sleep.

"An O'Fee puttin' herself above a Murphy, did you say?" he croaked.

Mrs. Murphy tried to keep him out by a mild disclaimer: "It's not so much that she puts the O'Fees higher, pa, but that she puts us Murphys lower. But, as I'm tellin' you, Delia—"

"Who is it puts the Murphys down?" the old man shrilled. "Bring her here and I'll tell her who the Murphys are."

"Yes, pa, sure and I will that. And, Delia, what I stairted to say was—"

"What counthry did the O'Fees iver save, will you tell me that?" Terence demanded. Then he laid claim to the rescue of the country from destruction, and Mrs. Morahan, who had never heard the story, brought his wrath about her by her skepticism.

Mrs. Murphy rescued her from the old man's one story by beckoning her out into the kitchen. And there they found the boy Thady slumped in a chair and absent-mindedly peeling potatoes. His thoughts were so far away that he had cut his thumb and did not know it.

His mother ran to him, crying: "Is it a beet that pitatie

is? I don't know. No, it is not. It's himself he's after parin'. Och, boy dear! what's on you at all?"

Thady, startled back to earth, stared at his mother, at her guest, then at his thumb, the while a rush of scarlet ran up his peppery face into his burnt-clay hair.

His mother fussed about for a rag, dragged him to the faucet, washed his thumb, and put a large nightcap on it, scolding him lovingly.

"I'm sorry, ma," he said, "but I fell to thinkin'."

"Which of the two was you thinkin' of, the gerl or the rigiment?"

"The two of them, ma."

Mrs. Morahan gazed at him so woefully that he turned to her for sympathy.

"You see, Mrs. Morahan, ma won't let me go to the war with the Sixty-nint' like I want to. I'm not twenty-wan yet and I had to have her consint and I'm over young for to be drafted. And now the Sixty-nint' has gone to France, and I not wit' them. The Sixty-nint' has gone to France and I not wit' them!"

That thought kept keening through his soul like the incessant refrain of the mourning women at a wake.

Mrs. Morahan understood the boy's sorrow, but she understood his mother's sorrow better, for she had three sons of her own gone or going across the long water. She shook her head bewilderingly between the two sympathies.

Mrs. Murphy spoke in: "He's needed here at home. And I'm not like some of these mothers that sinds their lads off and cries aisy and comfortable and gits used to it. I cannot give Thady up. Besides, he's not able for going, he fallin' off the thruck he dhrove and the harse dancin' on him only lasht week. And how would he be goin' away to wars and lavin' his bit of a colleen dhu to mourn for 'um?"

"My colleen! mourn me! Divil a much she'd that. She that won't look at me for not havin' a uniform on."

"And if you had one on it's little seein' she'd see of you, for wouldn't you be off to France this instant minyute? That you would! And she a Prodestan', of all things."

"No!" gasped Mrs. Morahan. "It's onpossible." She considered, and gasped again: "'Tis true the O'Fees are Protestants. Oh, Thady, and are there not nice gerls enough to be had without goin' among the haythen?"

Thady writhed in his withes. "I'll give her up if ma will let me go to the war."

His mother laughed in her security. "It's much you would give up, you that's just after sayin' she won't look at you."

This hurt him so cruelly that Mrs. Morahan interceded for him.

"Be aisy with him for a while just. He'll grow past that gerl and he'll forget the war when he gets to earnin' the big money on his nice high truck again. Sure, he is as ilegant a truck-driver as iver I seen."

Thady was inconsolable under a burden of humiliations. His wild young heart flung from battle-zest to love-longing, and he was denied comfort in either quarter.

Mrs. Murphy was used to his moping. She turned to Mrs. Morahan with a cordial, "Let you sit down and take the weight off your feet while I wet you a dish of tay."

Mrs. Morahan looked at the kitchen clock, said that she ought to be gone, and sat down.

"That clock is fast, if any," said Mrs. Murphy, answering her look.

She was just rattling in the tea-caddy when a fierce pounding on the floor and the shrill voice of the old man shook the air.

THE MURPHY THAT MADE AMERICA

"Is it murtherin' the old one some one is, within in there?" gasped Mrs. Morahan.

"Och, blathers, it's his tay he wants, and you to listen to him talk. There'll be no kapin' him quite without you sit by him a while, the divil blisther him for an old nuisance!"

"Ah! sure! and it's me will listen to the child," said Mrs. Morahan.

The two women returned to the parlor where Terence sat in his daughter-in-law's house as if it were his own throne-room. She put a cup of tea in the hand he sent forth gropingly and shook her head over him in doleful patience.

The worst of all Ellen's miseries was the eternal presence of her husband's sickly father in the little flat they had. Old Terence was a "dark" man, being blind; and irritable, being old. He had also been irritable when he was young.

All day he filled the best window, though he could see nothing; he said he liked to "feel the view." He could feel the meals as well; his stomach was like a clock in him. And when food-time arrived he would go whacking to the dining-room and set him down at table whether the food was prompt or not, to the great annoyance of Mrs. Murphy, who had often good reasons enough for the lateness of her meals, one of them being the difficulty of getting food and fuel, and two of them latterly the bad legs she had on her.

Terence fussed over his meals as if he had earned them, as if it mattered much what he worried with his old chops. He had a high, quavering voice like a bagpipe with the wind failing in it. And his daughter-in-law hated him tenderly, but treated him with loving severity.

Mrs. Morahan had hoped to gulp her tea, exchange a

bit of weather complaint, and get home to her own supper, but as soon as Terence had wet his whistle with the first gulp of tea he returned to the story she had fled from before.

"Mrs. Morahan, ma'am kindly, did I hear you aright when you misdoubted a Murphy savin' this counthry?"

Mrs. Morahan could be stubborn at bay. She answered, stoutly, "If so he did, it's me has never heard of it."

"Then it's time you did."

"Another time, Mr. Murphy. I must be shankin' along."

Thady's sad face was suddenly aglow as if some one had stuck a candle in it.

"Oh, Mrs. Morahan dear, and if you've never heard grandpa tell how a Murphy saved the country, don't you lose no more time. Tell her, grandpa. I'll get the map."

Ellen angrily motioned the boy to sit still, but he hurried over to a shelf where there was an old chart of New York State. He hastened back with it to his grandfather's side and spread the map open across the old man's old crutchy legs.

Terence patted his shoulder with a hand like a frayed whisk-broom, and said, "He has the soul of a soldier, and we rade the newspapers thegither. Don't we, boyo?"

Thady fairly glistened with pride as he answered, "That we do! So listen now, Mrs. Morahan; ma, do you listen now!"

"Listen?" Ellen groaned. "And who is it but me has heard it this twenty times twenty-odd! Sure, I could tell it backward."

"And that's the way you understand it," Terence snapped. "Hould yer whist and hear it again. 'Tis that simple it can be made plain to a woman itself if Mrs. Morahan will have the sinse and raison to kape quite and pay attintion."

6

THE MURPHY THAT MADE AMERICA

There was no resisting so helpless a tyrant. Ellen with a grimace picked up her knitting and raced her needles at top speed. Delia sat by her watching the stitches she made.

Delia had a woman s nose for news in the sewing line, but she paid no more heed to Terence's lecture than was necessary to make him think that she was spellbound by his little family epic. It was a trick she had learned in self-defense from her husband's occasional chatter on uninteresting topics. Her ear and her tongue conspired to echo a few words here and there, leaving her mind free for its own wanderings.

Terence, like Thady, had the warrior spirit. It blazed in his rickety frame. He had lost his eyes at Omdurman as an old soldier in the British armies. A wounded Mahdist calling for water had knifed him in the face when he bent to empty his canteen in the gaping beard. Even Thady did not like to hear Terence tell what he did to the heathen.

But the lad loved to hear him tell of his campaigns, and the two of them followed the European War day by day, Thady reading the newspapers and Terence furnishing the comments.

Thady wrought devastation in the names of French, Belgian, and Russian towns, but Terence never knew the difference.

When horrors failed in Europe, the boy would read pages from a bleary copy of Creasy's *Fifteen Decisive Battles of the World*. He had bought it for ten cents from a pile of books in front of a second-hand book-store, and it had furnished them with many a thrilling hour during Thady's convalescence from his accident. When they found that among the fifteen battles was one of those celebrated in the Murphy family traditions there was no end to their excitement.

And now the both of them—the veteran too weak to
fight and the lad not yet permitted to go—approached the
wonderful narrative with religious awe while the two
women made signs and exchanged silent lip-language over
Ellen's knitting.

Terence began by orienting himself on the map. "Put
me finger on the Hoodson River, there's the biddable boy."

Thady lifted the bony pointer to the line. The old
man cracked his regular joke:

"I can feel the wet of it."

Thady laughed and repeated it to Mrs. Morahan,
"Grandpa says he can feel the wet of it."

"He can feel the wet of it," said Mrs. Morahan, vaguely,
not knowing enough to laugh. Terence and Thady
waited eagerly, then subsided into despair of women.

"Now, Mrs. Morahan," Terence began, "and did you
ever hear of Saratogy?"

"Of Saratogy? Where the pitaties come from?" said
Mrs. Morahan. "Yes, but I do not care for them. I'd
liefer be eating a pack of cards. But they tell me the
harse-races there is grand. Himself, Michael, did nearly
win some money there one time, but only for the harse
bein' scratched, he said—how badly scratched, I disre-
member, but—"

"Shoo-whist, woman!" cried Terence. "The Saratogy
I'm pointin' at is the spot where the fate of this counthry
was settled by a Murphy."

"Well to goodness!" Mrs. Morahan gasped, politely.

It was Schenectady he was pointing at, and not Sara-
toga, but Mrs. Morahan was not looking, and Thady did
not want to hurt his feelings by correcting him. Terence
proceeded with grandeur.

"Forby I'm not a direct descindant of this Timothy
Murphy, glory be, him havin' married a Prodestan'—"

8

THE MURPHY THAT MADE AMERICA

"Married a Prodestan'!" said Mrs. Morahan, and was startled by her own words, enough to repeat them. "Married a Prodestan'! A Murphy? Why, Thady, what at all now! It's in the blood belike."

"He married two of thim, in fact," said Terence, "though not at the one time; yet the Murphys was always the grand gluttons for throuble."

"Gluttons for trouble," said Mrs. Morahan.

"However, the way I come by the histhry of it was not from the lips of Timothy Murphy, he being dead fifty years and better before I let me first keen on this earth."

"Your first keen on this earth," said Mrs. Morahan.

"My Gawd! the echo in this room would bet the worruld," Terence growled, then went on: "He had a letther written—not be his own hand—wrote for him, it was, and was sint home to Ireland and cherished be his people. And I seen it with these two hands, long after, where it told the great man he was held to be here in the America he saved. For, being Irish, he could save anny counthry but his own."

"Any country but his own," said Mrs. Morahan.

This deadly reiteration provoked Terence to a fierce protest. "Stop bouncin' me words back on me! And if Ellen does not quit clickin' thim nadles thegither I'll ate them." He fell to gnashing his gums dreadfully.

Ellen put her knitting away with a sigh, looking at it regretfully as a man looks at a forbidden drink.

Terence growled a bit softer. "Of all the n'ises a woman makes, I love best to hear her silence." Then he pressed on with the doleful drudgery of a man trying to tell a woman a long story. "Might I be let have a minyute to say me say out?"

A "Go on, for the love of mercy!" from his daughter-in-law.

9

LONG EVER AGO

"It was in the old ancient times when this counthry was like Ireland for bein' in the power of the Sassenachs, bad scran to them, that the American insurriction arose, Jarge Washin'ton was fatherin' this counthry and ladin' a flock of scared sheep around tryin' would the dust of their heels choke the roarin' old British line to death.

"Things wint from worst to worser for the Colonials and in siventeen siventy-siven the time seemed ripe for a masther-sthroke on the part of the British. Bould Gineral Boorgoyne gethered a worruld of throops in Canady for to come pilin' down upon top of the Colonies, while ould Gineral Clinton was to poosh up from below to jine hands with him.

"It was the Hoodson River they were afther choosin' for their stradegy, the same river you would see rollin' down along beyant thim buildings if it werrunt for the buildings. Could the English lay hould on the len'th of that river, they would be splittin' the counthry in two parts and privintin' anny union. It was like somebody would hould the stairway in this house so's nobody could go up or down or in or out."

"Up or down or in or out," Mrs. Morahan murmured, before she could stop herself.

Terence pretended not to hear.

"'Twas a dark hour for liberty, and I mind what the boy Thady here is afther r'adin' to me out of Crazy's *Histhry of the Decissuf Battles*—the verra words I remimber. 'The war,' says he, 'was comminced in inickity and folly and it was concluded in disasther and shame. Nor can anny milithry evint be said to have ixercised more impartant infloonce on the future fortunes of mankind than the complate defate of Boorgoyne.'

"Thim is his words, and though he is English, he has the thruth spoken for once.

10

THE MURPHY THAT MADE AMERICA

"Well, here comes old Boorgoyne down through the woods wit' a gang of Sassenachs and Hissians and Indian saviges and Tories, and down to the river he comes. And the Americans can't seem to stop him whativer. Giniral Schuyler was a grand man, but he could not hould an airmy with his one pair of hands. The min of New England was that jealous of New York they would not sind him anny min. So Schuyler kapes droppin' back and hittin' back and side-steppin' and shootin', but he can't stand annywhere for long.

"And up the river comes ould Clinton, capturin' forts and ships and stores and all. And now who's to save America? I'm askin' you, Mrs. Morahan, who's to save America?"

Mrs. Morahan was startled and caught napping among her reveries. She made a foolish hazard:

"Giniral Goorboyne, of course."

"Giniral Boor— Giniral— You poor sinseless faymale woman, he was the inimy!"

"Oh!" said Mrs. Morahan.

The old man came so near to apoplexy that he checked his wild rage lest it end him. He kept silence till he regained control; then he mumbled on, more to finish the sacred chronicle than to instruct the woman:

"Giniral Boorgoyne had one grand giniral with him. Fraser was his name, and he was the life of the airmy. A tall white harse he rode. And on the siventh of October, siventeen siventy-siven, the Americans had backed up till they could go no furtherer wit'out fallin' into the Hoodson River. So they stud fasht. So Giniral Boorgoyne says to Giniral Fraser: 'We'll finish 'um up to-morrow and call it a day. I'll smash in their cinter, and let you work round to their flank, and so bechune the two of us we'll bag the lot of thim!'

"'Well and good, milord Gineral,' says Gineral Fraser; and the next marnin' he sets out to creep round the Yankee flank. But Colonel Morgan was there on the American side, and he's an airly riser, too, an' he's tryin' for to creep round Fraser's flank. And the both of them might have been workin' round aich other's flank till Tib's Eve but only that Boorgoyne would have finished the cinter and turned on Morgan's other flank while Fraser flanked his other flank."

Mrs. Morahan lifted her head and pondered his words. Not that their message interested her, but because she thought she heard a familiar name.

"Did you say Colonel Morahan was there?"

"Morahan me fut!" growled Mr. Murphy. "Morgan! Morgan!"

"'Twould make the story more betther if it was a Morahan was in it," she insisted. "It was Morahan, likely, in the old country, and he changed it like some of these bog-trotters gets rich over here and throws away their O's and Mc's. What became of Colonel Morgahan?"

"He was kilt."

"Oh, the poor man! Perhaps 'twas for the best he was not a true Morahan."

"As I was goin' on to say—"

"But at that he'd be dead by now, annyhow, so he might as well have been a Morahan. One must die."

"Some gets talked to death. And now to get on—"

But even Thady broke in now: "That's what I'm tellin' you, ma. One must die somewhere, so why mightn't I be let die in France?"

"Oh, my boy, have you no heart in you for your mother?" said Mrs. Morahan.

But Terence was furious by now.

"If you've a pocket, put your tongue in it and hoosh

yourself," he protested. "There was no Morahans I iver heard of in the Rivolution. They left it to us Murphys. Well, Morgan, as I'm tellin' you, was tryin' could he flank Fraser, and Fraser, Morgan."

Thady, who understood the frightful crisis, was breathing hard, but the two women exchanged glances of patient pity. They did not even know what a flank was, and they did not care. It did not seem proper, anyway.

"It was a dairk hour for America," Terence shoved on, "and Gineral Binedict Airnold, who aftherwards turned informer, was gallopin' round like mad.

"What put the heart across in him was knowin' nothin' could save the day. America was that desprit there was nothin' could save her but an Irishman. And so Hivin sint wan, as she always doos—to ivery nation but Ireland.

"Colonel Morgan calls up the shairpshootin'est shairp-shooters he had, and he says, s'he, 'Shairpshooters, do you make out that gineral on the tall gray harse?'

"'We doos,' says the shairpshooters.

"'Mark him good,' says Morgan. 'That big gomeral of a gineral is ould Fraser; he's the hope of the inimy, and a grand man entirely. I admire and honor him that much I wouldn't wish him nothin' less than the most comfortable funeral iver injyed by a haro of war. I would not say,' says Morgan, 'pick him off,' says he, 'but if annybody was to pick him off we'd all rest more aisy here on the flanks.'

"So the shairpshooters hand him a wink and a salute and off they go about their business. And Gineral Fraser rode up and down the line, makin' ready for a grand chairge. And is it clare to yous up to there?"

Mrs. Morahan was afraid to perjure herself.

He snorted and continued: "Whin the shairpshooters

13

had their post taken—wan here, wan theyre— I forgot to tell yous that Tim Murphy was among thim and
ginerally rated as the shairpest shooter that iver shot
shairp. And Tim, the grand bouchal, picks out a nice
young three and climbs up intil it, and so, as Giniral
Fraser is ridin', a bullet cuts the crooper off the harse.
He says nothin', but goes on ridin' up and doon. But
phwat's this? Another bullet cuts through the mane of
the harse. The giniral says nothin', but his adjutan'—
which is a kind of private sickerty—says: 'Gineral, I
misdoubt somebody has taken a spite to you. You'd
best drop back. I see a man up a three beyant who keeps
aimin' on you.' In thim days the guns was not the
same to what they are now, but that short of range and
that long of bar'l, if a man missed whin he shot he
could come nare to knockin' his inimy over wit' a
swipe.

"So the adjutan' requests Fraser kindly would he drop
back. But the giniral shook his head and says: 'The
only droppin' back I'll do will be droppin' forward on those
Yankee Doodles. I think it's about time to be thryin' a
little chairge on thim.'

"He opened his mout' for to say the word, and with
that same off he wint from his harse, and flat on the
ground he lay."

"The creature!" sighed Mrs. Morahan. "And was he
hurted?"

"No; he was kilt. And it was Tim Murphy done it,
and not a word a lie in it. And now what say you to our
Timmeen?"

Mrs. Morahan was horrified and said so. "Well, I
think it was somethin' ahful. It must have been the
divil himself—God forgive him—that put such a crime
on Mr. Murphy. And if I was a Murphy, as I am a

Lynch, and on me mother's side a Joyce, sure you'd never have a word out of me about it."

"So manny foolish words out of you and not that one! Not tell it, says you," Terence screamed. "God save your head, you onfortnit thing—Saint Patrick's mother might be proud if Tim Murphy was her younger son. If it were not for that same Tim Murphy and the cliver and inganious lad he was, where would you be now? You'd be mushin' your bare feet through the bog. I misdoubt Michael Morahan would 'a' picked you out of a dry ditch.

"For, believe you me, if Giniral Fraser had utthered that 'Chairge!' he had in his throath, he'd 'a' won that battle, and with it the war. And Timmeen would have been kilt, to say nothin' of all the other Americans, such as was not prisoners taken.

"And so it fell out that whin Fraser fell it was his own min broke, and not ours. Back to their trinches they flew, and the Americans on top of thim. A nice man was Fraser, but he was on the wrong side of the ocean. The Murphys was one too manny for 'um. Tim it was saved the counthry."

"And all by his lone!" Mrs. Morahan murmured, to appease him. That was rather overplaying the compliment. The old man retrenched a whit.

"Well, he had help. In other pairts of the war there was others done good work—for min not Irish. Jarge Washin'ton and Wayne and Greene and the Frinchmin, and of coorse there was no ind of Irishmin, but none so good as Timmeen."

He smacked his lips over the memory, and Mrs. Morahan felt it safe to make a try at escape. She was thinking more of her husband's rage at a late supper than of the belated feast old Terence was making of the cold meats of glory long forgone.

15

LONG EVER AGO

Man-like, Terence suffered acutely at the end of his story of war because Delia, woman-like, had no comment to make on it. He sat wagging his head in defiant pride between contempt for the sex and longing for its approval.

Thady prompted him to finish the recital.

"Tell her what became of Mr. Murphy," he pleaded.

Terence required no urging. "He wint on fightin' Indians and white min. But a year later he lost his head over a gerl, a Prodestan'."

"It's a way the Murphys has," sighed Mrs. Murphy, who was related to the same only by marriage.

"But only for her not bein' of the faith, she was a nice colleen. Barefoot she was, too, whin she run away and clumb on the harse he had. But he bought her silk to be married in. And it was in Schenictady they was married. She lasted him thirty years."

"It's a long while to be married to a Murphy," said Ellen.

Thady winced at this thrust. "Oh, mother jewel, and a Murphy savin' this grand and glorious country! If I could only do like him."

"The Murphys saved it once. Let somebody else save it next."

But Thady was all aquiver with zeal to fight. He rocked in misery and groaned his old refrain.

"It's in danger now, and the Sixty-nint' is across the long water, and I not there."

The door-bell rang, and Ellen answered it. She came in aglow.

"Here's one will console you. Who is it but Miss O'Fee has come to call on you?"

Mrs. Morahan slipped away and went home as Miss O'Fee came in, blushing and giggling.

"Oh, Mrs. Murphy, it was not on Thady, but on you,

I'm calling—te-he! Do I look like a girl would go calling on a young man?"

"You look so to me," said Terence, who could see some things in the dark.

"Sir?" said Miss O'Fee. But Terence did not repeat. He sat listening eagerly to her voice and noting with pride a certain chill in Thady's answers.

The true purpose of her call slipped out when she explained that she was one of a group of the lady managers of a grand ball to be given to build up a Christmas fund to buy gifts for the "Hundred and Sixty-fifth," as the Sixty-ninth had been sacrilegiously rechristened. And she was hinting round for Thady to take her to the dance. But he was either extraordinarily obtuse or he had lost his taste for her sirupy voice.

Perhaps the thing that froze him was her careless confession.

"It's so hard to get men to the dances now. So many have gone away. You don't see many uniforms around town now. Had you noticed it?"

"I had," said Thady, with a certain acridity. "It makes it hard for yous girls that must contint yourself with the l'avin's."

"Why, Thady Murphy, how you talk!" said Miss O'Fee. "I'm sure your mother ought to be mighty glad you're one of the stay-at-homes."

Mrs. Murphy had been mighty glad, but she was not so glad as she had been before Miss O'Fee told her how glad she ought to be. She did not exactly like being what Miss O'Fee thought she ought to be.

So much frost formed upon her hospitality that Miss O'Fee felt the chill and took herself off.

Ellen came back from the door to upbraid her son for his choice of women.

"And is that what you've taken such a kindness to that you'd give the black of your eye for? The back of my hands to the likes of her."

"And mine, too, ma, would you but let me go to the wars. Oh, ma honey, you scald my heart holdin' me here. I'm a Murphy and I belong over there."

"But, Thady, avourneen, how could I sleep nights with the best boy iver graced a mother's name layin' out in thim terrible trinches with no mother to tuck you in of nights?"

Thady's heart was wrung with sorrow for her. and for himself. Old Terence spoke up:

"Now, Ellen woman, where's the Irish in you whativer? Sure and the lad would be as safe in the trinches as here. There's min has wint through many's the wars and come back with niver a scratch taken, and did not Thady here stay home and fall in love with a Prodestan' and fall off the thruck? And would you be sindin' him back to thry for to fall off again? and under a street-cair next time, belike? If so be he don't wither away entirely, he's that sorrow-struck."

Mrs. Murphy offered a desperate bribe.

"No, boy honey, stay at home and marry your Miss O'Fee. She's a right pretty gerl, and you can have a nice flatteen and be happy, maybe, for all she's a Prodestan' I'd risk that aisier than the wars."

She looked up to see the ceiling fall on her for her blasphamiousness. It is hard to dodge a ceiling, and she had a frightful moment waiting for the thunderstone that did not fall. The ceiling held, but she realized what a strain she was putting on heaven as well as on her son.

Thady shook his head: "Miss O'Fee was right to honor the min in uniform, but if she's lonesome now she must look elsewhere, for I'm done with women, ma, and with happiness."

THE MURPHY THAT MADE AMERICA

Poor Ellen twisted her hands together a long moment; then she cried:

"Ah, God break nard fortune! the two of you has me flanked entirely like that poor Gineral Gurboon ye're always maunderin' about. There's naught for a poor woman to do but surrinder. Thady boy, you're more Murphy than I am. I'd give you the veins of my heart for to make you happy, and there's only one way, that's certain sure, so go you and be a soldier, and the lovin' grace of the saints shield you round, O my maneen, O Thady avic."

A great agony of laughter broke from him as he sprang to his feet and crushed his mother to his breast in the sorrowfulest happiness a man can know. He was afraid to tell her how sad he was in his joy, for a word would have set him to blubbering like a child. And now at last he was a man.

He looked it, indeed, when, a few days later, he came home in his uniform. His mother felt a lump of pride in her throat that made her laugh while she wept. But his uniform was of a rain-proof material. Soldiers' uniforms must be, or what stains they would show from women's eyes!

Old Terence had to pass his hands about the boy's shoulders and the buttons and the cap, and the belt and the collar ornaments. It had been a long while since he had so missed the privilege of sight, but he would have seen too much had he got his eyes back, for he would have seen the faces of the boy who gives up his mother and of the mother who tries to fill her eyes with perhaps the last vision of her boy.

He heard their voices trying to cheer each other and he promised Thady that he would take care of Ellen. But his last words were said with a patriarchal gravity.

3   19

LONG EVER AGO

"Remimber, Thady, you're a Murphy. Keep your eye shairp like Timothy done, and if you should find a sizable three, climb it; and if up there you should get a good sight of— Well, it's bad luck to name names, but remimber the world wants savin' and it's callin' for a Murphy."

II

MICHAELEEN! MICHAELAWN!

HE sat at the head of his table with the look of a king trying to overawe his unterrified ministry. He was in his shirt-sleeves, and his two fists, set on end at a wide interval on the. table-cloth, gripped his knife and fork erect like scepter and ball.

From under the thick furze of his eyebrows he glared at the butter as if he would dominate it; at the sugar as if he would turn it to salt. His long and markedly convex upper lip trembled on a shelf of lower lip. But all he said was—and he said it with a quaintly tremulous crackling letter "o":

"I do-ont suppo-ose I could have another coop o' cahffee?"

His wail was lost in a tremendous roaring billow of sound that swept the house and shook everything within or upon the walls. At the same time a quivering gloom, broken with spaces of light, quenched the snow-mottled daylight and veiled his baleful mien.

A train was passing on the elevated road just ferninst the windows. He raised his voice in an angry howl and the train tornado, dwindling rapidly, left his last words unsupported—sticking out in the air like a beam:

"I sa-ay, I don't *suppose* I c'D HAVE another COOP O' CAHFFEE!"

LONG EVER AGO

A fat, pink-faced, gray-eyed woman at the opposite shore of the table answered with unruffled sweetness:

"And why couldn't you, Michael?"

She rose with patient labor, but another woman, also fat but not so rosy-faced, nor so gleaming-eyed, rose, too, and said:

"I'll get it, ma."

Delia pressed her back and answered:

"Set where you are, Katie."

As she would have left her place, a big man in shirt-sleeves reached up a big hand to check her. On the back of his chair was a policeman's coat.

"Ah, leave me get it, ma," he said.

While she resisted the police, two younger men across the table bobbed up. Both were in shirt-sleeves. On the back of one chair was a fireman's coat, on the other a coat with the badge of a building inspector.

Both shouted, "Let me get it."

Now the old lion roared again:

"Set down, the all of yous. Is it an airmy it takes to fetch me me cahffee? It's meself 'll get it!"

He rose so briskly that he flung his chair over with a racket. He might have followed it backward to the floor if "ma" had not steadied him with one hand, picked up the chair with the other, and pressed him back into it with both. Then with a flap of her palms she drove the others back to their chairs as if she were shooing chickens.

"Is it a riot you're startin'? Give me the cup."

She took the cup and moved to the sideboard, where a large tin pot sat squat on a plate.

Myles, the policemen, wailed in his high, shrill voice:

"Well, I think it's a shame that ma has to be cookin' and waitin' on table at her time o' life."

22

MICHAELEEN! MICHAELAWN!

Delia turned so sharply at this that she poured some of the coffee on the floor.

"And what's my time of life?" she demanded.

The big officer hastened to explain. "Oh, you're just in full bloom, darlin', but I mean that pa can afford a cook, and if he can't, us boys can."

This brought a bellow from the lion:

"And can you now! What wonders you are, arrunt you? And haven't I had in a hundred cooks for her? Yis! And would she keep th'm? No!"

Ma set the replenished cup at his plate and retorted:

"And what should I be wantin' with hired help? If they're foreigners, I can't abide them; and if they're Irish, I can't boss them. And I have my health, thank God for all things."

"All the same," the policeman began, "I think—"

But his mother ran on:

"Katie's help enough for her mother—ain't you, Katie?—of course you are! And, besides, your father's not so strahng as he was."

"What! Me not strong! Me that on'y yisterday week—"

With the most delicate irony, Delia suppressed his uproar:

"He has a strahng voice, and a strahng timper to that; but it's the wake stummick he has on him."

This made the lion almost weep:

"Me, that could digist—"

Myles tried again:

"All the same, I think—"

The lion was not afraid of a mere policeman, and he rounded on him as if he would bite the heart out of him:

"Stop thinkin', will ye? Who asked you for to think? If there's anny thinkin' to be done in the family, lave me

23

do it. And lave your ma and me run our home our own way. If you childer don't like it, get homes of your own —and high time it is you was doin' it, instead of makin' your own poor mother carry you in her airms—and at that all the time pickin' on her."

"Picking on their mother, is it? As if they would do such a thing! As if it weren't the blessin' of Heaven that we have them and they can all take dinner with us. They're good children as ever was. What call have you to be—"

The pacifying officer threw his weight into the other pan:

"Now, mother, father means all right; he—"

His reward was a snarl from father:

"I don't need your definse, I thank you. Keep it till it's called for, will you?"

"Why, pa, I was only—"

"You're always onlyin'! Quit onlyin', will you?"

Delia quieted him with a gentle:

"'Ssh! Such talk you keep! The neighbors will be raisin' their hopes to hear bones broken. Let's have a little quite now."

The old lion's ferocity was magically altered to an unimaginably gracious smile. He reached out and pinched her pink cheek scarlet and said:

"Ah, you're still the colleen 'gra!'"

She screeched with comfortable anguish and slapped his hand.

His laughter out-thundered the passing elevated train. He began to brag:

"You boys will never be gettin' wives the like o' this one. Sure, and when the Lord finished her, the patthern got busted on Him."

Moods shot across him like the alternations of an April day, when burst of sun and shroud of dark pursue one another incessantly. The children had long ago learned that, however black the cloud might be on their father's brow, the sun was always behind it.

They paid hardly more attention to his uproar than to the mock growls of a playful dog that makes much threat of fangs, but never fleshes a tooth.

Finally the noontime dinner was finished with sighs of repletion, toothpicks were plied with vigor, and each of the men lighted a cigar of his own.

At length the chairs were pushed back. Hands were slapped on the table in a kind of ritual of farewell. The three sons rose and put on their coats with long semaphore gestures, and their overcoats after that. Ma ran up to each of them to help, arriving just too late to hold the coat and just in time to be caught in the arms as they emerged through the sleeves. She had a kiss from each of them, and the father had a pleasant:

" 'By, pa."

Michael grunted his responses and stood glaring at them. Then his dour face suddenly glowed with a heavenly smile.

"Ah, thim boys is the ones! Finer lads was niver made." He worried his cigar a moment and shifted his cargo to a squeaky patent rocker before the steam radiator. He smoked contentedly for a time. Then his face suffered a look of peculiar sorrow.

His wife and their old-maid daughter cleaned off the table, making a dozen trips to the kitchen. Kate hurried eagerly to the window as she heard an elevated train approaching. She watched it pass, then went to the kitchen heavily.

At length Delia came in, bearing the last stack of dishes and the silver. As she set them down on the sideboard Michael sighed tremendously and shook his head in hopelessness.

Delia went to him. "What at all ails you, Michaelawn?"

He shook his head and moaned. "Nothin', nothin'," and sighed again, more dolefully than before.

Delia fetched a chair from the table and sat near him, in silence, waiting for him to tell her, and knowing that urging would only delay the confession.

It is a strange communion, the long silence of a man and woman who have loved and married and all, and brought children up to their full growth, and who have broken the same bread, sipped the same sup, shared the same news, ill and good, the same skies, roofs, weathers; thought the same thoughts over and over. What need have they for talk? They think forward and backward in the same yoke.

Romance seems to have little of its power left over them, yet their hearts plod along together, although forgotten, as hearts are when they do their work—and are only remembered when some thrill of fear or joy or some ache of regret sets them to leaping.

So Delia sat quiet in inarticulate sympathy with her mate. Now and then the elevated trains would pummel the rails outside and the house would rattle and jingle. This began to annoy Michael. He winced a few times, abruptly sat up in his chair, and snarled at the windows:

"The devil blisther those dom' trains. Sorry the wink of the sleep mother 'll be gettin' and them flounderin' and bangin' and whangin' the night through."

When they were among their children their language was more or less of New York. When they were alone they fell back into their own childhood language as into a pair of old brogues.

Delia answered calmly: "She'll grow used to the n'ise as we have this long while. It's so now that when I'm away I can't sleep for lack of it. To think of you quarrelin' with the ilevated! What at all ails you, Michaelawn? And are you takin' sick, maybe, that you're worryin' yourself to flitters?"

"Sick? No such luck! It's the black thoughts I'm thinkin' when I think of me mother here."

"Oh, it's wanderin' you are; take shame to you for such words. Give thanks to the saints in glory that you have your mother on this side of heaven and on this side of the ocean."

"But I haven't her on this side of the ocean and a storrum is kickin' up the waves and thrashin' the boat around. And she crossin' in winther! And this the worst winther on all the records!—narely as cold as last winther!"

"She'll call anny weather good that brings her to her boy. There's no fair weather whativer could bring my mother home to me—heaven shine on her soul."

Her apron went up to her eyes and she sat chewing a corner of it and rocking silently, while her heart was keening within her. Michael put out his hand and patted her fat arm with the awkward sympathy of a big dog. He tried to make haste past that theme to other memories.

"I'm remimberin' the day I put out from the old counthry and me sayin': 'Don't cry, mother, now, I'll not be long away. I'll be back before I'm gone, and that rich you'll have tay enough for to dhrown you, and a silk dress to milk the cow in, and there'll be a cow to milk, too, and I'll build you a cashle that 'll make Kylemore look like a raided shebeen.' That's what I said thin. And here I am this day."

"Ah! she knew it was but the wild talk of a boy comfortin' his mother."

"And I said I'd buy or fight Ireland free."

"Well, Ireland 'll soon be free."

"From no work of mine."

"Who's done more? You have but to think of the money you've gave and the work you done on the com-mit*tees* on this side the wather."

"But niver a fut have I set on the soil again. Niver an eye have I laid on the hills of Clare."

"You've sint money home regular."

"What's money!"

"It's a help. It's been good food to her, and tay and fresh thatch to the roof. And now, thin, haven't you sint for her out?"

"Yes, it's herself that's crossin' the ocean to me. And what 'll she find when she finds me? It's that that's the black thought. She gave me up when I was a big up-standin' gomeral, and she'll have back an old man with sons older than I was when I left her. Where's the cashle I promised her? She'll find me in this old flat up three flights o' shteps, and I misdoubt she'll ever get this far up till she wins on to heaven."

A train went by along the snow-laden trestles with a thumping tread. Delia raised her voice and lowered it just to fit the crescendo and diminuendo of the noise, as she had learned from long habit.

"Why, Michael, who could be wantin' a finer place than this? Always somethin' passin' the windies. There's no end to the vari'ty."

"It's yourself has called it a b'iler-facthry."

"Oh, well, that was only by the way of findin' fahlt."

"Nobody knows betther than me that it's not good enough for you."

She extracted all the honey there was in the compli-ment and turned rosy.

"Ah, don't be flattherin' me. Usedn't you to know the cabin I came from over Killfenora way? And I'm not forgettin' the little place your people had outside

MICHAELEEN! MICHAELAWN!

Lisdoonvarna. Thim was the raw winds that come over the ocean and blew the rushes off the roof. You've gone far and done good when you count where you started from."

"Where I started from, is it? What finer people was ever in all Munster than the Morahans, since the world was a world? And wasn't me mother's people O'Brines that was Lords of Aran Isles in their day, and me father's mother from the O'Flaherties that druv out the O'Brines."

She had pulled all his ancestors off the shelf on her head.

"Yis, yis, yis, yis! I know—I know—I know. But it was a long whiles back since your people was kings. Finer people was niver, but there's been richer. My own people was from the Lynches and the Joyces, but I'm not tahkin' of histhry, I'm tahkin' of modderen times. And there's no denyin' that you and me are rich now to what we was thin."

But comforting Michael was impossible when he had made up his mind to be dismal.

"Rich to what we was, it may well be. But not rich to what we'd ought to be. Look at Mattoo Carmody. Carmody he come out in the same boat with us and now he owns a fleet of boats. He owns banks and stores and he's got a pocketful of railroads."

"But think what a start he had."

"A start is it? Didn't I lind him the shoes he wore onto the boat? And now he's shod with gold shoes. And Roger M'Murtha—in the same steerage he come—he's a supreme coort Joostice, and Jawn Giluley is makin' scads of money—he owns this buildin'. I'm payin' rint to him—now and thin. But I'm a conthractor only, and the hard times—and this war on top o' thim—has conthracted me till if the conthraction expands anny furtherer I'm a squeeged limon."

29

"You have more sons than anny of them; all of thim workin'—and workin' for the city. You could lane on them if need was."

"A fine thing to lay back on me sons."

She lashed back at him: "Man, man, what's wrahng wit' you? I'd think you were some old hound yelpin' in the cold. There's manny out in that snow would be wishin' for to change places with you, only they have no places to offer you. And if your mother has been waitin' all this while she'll be so much the gladder to have you in her eyesight. Manny's the mother has sent her sons to America and never laid finger on them again whativer. And look at the mothers that's sindin' their sons out to the wars. It's not her that 'll be the unhappy one, and you ought to be down on the pier this mortal instint watchin' for her. When does the old boat boomp the dock annyhow?"

"She's doo in to-day; but that always manes to-morra. What with the big win' and the snow she'll never think of dockin' till Winsda—if thin."

"Maybe they'll put a spoort on," Delia suggested. "What if she'd steal in on you unbeknownst?"

Michael laughed patiently at such childishness.

"Sure and I've looked out for that. I paid the tele-graft coompany to notify me in full and plinty of time."

Delia retreated, murmuring:

"All right, all right, but you've a way of gettin' to a place too late. Hadn't you better call up the dock and ask them would the boat get in to-night at all?"

"Ain't I just after tellin' you the telegraft coompany has promised to sind me word the minyute the boat passes Sandy Hook? That gives me three hours to get to the dock."

Deiia took another and final farewell shot:

30

MICHAELEEN! MICHAELAWN!

"I don't suppose one of the boys could ferget. Messenger-boys doos ferget and they're slow."

"But ain't I tellin' you I paid the coompany—" Michael roared.

"I know, but it wouldn't be a nice thing to have your mother settin' on the dock waitin', not knowin' where in all this country you was—a cold welcome for her, that."

"Nonsinse! You'd worry after you got to heaven for fear the gold sthreets would cave in. I'll take a chance on the telegraft coompany."

Delia sighed, unconvincedly, "Maybe you know best."

"I paid the coompany!" Michael snarled. His voice stopped short at the sound of a telephone bell skirling suddenly. He looked at Delia and she at him. They looked anxiously at the telephone. It rang on till Michael, with some timidity, went to it and lifted the receiver from the hook.

"Hello!" he said in the tone of an invalid. "Is this the dock? No"—he turned triumphantly to Delia—"it is not the dock."

"Who said it was! And who is it?"

"Who are you?—Oh, it's you, Giluley." He turned to Delia with triumph. "It's John Giluley. How are you, Giluley, and where are you? Oh!" He turned to Delia with all shame. "He's on the dock. She's on the dock! Me mother! Down there in the cold and all alone with herself. Oh, the creature!—tell her not to stir—you stay by, Giluley. I'll be there just as soon as I've murdered one messenger-boy. Tell her I'm better than half-ways there now."

He slapped the receiver back and began to run blindly about.

"It isn't your mother?" Delia faltered.

31

"And who else should it be? Do you think I've a date with Queen Mary?"

"The boat isn't in, is it?"

"How else should she get here? Is it walked you think she did?—or shwum? The boat passed Sandy Hook these three hours. If I had the telegraft coompany here!"

"Oh, musha, then! Why, what at all! Och, meal and murder!" Delia groaned. "What are you lookin' for?"

He was blundering about like a bear in a cage.

"Me coat! Me coat! D'you think I can go to the dock in me shirt-sleeves?"

"And where should your coat be but where you left it off—on the chair there!—on the chair there!" He thrust into it, mumbling. The door-bell rang. Delia hurried to the door. A small messenger-boy with a large voice poked a telegram at her.

"Does M. Monahan live here?"

"Mr. Michael Morahan lives here!" she answered with dignity, and seized the envelope and ran to the dining-room, where Michael was now charging about for his hat.

"Here, Mike, open this," she said.

He took it grimly. "I've no need to open it." He opened it and read the insulting line: "Steamer *Hibernia* just passing Sandy Hook!" He made uncouth sounds of ironic wrath and clenched and unclenched his big fists.

The small gum-grinding messenger swaggered in.

"Hay, you gotta sign t'e book."

This exploded Michael. "Sign the book, is it?" He towered over the lad with Cyclopean rage. "He says I gotta sign the book! Oh, I'll sign the book."

The boy looked up into the storm and began to cringe a little. Delia dragged Michael away.

"He ain't the prisidint of the coompany, now."

MICHAELEEN! MICHAELAWN!

Michael surrendered his prey with reluctance. He snatched the book and pencil from the boy, scrawled a violent signature, drove his hand into his pocket, fished out a dime, and said with gnashing gentleness:

"Here you are, my little maneen; that's for yourself. As for your prisidint, tell him I'll slaughther him six different ways if I find him."

"T'anks," said the boy, resuming the milling of his chewing-gum. "Any answer?"

"Answer to who? For what?" groaned Michael.

Delia urged the boy out, murmuring, "Run home and tell your mother to thank her saint she has you back."

She thrust the boy out of the door, caught Michael's overcoat from the rack, pushed it on his wavering arms, and stood aside as he dashed through. She ran out into the hall to watch his noisy descent. She saw the messenger-boy flatten himself against the wall in time to escape being run over. Then she hurried back to a window, opened it, and stared down into the street.

She saw him emerge into the storm and struggle fantastically for his balance on the slippery pavement. She saw him brush aside all interferers and swing aboard a surface car on which a passing elevated train shook down lumps of snow.

Then she drew back into the house and brushed the snow from her own head and shoulders. She was praying for his safety in the crowded, slippery ways. At the same time she was calling to Kate to help her make ready for the ancient and honorable visitor from overseas.

"Oh, Kate, Kate! Herself is in town!"

Delia had been Herself in this household all these years. Now she was abdicating the throne.

Making ready for the guest of honor consisted chiefly in a frantic rearrangement of things already established—

33

the mighty pother that passionate housekeepers make out of things of no particular importance. Delia and Kate wrought like mad for an hour, yet they were caught still unready by a great pounding on the door, a jabbing of the shrill bell, and the familiar rumble of Michael's voice.

"My soul to the saints!" Delia squealed. "Herself is outside and the tay not drawn."

She made her way to the door, giving a chair a shove, a table-cover a yank, and the pictures on the walls a push to square them in the positions the trains kept shaking them out of.

She flung back the door and found Michael supporting a mass of clothes which she assumed to be his mother. Over the face there was a veil with frozen breath glistening on it.

Michael warped her through the casement gently, growling:

"Sure I thought you was all dead within in there. Aisy now! Do you think she's a load of coal, that you're so rough?"

They worried the old lady to a chair and proceeded to unwrap her as if she were a mummy, and when she came forth she had something the look of one, if it were not for the black glitter of her little eyes.

Her incredibly wrinkled face was all patterned into tiny diamonds and squares.

She put up two trembling mittened hands to clasp Delia's and kissed her warm cheek with thin, cold lips. She was panting too hard to speak at first, then she whispered:

"Ah, Delia, agra, how's every bit of ye?"

"Finely, thank you, ma'am honey, and it's you that have made the lahng v'yage and lookin' that fresh as if you'd been only steppin' from one room to another."

MICHAELEEN! MICHAELAWN!

Mrs. Morahan, senior, smiled at the amiable flattery.

"Och, agra, it's more like steppin' from airth up till heaven for these ould bones. It's a power of stairs you have, but once you are here you've no ind of comforts."

"Thim stairs is the divil's own bother!" Michael growled. "I'm thinkin' of havin' them out."

"You've been takin' good care of Himself, Delia."

Delia blushed with pride. "He's alive; that's much these days. But he needs a good bit of motherin'."

"A man never gets past the needin' of that, I'm thinkin'," sighed Michael.

And his wife, a little hurt with the oldest jealousy in the world, made an excuse for flight.

"But where's Katie? She should be here with the hot tay. Katie, Katie!"

She made off in girlish confusion and found Katie trying to untie the knot in her apron-strings, and the tea not begun.

Left alone with her child, the old woman stared at him, seeing rather the lad she had last seen than the heavy old man he had become.

"Ah, Michaeleen, my little Mickeen!" she sighed.

He dropped with a thump to one knee and embraced her and her chair with his burly arms.

"Ah, me little mother!"

"A better boy never broke the world's bread," she sighed, caressing his wrinkled cheek with a more wrinkled hand. "And he remembered his ould mother all this lahng while?"

"And she didn't forget her useless omadhawn of a son?"

"Forget him? It's me that has crossed oceans of say just for to have a look at him."

The roar of the blood in her ears had stilled now with

4   35

repose so that she could hear the cyclone of a passing train. She clutched at Michael's sleeve. "The saints take thought on us! What is it at all?" She caught sight of something shooting past the window. "Is it wan of thim flyin'-machines there's such tahk of?"

"It's only the ilevated train, ma honey," he smiled. "We have another that's like it, only underground."

"It's a grand city this New York," she said, trying to maintain her dignity. "Bigger than Dooblin, belike?"

"There's more Irish here than in all Dublin, let alone the foreigners and a sprinklin' of natives."

Bridget's pride held the curb on her astonishment. She had lived in the outskirts of a small town, and of later years had hardly visited even Lisdoonvarna, though the rumor of the gaiety and excitement of its sulphur baths had been a cause of much gossip from cabin to cabin. She had hardly seen a railroad till she took the stage from Lisdoonvarna to Ennistimon, and the train from there to Queenstown, and a lighter from there to the ship, and a taxicab from the ship to her son's home. That was all the travel she had had in her threescore and sixteen. But she was not going to betray her amazement with any gasping stupefaction of crude ignorance.

The Irish peasantry is generally credited with more aristocracy than any other. The poorest are fed on royal legends even when the potatoes fail, and they sweeten the sour milk on their stirabout with grandeur of manner.

Mrs. Morahan, senior, had spent her life in the very heart of the country of Brian Boroihme. She had seen the ramparts of his fortress at Killaloe on the banks of Shannon. With no more area than Maryland and no more population than Grand Rapids, County Clare boasted a hundred castles and ruins a thousand years old. Why should she truckle to an upstart like New York?

36

MICHAELEEN! MICHAELAWN!

She did not. She would not let herself express more than a polite approval. It was a strain, though, and she was glad to be restored to easy majesty by the shy approach of Kate.

Kate came in, fat and awkward, and so timid that she could hardly hold the tray of tea. She shoved it onto a table, knocking off a book, stooped for that and bumped the tray. Then she came forward, scarlet, and turned to the tiny old woman who had something of the air of a withered queen.

Bridget lifted her little head and Kate bent down and exchanged kisses with her, but could think of nothing to say. Katie had visited Ireland as a young woman of twenty some fourteen years before; time and lack of love had dealt harshly with her since, but the old woman did not hesitate to greet her with outrageous flattery.

"Katie dear, and how is yourself? But for why should I ask you? You're not changed the one whit since you come breakin' all the hearts in the eleven baronies of Clare."

The unwitting irony of this was pitiful in its effect on Kate and her humbled parents. Fortunately the little sharp eyes were too dull to see the dismay she caused.

Delia, with great presence of mind, whisked forward the tea and made a royal ceremony of serving it.

"It's the grand tay," said Bridget. "It's the same tay you've been sindin' me all these years."

Michael nodded; that had been one of his little tributes.

"But where's the other childer? Katie's not all you have left?"

Delia cast up her hands at the very idea.

"Sure we've a flock of them," said Michael. "I'll see can I lay holt on them. We maybe might ahl have soopper together."

He went near the door, lifted a black rubber ear-piece and spoke into the wall—a number he said, and a name. The Ould Black Boy himself must have been within in it, for in a moment Michael was hopping mad and contradicting the thing, shouting at it, "No, I did not say four-two-wan-six. I said four-tree-wan-siv'm!"

Bridget was hard put to it to pretend that she had been used to telephones all her life. At length Michael's voice ceased to quarrel with his invisible, inaudible tormentor, and he said: "Is this the station house? Is Lootinant Morahan there? Tell him his old man wants a worrud wit' him. Yes, this is Himself. Oh, hello, Cap'n, you're lookin' fine. Yis—sure! Thank ye— Is that you, Myles? Say, can't you quit out of that a while and run over home? Your grandmother is in and dyin' for to see you. Ah, tell the Cap'n there's burgulars here! Fine! And say, Myles, round up the other boys, why not?—and—whishper!—bring thim along ahl at the wan time. I want to—to—what you might say spring the boonch on her—er—all in a boonch. Fine for you! And say, be quick about it. Good-by."

He hung up the receiver and turned to Delia:

"Myles says he'll run them ahl in. Sure, they'd fill a pathrol wagon, and at that there's a couple o' gerls missin', Nora and Mary, that married and wint West. Say, Delia, if that gang of lads is to ate here, you'll have to be ordherin' in a pile of thruck."

Delia bustled out with Kate, and mother and son found themselves alone again. They chattered a long while, exchanging gossips of old acquaintance come to America or left at home, or returning thither. Michael seated himself in a chair by her side and took her hand in his and stared at it and smiled at her with a world of love. He could find no phrase to express the welling of the long-stored waters of his affection—nothing to do but to shake his head and maunder:

"Och, you little old villain, you."

She smiled back at him and squeezed his hand as with a bird's claws, helpless to say the things she felt. She masked her confusion with a sarcastic, "Have more respeck for your elders."

"Elders is it, the devil admire me if I'm not the elderer of us two."

"Wirrasthrue, Mickeen," she moaned, "I'm a long ways from the old home—and a short ways from the new."

The thought was a knife in his heart. He clutched her hand as if he would hold her back. He shivered, and a little tremor ran faintly through the rickety tenement of her tired soul.

"It's growin' chill, Mike avourneen, with the sun gone."

He caught her hands tighter in his and gasped: "Why, you're fairly starved wit' the cold. Come over here and have a taste of the heat off the radiator."

"The what-iator?" she said, as he shoved her chair across the room. "What have you within in there?"

"Stame."

"Is it an injine that you have stame to it?" He put her feet against it and she wondered. "Och, musha, there's warmth there."

"Yes, in warrum weather there's warmth."

She looked about. "And have you no fireplace here? No, you have none. How do you put the hate in this?"

"We don't, ma dear. Down-stairs there's a janitor— a kind of cellar king. He puts coal in a big foornace when he's not too busy, and the warmth mounts up.

"And does he now? And saves you the work! And I notice there's no smoke at all out of this. It saves your

39

eyes and nose a lot of throuble. There's a pile of con-
vanience into it; it's cliver and clane. And that thing
in the wall there you talk to; that's injanious. It bates
the way I used to go out on the hills and call you childer
home when the night come crawlin' over the say."

"Oh, well, they have points. But, ma, acushla, I'd
rather than all the radiators and telephomes in the
worruld be a wisp of a lad again, droppin' at your feet
before the old kittle over the turf fire, and you tellin'
me about the fairy people—Thim Ones."

She laughed uncannily. "It was long iver ago and
me hair was woild and red, and none of the bog-cotton
it is now."

"And I'm no wisp of a lad be some two hundred pound.
I'm wonderin' if you call to mind the story of how the
wild flowers come to be invinted. It's the further-
backest thing I remimber."

"Och, child, darlint, haven't you forgot that at all?
Ivery night you'd dhraw up the little creepy-stool to me
side, and you'd lane your cheek on me knee, and look
into the core of the fire, and make me tell it till you—
before you was smothered to sleep."

The wish to hear it again came upon him with a pang
of longing. It was so dark by now that he could hardly
see her or himself, and the gloom played magic with him.
Without thought of his cumbrous weight of flesh, he got
to the floor and laid his big head on her sharp knee, and
murmured:

"Tell it me again, mother jewel. I've a longin' to
hear it that's smotherin' me, now. Tell it me again."

Upon the dark their fancy painted the same picture:
the young widow in the shadow-furnished cabin staring
into the whispering radiance of the fire, and the barefoot
drowsihead crouched against her feet. Youth came back

to them both with a blissful sorrowfulness. The voice that quavered through the old legend seemed to them both the rich, deep singsong of a full-throated girl: "It was once, a lahng, lahng time pasht, whin God was feelin' tired afther a haird day's worruk. He put His head on His hand, and He wint to sleep. And clouds of gold gethered round Him for to prevint the disturbance of His rest.

"He dramed wondherful drames, and whin He woke, He looked round and waved the cloud off, and He saw the angel Michael standin' gaird. And Michael asked the Lord if He was wantin' annything and He said— He said—"

Her memory wavered, and the boy prompted her as of old:

"He said, 'No, t'thank ye, Michaeleen.'"

"He said, 'No, t'thank ye, Michaeleen.' Thin He— thin He—" She was only pretending to forget this time, to see if he remembered this also. To her strange delight, he mumbled:

"He swithered for a minyute."

"He swithered for a minyute, thin He says, 'Sind me a chariot and a charioteer wit' 'harses wit' wings onto thim.' And with that same there stands the chariot wit' the winged harses, and the charioteer stands ready for orders and saloots, and God says, 'Take this sack of seeds—'"

"'Of flower seeds,'" came the correction.

"'Of flower seeds, and take a thrip around the intire worruld and scatther these seeds by the roadsides, in the woods, in the bogs, in all the woild places whativer where the poor have access.'

"At that time flowers had only been newly invinted and they were very rare. Folk called thim 'livin', breathin' jewlery,' and none but the rich had thim. Which was not God's intintion, at ahl.

"So the angel took the sack of seeds, and hurrooshed his harses out o' that and wint and did God's bidding. And the airth was barren no more, and it was no more only the rich that had flowers, for from that day primroses, daisies, butthercups, and all the purty, wee posies of the worruld have grown in places where the poorest could have them for the throuble of shtoopin' down. Iver since then there is no mortial so poor he cannot find flowers along his pathway, wheriver, whativer, whoiver."

Her voice died away, yet the ghost of it seemed to float upon the air. The two souls hung aloof from time and place and fact and age swithering in a golden cloud of reverie.

The door-bell rang through it. Delia came in from the dining-room and stood in a nimbus of light, peering at them in wonder. Michael rose to his feet with difficult struggle, for the burden of his years fell back upon his shoulders.

"Michaelawn!" said Delia, "what's on you again? Why have you not made a light?"

"Why have you waked me from—" But he could not explain.

Delia lighted the gas and they sat chatting and brooding for a long while. Then Bridget was startled by a whirring bell, and Kate stole through to the door and admitted a parade of Michael's children, all talking, bustling, treading upon dreams.

There were Myles, the policeman; Shamus, the fire-man; Barney, the building inspector, and Dermot, the priest.

Michael did his best with the introductions. When it came to the young priest he was puzzled.

MICHAELEEN! MICHAELAWN!

"This is Dermot," he said. "He's the only wan that takes afther me. Kiss your grandmother, Father. Troth, the relationship is so twishted I don't know how to call him. If he is Father to his own father, what would that make him to his grandmother?—grandfather belike. Annyhow, Father Dermot, me son, kiss your grandchild."

Dermot was shy and his grandmother was a trifle afraid of him, but Michael shouted:

"Don't let his cloth put a chill on you, mother. He's the most janial Father I iver had."

"It's a grand family you have, **my bouchal** bawn. And it doos me proud," said Bridget.

The door-bell rang again. This time it was Patrick, who had hastened from the far-off Bronx. He bore a large bundle.

"It's you, Paudeen," cried Michael, "and where's the woman that owns you?"

"She's strugglin' up the stairs," said Patrick. "I hurried up to give grandma the first sight of—of this."

He unfurled a googling infant. Bridget was all a-flutter over it. She poked a lean finger at it, and it clutched it in a pink paw and gurgled.

"And what might his name be?" Bridget asked.

"Bridget," said Patrick.

"Och, murder in Irish. I'm a great-grandmother!" gasped Bridget.

Then the young mother stumbled in, breathing heavily and blushing with fury. Patrick introduced her.

"This is my Annie, grandma. She's only a Sligo woman, but she's all right in spite of that. And there's the proof."

He laid the infant on the ancestral lap and it looked up, waving hands and feet aloft to the down-staring witch whence its life had been, as it were, decanted thrice.

43

LONG EVER AGO

The ancient Bridget wondered over this promise of future generations, and her emotions overwhelmed her. She drooped back in her chair and Rosie bent to snatch her child away, but it clung to the old hand it held. Michael laid an anxious palm on his mother's brow.

She understood his fear, and with her free hand caught at his, whispering:

"I'm ahl right, Michael avic. I'm better than ahl right. I'm just that happy I'm drowsy wit' it. I'll have a few winks of sleep, then I'll come back till you."

A train stormed by and Michael grumbled:

"The devil fly away wit' those cairs; they'll murder your sleep on you."

"Och, no, honey, I'll rest the betther for them. They're like the long waves that used to come over the ocean from here and bate upon the cliffs of Moher, where I heard them the night through. Little I thought I'd pass over thim to this side of the big wather."

Her head sank to her breast and she was already asleep. Her child and his children stood about her in the shadow like ghosts. In the mystery of existence she had given them to the world. Beyond them in deeper shadow a future company of souls waited their turns in the clay.

III

SENT FOR OUT

I

"WHAT'S on himself at all?—I don't know," said Mrs. Delia Morahan to her sons. "So airly in the day, his dinner but only aiten, and he singin'! And he has no drink taken. There's something queer in it."

Michael Morahan, usually the last to finish his noon-day dinner, had been to-day the first. He had chased the last morsel of his second piece of pie up against his left thumb, forked it, stowed it, washed it down with the last swig of his second cup of coffee, and sighed the big, full "Ah!" that was the amen of his grace. Then he had pushed cup and plate back, planted his hands on the cloth, heaved himself erect, swept the faces round the board with a defiant and mysterious smile, winked at his fat wife, kissed his ancient mother on the lace cap, and stalked into the bedroom.

And now through the quivering door pealed the thunder of his song. It had the wild vigor of a war-chant, but the words were:

"Thin coom to thi-is buzzum, me own sthricken deer."

Myles, the policeman, winced: "Stricken deer, is it? He'd scare off a flock of buffaloes from restin' in Centeral Park."

45

LONG EVER AGO

"Katie," said Delia, "let you go tell him to hold his whist, and doos he forget his poor mother is near moidered with the influence?"

Old Bridget put up her shriveled hand and crackled:

"No, no, lave the boy sing. It's a pleasure to hear a man singin' about the house."

"Singin'? yes! would he sing," said Delia, "but it's auctioneerin' he is."

It was a kind of Irish headache old Bridget had on her, for she startled at the least clack of knife on plate, and every elevated train going by seemed to go over her, yet she smiled at the clamoring lyric of her son. And she fell asleep in her chair to his lullaby. Katie wheeled her into her own room, where she might sleep undisturbed.

Delia continued to wonder about her husband:

"And he invitin' Shane to dinner and nothin' come of it. And when Shane says he's lost his job he lets his face fall and says nothin'; then takes himself from the table, and now singin'! It bates all."

Shane O'Mealia smiled with self-derision:

"Ah, there's no news in me losin' me job. It's the one thing I do with regularity."

"Niver once through a fahlt of your own, Shaneen," said Delia, patting him on the shoulder as she bent over to clear off the débris of dinner. Shane put his hand on hers and muttered:

"Ah, aunt honey, when the coincidences coince too regular it quits bein' accident. It's me that's not worth a thraneen."

"Och, blathers, and you with a head of gold."

"Oh, I've a head, and so's a pin, but I can't sthick, and a pin can."

Shane O'Mealia was the son of Delia's sister Hannah, who had never left Ireland. Shane himself had come

46

over but three years ago.   He had a genius for bad luck
and for melancholy.   But he had also that magnetic
quality known as "a way with him."   He was one of
those night-haired, night-eyed, Spanish-looking Irishmen
that legend explains by the wreck of the Great Armada,
when myriads of Philip II.'s soldiers were drowned in the
race of Erin.

Shane had a picturesque Hispanian gloom that was
very effective with women; it made the old ones long to
enliven him and the young ones long to be the cause of his
further grief.   Delia loved him almost more than her
own sons, because her own were self-reliant and New
York born, and dictatorial.   They liked Shane, but they
were forever ridiculing him.   "We guy him for his own
good," Myles would say when his mother tried to hush
them.

Shane worked hard and earnestly, almost desperately,
but he was hounded by one of those amazing sequences
of luck that distinguish life and other games of chance.
His first job in America had been that of a digger in an
excavation that was never completed; the builder failed
before he reached his foundation.   The next job was
ended by an injunction.   The next by the death of his
employer.   The next was tied up by a stockholders' legal
war.   Even when Michael managed at last to warp him
into the haven of so many Irishmen, an appointment
in one of the municipal departments, Shane attained it
just as it became the fashion for politicians to boast of
their economies and the reduction of their staffs.

Shane was politely, and with many compliments for his
intelligence, successively squeezed into and squeezed out
of more or less important posts in the Bureau of Assess-
ments and Arrears, the Department of Bridges, the City
Chamberlain's office, the Board of Coroners, the Corpora-

tion Yards, the Tenement House Department, and the Public Service Commission.

Michael, who knew somebody everywhere, got him all the jobs, and Shane always made friends; but he could not take root. Michael always promised that the next job would mark the turn of his luck for the better, but bad luck sought its own again.

Only a month ago Michael had landed Shane in the office of the Commissioner of Public Charities, and had been assured that he was there for life. He lived but the one month, and only to-day he had sobered the jovial Michael with the news at dinner. When Michael was happy, however, he was happy in spite of mere facts, and when he was glum, dynamite could not unseat him from his gloom. He had recovered instantly from Shane's ill news and had promised him still another job, and now he was howling from the next room:

> "*Cushla ma chree,*
> Did you but see
> How the rogue he did serve me?
> He broke me pitcher, he spilt me wather,
> He kissed me wife, and he married me daughther,
> *Oh! cushla ma chree!*"

Shane hardly heard him as he raised his heartbreaking black eyes to groan:

"It's bad luck has the long legs. What blisters me is this thing comin' on top of me gettin' me commission in the National Gaird for to be second leftenant—lootinant in the Sixty-nint'. What do you think of that, Aunt Dalia!"

"It's a grand thing for the rigimint," said Delia.

"But grandeur pays no bills," said Shane, "and I've me uniform to pay for, and it ready these two days."

SENT FOR OUT

Michael, collarless and fuming, appeared at the door in time to hear this last. A scowl that would have done credit to Lucifer changed to a smile that St. Raphael would have been proud of.

"Shane, me boy," he said, "niver fret; it's me will lind you what cash you must give the milithry tailor."

Shane was joyed for an instant; then he shook his head.

"And for why should you, Uncle Michael?"

"I have me raisins," said Michael, with an occult wink at himself. He turned to his wife. "Dalia, where's that boondle of money I'm after lavin' on you lasht Choosda?"

Delia set down a spool of plates in alarm and gasped:

"The money you gave me for the rint?"

"That same."

"You gave it me for the rint!" she protested. "And Giluley's comin' for it this same day. And two months he's waitin' f'r it."

Michael was not disturbed. He laughed:

"Ah, tell him to cahl again, and glad for to see him anny day. And no haird feelin's on him for ahl he's a landlard. Tell him I'd forgive him did I owe him six months' rint, let alone two."

Delia was horrified at this shiftlessness and refused to give up the money till Michael explained:

"I want Shane in his uniforrum this afthernoon and night. It's va-ry impartant. And I want him here. Are you listenin', Shane?"

"Yes, Uncle Michael, and glad to be here, seein' I've no place else to go."

Delia's curiosity was not yet assuaged.

"But why for in the uniforrum? Will it help the boy to a job belike?"

"It will that," Michael grinned, "and to a life-lahng job I'm thinkin'."

49

This served only to mystify mystery, but when Delia almost squealed in her curiosity Michael guffawed, caught her in his gorilla arms, and crunched her bones, while he dodged the slaps she aimed at him. Then he returned to the bedroom and began to rival the noise of the elevated road with his blood-curdling rendition of another love ditty:

"Thou bidst me sing the lay I sang to thee."

Delia kept pausing in her clearance work and sighing: "What's on him entirely? Singin' and keenin'—is it sick he might be?"

"He has the sound of it," said Barney. "He'll have the roof in in a minute."

"Now, ma," said Myles, "what's the use of worryin' because pa is singin'? Why arrunt you singin' because he's not worryin'?"

But Delia was puzzled solemn:

"There's something in the win' and I can't abide him havin' secrets of his own. He's not to be thrusted wit' them."

II

The men pushed back from the table and got out their tobacco. Shamus, the fireman, offered Shane, the guest, his package of cigarettes.

"I don't use them," said Shane, and fished out a pair of cigars—a farewell tribute from his late chief. He proffered them to Myles, who absently accepted them both.

"Annybody could tell you were a policeman," said Shane.

"Oh!" said Myles in a trifle of confusion as he handed one back.

He tried to cover his retreat with a bit of sarcasm:

"You'll be a posituv danger to the ladies, Shane, in your brass buttons."

Barney, the building inspector, piped in:

"Judy Dugan will go mad."

Delia lifted her head. "And what's Judy Dugan to Shane?" she demanded.

"Nothin' at all, Aunt Dalia," said Shane.

"Nothin' more than the black of his eye," said Barney.

"Ah, whist and bad manners to you!" Shane growled.

Barney continued to prod him. "Weren't you sayin' you were goin' to the County Cavan calico hop to-night?"

"Maybe I might."

"But you're from County Clare."

"Cavan is in Ireland, too," Shane fenced.

"Judy Dugan is a Cavan girl," Barney mused aloud.

"So I belave—believe," said Shane, who was trying to shake off his accent. He tried to seem indifferent, but Barney followed him up.

"Are you takin' her to the Cavan hop?"

"Maybe I might."

"It's more like Judy takin' you," Myles sniffed.

Delia paused at the kitchen door with a load of dishes. "What chat is this of Judy Dugan and Shane?"

"She owns him, that's all," said Barney.

"Oh, wirra, wirrasthrue!" Delia wailed, as she pushed through the door dolefully and joined Kate at the faucets, but told her nothing of her fear.

Against a counterpoint of dish-washing in the kitchen and Michael's balladry in the bedroom the young men fell to battling for the pure Irish love of battle. Shane led off with a furious tirade, twisting himself in and out of his brogue.

"You're a fine gang of slandherers, puttin' bad thoughts

in your mother's mind. Have I no right to take who I
plase—please—where I please—plase—please!"

"Don't ask me," Barney laughed. "Ask the girl you
left Back There. What's happened her?"

Myles answered for him. "She's still Back There and
liable for to stay."

Shane's eyes narrowed to lines of glittering coals. "Are
you referrin' to Moyna Killilea, be anny chanst?"

"Oh, there was more than the one, then?" Myles
whooped, triumphant in his bear-baiting.

Shamus added his jab:

"There's less than the one now, I'm thinkin', over
there now."

Shane was flaming with wrath. He threatened both
the policeman and the fireman. "Keep your lahng
tongues from off her name, yous two, or I'll twisht them
out of you!"

The burly Myles laughed down at him: "You're not
mentioning Miss Killilea yourself this long while back.
We used to hear all the time about your going to send for
her out."

"You know why I haven't sent for her out. Where
would I be gettin' the money?"

"If I had a girl waitin' for me there, I'd get money,
if I had to steal it."

"It would be aisy enough stole, with police like you
about," Shane snapped.

Myles laughed unperturbed. Barney joined the hurl-
ing-match.

"The fare over is only fifteen dollars."

'That's steerage!" Shane answered. "Do I want to
be bringin' the gerl over in the steerage?"

"Steerage is better than not comin' at all," said
Shamus.

But Shane pleaded: "Suppose I had her here? Have I got a job to keep her on?"

"Ah, you'd find a way if you wanted to," said Myles, ruthlessly. "But why send for Moyna when Judy Dugan's so convenient?"

"You lave Judy Dugan's name out of this, I tell you," Shane stormed.

But Myles stormed back: "You don't leave her out anywhere. You're with her all the time."

Shane was staggered. It was an ugly situation. He had plighted his troth to Moyna; he had in his young loneliness taken delight in Judy's society. He had neglected to tell Judy about Moyna. Perhaps he had told Judy that she was the only girl he ever truly loved. It was as true, he was sure, as Judy's statement that Shane was the first man she ever kissed. Some cards have to be dealt before the game can begin.

But while these things are not unprecedented, they do not explain well, so Shane had recourse to an explanation that was entirely the truth, though it might not have been the entire truth:

"Well, I'll tell you why I've been with Judy so much, since your nose is so lahng. Her father's always out of work."

"Small wonder—seein' he's always in liquor," was Barney's contribution.

Shane went on, "And Judy keeps after me to get him a job."

"You that can't get one for yourself!" Myles sniffed.

And Shane answered, "Haven't you noticed that a man can get a job for others whin he cannot for himself?"

This appealed to reason and experience.

"But where," said Myles, "would you put old man

Dugan? He's that withered and wore out, he's as useless
and rickety as a busted umberella."

"That's why I'm trying," said Shane, "to get him a
place in the Board of Health."

Barney had not yet tired of the sport. He asked:

"Is it your intention, once you've got Judy's father a
job, to marry her and all three live on the old man, or
will Judy go on workin' at her shop, and the both of them
support you?"

Shane did not enjoy the post of target and his cousins
had wrought him to a passion. He broke out, hotly:

"Judy's nothing to me, I tell you, but a nice gerl.
She has a habit on her of acting like she owned a fella,
but she don't own me. Moyna is my Moyna, and when
I get a job that I can hold I'll bring her here by the first
boat. But I've had the devil's own luck. I've never
been able for to get settled annywhere. I've not dared
write Moyna for the disappointment it would be to her,
but I'll bring her out—don't you fear. Some day I'll
bring her out!"

"Some day it will snow stirabout," said Barney, who
was suspicious of eloquence.

Myles and Shamus were almost converted. When the
door-bell rang. Kate bustled through the dining-room,
drying her hands on her apron.

"Four to one it's Judy Dugan," said Shamus.

"You win," said Myles, hearing her voice at the door,
a sharp twangy Manhattan voice, with a perpetual color
of amusement and sophistication.

Shane's swart cheeks were suddenly daubed as with
red paint, and his indignation gave him the look of guilt.
As he had said, coincidences were always against him.

Judy followed close on the heels of the returning Kate,
and sang out:

54

SENT FOR OUT

"Hello, youngsters! Pleased to meet you—good-by!"

Their greeting was a trio of smiles and an almost decorative triple gesture at the uneasy Shane. Judy's tones and her eyes softened toward him and she cooed: "Hello, Shane! It's you I want to see."

The three brothers began to side-step toward the hall, when Delia bunted the door open backward and revolved in with a stack of plates in each arm. As she was unloading them at the sideboard, she was trying to forget her new grudge against Judy and be hospitable:

"Why, Judy, and is it you, now? And how are you? But it's no need askin', with you lookin' like all the money in the worruld. And so well, too! Sit down, do."

"Thanks," said Judy, and sat.

Delia, who was hoping she would not, was just sinking wearily into her own chair when Myles scooped her up and, pointing to the kitchen door, spoke in his most policemanly tone:

"Quit out of this—you're not wanted."

Judy jumped up with a gasp. "Why, Myles Morahan, the idea. I wouldn't think of it. Sit still, Mrs. Morahan. Shane and I can go in the parlor."

"It's dark in there," said Delia. "I'll turn on the electrickity."

"They'd like it better dark," said Barney, outrageously.

Shane could have throttled him, but Judy laughed aloud. Delia looked as if she had been stabbed in the heart.

III

Still, one has to be polite in one's own flat, and Delia managed to say:

"And how's your poor mother, Judy?—the saints give her aid!"

"Oh, ma's poorly, thank you," sighed Judy, her laughter turned to dreariness. "Poor soul, she goes from bad to worse, and back to bad again, but never to better, or even well."

"And your father?" Delia asked, with some embarrassment.

"Oh, pa is fine—for pa. But of course he's always a little—well, you know pa's pa."

She smiled it so pluckily that Delia, who was already softened with regret for the far-off Moyna, felt a sorrow also for this nearer victim of Shane's overpowering helplessness and beauty. One of her incessant prayers welled to her lips, and two or three of her swift tears ran out on her lids. "Ah, God mark you to grace, you poor child! You've been father and mother to your own father and mother since your poor ma got past herself and took to her bed. And you such a grand business woman at that! It's you that's the man of the family."

Judy was not used to being taken seriously or tenderly. She rarely took herself seriously or felt herself worthy of sympathy. Sympathy was for her bedridden mother and her bottle-ridden father and such dark souls as Shane O'Mealia, whom she had tried to cheer along his path.

Delia's unexpected tribute astounded her. Tears call out tears, and Judy felt her lashes suddenly wet. She shook off the unwonted drops and forced a hypocritical smile of indifference. "Ah, go along with you, you blarneyer."

As Delia always said, "Judy never looks herself," so now she suggested almost anything rather than the good, wise girl she was. She was not beautiful, but she added to the gaiety and the warmth of the landscape. She was dressed in the latest impudence of fashion. A joke of a hat was tilted over one brow with the effect of a general wink. Her hair was of a somewhat supernatural tint, and its arrangement was—as Shane once told her—"as full of I-dare-you as a poke in the eye."

Her skirts were short and hardly touched the light-colored tops of her patent-leather shoes, so high heeled that she walked like a toe-dancer. Her furs were a shower of imitation mink heads, with sly shoe-button eyes, and she carried her fluffy muff high on a convexly carried figure that seemed about to break in two forward. Her knees were bent and one foot trailed the other limply.

Judy was a dressmaker, and she had to dress in the very latest style. Women in the very latest style rarely look quite respectable, no matter what the style. Besides, Judy looked as frail and clinging and deleterious as a parasitic vine. Yet for all her swagger and her sophistication and her willingness to flirt a little to keep in practice, her heart was full of Irish ice, and her fist was quick to repel the first adventurer beyond what she called "the dead-line every lady draws."

Shane had more or less implied that when he got a steady job he would relieve her of the necessity of ever working again with her delicate hands. She had more or less accepted this as a more or less formal betrothal. But, knowing Shane, she had made no hasty preparations for closing her shop.

Though she looked as if she could hardly stand alone, she was a very busy business woman. Though she found strength somewhere to dance all night every now and then, she also got to Mass with fair regularity by setting her alarm-clock into her precious hours of sleep and accepting it as a trump of Gabriel to wake her from the dead.

Judy's dressmaking and milliner shop was nearly on Fifth Avenue. She had not forgotten her Irish birth and she was proud of her Hibernian name, but business is business, and she felt that "Judy Dugan" would not look enticing or authoritative on a window. So her plate-glass and her business cards read:

```
+-----------------------------------+
|                                   |
|         JULIE DU GANNE            |
|                                   |
|  MODES                 CHAPEAUX   |
|                                   |
+-----------------------------------+
```

And she made some money, too. But it was hard to save any. For her mother consumed an amazing quantity of medicine and invalid's foods and ran up doctor's bills unceasingly. But her father was Judy's one great extravagance. She really could not afford her father. But neither could she let him go. He cost her strength and suffering and time and money. She was always maneuvering him into jobs and out of trouble, and she was always protecting his pride at the cost of her own. To keep people from understanding him she was always getting herself misunderstood.

And never more so than now, when, in her brusque way, she tried to escape from Delia's sympathy with a sharp, "Come along, Shane."

Shane followed her into the parlor, wearing a craven look, plainly enjoyed by the three brothers, who buffeted one another with triumphant amusement at his conviction, and lingered to have further fun with him. But Delia sank into her chair, crushed.

When Judy had closed the parlor door she turned to Shane as if expecting to be kissed. He was in no mood for caresses, with those voices on the other side of the door. He vouchsafed a bit of perfunctory blarney:

"Well, Miss Judy, and how is it you are? You're lookin' fine."

Judy felt the rebuff and threw herself back coldly.

"I came to see if you had news of that job for pa?"

"Well," Shane groaned, "I've spoken to several of the big fellows in the Health Department—Pat Gartland, for instance."

"His wife is one of my customers," said Judy. "I guess I can work that pull myself."

"But he says what they ahl say: that while you are a fine gerl and charming and—"

"Yes, I know all that. One of them told me that so sweetly that I slapped the face off him."

"They all say that your father, while he is a very nice old man, he—he—"

"Yes, I know," sighed Judy.

"It's not only that he takes a little too kindly to the drop, but when he has liquor taken he always wants to whip everybody. And he's such a wake old man that he's hard to handle without breakin' him entirely. That last job I got him with the Public Works, remimber, he said he could lick the boss with one hand and the United States Airmy with the other."

"I know, I know," Judy groaned. "And he's so peaceable when he's himself!"

"That's the trouble. He's so rayrely himself."

"But suppose he promised not to look at a bottle again —if he promised solemnly"—she pleaded.

"Oh, Judy—you know he tosses off a pledge like it was a gulp of potheen."

"I know. He means well, but—O Lord! What can I do? What can I do?" She was gnawing her lip frantically and beating the carpet with her flippant little shoes.

Shane's heart went out to her in a rush of pity and he laid his hand on her silky shoulder.

"There's one opening yet. I pesthered Pat Gartland till he offered to give the ould boy another last chance if he promised—"

Judy leaped up in a flame of hope:

"Promise? Oh, he'll promise anything. I'll promise it for him."

"That won't quite do. Pat said he'd give the ould bosthoon a foine, aisy—a fine, easy job as inspecthor—inspector in the Board of Health, if—if he would go to a priest and take the pledge with all the sacredness the Church can put on it."

"Oh, that's splendid!" Judy cried.

Shane was not so sure. "The old felly is proud, you know, and he can be sthubborn as all the goats in Ireland."

"He'll have to do it—pride or no pride!" said Judy.

Shane's eyes grew softer on her. "I was thinkin' it might be nicer were we to keep it in the family. Me cousin, Dermot Morahan, bein' a priest, I might fix it up with him to throw such a scare into the old man as would frighten him off liquor like it was poison."

"Fine! Oh, that's wonderful."

"But will your father go to him?"

"Of course he will."

"Better ask his consint. Like all those wake ones, he's powerful sthrong on pride. You'd better ask him before I tahk to Father Dermot."

"I will, and I'll let you know right away. And promise me one thing more—that you will tell no one of this. I can't bear the shame of it."

"Sure I promise. I swear it!" said Shane, and in his eagerness to have the compromising interview ended and to get back into the public view, he opened the parlor door just as Judy, half blinded with tears and hysterical with gratitude, cried:

"Oh, Shane, you're the dearest boy in the world, and I can't tell you how happy you've made me. Umm!"

And with that she seized him in her arms, popped a kiss on his cheek, and ran away, nodding good-bys and dabbing her tears from her leaded eyelashes. Kate had turned from the window at the sound of the opening door and she saw the kiss. Delia, who had risen from her chair, saw it, and fell back with a groan. The three sons saw it and grinned angrily.

IV

Shane, embarrassed to stupefaction, understood how everything was misunderstood and was too angry to explain. It seemed disloyal to Judy even to discuss her conduct. He went for his hat.

Myles could not help saying: "You see? What was I tellin' you! And he saying she's nothin' to him!"

"It's thrue," Shane roared, rounding on him. "Judy is a fine girl, too fine for toads the likes of you to miscall out of her name."

There might have been blows passed if Delia had not stepped into the gap. She sighed with gentle reproach, "Thrue for you, Shane, but werrunt it betther for others to be sayin' it than you?"

"And why not me?"

Delia turned to her sons and drove them out, crying:

"For why are yous all loafin' here? Have yous no jobs? Get to them, and don't stay cluttherin' up the house."

They understood and laughed at her as they kissed her, and laughed at Shane as they waved him fare-you-wells. Delia closed the door on them and turned to her uneasy nephew. She put her hand on his arm. "And now, Shane, for all you're my sister's son, you're more like one of mine, and it's like a mother I feel toward you."

"And you've been my mother in America."

"Then maybe I have the right to say it, Shaneen avic, but it's the long sorry I'd be to see you turning away from one gerl to another. I'll ahlways remimber how you used to miss the old home gerleen when first you come out. You used to tell me and tell me how Moyna looked to you when you told her good-by at the top of the long hill there that falls away from Lisdoonvarna. You said she stood in the rain with an old petticoat for her only umberella, and barefutted at that, her people bein' so poor, and she wavin' you good-by as far as you could see her, which wasn't far for you cryin' so hard. You used to write to her every boat, and you used to tahk about no soul else. It's hard if you've forgotten her, but men doos forget. Still, if your heart's changed in you, Shanie, oughtn't you first to let Moyna know she's no cahl to keep on waitin' on you? I'm sayin' it that loves you and likes Judy, and have niver laid eyes on Moyna, only in me mind."

Shane checked her with a fierce cry: "But don't you understand? Can't you lave me explain it a minyute?"

And then Michael came forth from the bedroom, dressed in his best—dressed in the things he wore to High Mass on a Patrick's Day.

Delia put up her hand to silence Shane. If he had wanted to speak, he would have been overwhelmed by the domineering Michael.

"Well," he snorted, "here am I in me own uniforrum, disguised as a gintleman. And, Shane, it's high time you were gettin' yours from the tailor."

"What's this whillabaloo?" Delia stormed. "What's this you're gettin' so readied up for?"

"I'll pour it all in your ear, woman dear, when we're alone with ourselves. Hoostle your stoomps now and dig out the money for Shane's uniforrum."

He shouted down all her protests, even Shane's protests against accepting the loan. He assured the youth that he would learn all he needed to know in good time, and sent him off. And only then he consented to explain to his distracted wife:

"It's about Shane's gerl, Moyna Killilea," he beamed.

"Och, it's a sad day for Moyna Killilea."

"What talk have you?—it's the grandest day iver for Moyna Killilea."

"Thank God for all things," Delia groaned. "She'll not know of this."

"Not know of what?" Michael shouted, upset in the progress of the oration he had been composing as he dressed.

Delia tormented him further with her own torment:

"Praise to the saints, there's two thousand miles of salt wather bechune this and the salt wather will be in her eyes whin—"

Michael shouted her down in haste:

"Two thousand miles is it? And what would you say was she to walk in that door this minyute?"

"I'd say me prayers against the fairies would be in it."

"No fairies at all—whativer. Unless it's me that's one of thim."

"And now what?" Delia gasped in a smother of wonder.

Michael's gorgeous smile flowed slowly across his face like treacle and ended in a wink so tight that it seemed he would never unknot his features again.

"Listen, woman dear, whilst I tell you a tale. Shane has been mopin' away these three years now to get the money for to bring his Moyna out, hasn't he?"

"He was that, but now—"

"And ahlways losin' his job in the nick of time, hasn't he?—wasn't he?"

"That he did."

"Well?" He made three long syllables of the word.

"Well?" she echoed, fiercely.

"Well, use your brain, if you have anny."

"You're not standin' there tellin' me that you—"

"Come on, come on, you're gettin' warrum! I got in a little extra money a while back, and Shane fell in with a job I thought would be more permaninter than the others, and so—now can you guess it?"

Delia spoke in a ghastly, ghostly whisper:

"And so you sint her the money!"

"The money I sint her. Go on!"

"To come over here!"

"To come over here! Grand! You guessed almost wit'out help. You see, I had such blessed succiss bringin' me mother out, I got kind of addicthed to it, so I inclosed some money and wrote to Moyna that Shane was fadin' out entirely for lack of her, and I was thinkin' 'twould be fine for to have her land here unexpecthed and I'd have him here and she could come leppin' into his airms like. So she cabled she'd be here and I'm on me way to the dock and Shane is on his way for his uniforrum. Now tell me if he won't be surprised and plased to see her walk in?"

He tried another of his gorilla caresses, but Delia did not strike at him or resist. She groaned:

"Shane'll be surprised full and plinty; how plased he'll be when she walks in will depind on what she walks in in. Shane used to tell me she was as nice-lookin' a gerl as was in all Clare, but Clare's not New York, and three years makes a power of difference in a gerl's face, not to mintion the heart of a lad. Maybe Shane's heart ain't where it was."

"It 'd better be," Michael rumbled, his most ferocious face returning. "If his heart ain't thrue, I'll have it out of him. If he breaks her heart, I'll break his head. The poor trustin' colleen—waitin' and waitin'—and him lavin' her wait—and her pinin' away—ah, it's crool—that's what it is, it's crool. Her fare over was thirty-nine dollars."

v

Delia began to rock with an anxiety that was contagious, for Michael clutched her and demanded:

"What's set you to doubtin' Shane O'Mealia? He's as dacent a lad as you'll find in a day's walk—and your own sister's boy."

"Och, it's never a know I know what's in a man's heart," Delia mourned. "But I've seen manny's the young lad come out of Ireland lavin' his heart behind him, and scattherin' promises as thick as snow; but when he gets here and works hard and saves little, things costin' such a terrible cost, and he sees fine-lookin' gerls goin' past him in dhroves, and he lonely and young—and there's the dances and the hurlin'-matches and the futbahl, and the streets, and everywhere gerls laughin'—and he don't mane to be unthrue, but the colleen at home is out of sight—and he's lonely and—and it takes a lot of days to make a week, and a month is a lahng time to be lonesome and a year is an ahful lahng while. It's three years now Shane's waitin' and starvin', and him so handsome, the gerls annoys him with their smiles. I don't blame the poor lads for growin' desprut and takin' up with what beauties they find to hand. Maybe that's what's come over Shane. I don't know. I say maybe. But Moyna—

65

och, the heart-scald to her should she find him cold to her."

The experience was not unfamiliar to Michael among the thousands on thousands of Irish pouring into the country, but he could not believe it happenable to his wards.

"Ah, somebody's been puttin' bad stories on Shane," he smiled. "The divil sail away with you and your sorries. Ahl I'm sorry for is that I didn't tell it you before I sint for her out. But, howane'er, she's here and I'm to go to meet her."

"Arrun't you goin' to be late, as you were when your mother come in?"

"Not me," said Michael. "I niver make the same mistake but the wan time. I'll bate the boat to the dock by an hour at laste. You make Shane slip intil his regimintals and—well, I'm thinkin' we'd better give up part of the surprise. Too much surprise is a dangerous thing. Let you tell him she's to be here and tell him just to look surprised. That's safer. There's no knowin' what a man 'll do when he's reely surprised. Well, I'm gone now. Don't you fret, honey. It couldn't go wrong on me—and me squandherin' thirty-nine dollars on her fare. Good-by again, and I'll tiliphone you from the dock before we stairt from there for here."

He kissed her and left her in a slump of woe. He reached the dock just as the boat was reported at the quarantine station. Being too early has much the same peril as being too late.

Michael found upon the pier an old political crony now high among the officials of the Dock Department. Michael was inspired to urge this man to give Shane a position. It would be double joy to present Shane with his wife-to-be wrapped up in a new job.

Naturally Michael led the official across the wide street

66

to a proper counsel-chamber, where he poured into him beer and eloquence concerning the merits of Shane.

The best of it was that he gained his point and forced his friend to promise Shane a comfortable post. The worst of it was that by the time he had clinched the bargain and toasted its health, Moyna's steamer was docked and all its passengers ashore and passed through the customs gantlet and gone away. When Michael strolled back to the empty pier he was furious at "the dirthy thrick the shtamer played on him, shlippin' a-past him unbeknownst."

But that did not mend matters, nor did it forewarn Delia of Moyna's arrival. The first she knew of that was when she was startled from her almost comfortable despair by the sound of knuckles on the front door. She called to her daughter:

"Katie, would you see who that is knockin' like they'd never seen sight nor light of a door-bell?"

Katie trudged to the door, expecting some yokel of an errand-boy. Instead, she was greeted by a strange and frightened girl standing among her luggage and asking in all timidity:

"Does Mr. and Mrs. Morahan live here, and are they expectin' a visitor from over the wather?"

"Yes," Kate gasped, "they do—they are. You're not Miss Killilea?"

"Yis, ma'am, thank you kindly. And askin' your pairdon, but you're not Miss Morahan that come visitin' us in Lisdoonvarna some fourteen years back? Or are you?"

Kate nodded and the visitor went on:

"Ah, I remimber you. You've not oldered the one whit. But me—I was only out six years then—I've changed beyond your recollectin'. And plase, is Mr. O'Mealia home, if you plase?"

LONG EVER AGO

Kate was slow to understand, but now she shouted aft:
"Ma! Ma! Here's Shane's Moyna!"

VI

Delia came running to the door and enveloped the girl
in her arms and rebuked Kate for holding her there, and
ordered her to help in Moyna's huge old valise and the
bundles she had lugged up the stairs. Herself, she kissed
the cold red cheeks and brought her to the marvelous
steam radiator that had caused Michael's mother such
amazement. And since the girl had blundered into a
tragedy, Delia doubled her natural hospitality, kissed her
again, fluttered about her, helped unwind her out of her
shawl and pulled off the seedy old jacket and shook her
head over the coarse black serge skirt and the cumbrous
shoes.

"Is it an angel that's dropped through the skylight?"
Delia rhapsodized. "Sure you've had the use of the May
dew on your cheeks. And the roses in them! We don't
see such cheeks in this pasty-faced town. Oh, but you're
a born blossom—"

"And have you seen Shane?" said Moyna.

"Where's Michael, I'd like to know," said Delia.
"Didn't he meet you?"

"Never a meet he met me whatever, ma'am dear,"
said Moyna. "I waited and waited. I was that flut-
thered, I thought I'd fly away with myself entirely. I
asked a tahl man in uniforrum—one of the constabulary
he was—did he know where Michael Morahan might be,
and he knew him, and, seein' I had the addhress on an
old letther, he told me where he lived, and said I'd better
joomp into a taxicab, as he called it—it's a kind of an
inside-cair without horses, you know."

"Yes, yes, I know."

"So I thought I'd betther not linger on the quay; and for ahl the expinse of the carriage, I'd betther not be tryin' for to find me way in New Yark, and the bobby calls me a driver and helps me boxes in and lifts me in the cair and—whirroo!—I thought the Old Black Boy had me on his wings. But before I could straighten me hat and me backbone, sure here I was. I says to the jarvey, 'How much?' and he says, 'The clock says sivinty cints,' and I tould him that was a quare kind of tahk to have out of a clock. But I suppose it's the American language and I paid it and—where's Shane O'Mealia, if you plase, ma'am?"

"Sure Michael left here in time to be there twice," said Delia, sparring for her wits.

Moyna seemed to catch a note of evasion in her manner and clutched her arm, pleading:

"But Shane O'Mealia! I'm askin' you kindly. Where's my Shanawn? Has somewhat happened him belike?"

Delia gathered her in and soothed her. "Whisht, honey; he's never dramin' you was on this side of the wather, and he's gone for to get his uniforrum."

"Uniforrum? Is it a constable, too, he's goin' to be?"

"No, a soldier."

"Oh, the saints bind down to me," cried Moyna. "A recruitin' sergeant has got him from me before I'm here?"

"No, it's the Sixty-nint' he's officer in."

Moyna's terror fled instantly. "Oh, he used to write me manny's the letther about the Sixty-ninth—and he's an officer in it now like he was aimin' to be? Ah, that's the chat! And what is he now—a corpor'l or admir'l, or—"

"Lootinant."

"Och, blathers, he'll make a grand liftinant."

Delia breathed more easily and remembered to say:

"Bad manners to me for not axin' you would you like me to wet you a drop of the tay—"

"Oh, I'm that stirred up, ma'am dear, I could never take annything. The sight of you and news of Shane is mate and dhrink to me."

Delia called to the household drudge:

"Kate, take her things to your room while we fix up where she's to stay. No, Myles can sleep with Shamus, and she'll have his room, I think."

Kate took up the rope-bound valise and a big bundle and an ungainly umbrella and held out her hand for a lesser parcel in Moyna's hand. She shook her head.

"And what is it you've there? Your other shoes?" said Delia.

"It's something I brought you and Mr. Morahan from home."

"Oh, and is it now?" Delia exclaimed, like a child at Christmas. "Lave me a look at it."

VII

She popped the string in two and, unrolling the paper, took out a large clod of earth with wilted clover on it. She held it at arm's length and stared at it in silent tenderness, till her eyes turned to water and she smiled blindly; then her eyelids quivered and closed and she carried the lump of soil to her heart and sighed:

"Shamrocks!—on The Sod itself!"

Her tears splashed on it and set the little trefoils to bobbing about. Moyna explained, eagerly:

"They're from the knockawn just beyant your mother's cabin. They're destroyed with the dryness now, ma'am dear, but whin I dug them there were the fresh showers on them like what's fallin' now."

SENT FOR OUT

Delia, with her eyes clenched and still raining, was thinking aloud: "Oh, I can see them blowin' in the win'! They take me back again. I can feel them like when I was runnin' amongst them, and they was noddin' and whimperin' round my little bare feet."

She bent her head and lifted the sacred turf to her lips.

"It's not much they are, ma'am dear," said Moyna, "but—they're Irish."

"Ah, what could you bring with you," Delia laughed and sobbed, "betther than shamrocks? and yourself?"

Moyna waited till she had finished her good cry, then she began again:

"But, ma'am dear, where's Shane? He's had time for to uniforrum a rigiment, horse and fut."

"He'll be here soon," said Delia.

Moyna glanced down at herself and shook her head. "It's a disgrace I am to be seen in a city. Miss Kate dear, could I hide this old hat somewhere, and would you mind did I prink up a little and chase a comb through this hair?"

Kate led her into Myles's room, and she opened her valise and got out her paltry equipment. But when she let down her red hair she was rich as Queen Godiva.

"Come out here where it's warrum and not so dark," said Delia, leading her into the dining-room, which was also the living-room. "Ah, Moyna, but it's the beauty you are—and your hair—it's a wonder the comb don't burn up in it."

Without her ugly hat and her worn cloak, with just herself, she was indeed beautiful—her gray eyes charcoaled with black lashes, her cheeks unimaginably crimsoned with the sharp wet winds she had lived in, her hair flinging about her like a banner as she bent and fought it with the comb.

71

Delia attempted a further compliment.

"I wonder the min in Lisdoonvarna did not prevint you goin' away."

Moyna laughed a bit.

"There's wan or two been pestherin' me not to lave it, but the thought of Shane O'Mealia pulled me like a rope. It seems like it was that that drew the ship through the broad water. But Shane—it's little he thought of me, I'm thinkin'."

"What else had he to think of?"

"Och, meal-a-murdher, there was women in this country before I got here. I saw slathers of them in the streets as I come along, and betther dressed on a week-day than I'll be in heaven. The best in Lisdoonvarna is what the pigs in the New Yark streets would turn up their noses at."

"What eyes could Shane have for the likes of thim?" Delia protested.

But the girl was growing suspicious. "He'd hardly help seein' some of them. They dress that grand you'd hear them with your both eyes shut. Does he never go about?"

"Not much."

"To no dances?"

"What cahl has he to go to dances?"

"Och, he that used to wahk ahl day to dance ahl night!"

"But that was with you."

"Well, there was others he'd dance with, too, even there. We fought like fury over it. I was always quick of timper, bad manners to me. But I've been afraid—three years is a lahng while, ma'am honey. Are you sure he loves no other gerls—are you certain sure, ma'am dear?"

"Why, Moyna, what at all ails you?"

The door-bell shivered brazenly and Moyna jumped to her feet.

SENT FOR OUT

"What's that?"

"The door-bell!" Delia laughed, and motioned Kate to answer it. On Moyna's red cheeks there came a redder red.

"Is it a bell you have? Sure, but you're the quality here. And me knowin' no better than to knock."

Her blush of shame was scattered by the incursion of Judy Dugan in her same fashionable clothes, with the same dashing manner. She spoke briskly: "Oh, Mrs. Morahan, isn't Shane here?"

Seeing Moyna, she stopped short with a disinterested, "Oh, I beg your pardon."

"I want you should meet Miss Killilea," said Delia, sternly.

VIII

Judy, hearing a name that meant nothing to her, spoke as New-Yorkers speak to strangers, with a curt nod.

"And how is your honor? and hopin' you're well," said Moyna, looking her up and down with an instant terror of jealousy because of her use of the name of Shane and her outrageously fashionable clothes.

The contrast was complete between them. Judy, born in Ireland, but brought over as an infant in arms, was citified to the last degree, used to the sight and environment of soft things and no heavy labor; she was slim and limp and lithe and dressed in the glossiest, most feminine things, and she stood in the attitude of a feather boa.

Moyna stood squarely on her large feet in low-heeled shoes. She had been used from childhood to hard labor, to scrabbling for potatoes in wet ground, to carrying great creels of turf on hip or shoulder; she had gone barefoot and barehead through rain and mist the greater part

73

of her life, and her beauty was stalwart, big-thewed, broad-bosomed, high-colored, almost primeval.

She looked as if she could have easily twisted Judy into a bow-knot, but for experience she was a child in comparison. It was Moyna that was smitten with fear at the light chatter of the nervous Judy, who rattled on:

"Forgive me for rushing in on you like this and dashing off again," said Judy, never dreaming that she was scattering torpedoes, "but I thought Shane would be here."

"Will you wait—or won't you?" said Delia, afraid to live in such danger.

"Can't stop a moment," said Judy. "Would you mind taking a message for him?"

"Sure I will," sighed Delia.

Judy's face was suddenly wreathed with smiles and she cried: "It's such good news for both of us. Just tell him that I said I've seen my father, and he has given his full consent gladly, and that we'll all three go to the priest to-morrow noon together. Tell the dear boy that, will you? He'll understand and arrange it all and I'll be ever so much obliged. Good-by; delighted to have met you, Miss Killigrew."

She hurried out, leaving Delia and Kate helpless, and Moyna aghast. Delia and Kate exchanged glances of panic, and in Moyna anxiety and a wild fear grew like an oncoming storm. She began to put up her hair, jamming its coils together and stabbing it with pins as if they were knives; and she was yammering:

"Her father gave his consint! and they'll go to the priest to-morrow!—her father's consint—the priest! What does it mane? Who is she?"

"She's a—a friend of ours; and a neighbor."

"And a neighbor of Shane's, and a fri'nd of his! And she niver heard of me, nor me of her. And what, if you plase, ma'am dear—oh, dear ma'am—what do you make out of this goin' to the priest?"

"I—I don't know what it could mane," Delia stammered.

Moyna shuddered in a tempest of despair. "Oh yes, you do, ma'am, askin' your pairdon. And so do I. They're going to the priest to have the banns called. That's what it manes. They'll be asked out next Sunday. They're to be married in three weeks. For all I've waited three years, I'm not needed. For all my surprisin' Shane, I'm too late. It's too late I am!"

She broke down and wept with all her might, burying face in the depths of her hair, and tearing at the strands, till Delia was frantic.

"Oh, mercy be among us! This is beyant the beyants!"

Moyna's face came out of her hair in a revulsion to wrath. "Is it a heart he has in him, that Shane, or is it a hotel? Oh, it's the bitther day I ever set fut on the ocean. But I never thought Shane O'Mealia would go for to be makin' a fool of me like this."

Delia tried to reassure her.

"Ah, set no store by Judy's talk, avourneen. She's a lahng tongue on her. Shane's not the slieveen to play fast and loose."

"And is he not, now?" Moyna raved. "Did he lave me in Ireland three years? Yis! Did he sind for me out? No! Did he meet me at the dock? No! Did I find him here? No! Who did I find here? Her! Runnin' in with her, 'Tell Shane this and tell Shane that!' Was he her pig, she couldn't have talked more like ownin' him!"

Delia's wits were gone entirely; she could only offer random inspirations such as they were: "Och, Moyna, Shane wouldn't trade you for his pick of the stars."

LONG EVER AGO

"Well, he can have his pick of them," said Moyna. "I'll lave him the free hand of them." Suddenly her violence and her noise were at an end. She dashed her tears from her cheeks with the back of her fist roughly, and stood wrestling down the sobs surging in her breast. She fought herself to a standstill and then laughed softly and bitterly at herself with a meekness that was harder for Delia to bear than all the outcries of her pride.

"Well, afther ahl, what cahl have I to be carryin on like this? Who is it I am that Shane O'Mealia should be blind to the whole worruld because of me? And small blame to him. For why should he be thrue to an old-country goose like me when there's queens like her about? Where's my things?"

She reached about for her bundles and began to throw them into her valise again, packing in with them many a thumping tear.

Delia caught at her hands. "Moyna, my lanna, you're not quittin' out of this! Kate, don't lave her have her clothes."

Kate snatched away the scant wardrobe as fast as Moyna thrust it in the valise. Moyna gave up the struggle for the sake of manners and spoke with dreadful calm:

"Then I'll go without, and good evening kindly to you, ma'am dear, and no hard feelin's on you for what you couldn't help."

She moved irresistibly to the door, dragging the clinging women with her, Delia wailing:

"But, darlin' dear, where will ye spind the night?"

Moyna tossed her head high: "In anny hotel but the one Shane O'Mealia keeps under his coat. I won't stay in the same town at all. I'll wahk over to Chicago and spind the night there. And the next mornin' I'll move on to Philadilphia or Boston, or anny place where he'll

76

not find me. Not that he'll try. He'll be glad to be red of me. And at that it's no harm I wish him at his weddin' whin it comes."

Then the sobs broke from her, and in an irresistible frenzy she ripped loose the fingers of the clinging women and dashed out, leaving the hall door open.

Delia and Kate heard the diminishing whirlwind of her stampede down the stairs; they ran out into the hall and stared down at her, and then in hopeless helplessness returned to the flat. Delia dropped into a chair and threw her apron up over her face, groaning:

"Oh, wirrasthrue, and sorry on the day, and God break haird fortune!"

IX

Kate ran to the window and threw it open and called back: "There she goes runnin' down the street and people starin' at her. Moyna! Moyna!" she shrieked down into the cavern. But an elevated train ran by with long linked thunders and drowned her voice. She closed the window and sank into her own chair, mumbling, "She's turned the corner, and Heaven knows where she'll go now."

Michael's old mother began to call from her own room. She had been wakened by Moyna's tumult and had cried out unheard. Kate ran to her now and wheeled her back into the dining-room, where she was trying to explain to her when Michael himself came home.

Delia, who had seemed to be drained of strength by her ordeal, rose and went at him with a power that would have honored Moyna. The big man cowered before her like a whipped and whining hound. The only thing that saved him was the ringing of the door-bell.

77

Kate admitted a stack of boxes that walked in on a pair of legs.

Delia, seeing it, gasped, "The saints shield us, what's that?"

From behind the pasteboard tower came the words, "It's me—Shane, with me uniforrum." The boxes went toppling over on a sofa, revealing him in a glow of pride. "There's a fatigue coat and a dress coat, and a campaign hat, and two pairs of pants, and puttees, and a dress cap, and a belt and a sword knot and a sword."

A long, slim bundle in a leather case fell to the floor with a muffled clank. "That's the sword!" he said, and, picking it up, brought it forth with the thrill a sword always gives a man.

Delia glowered at him unmoved. "You'll be needin' a sword to cut the knot you're in."

"What's that?" said Shane.

"Moyna Killilea is here—or was."

Shane was struck by a very lightning of surprise.

"Moyna! Moyna Killilea! Here! In New York! When—where—how?"

Delia motioned to the abject cause of all the trouble. "Himself sint for her out."

"Moyna on this side—in this house?" Shane stammered, in a chaos of emotions.

"She was," Delia muttered. "And so was Judy Dugan. They met, and Judy told me to tell you that her father gave his consint, and you'd all three go to the priest together."

"And Moyna heard that?" Shane whispered.

"Did she hear it!" Delia laughed.

"But did she understand what Judy meant?"

"She did that."

"And what did she say?"

SENT FOR OUT

"She wished you luck at your weddin' with Judy—
and said she'd take herself off out of your way. And she
did."

Shane dropped in a heap on a chair, wringing his hands
and groaning: "O Lord! O Lord! And where did she go?"

"Out!" said Delia, bitterly.

"Out where? Out where?"

"Just out. She said she'd walk over to Chicago, but
I don't think she'll make it."

Shane went into a panic of remorseful alarm. "But
the poor soul doesn't know New York. It's grown dark
already. She'll be run over. Harm will befall her. O
Lord! O Lord! Judy has put a curse on me. Where
can I find Moyna? What can I do?"

"If you love her you'll hunt for her," said Delia.

"Love her! Of course I love her!" he cried, and, indeed, his old love came back on the full tide of pity and
fear. "I'll hunt the town through. I'll scour the world.
Oh, the darlin' that she is! And her heart must be broke
in her."

And so he dashed out.

X

Delia turned on Michael, who looked as if he would
like to follow: "And now, you big blundherin', slutherin',
deceptionable old gob of a natural, what are you goin'
to do to undo what you've been doin'?"

It seemed that nothing but a miracle could save Michael
from a beating. Heaven sent him an inspiration. He
slid along the wall past the threatening foe and reached
the haven of the telephone. Curiosity stayed Delia's
hand while he fumbled the receiver off the hook and called
into the transmitter in a weak voice:

"T'irty-wan hundred Spring. Hello! Is this P'lice

79

Headquarthers? Gimme the inspecthor. Say, is this you, Chief? This is Mike Morahan. MIKE MORA-HAN! Can't you hear? Are you gone deaf? Yes, it's me. I want you should sind out a gineral alairm. A gerl has roon off, named Moyna Killilea. She's just in out of the old counthry and she's—say, Delia, what's she like?" He repeated the dictation he got—"red-headed, bare-headed, gray-eyed, in a black serge skirt, wit' no hat on her, and Irish shoes on her feet, and a wild look in her eye would scare a copper up a lamp-post. Send out worrud and bring her in or I'll have you broke."

Having bullied the police, he sidled toward his hat and coat and backed out.

Delia's most unusual tornado frightened her as much as it did Michael, and she sank down in a whirl of shame and grief. Her rocking-chair cantered for miles as she discussed with Kate and old Bridget the perils that confronted an ignorant country girl like Moyna in the night mazes of the big city.

The women held a wake over the girl as if she were already dead. The sons came home for supper and found the women as mournful as the three Fates, and the supper not started. When the boys heard all that had happened, they took nourishment from excitement and set out to add their wits to the great pack of hounds on the trail of the runaway hare.

At nine o'clock, when Delia was getting tea and toast to replenish her strength for more grief, Judy Dugan came in in still finer finery. She was dressed for one of the numberless dancing parties the Irish girls and lads are forever getting up. Shane was to have taken her. She had wondered at his non-appearance. Delia was too weak to give her what she gave Michael, but she did her best in her weak woman's way.

SENT FOR OUT

Judy had a mother who was gifted at hysterics and Judy was trained to marvels of patience in trying to sell dresses to impossible women.

It was a hard blow to her to learn that Shane had cherished a sweetheart all the while he was philandering with her. She had taken a deep interest in him and she thought that it was love. It might well have been, but Moyna had come in time to nip it, if not in the bud, at least before it bloomed to the full.

Shane was so unpopular here that Judy did not need to add her own grievances against him. Her tears for herself sank back into her heart. She was there when Policeman Myles himself brought in Moyna, treating her with a mock severity that shattered her overspent temper and her overtired strength.

Delia and Kate launched themselves upon her with kisses of frantic welcome that made them infinitely dear to her in her need. And Judy saw her so lonely, so hurt, so pitiful, that she almost forgave her for having seen Shane first. Myles explained in his gruffest tones, while he winked across Moyna's shoulder:

"The cops found her out in Bronnix Park, askin' how much furtherer was it to Chicago, so they took her up for a suspicious character. I used me infloonce and got her off on parole during good behavior. She was all for not comin' with me, but I arrested her for resistin' the police and brought her down on the subway. I stopped in here to see could pa stand bail for her and would he. Of course, it's a serious charge they got against her, wanderin' in Bronnix Park without a license; but maybe if she promised to make no more trouble and if Shane was to forgive her and she'd promise to take shelter under his wing as his wife, I might get a suspension of sentence. I say I might."

Moyna had carried all the freight of woe and fear and

81

loneliness she could bear. She was as unresisting as a broken, bruised, and hobbled mustang.

She had no strength to flare up even against Judy, who took the same key, and upbraided her for her stupidity and her treachery in misunderstanding harmless words and doubting the faith of the faithful Shane. But Judy had too much pride to explain how it was on account of the strength of her father's weakness that the whole trouble arose. Trying to conceal that, she only confused herself and confirmed Moyna's despair.

Then Judy went to her own disordered home and cried all over her party dress, took herself out of her finery, and crept into her bed. The alarm-clock found her still awake, but she dragged herself to early Mass and thanked Heaven for having a shop to go to, and begged for blessings on the handsome head of Shane O'Mealia.

But long hours before this Michael had come home, bringing in the exhausted Shane, whom he had found half fainting on the street.

At the sound of his voice at the front door Moyna darted into the bedroom that had been assigned to her.

When Delia revived Shane with the miraculous news that the lost ewe-lamb was "within in there," Shane ran to the door and turned the knob. But he almost broke his excellent nose, for the door was locked.

He remodeled his nose with one hand while he rattled the knob pleadingly with the other. And he thrilled the panels with his prayers for mercy. He had back only the heartbreaking sound of Moyna's sobs for a long while, then a more hurtful silence, and after that grim advice in her deepest tones:

"Don't be wastin' your time on such as me. You're keepin' your grand lady from the party, and you've the priest to see to-morra."

"Och, Moyna," Shane implored, "quit out of that and come back to me arrums, or the only party will be the funeral of the one that loves you."

Moyna's voice faltered a little, but she answered, bitterly:

"It's sorry I'll be not to be there, but I'll be goin' back across the ocean the mornin'."

"Ah, Moyna dairlin', sure the ocean itself is no thicker than this dure bechune us, and I'll dhrown meself in the say if you tahk of sailin'."

Moyna laughed back: "You've shwum for three years now, and Madamselle Dugan will hold up your head for you. She shwims grand, too."

Michael tiptoed up to the distracted wooer and whispered:

"Try a bit of foorce; it's that that the women love."

Shane assumed his fiercest tone:

"Moyna, if you do not open this dure this mortial minyute, I'll break it through."

"Do!" said Moyna. "And the instiant you coom in at the dure I go out at the windy."

Michael heard this and it stumped him. He thought awhile, then he motioned Shane to a distance and held counsel with him. Shane yielded at length and went to the door again to call:

"Good-by, Moyna, and may the saints have softer hearts than you have. Good-by-y."

Then he gathered up his boxes and went sadly away, loaded with bundles and woes like an inconsolable expressman.

There was silence on the other side of the door, but the anxious watchers could vividly imagine the dismay that was there. Delia knocked and told Moyna that Shane was gone, and begged her to come on in out of the cold in there; but Moyna answered:

"Thank you kindly, but it's not fit I am to be seen, and would you lind me the use of the room till the next boat back? I'll pesther you no more."

So they left her to her gloom and sat down like doleful besiegers of an impregnable citadel. There they were when the telephone bell rang. Michael answered it. It was his son, the priest.

"Is Shane there?" Father Dermot asked.

"He is not, Father," said Michael.

"Then, father, would you get word to him for me? He and Judy were bringing Judy's father here to sign the pledge before me to-morrow noon, and I find I have a call out at that hour; so ask him, will you, would they come at eleven or at two? Either hour suits me and I'll have the pledge already written out in words would turn Gambrinus into a prohibitionist."

"I'll tell him, my son—er, Father—and thank you more than you know," Michael shouted, "and good-by to you, me boy—your Riverence!"

Father Dermot, whom Shane had not warned to secrecy, had unwittingly dissolved the mystery that Judy's pride and Shane's oath had erected between Moyna and her happiness.

Michael was on fire with joy. He almost blistered the door with the fervor of his language as he passed the explanation in to Moyna. It brought her forth at last in a completely altered mood of contrition. It was she now that had done wrong and dealt harshly, and it was Shane that had been noble beyond belief.

Moyna felt undeserving entirely now, and there was no need of the uniform Shane walked in in a little later. But it helped to complete the collapse of Moyna's resistance.

Shane was not prepared at all, however, for the enthusiasm of her surrender. And when she charged on him, crying, "Oh, Shane, my Shaneen beug, forgive me, forgive me!" he was so taken aback that his elbow knocked against the hilt of his unaccustomed sword and sent the scabbard between his legs, and he would have gone sprawling if she had not upheld him in her strong arms.

He was about to resume his attitude of groveling repentance, but he caught sight of Michael making terrible faces of stern suggestion, and he understood. He made some difficulty about pardoning his prodigal sweetheart, but at length he gathered her into his arms with a lofty condescension that made her feel small, and weak, and unworthy of his grandeur, and utterly dependent on his strength of character.

Which was the way she wanted to feel.

IV

EXCEPT HE WERE A BIRD

GOOD young Irishmen when they leave Erin for a
better world join the heavenly choir of New Jeru-
salem after due probation. All sorts of young Irishmen,
when they left Ireland for the next best place, joined the
Sixty-ninth Regiment of New York.

That was one of the first things young Shane O'Mealia
did when he came out to the States, and his first letter
back to Moyna Killilea had been full of the glory of his
acceptance into the famous organization. He spent most
of his leisure at the home of his uncle, Michael Morahan,
and it had been a brave day when he had arrived there
with golden news, and cried:

"Aunt Dalia dear, I've been thransferred from private
in Coompany Ah to sairgeant in Coompany Haitch!"

He had written that home to Moyna, too, and it was
the one bright chapter in his long chronicle of losing jobs
and postponing the blessed day when he could send for
her to come across the long water and marry him.

The week that brought him his commission to the
Second-Lieutenancy of Company N, Captain Kerin commanding, brought Moyna Killilea to America most unexpectedly. She could not resist the bravery of his uniform,
and she consented to restore him to her idolatry. She
agreed that the banns should be called the following
Sunday.

86

EXCEPT HE WERE A BIRD

But it looked as if the Old Black Boy was in it. Before the priest could "ask out" the couple the first time the devil sailed away with Shane's next job. The banns were recalled. In good time Shane found a new position—in a stove-store, no less, and the wedding preparations were resumed.

Shane's modesty prevented him from boasting to his new boss that he had the honor of employing a second lieutenant in the Sixty-ninth, N. G., N. Y. Shane decided to save that gorgeous surprise till the man was ready for it. He was a foreigner, anyway, and would have to be educated up to the meaning of the Sixty-ninth in the history of the nation, the achievements of its child, the Irish Brigade, in the Civil War, and other matters that have given the regiment a place all its own.

The stove merchant was born in America, but he was as foreign as only a man of Norwegian descent could seem to an Irishman. His impossible name was Bjerring— "Old Bejabers," Shane called him—at first—but stronger names later. O. O. Bjerring sold stoves of all sorts, furnaces of all sorts, radiators, gas logs, ice-boxes—everything relating to heat.

But the emotional, impulsive Shane found Mr. Bjerring even colder than employees are apt to find employers. Shane described him to Moyna: "For all his stoves, that Scandihoovian cannot get the warrumth of a fish into his soul. He has a snowball for a heart and ice-wather on tap in his veins. Troth and he was born with an icicle on the ind of his nose."

Shane put off telling him about his commission in the hope that the spring would thaw him out, but long before that Mr. Bjerring broached the subject himself:

"By the way, O'Meely," he said one day, "take a tip from me. Seeing that you're Irish, they'll soon be after

you to join the Ninety-sixth, or whatever it is. But don't
you do it. This militia business is all wrong. It's a
waste of time. Nobody but a fool would waste it. Besides, I don't believe in this militaryism. I fired a man
last year who had to go away for a week to camp. His
night work, too, was always being interrupted by the
drills. I simply won't stand for it. And I want you
should promise me you won't go and join."

The startled Shane promised that he would not go and
join. He was not asked if he had already gone and joined.
But now his plight was a trilemma; how was he to keep
his job, his military career, and his wife? How could he
live without e'er-a-one of them? He resolved to cling
to them all as long as he could. He would not let his job
know of his military career. He would keep his fame a
secret, and cast about meanwhile for another job.

There was one comfortable fact: his sweetheart was
not at war with his regiment. His uniform had been his
best argument with her, and when she saw him drilling
his men she was fairly destroyed with admiration.

That was a wonderful night when first Moyna came
down to the armory and watched his work. The Morahans, Michael and Delia, and their daughter Kate, were
invited along, of course. Shane took care not to invite
the sons of the family: they had enough fun to poke at
him without added ammunition.

Moyna and the Morahans arrived in time to look over
the armory before the assembly bugle. Moyna was
tremendously impressed with the building, especially the
magnificent furniture in the officers' room and with the way
everybody saluted Shane. Only two companies were
drilling that night, but Moyna thought the armies of the
world were gathering.

With duplex pride Shane introduced the officers to her.

EXCEPT HE WERE A BIRD

It was not difficult for soldiers to be courteous to a beauty like Moyna, but she was fluttered by their civilities.

"Ivery mortial wan of thim," she exclaimed, "is politer than the rist of them. And they're not ferocious whativer, for ahl they're such brave min. And they're handsome lads, too; but none of thim's as pretty as my Shaneen."

"Wait till you've seen Lieutinant McCooey," said Shane. "It's only fair to inthroduce him to you, for we come out in the same boat and we wint before the Examining Boord the same ahful night, and we both scraped through by the same narrow mairgin. But he's a grand looker and no mistake. I doubt I'll hold you for mine once you've laid your two eyes on him. Where is he now, I don't know. There he is—on the stairs. Oh, McCooey!—Oh, Lieutinant McCooey!"

Moyna saw a uniformed officer trudging up the stairs and she braced herself for a shock of beauty. But she told herself that, were the man Apollo himself, she must remember that Shaneen had her heart.

When Lieutenant McCooey turned, Moyna staggered in spite of herself. He was ugly to a magnificent extent. He was ugly enough to be handsome and on past that to being ugly all over again.

"The saints gather round us," Moyna said, as he came down the stairs, "is it a baboon you have dressed up for a mascot? Och, wirra wirra, how his face must hurt him at night when he's alone wid it."

"He's the best-hearted man in the world," Shane mumbled.

"Why wouldn't he be with the moog he has on him?" Moyna groaned. "Were he a saint, he has his martyrdom under his hat!"

By the time McCooey had reached the bottom of the

89

stairs Moyna had subdued her features, and she greeted him with the full candle-power of her enthusiasm. McCooey was infatuated at once, and his smile was not so bad as his serious expression. And he delighted Moyna by telling her that Shane was the pride of the regiment.

When he moved away Shane spoke gently: "He has ahlways the kind word for iverybody."

"And smahl wondher!" said Moyna. "Whin he was at Blarney Castle he might have bit a piece out with that jah he borried off a gorilly. His poor mother must have lived ferninst the Zoo-ological Gairdens."

Shane tried to be loyal to McCooey: "You oughtn't to miscall him, seein' he came out on the same boat with me."

But Moyna only smiled: "Ahl Ireland's the betther-lookin' for his absince."

"He'd do annything on earth for a fri'nd."

"Can't he do annything on earth for himself?"

Shane gave up the effort to win a word of praise from Moyna for McCooey, and asked only one favor:

"If you see him afther the drill, don't fail to remimber his name—McCooey; and he's a lieutinant."

"If I see him after the drill it 'll be because I can't bate him to the dure," said Moyna. "But have no fear of me forgettin' his name. While there's sinse and mimmory in me I'll joomp at the name McCooey."

Then the bugle blew all social thoughts away and the visitors scurried up to the gallery to watch the entertainment. As Moyna gazed about the expanse of glistening floor under the vast arch of the glass roof, she was lost in awe and cried:

"Ah, the grand railway station 'twould make were there but thracks in it."

Moyna soon picked out Shane's company. McCooey

was with the other. She was disappointed to note that Shane's post was in the rear of the rear rank. The captain gave the stentorian commands and Shane merely mumbled and prodded the inaccurate and indolent.

Moyna turned to Michael for information:

"For why would he be an officer and he workin' there in the back yaird all the time?"

Michael winked at Delia and answered:

"That's the place he holds. Out in the field of battle he would be carryin' the wather to the min and tidyin' up the tints."

Moyna believed him and her pride collapsed.

"Och, blathers, and that's a fine job! It's a chambermaid he is, then. And he tellin' me he was a leftinant."

But after a time Captain Kerin, catching sight of the squad of spectators aloft and realizing that it was Shane they came to see, was gracious enough to call Shane forward to take command while he joined First-Lieutenant Cavanaugh in the line of file-closers and took his orders from his subordinate.

Seeing this alteration of estates, Moyna was tremendously excited. She clutched Michael's arm:

"He's promoted already! Or is it a mutiny he started? Sure would yous look at the captain and lootinant slinkin' along behind with the sthragglers and takin' orthers from my Shane. Lave them to workin' the mop and makin' the beds. Shane is king now. I tell you people comes into their own in time."

Shane was making a brave show, but he was more afraid of the company back of him than of anything on earth except the little crowd in the gallery.

Shane was so terrified, so mixed, that Michael groaned to Delia:

"The poor stokawn doesn't know bay from a bull's fut."

He gave two or three impossible commands such as "Right front into line" when they were already in line and "Column right" when it led his column into the wall. In extricating them from one tangle he got into a worse. He got them so tied up that they stopped fast like cigar Indians while he tried to evolve them from their difficulty; but he had at length to give the hopeless command:

"Fahl out and fahl in again."

Moyna, noting how befuddled the men were, protested:

"Did you ever see the like of the lunkheads they are? I wonder Shane is that patient with them."

The captain and the first lieutenant were smiling; in their day they had also known the drill-fright of playing with toy soldiers that know a thing or two themselves and have the dreadful gift of laughter. The men were tormented with amusement at the mixed commands, for a misplaced word almost always proves irresistible to the human sense of humor. A man slipping and falling on the ice is no funnier than a word bumping unexpectedly into another. But the men all tried to keep from laughing aloud, since they knew who was in the balcony. And so they marched about, tight-lipped and shivering, till Moyna noticed it and asked Michael:

"See the poor things shake. Is it that Shane has scared them into a palsy, or is it a chill's on them? I doubt there's a powerful dhraught on the flure."

Michael was merciful, and doubted there was, too.

When the miserably embarrassed Shane had aligned his men once more he thought he would put them through the manual of arms to steady them and himself. He tried to make up in severity what he lacked in security and with a voice positively blood-curdling he shouted:

"Prre-*sint* HAIRRUMS!"

It was a very excellent presentation: the pieces went

into position with a snap and the company froze into a Noáh's ark.

Now Shane roared, "Ardor—hairrums!" and the muskets came down to the order in grim precision. And then success betrayed him and from his astonished lungs came the thunderous absurdity:

"Right shoulther—bay-nits!"

The company wavered and rocked as if a shell had exploded at its feet. The command was unheard of and impossible, and if that were not a double reason for laughter, there was no resisting the look on Shane's face when he heard his own voice rollicking round the armory like a sarcastic echo. Years later he would be known as "Old Right Shoulder Bay'nits."

Moyna saw nothing funny in Shane's command; she was merely dazed at the result. Solemnity was gone, rigidity was broken into flitterjigs. The men leaned on one another and whooped. Captain Kerin fell against his first sergeant and Lieutenant Cavanaugh slapped the right guide on the back.

The other company, standing at ease at the time, heard the command, and laughter ran along it in a seismic billow. Everybody laughed but dear old McCooey. He was too kind-hearted not to feel Shane's desperate dismay.

Moyna still could not understand. Then a light struck her and she smiled:

"Oh, I see. Shane's humorin' them the way they'll feel aisier."

"That's it!" whooped Michael, who was an old Sixty-ninther and was shrieking with the rest. "You have it! He's humorin' thim!"

Now Moyna laughed as hard as any, her eyes glistening with pride as she chuckled:

"He's a witty lad, my Shane. He can make a rigimint laugh—and hould his own face as straight as a funeral!"

"Thrue for you, Moyna!" Michael roared. "He's witty; you have the thruth of it there!"

"But what makes him so red? His face is red to the back of his neck."

Again Michael was merciful. He would not diminish Shane's prestige in Moyna's eyes. So he sobered down and muttered: "You're under young to know. No doubt Shane 'll tell you after you're married."

Then Moyna turned red. And she and her Shane were blushing in mystic kinship.

Disabled with disgust, Shane saluted the captain with his sword and the captain came reluctantly from the concealment of his men and, returning Shane's salute with a sweeping blade, took command of the company, while Shane prowled off to the rear.

"He's givin' the captain another chance," said Moyna, "afther showin' him how it's to be done."

Michael said to Delia: "That gerl is a wondher at graspin' milith'ry matthers. It bates all."

Captain Kerin tried to scare himself and the men into dignity by a wolfish snarl:

"At-*tin*-SHAN! Far-wurd-haow! Gui-drigh-tt! Squads ri'!—Col-yume ri'!—haow! Double time—haow!"

He dog-trotted them round and round the armory at the double till they were almost dropping. He jogged alongside, muttering:

"I'll sweat the snickers out of you! Close up there!"

At the far end of the armory he brought the straggling column on left into line, then opened them out into squads and then spread them clear across the floor in the thin line of skirmishers.

He moved them in extended order to the attack with

EXCEPT HE WERE A BIRD

frequent rushes and loadings and firings, kneeling and prone. And now the guffaws of ridicule were forgotten in the immemorial still laughter of the lust of combat in the supreme gymnasium of war.

Michael Morahan was breathing hard, though he smiled when he mumbled:

"It's a grand thing watchin' a battle from a balcony, and seein' the fearless lads shootin' imaginary inimies full of imaginary catthridges."

Shane got a chance in the fire by platoon, but he was lost as the control of fire passed to the corporals wriggling on their bellies and giving the ranges, as if the wall a dozen yards away were a line of trenches soon to be stormed for the sake of the nation's all-important life. It was childish in a way, the pretense of earnestness, the valorous abandon to the nursery make-believe; yet these men would go into shrapnel rain and bullet sleet with just the same exultant childishness for a cause perhaps as nursery-like, though the cannon whiffed them to shreds or the bayonets ripped them open. Only then their women-folk would not have them all back when the drill was over and the diplomats signaled "Dismissed."

So keen was the delight of the soldiers in their trade that when the captain made ready for the charge and called, "Fix bay'nets!" no laughter blurted at the fatal word. The knives rattled into their locks and at the wild command the line sprang up and came roaring forward with all steel glinting, and every face aflash with joy.

While man is man such things will thrill, and Moyna stood up and cheered. Michael yelped, and when they halted with their valiant officers on the captured line he moralized:

"By cripes, but thim boys is the boys! Sure and if it had to be I wint to war, I'd rather go with Irish than with

95

anny other, for I'd be safer; and I'd rather go ag'in' anny other or ahl the other than ag'in' the Irish, for I'd be in more danger. Us Hibernians has a kind of peculiar appetite for throuble. We're the on'y people I know of that begins to grin at the mintion of a shindy. Others fights hard and they're solemn or sad or desprut or contimpchous, as may be, but the Irishman laughs. He's the laughin'est fighter was ever in the worruld. If they can't get foreigners to fight, they'll fight among themselves for the pure love of the art of it."

"All the same," said Moyna, "I'm glad there's no danger here."

"Danger is it!" Michael protested. "Av coorse there's danger, in full and plinty. When it comes to chairgin' acrost that shiny flure, who knows what moment his fut 'll shlip and he come down on the inimy on the broad of his back? I done that once whin I was first promoted from high private to lance corpor'l, for gallanthry in the field of refreshments. And I got a lumbago I'd 'a' had a pinsion for it if the Repooblicans hadn't happened on an eliction. Sure it's dangerous."

"Thin I don't want Shane dhrillin'," said Moyna. "And he can quit out of this."

Michael shifted promptly: "Ach, Moyna agra, did you lave your sinse of yumor at home with your umbrelly? There's no danger at all. I'm on'y tahkin' to keep you from bein' bored by the tameness of it."

When the drill at length was over and the companies dismissed to their company-rooms and thence to their own clothes and homes, Shane was reluctant to face Moyna at all after his disgraceful slip of the tongue. But Michael seized the chance to reach him first and explain hastily that Moyna had taken his misfortune for genius, and Shane was wise enough to accept her congratulations with the modest grace of one who knows he is very good, but prefers not to admit it.

And then dear old McCooey came along, caught them at the big door of the armory, and with the noblest intentions in the world proceeded to slaughter Moyna's comfortable illusions:

"Miss Killilea, I'm glad to have met you, and I've told me old friend Shane here he was a good selecter, for of all the ladies I've seen him makin' up to, the one he's finally decided to marry is the jim of the boonch."

"I thank you kindly! Good evening kindly," said Moyna, turning aside and muttering to Michael, "Take him away before I murther him."

But McCooey's generosity was not exhausted. He followed along to add:

"And don't take it to heart about Shane's blundher to-night."

"Shane's blundher?" Moyna echoed.

"Yis, the unfortunate break about right shoulther bay'nits. The best of soldiers makes the moonkeys of themselves at first. But he'll get over it."

"Yis, Shane'll git over bein' a moonkey," Moyna groaned between her clenched teeth, "but there's others never will."

And she swept away, leaving McCooey blissfully unconscious that he had been annihilated. Moyna was so wroth at him that she forgot to question Shane about that list of girls he had made up to before he found the Jim of the Boonch.

Moyna went to other drills and Shane was luckier. He prospered at the armory and at the stovery and at the love-game. The wedding date was set, and he and Moyna selected an apartment that was just a trifle more expensive than they could afford, and Shane gave a

97

mortgage on his soul to an instalment furniture palace. And then the fairies that Shane had somehow offended began to sit up daytimes and form battalions to destroy him. Hosts of them fell on him right, left, and center, and attacked him at his job, at his post, and at his heart.

First came the boss, Mr. Bjerring. Shane broached the subject of a few days' furlough from the office for the sake of his honeymoon.

Bjerring drew a long face. "I don't believe in men marryin' so young," he growled. "Why not wait a few years? What you want to get married for, anyhow? Take my advice and not. Why, only last year I had to fire a man because he got married and his wife got sick— right in my busy season, too—and what you think he wanted?—to draw his wages in advance! Honest!"

Shane gently explained that all arrangements had been made for his wedding and he would tell his wife that if she got sick it must be in the late summer, when stoves are not so lively and ice-boxes have quieted down. Bjerring grumbled:

"Well, I'll let you off a few days for the honeymoon, but you got to work nights to make it up. I'm just goin' to begin stock-takin' and things are in a hell of a mess, because the bookkeeper gave me some lip yesterday and I fired him to-day. You make your arrangements to spend three evenings a week here for the next few weeks, and after that I'll let you off half a week to get your eyes open. But of course I'll have to dock your pay. You wouldn't expect to be paid for gallivantin' round the country, would you?"

Shane shook his head and said Mr. Bjerring was very ginerous to lave him off at all. But he wanted to bend a stove-lid over the villain's crown. And when he broke the news to Moyna that evening he said: "It's that old

EXCEPT HE WERE A BIRD

Bejabers that has no heart in him whativer. Would you shtuff him in a red-hot oven, you could use it for could could sthorage and keep eggs in it ilegant."

That night he went to the armory on his way to the shop, and found in his box a copy of a new order—General Order No. 20—from regimental headquarters, announcing that the annual inspection was shortly to take place— the yearly Judgment Day, when lockers were opened and all souls aligned for condemnation.

Shane had known the anguish of this fierce inquisition and the toil of preparing for it. It had been bad when he was a private; worse when he was a sergeant; it would be a persecution to him as an officer.

Every man jack in the regiment was expected to be present, dead or alive. Every shoestring, puttee-strap, and collar device was expected to be in its place in perfect condition. And Shane knew that the men had a genius for absenting themselves and the State properties intrusted to them. They had a genius for making mistakes in sheer terror when the inspector halted in front of them and waited for them to port arms and open chamber. They seemed unable to let go the rifle when the inspector took it or to take it back when he returned it, and the sight of a speck of grease on the white-glove finger was as a sign of the plague to them.

So it was like perusing his death warrant when he conned the fierce paragraphs of the order, each clause in it being a challenge and a threat. He would have sworn that Bjerring wrote it himself as he read:

II. The several subdivisions will parade for inspection under arms (except Hospital Corps detachment) without ammunition or rations, in service uniform, olive drab, dismounted, with field equipment, including first aid packets and pouches, and intrenching tools, and blanket-roll "packs," U. R. Schedule

A and C for officers and F for enlisted men, as prescribed in the "Table of Occasions," pages 34, 35, and 44, and the Appendix to I. D. R. 1911, in so far as they apply to issued property.

The uniform and equipment shall be worn as for field service: special care should be given to the placing and adjustment of equipment for uniformity in appearance and ease in carriage.

The property not carried on the person shall be arranged in an orderly manner for examination, verification, and inspection for serviceability.

Overcoats and identification tags will be examined in lockers or storerooms.

The blanket-roll "pack" will be made with shelter-tent half and blanket-roll strap, and shall contain blanket, bed sack, shelter-tent pole and pins; the pouch will be folded lengthwise and placed on the outside of the roll. Tin cup, mess kit complete, and field kit will be carried within the haversack, properly placed; the field kit will contain towel, comb, tooth-brush, housewife, soap, and one pair of stockings. The contents of the haversack will be displayed for examination and verification when the blanket-roll "packs" are opened for inspection. "Packs" will be opened and property worn will be displayed for examination in a uniform manner and according to the rules prescribed in the hereinbefore mentioned Appendix, pages 1 and 2, with the authorized modification.

·   ·   ·   ·   ·

V. Books and records, including financial records, property returns with required inventories, muster rolls in duplicate, with a complete résumé of all service performed since the previous muster, to show compliance with the law, will be submitted for examination.

·   ·   ·   ·   ·

VII. All military property not issued to the men and including field equipment, tentage, etc., will be displayed and arranged in the most convenient manner for thorough examination as to condition, serviceability, and for verification with inventories, with the total number of articles, displayed in mass, placed on a tag or suitable card, as an aid to verification. Accountable officers will have the required property returns and other papers requred by the inspecting officers filled out and ready to deliver before the property is examined.

IX. The army inspector will make a daylight inspection of property, beginning at 10.00 A.M. . . .

It is dry reading, doubtless, to the civilian, but to Shane every line was surcharged with drama. He foresaw what he had hindseen—the amazing number of things that could turn up missing, the blanket-roll and the blankets, the straps, the buckles, buttons, leggings, tent pegs, tents, ponchos. Private McGahey would have a tin cup with a hole in it and Private McCorkle none at all. Private O'Leary would have a senile comb, but no tooth-brush, and Private Garrity would howl that somebody had shwiped his unthershirt off him. A wail would go up for lost "housewives" whose disappearance nobody could explain.

He knew the toil of tracing mislaid articles and the difficulty of supplying the men with new equipment from the stores of the disgusted regimental quartermaster.

And then the labor of teaching the men how to arrange their belongings, the appalling problem of getting the blankets folded right and alike, the packs hung in place!

It was like mobilizing a foundling-asylum. The overgrown hulks were giant infants, confused about every least thing, incapable of remembering or accomplishing the smallest detail.

And the paper work! the books, the records, the files! and a weary on the blots that fell on the paper and had to be erased with infinite care.

The wonder was not that the Guard was not more efficient, but that it existed at all: that men could be found who would endure the endless grind for the sake of their loyalty, and get no pay for it except the privilege of spending their own money and their leisure, with the occasional reward of silent approval or the semi-occasional bliss of a brass-band parade.

While the order still trembled in his aspen hand Shane was summoned to a meeting in the officers room, and the colonel delivered a blistering harangue on the importance of the inspection. He was determined to attain a perfect record. The Regular Army officers always praised the regiment for its splendid vigor and fighting quality, and he wanted equal praise for their equipment, training, and attendance.

He demanded 100 per cent., or better, and he held the officers personally responsible for the presence of every man. No excuse whatever would be accepted for an absence except a certificate of interment. A doctor's certificate would not be looked at. If the man were too ill to walk in, an ambulance and a litter must be sent for him.

The officers staggered away, solemnized by their responsibilities. In Shane's company-room his captain delivered another and fiercer tirade. He divided the roster between his two lieutenants and insisted that each should secure a personal pledge from each of the men on his list. If there were any trouble with employers, the employers must be visited and compelled to let their men off for that night. The year before, the company had paraded with one man missing, and the disgrace was terrible.

Shane got away from the armory, at length, and hastened to his shop, where Mr. Bjerring came down on him like an avalanche of snow and accused him of having spent the evening spooning with his girl.

"Spooning with me gerl, is it?" Shane moaned. "Sure and if I ever get next or near her for two minyutes it 'll be only for to tell her I haven't the time to say good-by."

EXCEPT HE WERE A BIRD

These were busy days for Shane O'Mealia. He lived to go to chapel and hear the banns called the first time. He was told that they were called the second time, but he was pursuing a soldier that Sunday morning from one old address to another and another. His sole source of comfort was the angelic patience of Moyna, who was satisfied with an occasional telephone chat from the stove-shop or the soldier-shop.

At last she rebelled! And he received at the armory, where he was working on the books, this special order from the Headquarters of the Home Guard:

DEAR MR. O'MEALIA,—If it's an absentee I'm marryin', I'd be glad to know it sooner than later. Or is it the new fashion to get the divorce before you get married? I've droves of questions to be asking you about how I'm to furnish the flatteen, and the invitations to the wedding and the like of that, but you're never here. If I was your old wife itself these ten years, you couldn't be away more. This even you come up here and pay your respects to your Share of the World, or I'm no longer
Yours,
MOYNA KILLILEA.

Shane broke away from the captain and the battalion adjutant, who were trying to get the company paper to rights, and went to see Moyna instead of the waiting Bjerring. It was like a reunion after long absence. Moyna's temper was appeased and she promised to be patient with the distracted Shane.

The next morning the frigid Mr. Bjerring proved that he could heat up. He was red-hot, scarlet with wrath, and he said:

"Young feller, this is your last chance in this shop. You're here every night from eight to ten, or you don't get in here daytimes at all. Get me? One more absence and you're fired, and I'm givin' you your notice now."

Shane saw his honeymoon gone up in smoke, and his commission in his beloved regiment forfeited, and he cried:

"But I can't be here Thursday night whatever, for that's inspiction night."

"Inspiction of what!" Bjerring sneered.

"Me battalion!" said Shane.

"Your battalion!" Bjerring roared. "Where'd you get a battalion?" He paused with jaws agape, then nodded. "Oh, I see! You joined the regiment in spite of your promise, eh?"

"I'd joined before the promise, so I didn't join again."

"Oho, aha, uh-huh!" Bjerring jeered. "You're pretty smart, ain't you? Well, we'll see how smart you are. If you ain't here Thursday evening, I'll fire you so quick it'll make your head swim."

Shane's pride was nauseated, but he dared not let it rule him.

"But if I'm absent, we'll not have our hundhred per cint. of attindance. It'd be a crime."

"A hundhred per cint. of attindance, is it? Well, that would be a calamity! If you weren't there the country would go to rack and ruin, I suppose. Ah, you make me sick! You got a head full of stove-polish for brains. A hundred per cint.! Haw-haw!"

It is hard for an Irishman to be mocked by anybody, but to be imitated by a Scandinavian! The stoves began to dance around Shane in a fairy ring. He had lost too many jobs, however, and he had vowed that dynamite should not unseat him from this one till a better appeared, so he held his whist with super-Hibernian self-control.

When his noon hour off arrived, Shane flew to the Morahans to share his distress with Moyna. The whole family was at dinner and Delia thrust a plate and a chair into the circle for Shane. But he could not eat, for excitement, and he spoiled Moyna's appetite on her.

"The devil fetch me," he groaned, "but how am I to be at the shop and at the airmory the both of thim the same time?"

"There's just wan way you'd be able for that," said Michael.

"Then tell it me quick!"

"Be a bird!" said Michael, and when Shane knitted his brows in puzzlement, the old man growled: "Ah, you're not forgettin' the father of all Irish bulls?—Sir Boyle Roche's famous observation that a man could not be in two places at the wan time except he were a bird. Be a bird and you'll do the thrick handsomely."

Shane turned away to hide his anger, and Delia cuffed her husband over the jaw.

"Take shame to you for makin' light of the boy's trouble."

"I'm not makin' light of it," said Michael. "I'm takin' light to it. There's one way only and I've told him."

They all talked it over and under and round about, but Michael's solution was the single one—and that was impracticable. So Shane went back to his work no nearer a decision than before.

That evening Shane stole away from the shop for half an hour and ran to the armory to explain to his captain that he simply could not be present Thursday night. The first battalion was undergoing inspection. The men were drawn up in lines like lads at a hiring-market in the old country and the grim inspecting officers were going along putting their microscopes on them.

One of the companies had a man missing—a corporal

he was, too. He had promised to be there and a broken
leg had been his lame excuse. His officers were covered
with shame.

The colonel was so discouraged and Captain Kerin
so worried that Shane did not dare announce his own in-
tended desertion. He went to his locker to make sure
that everything was in place. He opened it and fell
back with a yell.

His uniform was gone!

Shane could not believe his eyes. He put his hand in
among the remnants of the contents. The fatigue cap
was there, but it was not to be worn at inspection. His
campaign hat, his olive-drab coat and breeches, his belt,
his sword, his puttees, his revolver and holster—all were
gone!

He called the quartermaster sergeant to make sure that
it was not an optical illusion. The sergeant confirmed
Shane's eyes and rivaled his dismay. But he had no
explanation to make, except that the fairies were in it.
He did not quite believe in the fairies, especially in the
United States, but this looked like evidence that they had
come over in some ship. While Shane was tearing
through all the other lockers to see if his things had been
shifted, the armorer came to him and saluted:

"Lootinant, you're wanted on the 'phone."

Shane's heart leaped: the thief, the Judas, was overcome with remorse and was going to make restitution.

"Who is it?"

The old armorer's eyes twinkled and there was the grin
of a laugh behind his long mustaches.

" 'Twas a lady's voice. When I asked her what was
her name, she answered, 'And does he get calls from so
many ladies he has to have their names?' "

"It's Moyna," said Shane. He dragged himself to the

telephone, and though he believed that a brave man should spare his dear ones the worst shocks, this last cataclysm was too vast to conceal. It would be like trying to break an earthquake gently.

"Och, Moyna, Moyna!" he moaned across the wire. "Me uniforrum! me uniforrum! The devil has stole it off me while it was safe within in me locker!"

Moyna's voice expressed amazement and sympathy, but there was not half enough horror in it to suit Shane. How could there be? A woman could not understand such disaster. In fact, there was a glitter of cheerfulness in her tone when she went on:

"Shaneen, quit out of there and come up here, for I've found the way for you to be the bird that's in the both places at the one time."

"What talk have you of birds! It's no time for such nons'nse. I've to get back to the shop or I'll lose me job for the lasht time."

"But you'll lose me and the rigimint if you don't come here. I'll keep you but a whileen."

"I'm on me way," he sighed, meekly.

He slunk from the armory and took a street-car. His load of woe was so heavy the car creaked under it and keened along the rails. He could hardly hoist his burden up the three flights of stairs to the Morahans.

Kate answered his ring, and she was smiling outrageously: "There's a gintleman here to see you, Shane." Then she snickered. Her flippancy was atrocious at such a time.

Shane dragged his feet into the parlor, and there facing him was his own uniform drawn up erect and saluting him.

"Moyna!" he stammered. "What the— How the— Where the— Why the— Who the—"

The rigid figure slumped.

107

LONG EVER AGO

"Och, blathers, he knew me at the first peep."

"Knew you?" he echoed, "and why wouldn't I know you!"

"Well, that's from bein' so well acquainted with me face; but nobody else would know me. And I'm goin' to the inspiction and stand in your place and name. And sure it's not deceptionable at all, for won't I be wearin' your name the next week and won't the priest make us one? So you see, don't you?"

"I see entirely too much," said Shane.

But Moyna would not give up. "Forget what you remimber now and look again. Who would know me for a gerl?"

She was a winsome, graceful figure, and lacked nothing but to be convincing. Under the campaign hat a bulge of red hair was wadded. The coat wrinkled over the shoulders and strained across the chest—and at the hips. The riding-breeches she could not button at all across her fat knees.

She saluted again after the British fashion, palm to the front.

Shane could do no less than click his heels and return the salute, bringing his right hand up smartly, palm to the left in the American fashion.

Then he brought his other hand up to hide his wide spreading smile. She was so funny in that gear that he smiled even through his heavy gloom. She was so funny that his moral indignation was late in arriving.

Moyna was flattered by his salute and she quivered with the triumph of her plan. When he said, "You'd never go to the airmory in the like of that," her answer was a ringing declaration: "To the airmory is it—wouldn't I go barefut on me hands and knees from Cork to Antrim for you, Shaneen! And at that they'd never know me."

EXCEPT HE WERE A BIRD

Shane could not keep up the game:

"Know you?" said Shane. "Why, you blessed little scandal, they'd know you as far as they could see you and fartherer to the back of that! You couldn't decave a blind man with that shape."

"What's the matther with me shape?" Moyna stormed. "Sure there was min in Lisdoonvarna said me shape was proper enough."

"And I agree with them only for wishin' to poonch their heads for darin' to know whether you'd a shape or not. What business was it of theirs?"

"Well, I'd hardly be livin' without cuttin' some kind of figger. Of course, if you don't like it—"

"Your figger is ahl right and betther than that. But it's too good for the duds of a man, and if it wasn't it's not me would be marryin' you. I'm lookin' to be wedded to a colleen, not a lieutenant. Step out here and take a look at yourself. Be careful! Don't breathe, or you'll be shootin' the buttons off me blouse!—and for the love of God go take off those pants or put somethin' over them for fear somebody would come wahkin' in on ye. They'd think it was a comic-opera house."

Moyna turned and ran, and ran so womanly that Shane forgave her her wickedness, though his whoop of laughter was not to her liking. She would not leave her room till Shane pleaded through the door that she had given him a wonderful idea.

Then she came forth as shy as Ruth and clothed in her right clothes. She brought back Shane's uniform in a great parcel—but she refused to tell who it was she had bribed to steal it for her, or with what bribery. Shane suspected the old armorer and his skeleton key, but Moyna was such a different thing in skirts that Shane could hardly be interested in such details. He smiled:

"I'm that glad to have you back, I forgive you your criminal pasht. I can hug you now and welcome. But can you see me embracin' what you was a few minyutes back? No, you cannot."

"I'm sorry I shocked you."

"Troth, and 'twas a shock I needed, for I've taken a grand idea from your masquerade. I'll get one of the lootinants in one of the other battalions to stand on the floor for me. My company is the last company in the battalion and they'll be a long while reachin' it. I'll wear me uniform to the shop. I'll work like the Ould Boy itself and I'll get to the airmory in time to be there before the inspiction officers l'ave off work, belike. Anyhow, they are strangers to me and me to thim, me being a new officer, and they'll never suspicion."

The next day Shane telephoned his captain and asked what would happen if he missed the inspection.

"I can't tell you over the telephone," said Captain Kerin. "They'd arrest me. But come out to the tannery and I'll show you."

Shane haltingly explained the situation and Captain Kerin almost overloaded the wire with his wrath as he thought of Shane's dereliction. He had hardly any anger left unexpended when Shane propounded his inspired invention of a substitute.

"I'll not hear of it," Kerin clamored. "It's dishonorable."

"But it's dishonorable of the divil to keep me away and to ruin the hundhred per cint. yous all have worked so hard for. I can't abide the idea of me bein' the cause of the disgrace."

"I'll not hear of a substitute," the captain roared, a little gentlier.

"Who would you suggest?" Shane wheedled. "Would Lootinant Clavery do it?"

EXCEPT HE WERE A BIRD

"He's in our battalion and he's well known to brigade headquarters."

"How would Liftinant—Lieutinant—you see I'm so new I don't know manny of the officers well enough to ask them would they do it."

"You're not asking me to ask them, are you? Good Lord! you've a queer notion of me. Would you lose me my commission, too?"

"I'm disthracted, that's thrue," said Shane. "Well, I'll bother you no more. I'll give up."

"Er-ahum!" said the captain. "If you should get old Sergeant Gavigan to find a man for you—he knows everybody—don't you let me know it. If I find somebody on the floor in your place, I could say I knew nothing of it, and I don't! And I won't! Good-by!"

As Shane hung up the receiver he winked with grave deliberation at nobody at all. Then he called up Sergeant Gavigan, who worked in the city water-works, and explained the problem to his understanding old soul.

"Leave it to me, Loot! I'm a first-rate fixer. I'll get you a good man, and don't you worry."

"He mustn't be in our battalion, you know."

"I understand, Loot. I'll rustle round among the young loots and pick one of 'em will be only too glad to oblige you and the company. You're safe in my hands."

The next day—the dreadful day of the inspection—Shane called up Gavigan again, but he was informed that the sergeant was out on the hunt for a man and left word for Lieutenant O'Mealia that he was not to worry.

Shane worried, none the less, and Bjerring worried him. Bjerring had set himself to win this point in his feud against militarism, and he kept a close watch on Shane.

When Shane appeared that evening at the shop he did not dare wear his uniform as he planned—at least not openly. He had it on under his other clothes, and it nearly choked him all over. His pistol and hat he had left in his locker.

He set about his stock-taking tasks with such enthusiasm that Bjerring was softened with success, and at ten o'clock he said with a yawn:

"Well, we'll call it a day's work. And if you're fired from the Ninety-sixth it's better than being fired from your bread and butter, and some day you'll thank me for saving you from wasting all your evenings and getting nothing for it. There's nothing in it, my boy!" And he actually said "Good night!" when he locked up the store.

Shane waited till he saw which way Bjerring was going, then he went the other way. He rounded the first corner, and ran to the armory, ran to his locker, ran out of his mufti, slapped his hat on and ran to the drill floor as he buckled his belt around him and strapped his pistol holster to his thigh.

The inspection was finished for all the companies but his. He paused to look the field over. In front of the first platoon the first lieutenant stood at ease, inspected and approved. The second lieutenant was hidden by a little mob of colonels and the like.

Shane wondered who his substitute could be. He hurried to a point of observation. He could see only that there was much excitement and that Captain Kerin was red as a British flag.

Shane, trembling with curiosity and dread, dared to join the group. He was unobserved except by the horrified row of privates and corporals in the line.

Shane peered between the heads of the inspectors and made out the substitute that Gavigan had provided him. He almost fainted.

It was Lieutenant McCooey!

EXCEPT HE WERE A BIRD

Never had he looked so immortal homely. His face reminded Shane of the hunk of corned beef in a boiled dinner

An angry brigade officer was saying to a horrified regular·

"I've seen this man before. I'd remember him in a million."

And Shane recalled Moyna's words. Colonel Van Nydeck thundered at the miserable wretch whose only crimes were his big face and his big heart:

"I never forget a face. I've seen you before somewhere."

"Yis, sor," McCooey burbled. "I'm often there."

"I inspected you Tuesday night in the first battalion."

"That's me twin brother, please," McCooey explained, with happy speed.

"And I never forget a name!" Colonel Van Nydeck thundered again. "That man's name was McCooey!"

"Yis, sor, so it is!"

"But your name on the roster is O'Mealia."

"Yis, sor, so it is!"

"Then how in—er—how in reason could you be twin brothers—with his name McCooey and yours O'Mealia?"

"Me mother married twice, if you please," McCooey was inspired to explain.

The logic of this chloroformed Colonel Van Nydeck for a moment. But from the way he blinked and choked and sputtered Shane realized that in a moment he would explode and probably scatter shrapnel enough to annihilate the entire company.

With all the bravery there was in his Irish blood, Shane pushed through the colonels and majors and, shoving McCooey aside, took his place and saluted.

When Colonel Van Nydeck opened his eyes he thought

he was bewitched, for in place of the red caricature of McCooey stood the pale white ideal of Shane's marble mien.

Colonel Van Nydeck began to choke again and Shane explained:

"Asking your pairdon, sir, but I was called away unavydably and Lootinant McCooey was kind enough to hold me place in the line till I could hoostle meself back."

"Do you realize, sir, what such an imposition means, sir?" Colonel Van Nydeck roared.

"That I do, but it was a matther of losin' me job and me wife or roonin' the record of the rigimint, so I took the chance. But lave the poonishmint fahl on me and not on poor Mac."

"We ought to take the shoulder straps off both of you, sir!"

"Then take them off me twice, if you plase. But don't go for to maltrate poor McCooey for the kind heart he has in him. Sure, he'd do the same for annybody, were it your honor himself."

"Well, of all the— Why, I'll— Who ever heard of such a— Whew! I'm choking."

Shane went on looking as beautiful as only a bad angel could look:

"And you oughtn't to be poonishin' the captain, ayther —nor the min. We ahl worked so desprit hard for the hundhred per cint. If you'll give us that, I'll resign tomorra or stand coort mairtial or anny damned—excuse it, plase—annything you think best. Only don't hould it against Mister McCooey. There's not so much kindness in the worruld you can afford to crush it whin you see it."

The colonels and majors looked at the benevolent McCooey. He was a very allegory of misguided philanthropy. There was no limit to his goodness. Even now in his ordeal he had the kind word for Shane: "Asking your pardon, sirs, but you should overlook Mr. O'Mealia's mistake. He's that new to the milit'ry, it was only the other night wasn't he ordering his min to 'Right shoulder bay'nits!'"

The colonels and the majors grinned and withdrew for a conference. At length they came back trying to look ferocious, and Colonel Van Nydeck glowered and growled:

"We have decided to forget what happened and we will overlook this offense in spite of its gravity. We think that you have both been punished enough."

"I thank you kindly, I'm sure—and so will Miss Killilea, who's perishin' in the gallery there. One thing more," said the amazing Shane. "I'd like to apologize before yous all for dragging Mr. McCooey into this. I wish it had been annybody else."

"Don't you do it," said Colonel Van Nydeck. "If it had been anybody else but McCooey, it would have been all day with you. And what is he up to now?"

To the astonishment of their High Mightinesses, Mr. McCooey was waving one hand at a beautiful girl standing in the balcony. And he was yelling through the trumpet of his other hand:

"It's ahl right, Miss Killilea! I fixed it!"

9

V

LONG EVER AGO

JUST once the impulsive Michael Morahan took his wife, the patient Delia, to the Zoological Gardens in the Bronx. It happened to be a day when the keepers were pulling a tooth for an old lion. They had manacled his claws and his jaws, but they had not manacled his voice, and Delia never forgot the beast's heart-curdling belches of rage and pain while the tooth was being evicted, nor the abrupt purr of bliss that afterward made silence audible and comfortable.

She never forgot it because her husband so often reminded her of it, especially when he was preparing for a celebration of some sort. He loved being dressed, but he hated getting dressed. He grew so wroth always that he could not see what was before him and was constantly hiding what he was hunting.

He was peculiarly ferocious to-night because he was putting on his "full-driss soot" and was to wear his high hat and a badge. He was to represent the men of his county—Clare, the Banner County, no less—and at the Clare Lady Hurlers' Annual Ball!

Michael was the vice-president of the "Clare County P. S. B. and A. Association"—P. S. B. and A. meaning "Patriotic, Social, Benevolent, and Athletic." The president was ill—"he having a sore throath on him"—and Michael was to lead the grand march with Miss

116

LONG EVER AGO

Belendia O'Rahilly, the majestic captain of the lady hurlers.

Delia would have been uneasier about this if Herself had not been the representative of the Clare Ladies' Benevolent Association, and therefore slated to march directly behind Michael with the tall and handsome Martin Kelleher, the manager of the famous Clare Hurlers. Other clubs of hurlers and lady hurlers and merely social associations of other counties were to be present, and there were to be two bands to play on two floors; one, American music, and one, Irish.

A grand night was sure and the daylight would doubtless surprise the dancers—or rather it would not surprise them, because the Irish are the tireless steppers, and every Saturday night and many another night they set buildings all over town to rocking with their thousands of jigging feet.

Michael had cause to be anxious about his important appearance, and he kept Delia and their old-maid daughter, Kate, jigging to find him and fetch him his equipment.

At length he was harnessed as far as his collar, and he was growing purple in his combat with that, trying in vain to make both ends meet. He had shoved his left fingers down inside the neck of his shirt to push the collar-button out, and he had bruised the fingers of his right hand trying to engage the buttonhole and the button. The only result was to derange his Adam's apple and to lacerate a number of collars.

Delia, who was in the bathroom, trying to wash her own hands after buttoning his big patent-leather shoes on his bigger feet, came back to find him standing among the ruins of half a dozen collars and trying to terrify his last one into forming a union with its other end. The hand at his throat impeded his articulation, but not his roar.

117

LONG EVER AGO

Delia smiled at his mien of fiendish malignance as if it were a harmless mask on the face of a child, and said:

"Oh, it's on'y you. I thought they were exthracthin' another toot'th from the ould African line in the Zoo-ological Gairdens."

With the fearlessness or a lion-tamer she reached up, pulled his paws down, and said:

"You poor little bouchaleen, for why are you trine to button your fisht into your neck? Have you no pockets to put it in or is it a new fashion you're startin'?"

Michael's eyes popped, but her cool deft hands had the collar buttoned before he could bite her head off, so he patted her fat back and cooed like a ring-dove nuzzling its mate:

"Och, Dalia asthore, it's a miracle-worker you are. You can button a collar or a shoe as aisy as sayin' a prayer. I'm wondherin' if I'm doin' wisely to l'ave you march with that Martin Kelleher. He's hardly betther than half my age and twicet my stren'th. But at that I'll have a go at him if you smile too sweetly on him."

"More betoken, it's you that had better be very careful how you make up to that O'Rahilly beauty. She's half my weight and twice my len'th and she's a wildcat in a quarrel, but I'll wallop her wit' her own caman if she don't wahk very correct."

The mutual flattery of mutual jealousy delighted both of their old gray hearts, and he hugged her till he threatened to break the ribs of her new corset. Then he noticed that it was the corset he was embracing, and he flared up again:

"You're not tellin' me you're not drissed yet? And me all readied up. And I've got to set round in this hot collar and miss l'adin' the march belike while you primp. And what you been up to this lahng while?"

118

LONG EVER AGO

She handed him a look that showed the strange power of the human eye. He remembered that he had kept her busy on his own errands and he laughed in time to save his scalp.

"Don't say it. I know it."

He brushed down his excited nair and announced that he would wait for her in the dining-room. He carried his long-tailed coat over his arm, put it reverently on the shoulders of a chair, pulled the patent rocker up under the center light, and sat down to reread the evening paper.

He had just got his forehead between the shafts of his spectacles when he felt a draught blowing on his white shirt-sleeves.

He peered over the rims of his glasses and saw that the window was wide open and half filled with the ample form of his daughter Kate. She was leaning out, as usual, gazing at an elevated train rumbling by with a glitter of lighted windows.

"Kateen!" Michael roared, "come in out of that, out of the street, will you?"

She did not hear him for the noise of the train. He slammed down his paper, and, stalking over to her, reached through the window till he had her by the shoulder and dragged her in.

The bump she took on her head startled her hardly so much as her father's voice:

"Whativer is it's on you, Kate, to be ahlways in and out of that windy? Have you never seen an ilivated train before? Begobs, you've seen a million. I've seen you see them! But you're ahlways hangin' there. I wondher your elbows ain't grew to the ledge. I doubt but you'll be havin' cairns on them. Have you a sweethairt's a train gaird, or what is it you're expectin' to see—a collision or a balloon ascinsion, or what at all?"

Kate walked away, answering, drearily, "Nothin', pa, nothin'."

His first anger improved to his second stage.

"And are you tellin' me you're not ready yit? The divil admire me! but you've your praskeen on still and your old driss. Is it to a barn dance or an apern-and-necktie pairty you think you're goin' to? No, this is a grand bahl—the grandest iver!"

"I'm not goin', pa!"

"And why are you not goin'?"

"I don't care to go."

"You don't care? And what have you to care? It's me that's doin' the carin'. I'll not be lavin' you here alone. I'd not thrust you not to go fahlin' out the windy. And for why would you not go?"

"I never have any fun, pa. I'm only an old maid. Nobody dances with me except some other old maid. I'd liever stay at home. The dishes are to be washed yet, and grandma sleeping in her room there ought not to be left alone."

"I'll speak to Mrs. Whoriskey across the hahl to keep an ear on her would she want annything. You're goin' to the bahl, and you'll have a good time or answer to me!" She shook her head and turned away, and for all his bluster he called for help: "Dalia! Ma! come heer, would you, and make this little-good-for obey me and go to the dance. Sure and haven't I the ticket bought for her? It says, 'Tickets admitting gintleman and lady, includin' wardrobe, fifty cints.' That's you and me, ma. But I didn't take the wardrobe. And it says, 'Extra lady, twinty-five cints.' So I bought her wan, and she would be wastin' the quarther, besides the gittin' in for the half price."

"I urged her and she said she'd not go," said Delia,

who appeared at the door. "And there's no makin' her move if she has not a mind to. She's very obadient in everything excipt what she doosn't want to do."

"It's a shame for you to be stayin' home," Michael growled. "You'll not see your ma thrippin' the light fanthastic nor me ladin' off at the hid of the percission. The balance of the family'll be there, ahl the byes and their wives or gerls."

"Thank you kindly, pa, but what am I at a dance? Who'd ever dance with the like of me?"

"Ah, Kate honey, I'll dance wit' you and proud of it, if you'll dance the Irish dances. I'd not disgrace my heels with anny of these moderen Yankee diviltries, these thurkey-throts, and tongos, and boony-hugs, and the like thrash. But lave me loose in a four-hand reel, or a *rinnce fada*, or a shlip jig, and I'll handle me feet as artistic as the best of thim. So come along wit' you now."

Kate shook her head with the obstinacy of the meek, and when Michael insisted she walked out of the room and locked herself behind her own door.

Michael was for breaking it down, but Delia checked him.

"Save your breath for your jigs. Katie won't dance the Irish dances, and she hates the Irish music."

"Then she's no daughter of mine," Michael raged.

Delia was calm even at that, and she smiled:

"Her sthubbornness alone would idintify her if she had not your jah. She takes her aisy and sinsible ways from me, so lave her home. She loves to be by her lone."

"She'd ought to go to dances and the like and meet the min. She maybe might find her match. How's annybody to marry her whin she niver stirs a fut outside the door? It's no convint I keep here to have a nun on me hands."

"Maybe her seein' the way you take on, she's contint not to tie herself up with anny of the min. Some of you seem to think that you're ahl a woman has to think of."

"And what else have you to think of? I ahlways misthrust these women that is too good for the min. A single woman's an accidint, I tell you, not an intintion. Break open an ould maid's heart and you'll find some lad's initials is cairved there."

Delia laughed: "What need have you min for flatthery from us when yous can ahlways supply yourselves? Katie's never been out of my sight for two days runnin' since she was born—lavin' out the time she wint over to Ireland to see your mother for a few months. And that was fourteen years gone. And niver a sign given of a ring or a letther written or resaved. Quit out of this now or you'll be late, and your lady hurler will be struttin' off wit' a younger man and I'll be losin' me beau Martin."

Michael thrust his big bulk into his dress coat and his overcoat, and put his hat on the side of his head, and looked at himself in the mirror with unconcealed satisfaction. He was so pleased that his heart softened generally.

He went to Kate's door and knocked.

"Good night, honey, and plisant drames. We'll be home soon afther daylight, so have me breakfast ready and I'll ate it in me driss soot like the swells doos."

Kate came out, and told him how fine he looked, and kissed him and her mother, and watched them go.

When she had closed the door on them she went back to the window, raised it, and leaned out again. She would have reminded one of the Blessed Damosel on the bar of heaven, she was so different.

Her mother looked up and waved to her and pointed her out to Michael from where they waited for the surface car.

LONG EVER AGO

She was there long after they had gone. She watched train after train go by. Then she trudged to the kitchen and washed up the dishes and put them in the cupboard and in the sideboard. Now and then she paused and listened at the door of the room where the old grandmother slept, or pretended to. But always when she went to the dining-room she paused by the window to watch the train go by.

At last the fatigue of another day at the tasks of a Martha overcame her. She said her unselfish prayers and stretched herself out wearily in her bed.

Michael came home fagged with enjoyment long before daybreak. He was sighing that he was not the man he was when he used to dance the moon down and the sun up. His finery was rumpled with exercise and he pulled it off regardless. Kate would straighten it up and press it for him later. He overslept, and waking him was like poking a polar bear, till Delia sprinkled cold water on him and ordered him out.

Kate waited on her yawning parents and asked them about the party as if she were their mother and they the youngsters. She listened to their rhapsodies with an indulgent smile of affectionate patience and far less enthusiasm than Michael's ancient mother revealed when Kate rolled her in her wheeled chair to the table.

The venerable Bridget had in her day danced barefooted on many a door taken from its hinges and laid down on the sod; and she dated back to the time when the pipers were men of honor and glory. She had seen the famine rage and the dances fall under the ban of the Church, and the pipers become outcast and vagabond. She had seen the better times come back and the pipers once more lifting their heads and the Irish language flourishing everywhere.

Her little eyes gleamed like liquid coal as Michael told

123

of his dancing prowess. Kate alone was indifferent; she stood near the window and every passing train caught her eyes away from her father's account of the numbers of old men and women he and Delia had danced to death.

"Och, ma honey," he was saying, "I'd rather than ten shillin' you were there last night. You're younger now than that old Kate-hang-out-of-the-windy. Come away from that, Kate, for the love of the saints, and lave the trains go by.

"Well, ma, everybody admitted I was the best man there except Dalia here. And she danced something outrageous. The way she bobbed to the cinter in the sets made the other women look like rags. She had their hair in their eyes and their combs hoppin' out of them and they sweatin' like thruck-horses and she fresh as a daisy. Her heels wint kickin' this side and that and her skirts flyin' the way you'd never drame she was mother to a priest.

"But at that it's more betther to be dancin' Irish ahl night than doin' them scandalous new fangles—thim Castile Wahks and lame dooks and Swedish movements that they was dancin' on the flure below.

"They had a band of white nagurs poundin' dhrums on the side and swattin' gongs, and the min and women wint round more like they was doin' a wrastlin'-match than dancin'. Kate, if you don't stop starin' out that windy I'll smash it for you. Have you no inth'rest whativer in your father's and mother's succiss?"

"Oh yes, indeed and I have that, pa," said Kate, trying to shake off her reverie and asking a question to prove her absorption in their experiences. "And who made the music up-stairs for the Irish dancers? Mr. and Mrs. McAvoy, or Mr. Hennessey, or Mr. Fitzpatrick, or who?"

"It was none of thim, but a new piper. I don't know

124

the name of 'um, a shrimpeen of a felly he was, but he could squeege the win' out of the Union pipes the way you'd swayre it was the fairies was in it.'

"I hate the pipes," said Kate.

Michael whirled on her with a gulping sound:

"What!"

"Fiddles and flutes are all right," Kate went on, "but I can't abide the noise of a pipe."

"The divil blishter us all!" Michael roared. "She hates the pipes, she says. And you sayin' she's my daughter. She's not even Irish. She's a—a Portugoose or a Zulu!"

Even Delia was aghast at the treason. She stared at Kate so knowingly that she saw something behind the dark look, something that implied more than a musical criticism.

"Lave her be, Michael," she murmured. "It's one of her headaches is on her."

Michael turned away from her in disdain and addressed his mother with exaggerated brightness:

"Of course, he was as nothin' to old Killilea—the granduncle of Shane's Moyna—you remimber him, ma, belike?"

"That I do," said Bridget. "He was a young bouchal whin I was a colleen. He played at manny's the 'pattern' I danced at. He played at the weddin' of me and your poor father—God give him heaven for his bed. He was blind, too, old Killilea."

"Most pipers used to be blind in the good old times," said Michael. "It was that kept me from takin' up the pipes meself whin I was a broth of a boyo—that and the hard they are for to be learnin'; and the expinse of thim. After seein' Dalia here, I had no wish to blow me eyes out pipin'."

"But why pipers should be blind I d'know, unless it's the win' that gets in their faces like. I niver understood it. Now a man who plays the war-pipes, or the Scotch bagpipes, is different. I could understand them goin' dark, for they keep up such a poofin' and blowin' you'd think they'd whoof the eyeballs out of their heads. But at that I niver saw a Scotch bagpiper blind. But the betther part of the Union pipers used to be blind. Old Killilea was a dark man in the eyes."

"Maybe," Delia said, "Union pipers was blind because they was blind first and took up the pipes for to comfort themselves with, or for lack of other thrades to work at."

Michael glowered at her admiringly. "Now it would be you would be thinkin' of that! Yous women is foolish and you can't keep to the main road of sinse and raison, but now and thin you take a short cut and stoomble on the trut'th be accidint. Maybe you have the right of it, Dalia. Yis, I do belave you have."

Kate broke in unexpectedly, "Was the piper who piped to you last night blind?" There was a trace of ill-suppressed excitement in her voice.

"No, he had a pair of eyes in him would outblink a weasel."

"And his name—did you say?"

"No; I didn't say. His name is a thing I didn't get. And what's it to you what his name is? You that have no likin' for pipin'." He turned to his mother again. "Somebody said he's been playin' round the counthry dances quite regular recent. He was pipin' for the Ballinlough Boys' Social Club lasht Saturda', and the Tuam Social Club of a Winsda', and the Manchester Martyrs' Cilebration the week before that. You was to the County Leitrim Ladies' dance, Kate. He was there. Did you not see him?"

LONG EVER AGO

"I didn't go into the Irish room," said Kate.

"And why werrun't you at the dance lasht night, Katie?" Bridget asked.

Kate shook her head and Delia explained:

"Sure, and we couldn't boodge her, though we tried. She niver goes to dances—or only rayrely."

Bridget's little eyes widened. "That's strange, Katie. Whin you come over to see me, long iver ago, I could hardly lay eyes on you for the dancin' you did. Ivery night most she was off to some parish patron or field dance or something. There was a lad in it, of coorse. What was his name, Katie?"

Katie answered only with a blush of rosiness unseen in her cheeks before. Michael and Delia stared at her incredulously. Bridget rambled on:

"He left home about the same time with you, Kate. I thought it would be he was follyin' you acrost the say. What was his name, now? I knew his mother. She died about thin. Who was she? You should remimber the name, Katie?"

"Oho!" Michael guffawed. "So Kate had a lover! Aha, she was human once. The deceptionable baggage she is!"

Delia was astounded: "Why, what at all? Musha then! Why, Kate my darlin'! and what happened him that you niver mintioned his name?"

Kate mumbled in a low tone: "Grandma is wanderin'. She remembers things all twisted. How should I remember the foolish things I did as a girl? I may have danced over there. Prob'ly I did. But nobody I knew was on the steamer with me. Nobody ever wrote me a letter in all these years. If I'd have loved any lad, wouldn't there have been letters? If there'd been letters, wouldn't you have seen them?"

Delia nodded and Michael looked solemn. But they were rather baffled than convinced.

Michael put Delia's thoughts into his own words when he said:

"You've your answer ready, Katie—and there's only wan thing the matther with it, and that is there's nahthin' the matther with it. It's just a thrifle too perfect—like yourself. And things that's too perfect isn't human like. So come and tell us ahl about it."

The stolid Kate was on the verge of an outbreak. She appealed to Delia as from a bullying brother:

"Ma, you better make him quit teasin' me, now."

The child-obeying mother rounded on the so-called master of the house:

"Go on about your business, Michael, if you have anny; the clock's been starin' at you this half-hour. Or have you settled down to be an ould woman with the rest of us and nothin' to do but sit in a chair and mind annybody's business but your own? Go alahng now, or I'll put the broom acrost your lazy shoulthers!"

Michael turned to his own mother. "Ma, are you goin' to set there and lave thim two ould hags pick on your little son?"

Bridget knew the art of being a mother-in-law, and she laughed:

"Michaeleen, you quit out of where you're not wanted, or I'll take you over me own knee."

Michael was pouting like a spankable boy as he took his hat and coat and sulked away to his office.

The two women turned to Kate with hungry curiosity, but she went into her own room and busied herself with making up her spinstral cell.

A few days later, after the noon dinner, when Delia and Kate had carried away from the table the dishes they had set out on it with the same thrice-daily ritual they had used for years, Kate went to the window and raised it, though the day was none too warm.

Up and down the trestles the elevated trains went rumbling, watched by thousands of others in the elbow colony along the tracks. A few of the gayer passengers on the platforms attempted to start the briefest imaginable flirtations with Kate and waved to her or lifted their hats with ironic courtesy. But Kate regarded them with blank indifference.

Delia looked at her sadly and shook her head over the lonely old thing she was, and the undercurrent of sorrow that was somehow different from the abundant sorrows of wives and mothers. The pity of it seemed to be that Kate had never known these anguishes. They are the only griefs that mothers do not pray Heaven to spare their daughters.

Suddenly Delia saw Kate's broad back waver; she saw her elbows leave the sill and her hands reach out into space as if to clutch at something. A train was booming past, but Delia felt sure that Kate was shouting something to somebody borne by.

She lunged so rashly outward that Delia ran and seized her about the waist and hauled her into the room, yelling in the abrupt stillness left by the vanished train:

"Have you turned disthracted entirely?"

Kate tore her mother's hands loose with unfilial vigor and darted back to the window, shrieking:

"Oh, he's gone! He's gone!"

Delia dragged her away once more, while the passengers on another train stared and wondered at the scene, and old Bridget rose from her chair and tottered forward in panic.

"Who's gone? And where gone?" Delia shouted. "The saints be among us, but it's you that's gone."

LONG EVER AGO

Kate flung her arms about her mother and began to sob:
"And all the years I've watched and waited!"

Bridget sank into the nearest chair and whispered what Delia howled:

"Who's gone? Who were you waitin' for?"

But Kate wept in a storm till Delia's curiosity changed to anxiety and she began to soothe her like a child in convulsions with many a "Hush! whist! child jewel! Och, avourneen! Shoo! shoo!"

She led Kate to a chair, where Bridget and she caressed her and gave her salts to smell and wet a cup of tea for her and finally had her facing the world again with something of her old-time calm.

And at last, though they forbore to question her, she answered their devouring need with an explanation:

"You know, ma, how I've watched at the window so long?"

"It's little else I know," said Delia.

"You've all made sport of it, and a joke it's been to pa. But no joke to me, I tell you that, for I've always been hoping that some day he would go by on the street or on the elevated trains. So many, many people are forever passin', I felt in my soul some day he would go by, too."

"He—he?" said Delia. "What he?"

"When pa sent me over to Ireland to visit you, grandma, I was only a little young slip of a girl, but we loved each other at the first glimpse like."

"We—we?" Delia repeated, like a refrain. "And who's we?"

"Floyd O'Gara and me."

"Of the O'Garas across the hill?" said Bridget. "That's the name I was tryin' for to say the other mornin'."

"The same," said Kate. "Some of the others made fun

130

of me for my New York ways and clothes, and called me the Yankee, and said I was stuck up, but Floyd O'Gara told them what he thought of them, and that it was no fault of mine being born out in the States, and that they were only jealous of me and my dancin'.

"Then they turned on him and called him out of his name. At that the pipers were in disfavor still, and his father had broken the first set of pipes Floyd bought with his own hard earnings, for his father said it was a disgrace to the family. But Floyd had the music in him and he had bought him new ones and begun to earn good money pipin' for all the dances and weddin's round about.

"So when they began for to pick on me—you see Floydie had taken a kindness to me from the start, and he told them that he wouldn't play for them whatever till they learned better manners. And they laughed and said little they cared.

"So for a while he had nothing else to do but pay attentions to me, and he would pipe for me alone, and I danced for him alone, and he piped the heart out of me. And he said I was dancin' on the heart of him under my feet. And by and by the others crep' up to listen, and they grew that heartsick for dancin' to his music, they begged him would he forgive them, and we patched it up, and the whole village of Lisdoonvarna was friends again.

"Only Floyd, for all he loved to see me dance, couldn't abide seein' me dance with any of the other garsoons and he pipin'. So we quarreled, for I was young and wanted to dance with all the lads, and I didn't prize his jealousy.

"It was a fool's quarrel, but never a chance had we to make it up. For after a week of not speakin' I had to take the boat home. Once I was out on the lonesome sea, my pride broke in me. I wrote him a long, long letter, tellin' him I was in the wrong and I would dance only for him and with nobody else. The letter never came back to me. He'd gone away to South Africa or Australia. I learned it from a girl came out later on another ship; she said nobody knew where he went, for his mother died about that time.

"I began watchin' for him, always hopin' he'd come to New York. Such millions come here, and go by our window. Why wouldn't Floyd? I was always afraid he would be on the train I didn't see. Sometimes I've sat all night at my window watchin'—watchin'."

Delia and Bridget had sat out the long story like watchers beside a coffin, shaking their heads and pursing their lips with sympathy.

"You creature, you," Delia moaned. "I'm destroyed wit' sorrow for you; and I never knew! And we ahlways jokin' at you."

"Just now—he went by!" said Kate, sopping her wet cheeks.

"The saints be among us, no wonder you were for leppin' out on the train!"

"Floyd was standin' on the platform. He's no longer the lad he was, but I knew him. And he saw me, and I waved to him—and he stared hard, then he waved to me. He waved to me, and I could see by the look in his eyes he knew me. And he'd forgiven me. He was that hungry to see me, he nearly climbed over the gates."

"But why is it cryin', not laughin' you are?" said Delia. "You've found him and he's found you."

"But we haven't found each other!" Kate screamed. "He's gone once more. I've lost him again."

"As if he wouldn't be gettin' off at the next station and runnin' back to you? Listen! I think I hear him just goin' to ring the door-bell."

"But it was an express train! It won't stop till it gets

to a Hundred and Twenty-fi'th Street. That's miles away. He won't know the house. They're all so much alike along here. Oh, I'd rather not have seen him again if it's only to be losin' him."

Old Bridget put her lean hand on hers and murmured:

"Be aisy on hope and be aisy on despair is a good motto, my lanna. There's plinty of ways of findin' the daughter of Michael Morahan. Let him ask anny policeman. But if you find him he may not be free. It's not likely he's stayed an old maid like you. Maybe he was on the way home to his wife."

Kate writhed at this as if a javelin had been hurled through her body.

"Oh, don't say that! It wouldn't come out so cruel after these years, could it?"

"It's a crool world, agra," Bridget murmured, "and there's no sweet but has its bitther, though there's manny's the bitther that has no sweet."

Perhaps in her ancient wisdom Bridget knew that the best way for the old to encourage the young is to croak to them despair. They resist automatically whatever is imposed on them and fly to the other extreme. So while Bridget prated against hope, Kate took fire from the friction and cried:

"I'm goin' to keep watch till he comes by again. He's livin', he's in America, he's in New York, he's on this street! He'll come back—I know he will!"

And old Bridget gave her for a benediction:

"Heaven shine on your soul and bring you your heart s hope; you've supped sorrow with the spoon of grief the long while. Sure and that you have!"

One thing Kate demanded with a peremptoriness new to her. She had authority already, for she was a woman like others, with a love story and a man on the horizon.

"Not one word of this to pa or the boys or anybody. I might lose him before I found him. What grandma says may be truth, that he has a wife and was going home to her. And children he might have—her children!"

But she determined to give Floyd every chance, and she rolled a chair up to the window and established herself there. All afternoon she played sentinel, her head turning this way and that to follow every car, and craning out to keep the street under espionage. The sky gloomed and glowed with the sunset. The people on the trains grew vaguer and duller and they all looked alike. The windows had lights in them. The sparse crowds of the afternoon thickened on the upward trains till the people were squeezed into a kind of human jelly. Still Kate watched.

When Michael came home for supper he found Delia setting the table and Kate playing the Lady of Shalott at the window.

Michael insisted on knowing the cause of such behavior and Delia answered:

"Hould your whist or go away somewhere. Haven't you a meeting of the Friendly Sons or the Knights of Columbus or some *com*mittee or something?"

For a wonder Michael had no excuse for leaving home that evening. In fact, he was expecting a call from John Giluley, his friend and landlord, who was urging a real-estate investment on him.

When Giluley came he wondered at the open window and Kate ensconced there. He shivered a little and with doubtful altruism advised Katie to look out or she'd catch cold.

When the window in front of Kate could not be hinted down he sneezed and suggested:

"Maybe we might go in the pairlor?"

LONG EVER AGO

So he and Michael left the comfortable dining-room and went into the uncomfortable parlor.

Michael had to go through the dining-room to the icebox of hospitality several times in the effort to make the parlor more comfortable. On one of the trips Kate had another attack of excitement. She stretched herself prone across the sill and shrieked wildly well:

"Floyd! Floyd avic! Here!—here!"

"Here yourself!" cried Michael. He rushed to her, grabbed her heels, and restored them to the floor, where an old maid's heels belong.

"Leave go! Leave go!" Kate cried, fighting so hard that Michael could hardly hold her.

Delia ran in from the kitchen, and when Michael called to her for help she also attacked him, commanding: "Lave her loose! Lave her loose!" so loudly that Giluley came running in.

Michael reasoned with Delia: "Can't you see it's a fit she has! Get me a rope and a docther, quick! Troth, she was yellin' the way she'd rise the police."

But Delia and Kate outfought him, and Kate ran back to the window and leaned out farther than ever, shouting louder than before, "I'll be down there in half a minute."

"You'll be down there a dom' sight quicker than that," said Michael, seizing her again. "Is it ippilipsy she has, or hydrophoby? I don't know. She'll be frothing at the mouth anny minyute now."

John Giluley had an idea.

"Try her with a glass of water would she run from it. If she does, it's the ginuine hydrophoby."

He turned to the faithful pitcher on the sideboard, and, filling a glass, held it out to Kate from as far as his arm would reach.

Kate was just leaving the window. She gave the water

a glance, knocked the glass aside, and ran from the room. Giluley damply answered his own questions.

"She did it! She has it!"

Michael was about to pursue the flying Kate when Delia checked him and, bidding him and his guest sit down, recounted the whole story. There was time enough for that and for Michael's "I-told-you-so's."

"But what keeps them so long gone?" he wondered.

"Och!" said Delia. "They put hard words on each other; it's years ago; they'll need manny soft words to make up for them. They're lingerin' on them long stairs, belike, thinkin' it's a lane in Lisdoonvarna."

Mr. Giluley's only comment was a sneeze and a suggestion:

"Maybe we might close the windy now?"

Michael closed the window. At last Kate came shyly in, but alone. A terrible fear froze the parents' hearts, beating for once as one.

"Did you lose 'um?" Michael gasped.

Katie chuckled. "No, I have him outside. We've made up, ma!"

"Have you, now? Then have him in."

"He's afraid," Kate said, like a shy little girl.

Michael did not fancy her in the rôle, nor timidity as her lover's first trait.

"What's he afraid of?" he growled.

"Of you and ma," Kate simpered, with belated foolishness. "He's afraid you won't give your consent."

"Small danger of our refusin' that," said Michael, not realizing the violence of the language till the words were out. He redeemed himself handsomely. "I'll not give you up, Kate, to anny one who isn't a fine man."

"Floyd's a fine man," said Kate. "He's traveled the whole world since we quarreled. He went first to China, but for the most part it was Australia he was in. He's had adventures would make your blood run cold, but he says he never got over lovin' me. And he wants to marry me. May he, ma, please? Can I, pa, please?"

She looked as if she were a child again, asking for a bit of sugar on her slice of the bread of life.

"I'll not consint till I see him, I tell you," Michael growled, to keep from crying. "For ahl your tahk of Chiny and Austhralia, what proof have I that there is such a man?"

"Oh, there is!" Kate answered, with a swagger.

"And what business is he in?"

"I never asked him that," said Kate. "That would be a nice thing to ask, now, wouldn't it? You can ask him."

Michael and Kate would have been glad to be rid of Mr. Giluley, but there he was, and when he said, "I'd bet ther be shankin' on home," they had to insist on his staying. They were bracing themselves to receive Kate's sole wooer, this wondrous being who had held a woman's heart captive for fourteen years.

The preparation offered a splendid entrance for six feet of hero, but it was a good deal of fanfare for the frightened little brindle that Kate brought into the dining-room. His head hardly reached her shoulder and he had wild hair and fidgety ways with his feet and hands.

Michael and Delia groaned inwardly, and Giluley felt the mixture of sympathy and triumph that we feel for our neighbors' mishaps.

Kate, however, was so dazed with rapture that she assumed her treasure trove to be as beautiful in all other eyes as he was in hers. She presented him with as much pomp as if he had been Apollo:

"Ma, this is Mr. Floyd O'Gara. Floyd, this is my mother—our mother."

137

LONG EVER AGO

At this last Delia nearly withdrew the timid hand she
was putting out, but Mr. O'Gara seized it and clung to
it, and Delia did her best.

"Our mother? Already? Well, annyhow, you're
heartily welcome, Mr. O'Gara, for Kate's sake. She's
told us all about you."

"And has she, now?" said Mr. O'Gara, with a kind of
small barking sound.

Delia turned to her husband. "Michael, this is Mr.
O'Gara. Mr. O'Gara, this is Katie's father."

Michael put out his hand and spoke in his most ponder-
ous tones:

"How air you?"

"Oh, I'm iligant and grand, I thank you kindly," piped
Mr. O'Gara.

Michael tried to be brave and console himself at least
with the brogue.

"Well, he's no dago, annyhow," he said. "So you're
the absentee that's been takin' up all Kate's time."

"And have I, now?" said Mr. O'Gara.

"Indeed, and hasn't she been settin' by that windy
watchin' for you till she's almost wore the sill off?"

"And has she, now?" said Floyd, and stared with
idolatry at Kate, who worshiped him with a look.

Michael and Delia were plainly so depressed that
Mr. Giluley had the decency to rise and take himself home. Delia and Michael went to the door with
him. It made an easy excuse for a few words together.

When they had put out Giluley they turned to each
other with the same thought. Michael spoke it:

"Poor Kate! and that's what she's waited for! That
little shriveled sprissawn of a maneen. I wouldn't have
him for a toby on the mantelpiece."

138

LONG EVER AGO

"Be slow about breakin' Kate's heart in her," said Delia, miserably. "Betther ask him what business he's in."

"I don't care what his business is. I wouldn't have him round the place. Sure and what did they do to him in Austhralia? They condinsed him, that's what they done. And what's this, now?"

In the hall on the complicated hat-rack, umbrella-stand, mirror, and table was Mr. O'Gara's hat and a large, long, green baize bag.

"What's this?" said Michael. "It looks like a set of pipes!"

He massaged the cloth and finally opened it slyly. He exclaimed:

"It is a set of pipes. I wonder doos he play them? If he doos, there's more to him than you'd think at a glance. I couldn't learn them myself; they stoomped me complately whin I was young, and afraid of nahthin', too."

He paused and rubbed his jaw in thought and frowned again.

"But he's prob'ly only shtole them off somebody, or borried them to be learnin' on them. He'd betther be attindin' to his business, if he has anny, and not wasthin' his time on what's beyond him. I'll ask him can he play thim, and have the thruth out of him. But don't let on we've been inspectin' his kit."

They went back to the dining-room. As Michael opened the door Floyd O'Gara made such a quick escape from Kate's immediate vicinity that Michael dragged Delia back into the hall to say:

"Did you see the fine standin' lep he took! He learned that from the kangyroos, belike. I misdoubt his arms was around Katie's waist—as far as they'd reach."

Delia sighed deliciously: "It's a quare sinsation, happenin' in on Katie spoonin' with a stranger."

But Michael had more important news:

"I've just had a suspicion. That Floyd O'Gara in there might be the very same shrimpeen piped for us at the Lady Hurlers' bahl."

"No?"

"Yis!"

"The saints be among us!"

"I'm sure, but I'm not certain sure. And now instead of askin' him can he play, I'll ask him will he."

After a premonitory clearing of throats the guilty old spies returned to the dining-room, where Floyd and Kate were blushing like mad some distance apart.

Michael and Delia sat down and felt themselves very much unwelcome, but necessary. They mentioned the usual topics of people who don't know what to say, and finally Michael led up to what he was leading up to.

"Was you, be anny chance, to the Clare Lady Hurlers' last Saturday, Mr. O'Gara?"

"Well, yis, I—"

"You wern't the gintleman done the pipin', were you?"

"Well, yis, I—"

"I thought I reco'nized you and I'm proud to meet you." He rose part way and put out his hand. Floyd O'Gara, greatly flustered, took it with enthusiasm. Kate almost expired in a rush of pride to the heart. Michael sat back again.

"I don't know whin I've heard pipes piped betther than you piped thim."

"And don't you, now?" said Floyd.

"Do you pipe about much?"

"Yis, I keep busy evenings, and I take pupils day-times."

Kate spoke up: "You didn't pipe, Floydeen, did you, at the Leitrim Ladies'?"

"Yis, I did. I piped there. It was a month back. Why?"

"Oh dear!" sighed Kate, as if she would swoon.

"Why, what at all now!" Delia gasped.

Tears began to patter on Kate's cheeks and breast and knees. And her mouth crinkled as she sobbed:

"I was at that dance. And people asked me to go into the Irish room, and I wouldn't. Had I gone, I'd have seen you there, and a month of sorrow would have been a month of joy."

"But why would you not go to the Irish music?" Floyd asked, amazed.

"Since you piped to me, I've never been able for standin' the sound of it. And I wouldn't go with pa to the Lady Hurlers' for the same reason. Oh dear; oh dear! When we run away from sorrow we never know what else we're runnin' from."

Michael frowned on O'Gara for the vain suffering of his daughter's wasted life. "And now, Mr. O'Gara, why was it you never tried for to find Kate all these years?"

Floyd was frightened by his manner and hastened to explain:

"Who was I to be thinkin' that Katie would be re-mimberin' me all this while? She wint away without a word, and it is only a few months I come to this counthry, and for ahl I was perishin' to see her, I naturally supposed that a colleen like what she was would have been snapped up by a dozen min long ever ago."

"What, do you think she is? a Mormon?" said Michael. "But it's not likely yourself has not been married ahl this while?"

Floyd blushed, his hair almost afire as he shook his head and mumbled:

"I won't say I haven't tried to be, but I thank me patron

saint the women I thought I wanted was sure they didn't want me. Heaven was savin' me for Kate, and Kate for me. So we've decided not to waste anny more time."

He and Kate exchanged glances of such excruciating ecstasy that Michael said to Delia:

"Whin I was a lad, the old folks used to be consulted before a match was made. But now it seems parents is insulted instead."

"Why, pa!" Kate gasped.

"Michael!" Delia scolded. "Whist and bad manners to you for sp'akin' so to a guest."

"I can be as polite to a guest as the nixt man, but whin it comes to a son-in-law I have a mind to have a word to say. Howaniver, I know my place, and I'll go to bed—if so be I'm permitted to sleep here."

The women regarded him with stupefaction and Floyd O'Gara was ready to leap through Kate's window, but Delia motioned him to sit still and said to the departing Michael:

"Aye, take yourself off to bed, you ould line. You've got another sore toot'th, I'm thinkin'."

Michael had not meant to make a real exit, but he was committed to it and he could not think how to change his mind gracefully. He was doubly surly as he slammed the door of his own room and slumped into a chair.

Floyd O'Gara rose to go, and Kate was in too much dismay to keep him, so Delia hastened to use her wits.

"I saw a set of pipes on the hahl-tree, Mr. O'Gara."

"And did you, now?"

"Would it be askin' too much to ask would you let us hear you use them?"

"I'm afraid it would disturb Himself," said Floyd, cravenly.

"Pay no heed to him," said Delia. "It's my ears

are starved for a taste of them. I'd greatly fancy to hear you."

"And would you, now? Sure, half the success of music is the audience wishin' for to hear it. I'll have the pipes out and give you a toon or two."

He went to the hall and brought the instrument back in his arms as if it were an only child. He unswaddled it, strapped the bellows under his right arm and about his body, nursed the bag in his left arm, and set the chanter on his right knee, fingering the holes in it with his left hand, and laid the drones and regulators across his right thigh.

After a few preliminary croaks and tootles, and a flourish of curls and crans, he looked up to say:

"And now what would you have—an air or a dance?"

"Some ould air," sighed Delia. "I don't suppose you remimber 'The Little Heathy Hill' or 'Raking Paudheen Rue'?"

"And don't you, now? Do you think I'm not Irish at ahl?"

He played for her the sorrowful old tunes that brought the wet to her eyes and to Kate's. And the door to Michael's room had a look as if some one were leaning an ear against it. It seemed to shake tenderly. Then Floyd played a kind of plaintive jig that Kate alone remembered. Floyd had composed it for her during the time of war when he would play for no one else. Kate seemed to see herself flinging her slim body and her bright bare feet in girlish frenzy. It was long ever ago, but more vivid than anything else in the room or in the world. And Floyd saw her, too, as she was and would be forever in his soul.

He broke away from melodious regrets into one of the great bard O'Carolan's plangsties.

Now the bedroom door began to quiver mysteriously. Delia kept an anxious eye on it, and finally she whispered:

"You don't chance to know 'Crabs in the Skillet' or 'Shins Around the Fireside,' do you?"

"And don't I, now?"

He began to skirl. The bedroom door shivered, then flew open, and Michael issued, dancing like a jumping-jack. He brought his feet down with a slapping, clicking rhythm that must have startled the people below. But little he cared. Floyd kept reiterating the tune till Michael was breathless and sank into a chair, gasping:

"You have the advantage on me with that bellows under your airm there. Me own is bushted. But once I used to batther so tidy a clog to that, it was the piper and not me that gave out. Do you remimber, ma?"

Old Bridget had risen from her bed. She stood in the doorway in her nightgown, and a petticoat she had caught up in the dark for a shawl. She laughed shrilly:

"Aye, Michaeleen, you bet the flag of the fire to bits wit' your jiggin'. The ould cracks in the stone was there whin you sint for me out. And time was I could do me own share of cloggin' with the rest of them."

Floyd was almost popping with his unexpected glory, and Kate was pouring tears into the broad laughter of her mouth. Then Michael, frowning savagely, beckoned Delia into their room, and said with a kind of apologetic ferocity:

"I been thinkin' maybe we've been doin' Floydie an injoosthice."

"We!" Delia gasped. "You ould line, you! And is the toot'th out?"

Michael grinned evasively. "Maybe Katie has picked a good one, afther ahl. It wouldn't be so bad havin' a man about the house to pull the heart out of thim blessed tubes now and thin. It would save docthors' bills. And it would bate ahl the piannies and victhrolys in the worruld. In the older times, whin my people was kings in Ireland, we used to have aich of us his own piper for to play to him thin—like David done to Saulomon—or whoiver the divil it was. It's what us Morahans used to be used to."

Delia was glowing, too. "It would be plisant, when coompany was in, to say, 'Katie, ask your husband would he oblige the guests with a—'"

But Michael was back in the room, where Bridget was cowering by the steam radiator asking Mr. O'Gara if he could play "Spatther the Dew." He said he could and was just pumping up for it when Michael broke in with a terrifying severity:

"Mr. O'Gara, you've kept my daughter Katie waitin' on you some fourteen years now. I don't know the cushtoms in Austhralia, but it's a lahng ingagemint for our family. Have you or have you not anny intintions of havin' the banns called, and if not why not? and if so— whin?"

"What would you say to next Soonda'?" said Mr. O'Gara. "That is, of coorse, if Kateen has no objiction."

If Kateen had any objiction it was drowned in the noise of two elevated trains passing the window with a rattlety-bang. Kateen paid no attention to them at all, at all—then or thereafter.

VI

AT THE BACK OF GODSPEED

I

WHEN Mrs. Van Dusen went through her mail she usually tossed the invitations to her secretary with a word: "Put this on my calendar." "Can I accept that?" "Remind me to decline these very politely." "You answer that one—coldly. What right have they to invite me?"

But she got one invitation that she did not toss. She jumped as she read it. She blushed. She considered. When Miss Hubbard's hand went out for it, as of habit, Mrs. Van Dusen recoiled. She clutched the invitation with so miserly a grasp that her secretary, who went to the theater a good deal, assumed that this letter was one of those fearful things known as "the papers."

Miss Hubbard was delighted with horror, for life was rather tame in Mrs. Van Dusen's employment. Invitations to send out and to acknowledge; charity moneys to give or refuse; bills to pay; check-books and bank-books to arrange; appointments to be kept in mind; money to lend her son and never get back—such things about exhausted her excitements. She had not even a husband to quarrel with. And her handsome son rarely called when the secretary was there—except on the telephone,

146

when he grew flirtatious in a harmless, amusing fashion, impossible either to rebuke or to encourage.

Mrs. Van Dusen bit her lip, tapped her right mule on the floor, read the letter again, and then stuffed it into the envelope, and the envelope into that filing-cabinet which a woman keeps between her corsets and herself.

Then she said to her secretary, "Remind me to speak to Mr. Carmody about—about—just remind me to speak to him without fail."

This was discouraging; for Mr. Carmody was only her brother. He was stupendously rich, and so powerful that everybody spoke of him with contempt and would have been very proud to know him.

And that was all the secretary found out about the invitation, though she duly made the reminder. When Mrs. Van Dusen got round to it she went to see her brother. It was a long trip down-town, and she was in such a temper that she fairly scorched her way through the outposts and the front-line trenches guarding the great Carmody.

When she reached him he was up to his ears in work. He had six telephones on his desk, and he kept three of them going at once while he conducted a conference in a long-distance quartet.

He looked up at last and said, "Well, Margaret, what brings you down to this end of the world?"

"I want to see you."

"Feast your eyes."

"Alone."

"I'm alone." To Carmody, his secretary was only furniture.

"I said alone," said Mrs. Van Dusen.

"Oh, all right!" Dakin, the perfect secretary, who never heard anything and always heard everything, was on his way out before Carmody could boost him with a glance.

"Will that suit you," said Carmody, "or shall I plug the keyhole? What's wrong now? Broke? Or is that darling child of yours in wrong again? I don't want to hurry you, but I'm half an hour late to a board meeting, and I make it an infallible rule always to be on time—next time."

Mrs. Van Dusen settled herself comfortably in a chair, admired the skyscape and roofscape through the lofty window, then asked, casually:

"Did you get an invitation signed by somebody named McDwyer?"

"Did I? McGuire? What about?"

"About a reunion at the home of Michael Morahan."

"Oh yes, I believe I did! Yes, I know I did."

"Did you answer it?"

"I had it answered, I think. Why?"

"I got one, too."

Carmody laughed. "You accepted, of course."

"Oh, of course!" she assented, with irony. "Of course I can't go, but I don't know how to decline it gracefully."

"Why decline? Why not accept?"

"Don't be absurd. You know I couldn't go there. I'd embarrass those people as much as they'd embarrass me. And I'd never dare let the chauffeur take me there. And, besides, I have another engagement."

"I believe I used that excuse myself."

"But it's true. You have an engagement with me. We're dining at the Schuylers' and going on to the opera."

"I think I said I'd be out of town."

"You might as well be. They'll never know the difference."

"Well, so long as we have a good excuse, what are you worrying about? Why take this long trip?"

"Because I hate to decline. They may think I'm uppish. I don't mind being a snob, but I hate being thought one."

"I see. You want me to invent some real excuse?"

"I thought you might help."

"Let me see. Dakin does most of my lying for me—in that line. I'll ask him."

"In Heaven's name, no!"

"Well, suppose you get your doctor to order you to Florida."

"But I've got to be at the Schuylers' dinner, and the following day I've a reception that will be in the papers."

"Oh, well, I haven't got time to do any fancy lying. Just send 'em your regrets, and if they don't like 'em they can lump 'em. We're under no obligations to go. We haven't seen any of the people for over twenty years."

"I know, but—"

"Good-by. I'm off. You can dictate your answer to Dakin."

He pressed a spot on the rim of his desk and his secretary entered like a bottle-rubbed genie.

Mrs. Van Dusen said, "I'll write it myself at home."

Carmody nodded and returned to the tune he was playing on his various telephones. His sister's troubles did not trouble him. Being always in trouble, he was never in it, for one vexation chased another off.

His sister suffered more because she was always chasing that sad thing called pleasure. She was caught in an eternal game of tag, running herself to death.

She had forgotten her humble origin. Her brother's luck and pluck had brought him quick money. Carmody had found the pot of gold at the end of the rainbow. In fact, he was accused of monopolizing the rainbow, playing both ends against the middle. His abilities had commended him to bigger and bigger people, and his sister's social paces had commended her to their wives and daughters. So they had gone up like rockets and stayed up like steeples.

The accents they had brought from Ireland had faded from their voices as completely as the odor of the peat smoke from their hair.

Such Irish people as they had known for the last decade had been the high Irish, millionaires, generals, cardinals, archbishops, peers, visiting poets, scholars, judges, bankers. Mrs. Van Dusen's best friend was a countess from the Papal court.

They knew, of course, a little of the poor, the peasants, but of the middle class in Nova Hibernia they had no knowledge. They had long since forgotten that they had themselves risen like bubbles from the lees through the middle liquor to the gilded brim of life's glass.

The invitation to meet their *ab origine* acquaintances came as an unpleasant shock. They had no intention of returning to their old stratum, but they resented the difficulty of refusing without giving a handle for criticism. They sent their regrets and felt that the matter was closed. They counted without Michael Morahan.

II

To Michael Morahan the reunion was a tremendous event. One glory was that it was to be held at his "house," as he called his flat.

It made him feel good because, when his ship-load had sailed from Queenstown, twenty-five years before, he had been the leader of the crowd, the biggest lad among them, the one of most promise. It had been natural, then, that they should elect his home twenty-five years hence for the tryst. They had laughed and blarneyed his poverty with the assurance that he would have a castle on Broadway in five and twenty years.

He had not the castle. Many of his companions had distanced him in the struggle for wealth and power.

"Some of them has distanced me on the way to heaven, too," he would say. "But none of them has distanced me on the way to health and happiness, though at that I've had more sickness and throuble than most. But I've got as long a family as the best of them—and a wife that's more betterer than the best that iver came out of Ireland whativer."

Delia slapped his hand away, but a warm blush of pride encircled the white spot his pinch left on her generous cheek.

There was great stir in the Morahan apartment the afternoon of the celebration.

There was much cooking to do, and extra china and silver to be borried off the Dugans and all the other neighbors, and a world of folding-chairs had in from the jovial undertaker's; these must be snapped open and set about. Ice-cream freezers had to be rolled in, and cakes iced, and no end of bottles arranged, to say nothing of a damp, disreputable "quarter"—i. e., an old keg—that Michael insisted on depositing on a kitchen chair, with a washtub under the spigot to catch the suds.

Michael was home early from the yards where he kept his teams and the odds and ends of his business as a small contractor.

The house was already full, and the kitchen so crowded that the workers had to pirouette about one another. The sons' wives were on the scurry everywhere, as was

LONG EVER AGO

Kate, who was still thought of as the old-maid daughter, though she kept referring to her husband, "Mr. O'Gara," and brandishing her brand-new wedding-ring.

Everybody was in a grand fluster and nobody noticed that pretty Moyna Killilea, recently become Mrs. Shane O'Mealia, was quietly weeping into the dish-water where she soused the neighbors' china. Michael, who kept returning to offer his help as often as he was evicted by his wife, was the first to notice the tears splashing, and he nudged Delia as she was passing him with a delicately equilibrated arrangement of borrowed cups and saucers that would have made a juggler envious. She got to the table before the collapse and rounded on Michael. He saved himself by his mystery.

"Whisper! Moyna's cryin'."

"She is not! Is she truly? She is! The creature!"

Delia went to her and asked her why. Moyna brushed the tears away with a wet hand and left soapy water in place of brine.

"Och, it's nothin' much, only Shane lost his job in the stove-shop and we'll be turned out in the cold, and I told him he'd ought to have married Judy Dugan and been rich, instead of this old Me. And one word led to another and hard names were passed, and I'd have run off and left him, but he run off first, and I don't know where he wint—not that I care, for I'll never look at him again."

And then she belied her words by sobbing her pretty head almost off.

This family quarrel made no impression on Michael. He was used to the squally weather of landlocked waters, but he gasped: "Hasn't he got out of the habit yet of losin' jobs? I thought marriage would reform him, but it looks like he was set on bein' the champeen job-dropper of the world."

152

AT THE BACK OF GODSPEED

He felt responsible, since he had sent over to Ireland and imported Moyna, and, now that Moyna's tears began to spatter the dishes like bird-shot, he changed his tune:

"Ah, don't mind, Moyna honey. I'll get him another and a betther. This very night I'll make Matt Carmody give him a job—no, I'll make him give him a position. He's grown past jobs. You wait! As soon as Carmody comes—"

Delia echoed his words with an intonation of ridicule, and added, "If Shane waits for that he'll do a bit of waitin' will bate all records."

"For why would you say that?" Michael roared.

"Because Carmody is never comin'."

"Of course he's comin'! And why wouldn't he?"

He brought on himself a landslide of reasons. Delia put down her burden and smothered him with them.

"Why wouldn't he? say you. Why would he? says me. As if a man like Carmody, who's got millions where we've got hundreds, had nothin' better to do of an evenin' than forgather with a lot of plain people—just every-day Irish that hasn't an ahtomobile to ride home from work in nor a bank to call their own. And his sister one of the swellest of swells! Widdy of a man whose brother-in-law's a duke and his aunt is an earl, and— Wasn't it myself saw her own son drivin' a stage-coach up Fi'th Avenyeh one day, with half a doozen of harses in front and harns blowin' till you'd think it was an army—or somebody sellin' fish. And his mother herself, didn't I see her photograph in the paper along with famous murderers and politicians and—"

Michael tried to escape. He kept putting in vain phrases: "Well, of coorse—that may be, but—but—well—howanever—here! wait—say! back up! shut up!"

"Such words before the others," Delia protested. "But what I was sayin' was—"

An elevated train roared by the windows just then with prolonged thunder. Delia went right on talking, unheard but eloquent. When it had gone by, her voice emerged again abruptly, "—and diamonds on her till you'd be sayin', 'Is it a new kind of a disease she has?' and Carmody so famous the President itself is afraid to speak to him, and—"

Another train went past the other way with the same uproar. Delia moved to shut the window, but Michael stopped her and yelled into her ear, "I prefer the ilevated." He shouted to it: "I'm much obliged to you. Come again!"

Delia subsided with a triumphant: "And that's why Carmody will forget to be here. He's forgotten the likes of us long ago."

"Forgotten, is it?" Michael continued. "Wasn't he a lad with the rest of us? Didn't he come over in the same steamer? Didn't I lind him the loan of all the shoes he had to his feet? A man may forget much, but he'll not aisy forget the place he was born in. He may forget the man he met yesterday, but niver the boys he grew up with. He'll be here or I'm an Orangeman."

The telephone whirred faintly from the other room. It had a way of following up Michael's boasts unless he spit for luck. He had neglected the exorcism and he was uneasy.

"Now who's that?" said Delia.

"How should I know his voice from that dom' bell?" Michael blustered. He usually blustered when he was afraid. He went into the living-room like a school-boy going up to get what-for. Delia held the door ajar and listened in.

AT THE BACK OF GODSPEED

"Hello! hello! hello! Well, well! Mr.—who? Mr. Morahan?" Michael stormed in an artificial voice. "I'll inquire is he in. Who is it that might be wantin' to see him? McDwyer?" Delia could see his grin from the back of his neck. "Hello, Mac! It's me all the while. Well, how's things comin'? Are all the answers in to the invitations, and is ivery wan comin'? . . . That's grand. . . . All but who? . . . He's not? . . . Ah, that's a . . . He regrets? . . . He did like . . . Well, I'll be . . . Well, for the love of . . . Not comin' . . . A previous ingagemint! I'd give him a previous ingagemint on the nose could I find him. I wouldn't take tin dollars for the grudge I owe that man. Well, you're comin' round yourself, of coorse. . . . That's right. We've got along so far without that felly, we'll try to sweat out a day or two more."

Delia saw how his big head drooped and heard the false cheer in his voice.

"I'm glad he's not comin'. He'd put a damper on the rest of us. I never liked him. I sometimes think that some of the things the paper says about him is true. Well, I'll see you later."

He hung up the receiver and stood gazing blankly at the transmitter of such bad news. Delia was merciful:

"I told you so, but I'm sorry I told you so."

"A previous ingagemint!" Michael barked, as he whirled. "What right has he to a previous ingagemint? Sure he made this one twenty-five years past. If I could lay hold of him." He seized the telephone-book. "I wonder what's the noomber. Previous ingagemint!"

Shane O'Mealia, the luckless, the jobless, came in now to add to the gloom. When he learned what Michael was up to he said: "It's no use, uncle. I tried to get to him meself once, when I was looking for a job. There's about a thousand office-boys between him and the world. Why, his secretary's got a secretary."

Michael growled as he went on rummaging the telephone-book: "I'll go through thim office-boys like I was a cyclone. Here we are, 'Carmody, Abigail, Chiropodist.' What's that, I don't know. 'Carmody, Abraham, Pants.' Say, what's happened the Carmodys?" He ran his thumb down the index awkwardly. "'Carmody, Bridget.' Ah, that sounds better, more home-like. 'Dinnis—Emmett—Ignatius.' Ah, 'Matthew Haitch, Truckman.' There must be two of them, for he's not here. Is he not able for a telephone, I wonder? Mayhap they've taken it out on him."

Shane explained: "He's so important, he's not listed. You'd better try the Coagulated Steel; that's Broad, twenty-wan hundred."

"That's a divil of a note—to have a telephone and ashamed to say so." He took up the receiver for one of his usual bouts with the operator. "Hello! hello, Cintheral! Are you asleep at the switch? Give me Broad twenty-wan, oh, oh. . . . No, not tin to wan—twenty-wan, oh, oh. . . . No, no. Oh—oh—wow, wow. Yis. . . . All right. Thank you, plase! much obliged! you're hairtily welcome." A pause, then: "Hello! Is this twenty-wan, oh— I'm ashamed to say it. Is this the Granulated Steel? . . . I want Carmody, Mat-too Ah Carmody. . . . All right; I'm holdin' the wire as fasht as I can. . . . Is this you, Carmody? Ah, what does it matter who I am? I'm not askin' you to call me. I'm callin' you. . . . Oh, you're his sickrety, are you? Pl'ased to meet you. And how's *your* sickrety?" He turned aside to sniff: "An extra sickrety. And I knew him when he hadn't an extra shirt."

He reverted to the telephone. "I'm waitin'. . . . So

are you? Well, I'll hold the 'phone till I see Carmody, if I have to set here all night. What's my business? That's my business. It's none of your business. . . . No, I'm not a reporter. Say, tell him it's personal, and it's scandalous, and I'm Irish, and—I used to know him when . . . All right. Sure I'll hould the wire."

Having won thus far, he chortled as he put his hand over the mouthpiece. "The sickrety has gone to chase up Carmody. I hope I don't have as much work as this gettin' to Saint Peter." He started suddenly: "Hello! hello! Is this Mr. Carmody? Mattoo Ah Carmody? . . . Himself? . . . Is it yourself that's talkin', or somebody for you? . . . Oh!"

In a glow of success, he grinned, winked, snuggled to the telephone, and spoke in a voice of angelic geniality:

"Hello, Mat! You're lookin' well. . . . You don't know me voice? You used to when I wint by your cabin on the way to the big bog-hole for a shwim, and I'd holler, 'Hello, Mat! Quit out o' that and go shwimmin'.' . . . Ah, that remimbers you, doos it? . . . Yis, it's me. . . . Oh, she's well. She sinds you her love."

Delia cuffed him.

He yelped: "Ouch! She's very strahng. You'd hardly see a change in her, for all she's the mother av a rigiment. . . . Ah, hush your blarney! You'll have the Cintheral blushin'."

He lowered his voice to his old crony: "Say, Matt, listen! There's a little gang of us gettin' thegither the night at my . . . Yis, McDwyer told me you wrote him you had another date, but I said this ingagemint was made twenty-five years back. Sure, when I lent ye the loan of the brogues you walked the deck in, it's little I thought for to see you ownin' fifty-sivin vari'ties of railroads an' a couple o' judges for stenographers. . . . Ah,

go on, you old fox, wasn't I in politics once meself?—til
I got nare-sighted and dursn't trust meself amongst the
gang?

"Judge McMurtha 'll be here. You won't fergit the
little sprissawn of a man he was. And he a judge now
He's gettin' a bit old and feeble, so they're talkin' o
makin' a Sinator of him. You'll be needin' some fresh
Sinators now. Those ones you're afther usin' this long
time is goin' that stale, people holds their noses whin the)
rades the names of thim.

"Come along out yourself. . . . No, some other avenin
won't do whativer. What talk have ye of ingagemints
Lave your board of directors go to . . . If you lose a
million, I'll lind you another. I'll tell you wan thing
and that's not two—it's sorry the chanst again you'l
have to come to a twinty-fifth anniversary. I hate to
think where you're li'ble to be twinty-five years from this
Some of us that come over on the boat won't be here—
they wisht they could but for the weight of the sod that's
over thim."

His griefs mobilized as rapidly as his joys. "Fine lads
they were, too, some of thim—those that wasn't girls. . .
Yis—true for you!—too bad for thim. So come along
now, or I'll hang on here till you do. . . . Ah, now you're
tahkin'!"

He nodded to Delia and whispered, "He'll come!"

"You don't mane it!" Delia gasped, and Michael
parroted it:

"You don't mane it—I mane you do mane it!" He
whispered to Delia: "He says he doos mane it. . . . Al
right, Matt—we'll expect ye. Good-by—"

Delia prodded him with a plate. He cried out: "Wait
—wait! Say!" He turned to Delia, "Well?"

"His sister."

AT THE BACK OF GODSPEED

"Your sister! We're expectin' her, of coorse. She coom over on the boat, too. . . . Yis, I heard she was married—to who, I disremimber. . . . Mrs. Van—what? . . . Van Dusen? That's a hell of a name for an honest Irish girl. Still, we'll forgive her that if she comes. Ah, make her come. Tell her to lave the dishes till afther she gets home. Goin' to the opera? What opera— Caruso? Oh, be the powers of smoke! Dagoes can't make music—only n'ise. Tell Maggie we're goin' to have some rale music—Irish. I have a new son-in-law plays the pipes. Shame her into it. . . . That's right! We'll be expectin' the both of you. Good-by, Matt."

He set the receiver back and caressed the telephone as he murmured, "Nice felly, Matt!"

Delia masked her pride in the conqueror with an impatient, "Well, you've been settin' at that insterment long enough to hatch a clutch o' eggs."

"Annyhow, I hatched Carmody," said Michael.

His work was done. But Carmody had still to persuade his sister.

III

The elevated railroad that had drowned so much conversation in the Morahan home was drowned itself in the hubbub of the party that night. The house was so shaken with laughter, the fetching of jigs and duels of laughter, that the agitation of the Elevated made no impression. The trains slunk by discouraged.

Michael's wife, an honest Irish-lace fichu about her shoulders, was trying to greet the guests with one merry eye while the other anxiously watched for her husband. Michael's mother was not worried. This ancient Bridget kept her state in a large arm-chair she did not rise from. She had on her best black gown, and a bit of lace stuck in what hair she had to conceal what she had not.

Out in the dining-room Kate, very much dressed up, was making the last frantic revisions of the food display. The tables were staggered under towers of substantials. On the sideboard were sandwiches of every kind, and even olluvs, as well as flowers, little green pigs, and tiny green flags with golden harps—the emblem of a singing race. In the kitchen, like a forlorn Cinderella, sat Moyna O'Mealia, her face so blubbered with tears that she would not go into the parlor at all. She went about crying into everything, and alternately vowing that she'd die if Shane did not come back soon from wherever he was, and that if he did she would never speak to him again.

In the crowded parlor Michael's landlord, John Giluley, was prominent. Like most landlords, he was chronically sick with hopes deferred mitigated only by deferred repairs. He wore a long frock-coat and kept unconsciously putting his foot up for the bar-room rail that was not there. He talked down to Justice McMurtha, a small man with a large cargo of distinction. The justice was right smart for his size, with evening dress of the sort called impeccable.

His sweet and sugary daughter, Rosie, looking as if she were a candy-box picture come to life, was seated on the stool of the upright piano. Two of the Morahan sons, Myles and Shamus, both very swell in their "Tuxedas," were carelessly seated on the piano-keys on either side of Rosie. Loving each other like Cain and Abel, they were alternately jangling the upper and the lower ivories as they bent to speak to Rosie and sat back.

Delia, in a stew of impatience at her husband's bodily absence, was mentally absent in pursuit of him, while she tried to make Mrs. Giluley feel at home. Glancing at

AT THE BACK OF GODSPEED

Mr. Giluley, who was just rebuking his scandalous foot for giving itself away by making for that rail again, Delia said:

"It's a joy, sure, to see how well you keep lookin', Mrs. Giluley. And what way is Himself?"

Mrs. Giluley cast a despairful look at her spouse, caught him with foot in air, and moaned:

"Oh, himself is scarce fit to hop the len'th of his own shadder, the rheumatics is that strahng in him. But it's only your good kindness that says I'm lookin' well. Surely you've took note of me jah."

Delia, too distraught even to notice that protuberance, made capital of her neglect.

"It had not caught me eye. Now that I look close, it is a trifle swole. What's on it, at all? Moomps!"

"Oh, saints shield us round! I'm nearly destroyed with the faceache."

"It's neurology, belike, or maybe a tooth that's in it. Have you tried Doctor O'Halloran, the painless dintist?"

"Oh, he may be painless, but me, I'm not. You'd think he thought I was a boulder of the granite and he makin' ready to drill a blasht-hole. I let a screech you'd heard from Bantry to Boyne, was you there."

"Och, musha! if there's annything worser than a joompin' tooth, just get me it."

Mrs. Giluley felt it only polite to note that Delia's Himself was absent. "But where's Michael this while?"

"Oh, that Michael!" Delia sniffed. "He's always behind, like the cow's tail. Sure, but gettin' a pig to a fair is less than leadin' him into a dress-soot. I'll try him again." She went to the sliding-door and beckoned Kate to her whisper, "In the name of all, Katie dear, go see what's happened your pa!"

Kate shook her head hopelessly. "I've spoke to him

twice, and such words as he put on me through the door!"

"I'll put words on him, keepin' the guests waitin'!" She went resolutely to the room where Michael writhed in a death-wrestle with his linen.

"Is this a dog-collar you laid out for me?" he snarled. "I can't git half me neck in it at the one time."

"And why would you?" Delia snapped, as she whipped it off. "It's not your collar by four sizes. It coom home in the launthry. Some child's collar it is."

She found him one of his own and fastened it round him, then picked up a forlorn strip of white.

"Is this your tie?"

"It was. It's a thrifle roompled."

"Roompled, is it! It looks like the cats had foughten over it."

She made the best bow she could of it, and he grew so proud of himself that when she called him "a little-good-for" he embraced her and chortled:

"That makes two of us."

Then he broke into song,

"If thou'lt be mine, the threasures of air, of earth, and say shall lie at thy feet!"

Delia struggled to repress him. "Hush and hurry up. The pairty is all assimbled."

His spirits were not to be quenched. He cried: "All the more better. We'll make a triumphal intry. Come on with you now!" And despite her resistance. he dragged her into the crowd as he sang:

"Saint Patrick was a gintleman;
He came from dacint people.
In Dooblin town he built a church
And put upon 't a shteeple.

AT THE BACK OF GODSPEED

> His father was a Callaghan,
> His mother was a Brady,
> His aunt was an O'Shaughnessy,
> And his uncle was a Grady."

He marched forward, shaking hands with his guests, and swept them into an eddy after him. They joined the song, and he led them round his mother's chair with a wild hullaballoo in the refrain:

> "Thin succiss to bould Saint Patrick's fisht.
> He was a saint so cliver,
> He gave the shnakes and toads a twisht,
> And banished thim foriver."

Everybody repeated the last line with a breakdown that frightened Giluley for his building.

There was a terrific clatter, but Michael topped it with a howl:

"Who says it's twenty-five years since we were lads?"

Justice McMurtha wanted more music. He shouted: "Encore! There's a second verse to that. Encore!"

Michael rebuked him. "Who is it uses a dago word when there's the good Irish AREESTH! But I've neither the win' nor the mimory for it. You sing it, Judge. Ha, you a judge—you young rogue, you! Go on and sing it or I'll tell what I know of you."

The little judge, in an astonishingly severe basso like a lyrical death-warrant, roared, in a brogue cruelly compromised by years of New York dialect:

> "There's not a mile in Iahland's isle
> Where the doity voimin mustahs.
> Where'er he put his deah foot down,
> He moidered them in clustahs;

163

LONG EVER AGO

The toads went hop, the frogs went flop,
Slap dash into the wawtah,
And the beasts committed suicide,
To save themselves from slawtah."

All joined in the chorus again:

"Thin succiss to bould Saint Patrick's fisht.
He was a saint so cliver,
He gave the shnakes and toads a twisht,
And banished thim foriver."

A breakdown like a bombardment followed, till Delia
protested with horror:

"For the love of the saints, will ye have the pairty
pulled before it's begun?"

"Who's to stop it?" Michael retorted. "Haven't we
the police with us?" He put an arm around his son
Myles. "And the fire department to put disturbers out?"
He put an arm around his son Shamus. "And a mimber
of the judiciary to suspind sintence?" He kicked amiably
at the judge. "And a future ripresintative of the State
Legislature to amind the lah?"

He swung the other foot at Giluley, who limped out
of reach. Michael raved on. "And if those are not
enough, haven't we ahl the beauty in the world to chairm
the invader and loor him into a fatal slumber?"

Delia admired his gigantic hilarity with terror: "Oh,
Michael avic, for the love of the saints and the neighbors,
hold your whist!"

Judge McMurtha pleaded for him: "Don't spoil him,
Mrs. Morahan. After my years on the bench, it's like
heaven to unbend, and, by Heaven! we're going to unbend to-night. He ought to be here now."

"He? Who? Carmody, d'ye mean? Where is the big

gomeral? Isn't he here?" Michael fell from the clouds
with a thump. He had relied on Carmody, and boasted
of his capture.

"Carmody nothing," said Judge McMurtha. "The
old blind piper that piped for us at the patterns in Lisdoonvarna is the guest of honor."

"Who was that, now? I forget." Michael pondered.

Delia found the name as she ransacked her memory.
"That wouldn't be old Dinnis Killilea?"

"The same," said McMurtha, grandly.

"But I've had him dead these long years," said Delia.

Old Bridget confirmed the tradition: "That's the story
we have at home—that he fell in a bog-hole, ten-odd
years past."

"He fell in a bog-hole," McMurtha conceded, "but it
was filled with something stronger than water. He's
wandered all round the world, wherever there were Irish
to listen to his pipes. I heard of him being out in Chicago,
and after much correspondence with the chief of police, I
had him shipped East."

Mrs. Giluley forgot her tooth and smiled lopsidedly:
"Old Killilea, eh? Sure, he must be a thousand years old
if he's a minyute."

McMurtha nodded. "Very old he is and very peevish,
and prouder than the Old Boy himself. But he can still
play the Union pipes past anything I ever heard."

"But if you have him, where have you him?" Michael
demanded, impatient for more music.

"He's like you," said McMurtha, "he has to make a
grand entrance. I didn't want to miss anything, so I
asked my secretary to bring him over later."

"And you have a sickrety, too?" said Michael. "Murder in Irish, Delia, we'll have to git one of them."

Delia was afield in the back pastures.

"Old Dinnis Killilea! he piped for our wedding, Michaelawn."

Michael nodded dolefully. "That he did—that he did! And wouldn't he be the granduncle or greataunt or something to Moyna?"

Bridget bobbed her head: "Her father's cousin's step-mother married her uncle's nephew's father—or something like that."

"Oh, is it so close of kin they are?" said Michael. "And where is Moyna and her man Shane?"

Delia made mysterious signs that he had learned to obey. He changed the subject at once.

"I had hoped to see Peter Kehoe to-night. He was on the ship with us. Will he be here?"

"Niver an answer he answered my letter," said Mr. McDwyer.

Mrs. O'Rahilly broke in: "He made tubs of money, and the last time I saw him he told me he was running over to the old country for a visit. He must have stayed."

"Aye, stay he did," Bridget croaked. "Wasn't I one that saw him took to his grave there?"

All the old eyes widened with funereal fascination as children's do at a ghost-story. Bridget told the tale:

"He came back to us and made his mother's last years happy, and whin she wint he was not long follyin' her."

"Oh, the pity!" sighed Michael; "and him the liveliest lad on the ship. He brought along his concertina and played the dances for us. Do you remimber?"

"It's well I remimber the burryin' of him," said Bridget. "It was in the greatest storm since the Famine. Troth, the sky had a look on it like it would be a bog was turned upside down and the air full of the emptyin's."

The pink Rosie did not like this picture: "The poor fellow, to be buried in such a storm! Ugh!"

166

"Och, merry-come-sad, honey!" Bridget smiled tenderly. "Don't you know the sayin'—'Happy are the brides the sun shines on, happy are the dead the rain rains on'?"

"I never heard that," Rosie murmured.

"The sun will be shinin' on your weddin', one of these days soon."

"I hope so," said Myles and Shamus together.

Michael meditated aloud on it: "So Peter Kehoe's dead. That's too bad! He owed me nine dollars. Well, lave it go. I suppose his bein' burried is why he niver answered the letter I sint him. I sint it to his old New York address, but I marked it, 'Kindly forward if not there.' I misdoubt they forwarded it."

Rosie returned to the piano-stool. Myles and Shamus returned to their posts on the keys. They sat down with a jangle that startled Michael. He rounded on them.

"Come off that pianny, you lumb'rin' hulks! Is it a park binch ye think it is? And it's fresh tuned, too. Cost me two dollars."

"Oh, all right, pa," said Myles. "Don't get excited."

But that was what Michael most wanted to do. He had an old feud with Carmody, and he had his heart set on recalling it to life. He moped about, doing the work of a host perfunctorily. It was a long while before the ringing of the door-bell revived his hopes. He sent Kate to the door and tried to look indifferent. Delia peeked into the hall and gave the warning with a shrill whisper.

"It's the Carmodys!"

IV

Guests of honor do well to come late, for they usually bring constraint with them. It was so with the mere rumor of the Carmodys. Instantly all ease disappeared.

The famous plutocrats who had been little more than a misty tradition had actually materialized. Everybody felt small and unimportant and yet resentful. Even Michael took on a stage-fright.

Delia made another confidential pronouncement.

"They act as if they didn't know where to lave their things. Why doosn't Kate take them? It's a butler they're used to."

"A butler is it?" Mrs. Giluley shrilled. "When Mag Carmody come on the ship she had nothin' to give a butler but the old shawl on her head. And her brother Matthew he had hardly a hat. I could 'a' had him, but I chose Giluley."

Giluley straightened up as straight as his rheumatic joints would let him, and crowed:

"She did so. She chose me."

"She's a good chooser," said Michael. "Carmody has twinty million dollars."

Delia whispered again: "Maggie Carmody is still puffin' like a whale. She's not used to stairs."

"No wonder," said Michael, relieving his pride. "Her father's cabin had but the one story, and hardly that. The Carmodys were poorer than the poorest in Lisdoon-varna."

None the less, there was a hasty straightening of ties and smoothing of skirts as well as faces to greet the advent of the quondam paupers.

Mrs. Van Dusen, gorgeously dressed for the opera, floated in like a swan among geese. She was as ill-at-ease as the homely fowl, and as much afraid of them as they of her.

Delia had an attack of lockjaw. Mrs. Van Dusen was the first to speak. She recognized nobody.

"Mrs. Morahan?" she said, gropingly.

Delia, startled into action, came forward with a shy, "How are you, Mrs. Van Dusen?"

Mrs. Van Dusen felt the chill and tried to thaw it with a majestic condescension.

"We used to call each other Delia and Margaret, didn't we?"

"Maggie, I think it was," said Delia.

Mrs. Van Dusen winced at the name, but her confusion was masked by the reception of her brother. Carmody could roar down a board meeting of financial Titans, but he was roaring very small here. He was under the scrutiny of people who had seen him as a gawky young buck, and he did not know how to act.

Michael was shy with him, and gladly passed him on to the highest dignitary present:

"You remimber Patrick McMurtha?—Judge McMurtha he is now."

"Indeed I do!" said Carmody, bluffing to hide his chagrin. "He had me before him on those trust investigations. He ironed me out."

McMurtha smiled up with a downward grace. "I hope you are not still suffering the same appalling loss of memory that afflicted you on the witness stand."

Carmody laughed with more comfortable depreciation, "I'm better now."

"He had iver a bad memory," said Michael, also recovering with an effort. "I loaned him ten shillin' on the boat out. I've not had it back yet."

Carmody grinned. "With interest it would be about a million now. I'll turn my business over to you."

This put Michael in a position where he could be genial.

"Ah, it's little changed you are, Mat."

"You think not?"

"Well, you hadn't that," said Michael, as he smote Carmody in his capitalistic paunch.

Carmody grunted and retorted with a punch in kind. "And you never brought that out of the old country."

Seeing blows passing already, Delia intervened, for dignity's sake. "How are you, Mr. Carmody?"

"My first name is Mat, Delia," said the great man, "and I wish I were as well as you look."

Michael glowed with incandescent pride. "Delia hasn't changed, do you think?"

Carmody had enough native grace left to respond, "Not a bit, except for the better, if that could be."

Delia flushed. "You were ever to the fore with the treacle. I wonder you never married."

Carmody rose handsomely to this. He groaned, "When Michael got you away from me, I felt there was nothing left for me but work."

Michael interposed now: "This flirtation is growin' disrespectable. I want you should meet me mother. Mother honey, two very old, ancient friends of ours." He gathered the brother and sister Carmodys in. "Mrs. Van Dusen, me mother; me mother, Mrs. Van Dusen."

"Did he say Van Dusen?" said Bridget.

Miss Carmody-as-was had once been very haughty about her new name, but she felt called upon to apologize for it here.

"Oh, that's my poor husband's name. I was a Carmody."

The excitement of the family about the coming of the Carmodys had rather passed over old Bridget's drowsy head. She recurred now to early times: "No relation, I suppose, to Red Martin Carmody of Lisdoonvarna?"

Mrs. Van Dusen flinched visibly as she confessed, "Martin Carmody was my father."

AT THE BACK OF GODSPEED

"Saints alive!" Bridget keened. "Red Martin your father! And your name's Margaret! You wouldn't be little Maggie Carmody?"

Time had made a sarcasm of that "little." Mrs. Van Dusen moaned from an ample bosom, "I was once."

"Oh, it's well I remember you now," Bridget chuckled, like a witch. "Your people was poor—poor even for Lisdoonvarna, where a man with a hundred pounds saved would be a millionaire here."

"I'm afraid so," said Mrs. Van Dusen, who was enjoying the ordeal less and less.

"I remember the houseen you lived in—a little cabin at the back of Godspeed. And I remember when you and your brother put out to cross the ocean say. I used to hold your mother's hand when she cried. After a long while she began to get money from America. Most like it was you sint it."

"My brother and I." Mrs. Van Dusen was glad to have that remembered of her in her home town.

The far-off years were lighted up like peaks in the old crone's memory, though the valley-years between were thick with fog. She was vividly back in Lisdoonvarna now.

"After that your mother had tay when she wanted it and the old man smoked himself to a dried herring. He had tobacco always and to give away. He was more popular. They died happy in their beds. I was one of those that waked thim—heaven be their portion."

Mrs. Van Dusen felt a misery of guilt now, and she sighed, "I always meant to go back to them before they— before that—but—"

"Manny goes from Ireland," Bridget said, "but not so manny comes back. Oh, I see you like we was both there again and five and thirty years rolled off." She

171

began to snicker uncannily. "Little Maggie Carmody! Musha, child dear, I'm just callin' to mind the time I was interferin' bechune you and one of your father's pigs. You and the pig was fightin' over the same pitatie."

"Oh, great heavens!"

"Which had had it first I don't know," Bridget shrieked, "but you made off with it."

This was too much—much! Mrs. Van Dusen had left her friends at the opera and had lied to them elaborately in order to get away. She had expected the discomfort of grandeur among the lowly, but to be so haled back into the dust of humiliation was more than she was mortgaged for.

She looked for her brother, who had drifted aside into a colloquy with Michael.

"Matthew dear," she said, "we must go now." She explained to the staring company: "You see, we were at the opera and we ran away just to say hello. We promised to go right back. Come along, Matthew dear."

But Michael waved her away. "The stories we're tellin' are not for the ladies."

Delia's big heart understood something of Margaret's torture, and, seeing her stranded, she warmed toward her and took her arm.

"If you must go, don't let us be holding you. It was nice of you to take the long thrip to our poor home. It's been a taste of honey to see you. You was always the fairest colleen in Lisdoovarna, and now younger than ever."

Mrs. Van Dusen was pleased in spite of herself. "Young—look at my hair, Mrs. Morahan."

"The white of it is that becoming, I'd suspicion you bleached it," Delia protested.

"That's very sweet of you—Delia."

Delia was not satisfied to send her off only half warmed.

She plied the compliments like generous alms to a hungry waif.

"Small wonder the rich and the high here and abroad should be payin' court to you. You had always a way of bringin' the lads to your feet."

The generosity was contagious.

"You got Michael away from me," said Mrs. Van Dusen.

"Oh, Michael!" Delia scoffed. "It's much if he's not regrettin' it, now that he sees you."

Unwittingly Michael walked into the history of his own conquest. He put his arm around Delia and took Mrs. Van Dusen's exclusive elbow, to say: "Well, Mag, ain't Delia here the wonder? Younger and nater than iver. And that sweet we've niver passed a cross word. Have we, Delia?"

"Well, I'd hardly say that," Delia had to admit.

Michael flared instantly. "Listen at her! She's always for contradictin' me. Niver a word can I say but she comes at me with the back-slap." He calmed down as quickly: "Ah, but she's all right. And so young actin' I sometimes suspicion she's not the mother of me childer whativer."

"Michael!" Delia protested.

Michael threw his other arm about Mrs. Van Dusen's very shoulders now. "You're not such a scarecrow yourself, Maggie. Say, Maggie, do you call to mind the time there was two dances the one night, and there was crowns cracked because you couldn't go to the both of them with different lads?"

Mrs. Van Dusen forgot her impatience to depart.

"No, I've forgotten. Tell me."

Carmody escaped from Mrs. Giluley's mournful company with a wrench and made an effort at retreat.

"Margaret, we'd better be getting back."

"Hush!" said Mrs. Van Dusen. "I can't go now. Michael is telling me a story."

V

Before she could hear the pleasant details of her early prowess Michael's priest-son, Father Dermot, came in, and introductions had to be made. Before Mrs. Van Dusen could demand the story again, Kate's husband, Floyd O'Gara, arrived from a dance where he had been playing the pipes. Here was an artist to be proud of, and Michael forgot Margaret's needs in the ceremony of presenting the family marvel to the crowd.

Judge McMurtha was reminded that Killilea, the star of the evening, had not yet appeared. Michael was not worried.

"Perhaps the old villain has stumbled through the wrong door and can't find his way out again. Pipers have long throaths on them and they go easy dry. But if it's pipin' you're ready for, me son-in-law has few supariors and no aquals. Floydeen, oblige the ladies and gentlemen with a few choice screeches."

Judge McMurtha was not eager to have his client anticipated. Sparring for time, he said:

"But before we have the piper, where is that speech you promised to deliver to celebrate the occasion?"

"Oh yes," said Michael, "I did promise. And I'll feel aisier for gettin' it off me chesht."

He coughed ferociously: "Ladies and Irishmen, hold your noise, if ye can. In commimoration of this suspicious occasion [laughter], I have prepared a little address in commimoration of this suspicious occasion." [Groans.] He began to search his pockets as he felt his line slipping.

174

AT THE BACK OF GODSPEED

"I—er—as I stairted to remairk, in commima— Delia, for the love of Peter, what did ye do with the oration?"

Delia gasped: "That wasn't your oration on the type-writing paper!"

"It was. I had it wrote out special."

"Oh, the saints shield us!" Delia wailed. "I thought it was a circular for a patent lineament and I sint it down the doomb-waiter."

Michael opened his mouth for a tempest, but decided to spare Delia for the sake of the party. He almost brought on a stroke with his self-control before he could say, "Ladies and gintry, it havin' just come to me ears that me oration in commimoration of this commimoration has gone down the doomb-waiter, I will go whistle to that Scandinavian scandal in the basement and see has he sint it off with the gairbage. While I am gone Miss Rosie McMurtha, the talented daughter of a talented father, will recite— What will you recite, Rosie?"

"Oh, I don't want to recite anything," Rosie fluttered.

Judge McMurtha was stupidly honest enough to exclaim, "Why, Rosie, you asked me yourself if you mightn't."

Rosie transfixed him with a barbed glance as she giggled, "But I'd rather not, with everybody looking."

"Ah, go on, Rosie," Shamus urged. "It's grand, I'm sure."

"Oh, I—I don't feel in the mood."

"Spit it out, darlint," Michael insisted, "there's a good girl."

Rosie acquiesced: "Oh, well, all right. I'm not a very good reciter, though."

"We know that, dearie. We've all heard you." Michael meant to whisper that to Carmody, but his full

175

voice slipped out. Rosie flung a murderous look his way. He left the room and she piped in childish treble the sonorous classic, "The Fighting Race" by J. I. C. Clarke, with its stout refrain, "Kelley and Burke and Shea."

As she recited, Michael could be heard in the kitchen blowing the whistle and calling down the shaft in an altercation with the janitor. Nothing could have saved the poem from slaughter in Rosie's little voice, but Michael's ferocity did not help. Still, everybody knew the poem, anyway, so small harm was done.

Before the end of the recitation Michael returned and went right on with his explanations in spite of Delia's frantic gestures and Rosie's confusion. Said Michael:

"That Scandihoovian hyena says he put me speech in the furnace hours past."

He felt the radiator.

"Yes, he did. I can feel my speech warmin' the bronze. Fine for you, Rosie."

Rosie retired in chagrin to the solaces of Myles and Shamus.

Judge McMurtha, as master of ceremonies, spoke up:

"The next number will be a solo on the violin by Father Dermot Morahan, accompanied by a solo on the voice by Michael's other son, Shamus, with his daughter Kate at the piano."

Michael glowed with patriarchal pride. "Go on, Katie, whale the lights out of the piano. What's two dollars to me."

This trio suffered from a tripartite disagreement as to pitch, rhythm, and interpretation, complicated by the entrance of Shane O'Mealia, who brought a load of care with him. He asked his aunt Delia where his wife was, and she indicated the kitchen with her thumb. Shane hastened out joyously, and came back almost at once, slowly and sad.

AT THE BACK OF GODSPEED

He had the look of conspicuous vivacity a man assumes after an eviction at his wife's hands. Shane sat down near Michael, who was reminded of his promise.

He took Carmody by the knee and Shane by the lapel, and introduced them. He was deafly oblivious to the music and blind to the remonstrant glances of his son, the priest, as he said:

"Mat, this Shane felly is more like one of me own sons than a nevvy by marriage. He has just resigned a fine position. He's considherin' others, but, being as he's free for to-night, I'd like to do you a favor, Mat, for ould time's sake, so I advise you to grab him quick. The boy's a janius. He holds the records in jobs, and if you're as wise as you try to look, you'll ingage him for a position before you lave the room."

"I should be glad to at some future time," said Carmody; "at the present moment I have no vacancy."

"It's in your head you have one if you poshepone snappin' up this young Napoleon, and in your heart a vacancy if you pass by Delia's own sister's own son."

"All right, I'll make a place somewhere," said Carmody. "Come and see me to-morrow, Mr. O'Mealia."

Shane tried to keep from looking like a rescuee from drowning. He promised to oblige Mr. Carmody on the morrow, and hastened to the kitchen again with a new zest. He came back shortly with his old gloom.

Father Dermot, Shamus, and Kate finished their trio now, and the audience made up in applause for what it owed in attention.

Judge McMurtha rose to push through his program.

"The next on the program is a double jig by Senator-elect Giluley and his charming wife."

Michael had a suggestion. "And me son-in-law, Mr. O'Gara, will oblige with the pipes. Won't you, Floyd?"

"I don't mind," said Floyd, and he made ready. He
played a double jig and the Giluleys danced, he limping
with rheumatism, she holding her throbbing jaw.

Michael whispered to Carmody, "That would do
mighty well at an undertakers' convention. Do you
remember the dances we danced at the patterns in
Lisdoonvarna?"

"Do I? Wasn't I the champion?" Carmody bragged.
And Michael flared up:

"You a champion, you ould handless bosthoon! I
could dance you down with one foot."

"Could you, now?" said Carmody. "And since
when?"

"Since now!" cried Michael. Carmody tried to end
the matter with a magnificent disdain, but Michael's
blood was up and he challenged Carmody to a show-
down. Carmody thought of his fat and shook his head,
but Michael, reading his mind, said, "We're both carryin' weight for age. Come on now, or ate your words."

The crowd began to plead for a dance-duel, to insist
with violence. And Michael's swagger was so provoca-
tive that it was harder for Carmody to stand on his dignity than to risk its destruction. At last he rose, like
a martyr. He caught the horrified eye of Mrs. Van
Dusen, but it was not his nature to back out of an under-
taking.

He was greeted with loud cheers when he stood up.
The guests divided at once into two factions, the Car-
modites and the Morahaneers, and the partisans grew
quickly as frantic as lifelong Guelphs and Ghibellines.

"Mr. O'Gara will oblige with music, of course," said
Michael, "and for all he's my son-in-law, he'll play fair,
I'm certain sure. And do you happen to know a good
slip jig?"

AT THE BACK OF GODSPEED

"Manny a one," said O'Gara. "There's 'A Blast of Wind,' 'Give Us a Drink of Water,' 'Top the Candle'—"

Michael shook his head at each suggestion. "What was the one old Killilea was so grand at? He wrote it himself."

"Was it 'Strap the Razor'?" said Judge McMurtha.

"Nah!" said Michael. The judge tried again:

"Was it 'When Sick, Is It Tea You Want'?"

"No more that, but— Ah, where's me brain gone? The divil sail away with me mimory."

O'Gara spoke up, "Was it, by any chance, called 'Life in Lisdoonvarna'?"

"That's it!" cried Michael. "You're the boy for us. Play it."

"I don't know it," said O'Gara.

"Be all the goats in Ireland, why don't you?"

"Old Killilea was that jealous of it, he would niver write it out nor lave anny other piper hear it. I heard it from a distance once. It's gone from me now." He skirled a jaunty little phrase on the pipes and stopped.

"You have it," cried Michael. "Go along with it!"

"I'm not sure of whayre it goes from thayre," said O'Gara, tying his forehead in knots as he wrestled with his memory.

Michael was champing the bit and pawing the ground. "Well, play what you can, and what you can't remimber play annyway. Come on, Mat. Mother honey, would ye mind?" He rolled her chair to one side, while McMurtha cleared the table and the chairs were hustled back to the wall. Then Carmody, wishing he had stayed at the opera, was pushed into the arena, and Michael cried, "Begin to commince."

O'Gara began to play; the two big men began to whisper with their toes mysterious rhythms punctuated by their heels. Carmody's feet surprised him by remembering boyhood clog-tricks, and the native zest resumed its sway. But he was still a bit hazy and he stopped with a shake of the head: "There's something wrong somewhere."

"The divil's in it," Michael agreed. Then: "Oh, I know! We always danced it on a door."

Carmody nodded eagerly. "That's right. Too bad we haven't a door." And he moved to a chair.

Michael checked him: "Who says we have no door? We have manny of thim flappin' useless. Here, lind a hand."

At his direction Myles and Shamus completely unhinged a closet door and lowered it to the carpet. Michael stepped on it and smote a hole through a panel with the first salvo of his heels. Carmody breathed a silent, "Saved again!" but Michael would not be denied; he found a stout door from the kitchen to the back stairway and had it dismounted and set above the other. It stood the preliminary test, and he beckoned Carmody to come and take his medicine.

Michael ridiculed Carmody outrageously, shouting as he pounded:

"If you'd used your feet for writin' cheques, they'd fly faster. Stand on your hands and see can you do betther. Is it an ilephant that's dancin' or a rhinoceroose? I don't know." He was puffing horribly himself.

There was little to commend the contest except the intention. Age and adiposity could be imagined off mentally, but not danced away. The music of O'Gara was a thing of fits and starts, most of them wrong. He gave the old lads no help with his irregularities, for Irish dance music is innocent of syncopation.

In the midst of O'Gara's noisy blunders there was a

pounding on the front door that outclattered the racket of the dancers.

"It's the police!" Delia cried. "I knew you'd bring them! Let you open the door, Katie, before they club it down!"

Mrs. Van Dusen went to her brother's side and groaned: "To be caught in a raid! The crowning touch!"

VI

When Kate reached the door, with her eyes prepared for police, she thought she was bewitched by the more fearsome sight she saw instead—a blind and bent old goblin with a stick in one hand and a long green bag under his other arm. He was led by a terrified-looking young man, whom he deserted at once as he pushed straight for Floyd O'Gara and his music.

"Who is it that dares murdher my music?" he shrieked. "Lade me to him while I crack his scurrilous pipes over his crown. Where is he, I say?" He made a great swinge with his stick and everybody retreated, O'Gara gliding out of reach and insinuating himself behind the piano.

McMurtha moved forward. "Come in, Mr. Killilea, and welcome!"

Killilea greeted him with upraised stick. "Was it you, you villyin?" When the stick came down the judge was back in his place.

Michael put on a bold front: "Well, if you don't like the way the music is afther bein' executed, murdher it yourself."

Old Killilea laughed craftily. "Aye, and let the thievin' knave steal the rest of it, eh? Divil a much I like that."

Judge McMurtha put off fear and put on his most

judicial tone: "Calm down, Killilea, and behave yourself, or I'll send you up for disturbing the peace."

"Me disthurbin' the pace, is it?" Killilea howled. "And what of the silly gandher that's butcherin' my pretty melodies? I'll sind him up sky-high!" He began to cudgel the floor again and would not be appeased. Hearing all the clamor, Moyna had stolen to the dining-room door. She came forward a little to Mrs. Morahan and whispered:

"Who's that? It isn't the old piper from Lisdoon-varna?"

"It's him or his fetch," said Delia.

Moyna forgot her red eyes and her feud with Shane, at the sight of her old kinsman. She ran to him with a tender hand and voice: "Uncle Dinny, this is Moyna. Don't you remember me—me that you taught to dance when I was but a young thing?"

The old man put his bludgeon under the arm that held his pipes and ran his learned fingers over the rosy young face. He mumbled: "I call to mind the look of Moyna. That I do. My fingers remimber the face of you, but grown bigger, and your voice is taller than it was."

"It's the same Moyna, Uncle Dinny, only no longer a girl. It's an old woman with a heart of rusty iron."

Her words were bitter, but she was wondrous happy at finding some one of her own kith in this foreign land. She hugged the old man's arm to her side, and he laughed.

"Ah, but it was you could thrip it. At the patterns I could tell your feet from all the rest. I would rather than a hundred crowns hear you futtin' it now. Truth, I could niver tell whether it was you dancin' or the rain pattherin'."

Moyna was in a mood to enjoy her sorrow. She pouted.

"I don't dance any more, Uncle Dinny. I haven't

danced since you took off with yourself from Lisdoon-varna."

The time-beaten oldster was also comforted strangely to find a bit of his own family in the wilderness. He muttered in Moyna's ear: "Whisper, Moyna! if you'll dance me a little dance, I'll play you the tune they're all tryin' for to thieve off me. I'll play it soft and confidintial like and you shall dance in a whisper on'y for me."

Everybody made motions to her to accept the proffer, but she moaned, "Oh, thank you kindly, Uncle Dinny, but the lead in me heart is solid to me feet."

Michael whispered shrilly at her: "Go on! Go on!"

Killilea lifted his head. "What's that they're saying?"

"Pay no heed to them," said Moyna.

"Come alone with you, then. Had I a chair, I'd rest me four bones."

Michael slipped a chair under him.

Killilea beamed and nodded. "Thank you kindly, Moyna. Now had we but a door to lay out on the grass."

"There's a door here," said Moyna, in a yielding humor.

"Then shtep aboard," bade the piper, "and imagine the door is a drop of the dew on a small little rosebud, and you're Wan of Thim dancin' in the blue moonlight."

She was not cruel enough to oppose him and she was a bit wishful on her own account to dance out her heart. She grew impatient even of the fuss he made getting his pipes from the sack and fastened about him and pumped up. At last he began to play slowly in a minor scale with an urging cadence. And she began to foot it timidly on the door.

"Dance!" he shouted. "Let me hear you that can't see you."

Her fleet feet began to warm and flutter and his music

183

warmed with them. Up and down the range his melodies skipped, hopped, and glided, and the prattle of her nimble shoes both answered and evoked his skill.

She looked so winsome as she drifted back and forth along the door, hands on hip or up in air or arms akimbo, skirts aswirl, and feet like the hammers of a xylophone, that her husband Shane forgot to sulk and, assured that she who was so fair could not be cold, he went forward to her and put out his hand and cooed, "Acushla!"

"No!" said Moyna, and stopped dancing.

"For why do you stop?" cried Killilea. "Dance! Let me hear the rain."

Moyna's feet resumed their showering graces, but she turned her back on her suitor. He stood a moment disconsolate, then walked round the door to the other side. She turned her face from him in the reverse of the practice of the sunflower according to Tom Moore, Esq. Shane flushed, bit his lip, watched her dance longingly, till his own feet began to twitch. He began to dance on the carpet. He ventured to step to the door; she danced away from him. He danced after with a pantomime of pleading. She was less and less angrily defiant, then taunting, alluring, evading. She began to set him steps to copy. He was a broth of a boy on his feet and she could make no fool of him. He compelled her admiration of his dance-lore. He made so bold as to hand her a few steps to imitate. He had the advantage of metropolitan training. While she had been dancing at occasional countryside patrons he had seen the great clog-masters of the world developing the art to incredible agilities on the New York stages.

He had Moyna thoroughly whipped out before long, and that was the way she liked to have him have her. She hated him when he was weak, and wanted him superior.

184

Her instinct was right enough, and it was for his own good that she should discourage him into courage. She made a gesture of surrender and of homage and let him seize her in his arms before the whole company.

They stopped dancing, but old Killilea was at fever heat now and he shouted for Moyna to go on. He invited everybody to dance, and, like his protopiper of Hamelin, he played a tyrannical tune that could not be disobeyed. He led his own sacred melodies by little degrees into a tune that everybody began to guess at, to recognize, and finally with one voice and many feet to hail as "The Rocky Road to Dublin."

Shy little Floyd O'Gara was quickened to courage.

"That's as much mine as his. I was dandled to that as a baby." He crept forward to a chair and began to tootle his own pipes.

Old Killilea did not frown, but laughed and challenged him to a race.

The spring wind was changing to a summer storm.

Delia put Dermot's violin in his hand. He tuned it hastily and joined in the jig. Rosie McMurtha began to sing the air with a girlish zest. Kate dropped to the piano stool and battered the chords with a will. Shamus and Myles dashed out and returned, one with a flute and one with a cornet, and wood began to whistle and brass to chant.

The spectators were unable to restrain an impulse to yelp like Indians. Their feet ran away with them. Michael snatched at Delia and whirled her to the door, shoving Moyna and Shayne to the carpet, Michael howling:

"Take yourselves off and make way for the younger gineration."

Mr. and Mrs. Giluley gave evidence of a miraculous

cure. They charged on the door with a contempt for such bogies as rheumatism and neuralgia.

Carmody laid hold of Mrs. McDwyer and Mr. McDwyer formed a partnership with Mrs. O'Rahilly. Myles and Shamus fought an Arcadian battle about Rosie McMurtha. The rest of the mob broke into a panic. Everybody galloped and frisked and flung, leaped and sidled. The music raged, the musicians danced where they stood. Kate danced where she sat. The floor and the door snapped and sizzled like a gigantic popcorn-popper over a brisk fire.

Judge McMurtha tried in vain to remember his dignity. Mrs. Van Dusen was bitterly regretting her aristocracy and her other-worldliness. The peasantry in her blood began to boil again. The girlhood of old, ancient times derided the alien veneer of foreign customs. Her toes began to tingle and tap the floor. Her fingers jigged on the arm of her chair, and when at length Justice McMurtha cast responsibility to the winds of returning April, let out a whoop of boyish self-abandonment, and came capering before her like a young faun in the ridiculous disguise of an old judge, Mrs. Van Dusen sprang to her feet with a hoydenish:

"Hurroo!"

She caught up her skirts knee-high and went sidling and clogging. The muffling of the carpet so hampered her reviving virtuosity that she skipped to the door and cleared it of her rivals. She did not know that the rest had stopped dancing to gape at her; or if she knew she did not care.

The ice had not broken in her heart. It had not found time. It had suddenly fumed into steam.

When at last she sank into a chair, gasping and smothering and streaming with honest sweat and aching with laughter and hilarious toil, she was not shamed, but delighted, that the panting Michael groaned:

"Well, of all the ixhibitions I iver did see, Mag Carmody, yours was the most disgracefully graceful."

And she cried, "You flatther me!"

VII

The Schuylers at the opera had kept wondering why Mr. Carmody and his sister did not come back. The opera dragged out its harmonious length and the last curtain fell, and they had not returned. When Mrs. Schuyler reached her home she telephoned Mrs. Van Dusen's home to inquire if she were ill. A sleepy, resentful butler informed her that she had not arrived.

"I hope she hasn't had a motor accident," said Mrs. Schuyler.

When, along about 2 A.M., young Mr. Van Dusen stole into the house, the butler told him of Mrs. Schuyler's anxiety and her hope. The young man fretted and wondered. He called up the police and a hospital or two to ask if any disasters had been reported. There was no record of any that involved his hitherto respectable mother, who had never got into the papers for anything more distressful than a reception or a dinner.

The daybreak and Mrs. Van Dusen came to the house together. When the pale young man, in such a bathrobe as a Roman emperor might have worn, stood at the head of the stairs and saw her come dragging her heavy feet up the steps, he noted her general look of dishevelment, and ran down to her, groaning:

"Mother, what happened? Were you in a collision or something?"

He was dazed by her answer:

187

"No, me boy, I'm on'y after takin' a flyin' thrip to the old counthry."

"In Heaven's name, mother," he gasped, "where did you pick up that funny accent?"

"Just where I left it, darlin'."

He was genuinely terrified. "But, mother, why should you come home with a brogue?"

"Why wouldn't I? Amn't I Irish?"

"But I don't understand."

"How could you? And you half Dutch, you poor little misfortunate bouchaleen."

He spoke to her sternly, "Mother, where on earth have you been?"

"Home to the little cabin at the back of Godspeed."

He helped her up the stairs, and he was very anxious, because she was giggling mysteriously like a girl. But suddenly she sat down on the top step in the dim hall where the watery light of dawn wavered in conflict with the tiny electric stars, and she groaned:

"Och, meal-a-murder! I'm givin' a reciption this afthernoon to a whole world of people, and niver a soul invited from Lisdoonvarna!"

VII

CANAVAN

THE MAN WHO HAD HIS WAY

I

E VEN the horses were snobs. They swaggered along
the avenue with noses so high in air that the short
check-reins hung slack on their haughty necks. Whether
or not the street-sweeper got out from under their spurn-
ing hoofs was his affair, not theirs. On the box the
coachman and footman looked like a bishop and his
coadjutor, except that, as the whippletree grazed the
dingy street-cleaner, the coachman's mouth sagged with
an unspoken stable word.

In the swan-like scoop of the victoria sat a young man
and a young woman, patrician enough to loll without fear.
The girl—Miss Beatrice Newnes, it was—gave a gasp as
the canvas-clad scavenger just evaded the wheel-guard.

She was angry at him for giving her little heart a jolt.
Her horses had run down a man once before, and her
motor had bowled over a dirty newsboy with most
unpleasant results: she had missed an engagement at her
tailor's, and the newspapers had published her name and a
picture of her that was badly smudged in the printing.

"It's outrageous the way these street-sweepers dodge
in and out," she said to Rodman Cadbury, 3d. "We're
never safe from the danger of knocking one of them over."

LONG EVER AGO

"The worst of it is," said Cadbury, "that they think they are as good as we are."

"Oh, they are as good—perhaps," she smiled. "Better, I hope—as far as getting to heaven and all that, but—"

"I've no doubt that if they get there they'll be set to sweeping the golden streets," said Cadbury, groaning with the labor of shifting one knee over another. "The worst of it is, the dogs think that they are as good as we are Down Here. That fellow is probably wishing he dared heave a bit of Irish confetti at us."

But the fellow in the once-was-white suit was thinking nothing of the sort. He was dodging another carriage. The escape from a taxi-Juggernaut followed so hard upon the elision of a touring-car that each adventure crowded the previous one out of his mind.

At the end of the day, as he trudged home, scorching his thumb over his clay pipe, he sometimes reviewed what part of the kaleidoscope he could recall. This evening Canavan remembered his escape from the Newnes horses, chiefly because he had recognized the footman as the son of the aristocratic Honan, who lived on the ground floor of his tenement. Canavan knew that Patsy Honan worked for the Newneses, so he guessed that the girl in the victoria was the daughter of old millionaire Newnes.

"That Miss Noons is a bird," he told his wife, that evening; "purty as a pitcher."

"Shut up and ate your corn beef," said Mrs. Honoria Canavan.

The street-cleaner did not lay aside the robe of humility when he took off his white wings. In the street he was always almost run over; at home he was walked upon, sat upon, kept in his place. He was not so old as he would be one day if he lived. Indeed, if you had asked his age he might have answered, "If I live five years longer

CANAVAN, THE MAN WHO HAD HIS WAY

I'll be as old then as me old woman is now." He might have, but he would never have dared so to betray his wife.

Mrs. Canavan read the society columns of the Sunday papers and she was soon asking:

"What did she have on?"

"Who?"

"Miss Noons, of course. Who else?"

"What did she have on, did you say?"

"Yis."

"Clothes, of course—and a hat."

"Ah, you loafer, you! What kind of clothes?"

"How the divil should I know? I'm no milliner."

"The man who was with her was probably Mr. Cadbury—noomber t'ree—whatever that manes," said Mrs. Canavan, with dignity. "I'm after r'adin' that she's marryin' 'um next mont'. Or so the newspaper says, and it knows all that's goin' on."

"Marryin', eh?—the Lord help him—I mean her," he amended, hastily, as his wife glared his way. After he had pushed his pie-plate aside, and she had dumped the dishes into the sink, she settled back to read the last Sunday supplement, of which the society section had come round the fish for the morrow, which was Friday.

Seeing that she was absorbed in the doings of Upper-Tendom, Canavan timidly slid his hand to his hat and percolated through the door. If he left home meekly, he no less meekly entered the back room of the shabby saloon where a number of his cronies forgathered of evenings, and made a merriment of which he was a timid spectator. Among the humblest he was still humbler.

And so he lived his life surreptitiously, shunted aside at his job, at his home, and even in his cups.

But one day Canavan was brought home in a clanging ambulance. It was the first time in his life he had attracted so much attention. It is true they had refused him the glory of a bed at the hospital, and Mrs. Canavan read the next day's papers in vain to find a line about him, but the whole block turned out to see him carried in horizontally, feet foremost; and the many-windowed walls of the street were a berry-patch of heads.

"Well, that Noons driver got me at last, Honoria. It's t'ree times he's after missin' me," was Canavan's apologetic exclamation when he came to.

Mrs. Canavan was glad that, if her man had to be run over, he had chosen something aristocratic. An automobile would have been sweller, but a victoria was better than a dump-cart.

Mrs. Canavan nursed him in her rough-handed way, snarling at his peevishness, and taking for her standard the theory that the one safe way was to refuse everything he asked. When she tucked him in, her tenderness resembled the short-arm jab of a heavyweight, but there was a sympathetic idea behind it, and he found a luxury where another would have found rigor.

When he was strong enough to sit up and spit on the stove, Mrs. Canavan concluded that, being as the girl was growing up and needing more clothes and the boy coming through his shoes and his father's pants every few days, and meat going up every week in price, and all, it would be a real hardship to lose Canavan now. Having missed his weekly wage for a month, she realized his importance and decided for him that he must give up street-cleaning and hunt a job with a smaller element of hazard. Her ukase dismayed him for a time, as street-cleaning was the one trade he knew—if he knew that; but his ward boss, who would soon need his vote, got him a safer place with a blasting gang on the subway construction.

Canavan's job was to shovel and pick, here and there,

while the drills gnawed holes enough in the rocks, and then to stand off and wait until the dynamite had boomed and thudded. Then it was his job to go down in the sweaty earth-wound and clear out the shattered rocks, shoveling away what could be shoveled, and tearing with his hands at such blade-edged boulders as denied the spade.

Canavan's boss was unusually harsh with him, because he was as meek as he was willing, and the strength in him was a thing he had not discovered. He was as timid and hulking as a baby Pantagruel. Canavan stood every-thing—bruises till his hands looked like ragged gloves, and curses till he almost lost the right to call himself an Irishman.

Sometimes as he straightened the creaking thews of his back he would look with envy at the men who held the red flag to warn people and horses to keep their distance when the blast was about to thunder.

One day Sorahan, one of the flagmen, did not turn up. The day before, his step had been so unsteady that a friend had prophesied the return of one of his "period-icals," which recurred as regularly as a comet and boded nearly as much ill in its parabola.

So Canavan was detailed as flagman for the nonce. The standard was humble at best, but it made a brave spot of color. And Canavan loved red. And then the authority of it! One wave, and he put a stop to the progress of traffic of every sort; high-toned charioteers of brewery trucks, precipitant chauffeurs, presidents of corporations and parish priests, pushcarts and trolleys. Once he stopped a patrol-wagon! He almost fainted at the Tsardom of that!

Ah, but Canavan reveled in the red flag. It was his first sip of authority over other men. It was new wine, fire upon the palate and fume upon the brain.

LONG EVER AGO

Along about four o'clock the Newnes horses—no less—came clattering eight-footedly up. Canavan knew those horses. He had one or two of their hoof-marks still on him under his red-flannel undershirt. He owed them his demise from the White Wings and his shift to the blasting profession.

There was a strange joy in checking the Newnes team, of all. The coachman was for driving over him, as usual, but Canavan whacked one of the steeds over his haughty nose and brought him up standing, pawing the air.

The pretty lady leaned out and, in her aristocratic way, upbraided the coachman and the footman for not hurrying on. The sight of Patsy Honan's chagrin was precious ointment in Canavan's wound, spikenard to his downtrodden pride.

The coachman humbly explained over his shoulder, with a military salute, that, begging her pardon, Miss, he was held up by a flagman.

The pretty lady turned then on the flagman with a shrill volley of commands. Canavan, to her intense amazement—and to his—heard himself answering her with equal hauteur.

When she waxed dictatorial he was inspired to a great speech of defiance. The language was 1909, but the spirit was 1798.

"Ah, go chase yourself! I don't wear your dirty livery, and I take no orders from the likes of you."

The horrified Miss Newnes ordered the coachman to slash the dog with the whip and drive him down, but Canavan simply picked up a chunk of jagged granite and promised it to the coachman if he moved. He also invited Patsy Honan to come down from the box. But Patsy kept his arms folded in assumed disdain.

And then the dynamite let out a guttural oath somewhere, and there was a small Vesuvius of rock and dirt. Whereupon the Newnes horses began to rear and plunge, Miss Newnes to scream and cower. Honan leaped to the horses' heads by Canavan's permission.

In a moment the eruption was over, and Canavan lowered his flag as if it were a herald's trumpet. And he sneered:

"Git back to yer pulpit, Patsy Honan! And move on wit' your baby-carriage! You're blockin' the way."

There was a royalty about it that only an Irishman from the loins of Brian Boroihme could have attained. Cyrano de Bergerac would have improvised a sonnet on Canavan's gesture. The baffled wrath in the eyes of Patsy Honan and the coachman and Miss Beatrice Newnes was the tribute of the conquered. And they passed under Canavan's yoke.

Canavan enjoyed the incident as if he were an alley cat fallen in a barrel of catnip. The very savor of it intoxicated him for hours, days, weeks.

When that afternoon's work was over the Canavan who went home was not the Canavan who had left that morning. You could have told it by the cock of his pipe.

When he arrived he stalked up-stairs and entered without the usual treadmill shuffle on the door-mat. Mrs. Canavan ordered him to take his dirty feet out of her kitchen. Elate with authority, Canavan told her a place to go to, and laid his coat on the best chair.

Mrs. Canavan stared at him in a stupor. Her glower of inspection showed that he lacked the excuse and prerogative of being drunk. She went for him with the mop. For the first time in their connubial chronicle he did not duck and dodge for the door.

He received the mop on his upraised forearm, wrenched it from her brawny clutch, chucked it into a corner, and

14   195

proceeded to mop up the apartment with Mrs. Canavan. He made a thorough job of it.

His wife was too deeply astounded to resist. It **was** better so, for had she shown the ardor of a valkyr he would have prevailed, with the spirit that was upon him.

It was not a pretty fight, but it was lively while it lasted, and it ended with Mrs. Canavan in complete shipwreck amid a jetsam of pots and pans and chairs and plates, while Canavan lighted his pipe with epic magnificence, as if nothing in the slightest degree unusual had happened.

Mrs. Canavan stared at him from rapidly swelling eyes full of dazed admiration. It was a case of love at first sight with her.

And when he said, "Git offen that flure and wrastle me supper together quick, or round the room you go ag'in!"— when he said that she felt that here at last was the lord of her life.

He ate his supper with a contemptuous superiority. He called the coffee "swill" and the potatoes "mud," and she waited upon him like a captured Sabine serving the Roman who had toted her home over his shoulder.

When Canavan had eaten his fill he kicked his chair back against the wall, slapped his hat on one side of his head, and went to his saloon. Instead of trickling through the door and drooling into a chair, he entered with both feet, and yelled for the barkeeper to take the orders and have one himself.

Though he had sat among the gang off and on for years, he had been so meek and taciturn that he had been almost a stranger to the coterie. To-night he made himself host and, as the potations enlarged him, he led the singing. In fact, before the evening was over he had somehow managed to get himself invited to do a solo, and in a loud

CANAVAN, THE MAN WHO HAD HIS WAY

and confident tone, not afraid to err from the key, he had
sung this relique of Dublin days:

"Good evenin' to you, boys. I hope to see you well,
  As I consider meself to-night, as anny tongue can tell.
  I'm not out of employment, nor lookin' for a job;
  And you know me weekly wages is over eighteen bob.
  It's a twelvemonth lasht Septimber since I left Balbriggan
      town,
  And I helped me Uncle Barney to cut the harvest down.
  It's now I wear a ganzy, and around me waisht a belt,
  I'm a gaffer o'er the boys that makes the hot ashfelt."

  And the chorus was:

"You may talk about your sojers, your sailors and the resht,
  Your shoemakers and tailors to plase the ladies besht;
  But the only boys that have a chance the colleens' hearts to
      melt
  Are the boys around the boiler makin' the hot ashfelt."

  Second stanza, by request:

"A polisman steps up to me, and he says: 'Now, McGuire,
  Will ye kindly let me light me dudeen at your boiler fire?'
  Says I: 'Me honest polisman, you know it's gittin' late,
  And if you've anny gumption you'll go and mind your bate.'
  With that I drew out from 'um and I hit 'um such a welt
  That I knocked 'um in the boiler among the hot ashfelt."

  Chorus.   Third stanza, by wild acclamation:

"The boys they gathered round him and shtuck him in the tub,
  With soap and warrum wather they all begun to shcrub.
  In the Dub(a)lin museum he is hung up by the belt
  For an example to the boys that make the hot ashfelt."

When Canavan had done the asphalt chanty the circle
roared with the applause due to an unsuspected genius
long smothered in their midst.

LONG EVER AGO

It was: "Good bhoy, Canavan!" "Canavan's the la-ad!" "Give us another, Canavan!" "Shut up and lave 'um sing!"

Then Canavan roared out the ballad of "Nancy Hogan's Goose." It was even broader than it was long, but it went splendidly well with the beer.

It was late, late that evening before the crowd would let Canavan off, and when he swung down the street he found it suddenly too narrow for his swath. He climbed the stairs like an Irish bull, for whenever he had negotiated three steps he rolled down five; but he got all his dignity to the top at last, and he smote his door ajar like a costume-play prince entering a castle.

During the long evening Mrs. Canavan had mustered some of her old courage back, and when her man sprawled across more than his share of the bed she rebuked him after her old manner. Whereupon he placed his foot in the small of her back and catapulted her to the floor. The thud shook the house and ended her last resistance.

The next morning she let him sleep to the ultimate moment, helped him on with his clothes, and had his breakfast waiting for him. As he neared the place of his work and bethought him of the boss who had him completely cowed, his brief authority oozed. But Sorahan again failed to appear; again Canavan was established with the red flag, and the sip of command became a thirst.

On the following day the boss gave Canavan a bit of lip and Canavan told him where to go. The boss came at him with big fist clenched, and Canavan, seizing the spade, gave him the flat of it with such force that the boss's eyebrows showed through the gaping crown of his new derby. The boss fired him, from a distance, but election by this time was so imminent that Canavan demanded a new job of his ward boss, and got it. The fame of his prowess with the spade brought him, furthermore, an appointment as a poll-watcher with instructions to assure the safety of certain floaters, voting under the names of men who had removed to the cemetery or elsewhere. Canavan accomplished this false suffrage with such enthusiasm that the district polled eighteen more votes for his party than the total registration of both parties.

The ward boss cautioned Canavan against an excess of zeal, and there was some scandal over the matter. But prosecution was side-tracked and Canavan was recognized as too good a politician to be wasted on a blasting crew. There were political subways to build, and Canavan joined the municipal underground gang. The young fellow had acquired a lust for power and a taste for breaking a head when he saw it. He needed, and he began to acquire, the arts of waiting, of withholding the fist, and using the terror of its clenched threat, of manipulating people, and kneading a constituency like dough.

As Canavan came up in the world he came down in his tenement. It was one evening when he had reached the dignity of the ground-floor apartment formerly occupied by the Honans, whose son had lost his post on the Newnes equipage, that Canavan sat at his ease in a rocking-chair and thought backward.

On the window-sill his shoeless feet loomed large, and through them he could see a meek and lowly being in a dingy helmet and maculate white canvas, pushing the wheeled sack known as the can-wagon.

Mrs. Canavan sat in another rocker, with her somewhat smaller feet resting on the other sill, undergoing a painful incarceration in a pair of high-heeled slippers to which she was initiating them gradually.

Canavan imbibed a deep draught of smoke from a black

foot-rule of tobacco, shifted it to the larboard, and observed:

"That's Sweeney out there, whisk-brooming the pavement."

"Usedn't you to be in his squad?" said Mrs. Canavan.

"I used," and the big cigar jibed to the starboard. "It's not so long ago that I was diggin' peat in the bogs of Ireland and red-eyed with the smoke of it. And you was a barefoot colleen, peelin' praties for supper."

"Little we thought we'd be atin' mate t'ree times a day so soon," said Honoria. "You'll be President before long."

"Not till they change the Constitootion," he said from his superior political knowledge. "But I'll come as close to it as nominatin' him one of these fine days. It's America that's the country for the Irish."

"Sure is it," said Mrs. Canavan.

"If it hadn't been for them Noons horses, though," said Mr. Canavan, "I'd still be one of the White Wings, servin' as public chambermaid on the Avenyeh."

And Mrs. Canavan cooed, "Horseshoes sure do be lucky things, Danny darlin'."

II

All night long the crooked streets of London's many towns had been astream with citizens pouring one way, as if from another plague or another great fire. But it was not terror that drove them to the fields; it was sport that drew them. The annual hegira to the Derby was in progress; and those who were too penniless to book other carriage must e'en ride on shanks' mares.

All night long, then, the streets were murmurous with the rumor of feet and the muffled voices of the poor and pedestrian.

CANAVAN, THE MAN WHO HAD HIS WAY

Daybreak found the slopes about the classic hippodrome already populous with early squatters, while every convergent road was still swollen with footsore mobs. The later hours of morning brought a mêlée of motors of every shape and color, two-storied coaches, equipages of all designs, donkey-shays with bright-buttoned passengers, bicycles, more motors, more coaches, carriages, donkey-shays, and everything vehicular that could turn a wheel.

Everybody in England was there whom cruel necessity did not chain to a desk or a shop, and everybody who could beg or borrow or steal a top-hat of any bell or brim, or acquire one by entail, wore it on his head with perfect complacency as to any nether incongruity.

Even the horses seemed to be clothed in large sections of silk-hat cloth of various colors, black, sorrel, and bay. The King himself was there, accompanied by such princes, dukes, and others as made His Majesty's retinue.

With the exception of the King, who was correctness itself, *ex officio*, there was in all that crowd no correcter thing than Canavan.

What his old cronies of the Street-cleaning Department would have thought, had they seen him, it would be hard to imagine and harder to get into print. Some of them had advanced, some of them had lost even that job, some of them were still scavenging. Sweeney, for instance, had more white in his hair than in his uniform and he was still pushing the scraper. He would never have known Canavan for one of his former fellows, for that chapter of Mr. Canavan's history was one that he had torn out of his book as early as possible.

Least of all were the Cadburys aware of it—Rodman Cadbury, 3d, and Mrs. Cadbury, *née* Newnes. They understood vaguely that Mr. Canavan had risen from the people, and his occasional slips of tongue betrayed him;

but they knew that, whatever he might have been, he was now rich, potent, a personage. His enemies called him the King of the city and reformers were forever attempting to purge it of his influence. But still Canavan's influence pervaded and the knell of his dynasty was not yet sounded.

Cadbury had first come to know Canavan when an associate told him that a project in which they were engaged was being blocked by some mysterious influence. He learned that one Canavan had an interest in another company than that to which they had decided to let their contract.

"Who's Canavan?" said Cadbury, who did not read the papers.

"The most powerful man in the city—that's all," said his associate.

"What office does he hold?"

"All—and none. It's enough for you to know that you'd better not antagonize Canavan."

"And they call this country a republic!" sneered Cadbury. "That man Canavan ought to be in the penitentiary."

Cadbury had first come to meet Canavan in the flesh under circumstances of still greater meaning to his fortunes.

Cadbury had inherited as part of his personal property the control of a great company whose monstrous wealth, made up of the post-mortem trusts of numberless individuals, his father had handled as he pleased. Cadbury inherited the methods and the mental attitude of his father as well as the majority of the company's stock.

But he fell upon harsher times. The public began to mind its own business and to poke its finger into the books of the trustees. Uncle Sam's nose was offended at the habits of the Cadburys, dead and alive, and at the customs of the officials who ran the company while this Cadbury went dilettanting about Europe, making the whole world a pleasure resort.

To his disgust, rather than his shame, young Cadbury found himself and his lieutenants treated with scant courtesy by people and press alike. Previously to this, young Cadbury had never seen his name in the papers except in an "Among those present" list, or in the score of a polo-game, or on the occasion when he married Beatrice Newnes and found himself and his bride widely head-lined and half-toned.

But now he was universally advertised by his loving enemies. He and his sports and his business methods were omnipresent in news item, editorial, and cartoon. It was especially unfair to ridicule Cadbury's "business methods," for he had none. His appearances at directors' meetings were a bore to him and a joke to the board. He sanctioned whatever was simplest to vote for and whatever promised him larger dividends, since they meant to him another champion polo-pony or a motor-boat of higher horse-power.

And suddenly this hyacinthine youth found himself and his pleasances under the scowl of the mob; demagogues were howling the word Indictment. They were calling for his punishment, and Cadbury's own attorney could find no word to utter except his associate's password—Canavan.

"See Canavan," the lawyer said.

And Cadbury saw Canavan. He noted a curious look in the face that greeted him.

"Your face is familiar to me, Mr. Cadbury," said Canavan, "but I think we were never introduced."

Cadbury made known his errand in that tone of condescending terror with which a lord might beg his valet not to desert him in a shipwreck.

Canavan felt the snob's embarrassment, but his triumph was sufficient and he took no umbrage at what he felt to be a hopeless habit of mind.

"I'll use my infloonce—if I have anny," he said. "I'd rather like to help you if I can. I'll see what can be done."

Cadbury overflowed with gratitude and stumblingly offered any compensation his benefactor might demand. Again his manner was that of a man in a foreign country asking an obliging servant what he would consider an appropriate tip.

People of lowly origin feel manner by intuition, but again Canavan was smilingly superior to insult. He refused any gratuity.

"I'm owing you a favor for some years," he said, "and I'm glad to get it off my chest."

But when Cadbury asked what the unimaginable debt could be, Canavan only shook his head and laughed. He would not tell. But he told his wife afterward:

"That Cadbury chump was in the Noonses' carriage when it went over me. And I owe everything to that Noons carriage. There's one thing I'll never get off me chest—it's the scar their horseshoes left on me."

His brogue was fading away like a mist from Killarney of a fine morning, but when he was with his wife it settled down over his speech with its old-time thickness.

Mrs. Canavan was fading away too—in strength, but not in size. The brawn of her early life had softened to fat, and her husband's growth in power and pelf, though it brought him responsibilities and anxieties that kept him fine and taut, brought her only sloth and fatal luxury.

"Prosperity is not for the likes o' me, Danny darlin',"

she would sigh from the depths of a heart sinking in an opulent despair.

She grew fat of mind as of body, and gross of both. She did not react to the new conditions, and, while she bedecked her huge frame with the gaudy silks and weighty jewels that accentuated her plebeiance, she could not follow her husband up the narrow, steep ladder where his success pushed him.

Cadbury needed more than one saving from public ire, and he began to find Canavan picturesque as well as valuable.

One night he had him to dinner and displayed him to his guests, much as he might have diverted them with a famous chimpanzee trained to wear clothes and sit at table. But the people who came to be amused remained to be amazed. Canavan was no man's fool, and he had a way of gaining the upper hand of anybody he met.

Mrs. Cadbury was especially impressed with the barbarian. She could not stop talking about him.

"He's a new sensation," she exclaimed; "you feel as if he were a live wire dangling about you. He is positively thrilling."

And as the weary rich would rather be thrilled than anything else, Canavan found himself drawn into society, ingurgitated as in a quicksand of gold.

And so, as the years rolled on and rolled him deeper and deeper in potency, and as the appetite for ostentation grew by the thing it fed on, behold Canavan at last so far cleansed of his street-cleaning odium that he was a distinguished guest at the Derby, traveling *en prince*, hatted, spatted, gloved, and frocked like the King, with field-glasses slanting to his hip, and a brogue as faint as the tint of the soft gray gloves on the hands that had almost entirely forgotten the ungraceful tools of their early habit.

LONG EVER AGO

Canavan was not merely the guest of honor on the Cadbury coach, with Mrs. "Bice" Cadbury proud to be at his elbow, and Canavan was not merely a spectator at the Derby. Canavan was a participant as the gentleman owner of one of the race-horses.

"By the way, Mr. Canavan," Mrs. Cadbury was saying, "how ever did you come to name your horse White Wings?"

"Isn't it a pretty name?" said Canavan, cautiously.

"It's a beautiful name, but I was wondering," she mused. "Oh, I know! It's from the old song, 'White wings, they never grow weary,' isn't it?"

"Well, you can lave it go—leave it go at that," said Canavan, and added, hastily: "Besides, she has two white stockings. And you can take it from me, she's worth betting on."

All the people in the Cadbury party, including the Comte de Marmier and the Baroness Zumsteeg, bet openly on White Wings and privately hedged by laying equal or greater sums on the King's horse. For the King's horse was the favorite in the betting, and Canavan's animal was at the foot of the list, though Canavan said, "He's at the top according to the odds."

Two Derbies back, a horse from his Majesty's stable had nosed in first and knitted the empire a little closer by the good-fellowship that abounds when a favorite wins, especially a royal favorite. This year the King had entered another runner whose trainers vouchsafed him fit as a fiddle. Every loyal Englishman and Englishwoman laid on him every bob and quid he could muster, or she.

The favorite would not dare to lose—most of all to the dark horse of an expatriated Hibernian from New Erin.

But Canavan trusted to the pull of every four-leaved.

shamrock in snakeless Ireland, and he bet as much as he could get covered. Somehow he believed in the clean sweep of White Wings.

This is the story of the long, slow climb of a man, not of the short, swift run of a horse, and there is no place here for the brief, wild chronicle of that Derby. Only, after the jumbled chaos of the getaway, the shredding of the mass of horses into little scattered clumps of agitation, the great cavalry battle was gradually reduced to a duel of two leaders, with the rest nowhere.

The long-staring eyes of the field-glasses on the Cadbury coach made out in the distance one fact—that the hunched jockeys on the two horses in the lead wore the colors of the King and the colors of Canavan.

The man who was up on White Wings wore a jacket of green with a red, white, and blue sash. Canavan was the calmest man on top of the coach—the calmest outside, though the seethe within him was maelstrom. He hardly realized that Mrs. Cadbury was clinging to him for dear life, to keep from falling.

When the two horses came into the stretch, beating the resounding earth backward under their glorious hoofs, thousands of throats were split with the applause.

Two people alone, it seemed, were silent. They were too deeply stirred and too deeply concerned to make a noise. They were the white-bearded gentleman who owned the King's horse and the white-faced street-cleaner who owned Canavan's.

The thunder died in a gulp of national disappointment, and the frenzy of such Irishmen and Americans and Irish-Americans as were in the throng made hardly more than a little clatter in the universal silence of the broken-hearted, broken-pursed English.

LONG EVER AGO

Cadbury and Mrs. Cadbury and the rest of their party were riotous as only well-bred people can be when they let go. They beat Canavan with hands, umbrellas, parasols, fans. "Bice" (which rhymed with "Peachy") actually kissed Canavan before she knew what she was doing, but, as her husband's arm was round him at the time, and as the Comte de Marmier kissed him on the other cheek at the same moment, the incident lacked importance to everybody except Canavan. And all he said was:

"The best thing about White Wings is the long nose of her. An inch off that, and I'd have quit loser."

As he was clambering to the ground to run to his horse, Mrs. Cadbury called down:

"The King will send for you to congratulate you. He always does."

"If he does I'll not go," said Canavan.

"What!" screamed the whole coach-top in chorus. Mrs. Cadbury nearly swooned.

"Oh, don't make a scene, I implore you!" and almost unconsciously she added, "for my sake."

Canavan gave her a curious look, then turned and plunged into the crowd, fighting his way through with an old-time zest and an old-time expertness. He knew how to penetrate even a solid wall of mankind like that, and he spared no expense of other people's ribs, toes, or feelings.

The watchers from the coach followed his hat through the throng, and saw him reach the tossing head of his triumphant horse.

Canavan reached an arm round the reeking gloss of the throat and planted a kiss on the smooth, long muzzle. He pulled down the perfect profile and whispered certain things into the silken ear.

CANAVAN, THE MAN WHO HAD HIS WAY

"It wasn't for nothin' I fed you on shamrocks, mavourneen," he murmured. "Ah, but it's an angel, not a harse, you are, and you carried all Ireland on your back the day."

Then he reached up and wrung the hand of the giggling jockey, who was no German.

"I'll put something more in your hand than me fist, mind, Dennis, me boy," he said.

And at that moment the summons was brought him that His Majesty would receive him. Canavan wavered, but he was in no mood for rancor toward even a king, and he remembered Mrs. Cadbury's look and her phrase. So he left his horse's head and suffered himself to be led into the presence.

In the name of English sportsmanship the first of English sportsmen praised Canavan and his horse for their glorious victory.

"To win a Derby, Mr. Canavan," said the King, "is to make history, and to beat a horse like mine is to make great history."

"I'm much obliged to you, sir," said Canavan.

The King seemed not to notice the informality, and put out his hand as man to man. It is part of an Irishman's nature to let no person be politer than he, and the graciousness of the King set Canavan a pace. There is no courtesy more exquisite than that of two hostile warriors meeting under a truce, and, whatever may have been Canavan's mental reservations, he greeted the Sassenach with vizor raised and mailed hand unclamped.

As he walked off he looked out over the crowd-encumbered speedway and said to himself:

"Canavan, me boy, it wasn't for nothin' you took your start in the D. S. C. Sure and you're after makin' a nate job of that thrack."

LONG EVER AGO

With Canavan, success was absolution. He had learned the world from the seamy side out and the under side up. Conditions were to blame for his theories. As he saw it, the man who did his bit conscientiously and took his wage contentedly was usually allowed to go on doing his bit and taking his wage.

Canavan had set it down upon his tablets that the kickers, the pushers, the grafters, the takers of mean advantages, moved up; sometimes they moved up to Albany, sometimes they got only so far as Sing Sing—but they moved.

The man everybody spoke well of stayed in the well. The man on top had hard words and brickbats, editorials and sermons, shied at him, but "look at the view he gets," said Canavan. According to Canavan's experience, it was virtue, and not truth, that was to be found at the bottom of the cistern. Truth was to be found only at the top of the haystack.

For the Golden Rule he substituted what he found more practical, a brass rule: Do the other fellow and do him good, for he would do you as good as he could.

That was Canavan's philosophy. If it had led him to jail he would have cracked his rock with no more abjectness of shame than a man feels who takes a good tip and loses his bet. Since his philosophy had led him past the shoals into the lagoon, he felt no more Pharasaic pride than a man feels who takes a long shot and wins. The luck ran his way; that was all.

To offset the crooked entries in his annals there were countless anecdotes of decency, of bluff charity, of fine honor, of hard-working altruism.

He did good by stealth, often by lawless ways, and he

made no scruple to secure what he thought justice by perverting what the statutes call justice. For this reason there were many washerwomen who whispered the name of Canavan in the chapels and worked for him in the tenements. There were hundreds of laborers who would have died for Canavan, or, what was more important, would have voted twice for any man he favored.

And so he recruited an army that was as much his as Cæsar's legions were Cæsar's, and Canavan's gangs would have marched against Manhattan if he led, as Cæsar's veterans crossed the Rubicon and captured their home town.

Yet the effort of Canavan was all upward, outward. He was like some tuber planted in the muck and pushing to the light and the upper air with a blind, relentless instinct to crawl round, burrow under, gnaw through anything, everything that stood between itself and the light.

And all the while Canavan was growing in grace as well as in grip, and in subtlety as in strength. He wanted power, not notoriety; to keep the red flag and wield it, letting the others wear the uniforms and hold the offices.

When he was rich enough he began to sublet the uglier tasks, to depute authority to vicegerents, and to play the gentleman of leisure, the globe-trotter. Yet always he kept in touch with things, and on occasion, when his lieutenants and sub-bosses fell foul of one another, a cablegram that Canavan was thinking of coming home usually sufficed to dissipate the insurrection. If the rumor did not serve he came in person and quelled both sides till he could dispense justice or dispense with it, as he saw fit.

He assured his decisions by appeals to partisan patriotism, by a word of wit, by a promise or a threat, or, if need be, by violence. At least one prominent kid-glove

15   211

politician felt his fist and measured his height horizontally on a club-room rug.

It was during a period of calm when the halcyons brooded on the political sea that Canavan was taking his *otium cum dig.* on his yacht, for by now he had a yacht of his own. He had bought it outright from a decayed gentleman. Among its outfit was a library of books which every man of culture knows or pretends to know. Not one of them was familiar to Canavan.

On an occasion when Canavan's restless soul was desperately becalmed, though the boat was making her eighteen knots through a scudding sea, Canavan had recourse to the bookshelves, and his illiterate finger, roving among classics, stumbled upon Plutarch's lives.

"How many lives had this gazabo, I dunno?" Canavan mused, and pronounced the biographer's name as if it rhymed with "starch."

A preliminary whirring over the leaves showed him that the old Boswell was writing not of himself, but of others, most of whom were as total strangers to Canavan as was "Plootartsh" himself. He recognized Alexander the Great as a vague name. He had heard of Julius Cæsar. Indeed, he had once suped in a play of that name by Shakespeare. He had seen Cæsar assassinated eight times in one week, and had yelled, "The will, we will have the will," under Antony's fiery eloquence.

"The makin's of a grand old ward boss was in that felly Antony," he had said. It was approbation from Sir Hubert Stanley.

From Plutarch he learned of Cæsar's enormous debts and his enormous slaughters—a million men dead and a million made slaves to be condemned to mutual slaughter in the cockpits of the arena.

"And they holler if we break a few heads at election-time!" said Canavan. The circuses Cæsar gave to tickle the mob reminded Canavan of the chowder argosies of his own practice. It amused him to learn that Cæsar, for all his glory, was bald-headed, and sensitive about it.

He dipped into the lives of those two merciless Rome-renders, Marius (accent on the penultimate) and "Silly." They were to him only two rival sachems, knfiing each other and ripping up the city to satisfy their own feud.

"They were but Tweeds and Crokers and Sullivans and the like then as now," he thought. "A lot bloodier, but not half so clever. There ought to be some Plootartsh to write our lives the same way."

He had come to feel himself of a bookish bigness. The newspapers had long ago exhausted their heaviest block type on him, and, like Alexander, he sighed for more worlds to conquer.

He was up betimes this morning and the sailors were still holystoning the deck. It reminded him of his early days, and he took off his white yachting-cap with its gold cord and compared it with an imaginary helmet bearing its humble legend, "D. S. C."

"What are you staring at, my dear?"

The voice over his shoulder was his wife's. It shocked him because he was thinking of Honoria as well as of the young street-cleaner who had come over in the steerage with her and now was master of his own yacht.

But Honoria was not mistress of this yacht. Canavan's wife of now was Cadbury's wife of then. It was Beatrice Newnes that Canavan was wedded to now. She was always seeking a new experience, and when the insipid, time-slaying, time-slain husband of her own breed and breeding had got his neck cracked in a polo scrimmage, she had hardly grown used to the monotony of mourning before she was casting her eyes Canavanward.

LONG EVER AGO

She and Rodman Cadbury, 3d, had known each other from infancy. They had bored each other as children and they had stuck together from lack of strength to separate them from any other congeniality, like two pool-balls knocked into the same pocket. Cadbury had been good to her in his superficial way, and he had been true to her so far as she knew. Yet their life had hardly been so much a communion as a paying and returning of duty calls. She insisted that their wedlock had been only a padlock.

Canavan had struck into the well-ordered orbit of their system like a rowdy comet previously unobserved. One never knows what a new comet or a Canavan will do next. This fact upset Beatrice Newnes at first, but it excited her; and that was in itself a final recommendation.

She had learned from certain allusions that Canavan had once had a wife. Eventually she had known him well enough to venture a natural question:

"You speak of your wife," she said. "May I ask if you are divorced?"

"Divorced!" cried Canavan. "Divorced! My name's Canavan. The only alimony I've paid Honoria has been for masses to rest her soul."

And so, when Cadbury had joined Honoria in that region where Blue Books do not prevail, Cadbury's widow felt a right to annex Honoria's widower. By an ancient method more easily practised by women than explained by men, Mrs. Cadbury managed at the same time to lasso Canavan and make him hers while giving the impression that she was being pursued and overpowered by the man's all-conquering will. Action and reaction are equal, they teach us, and you can never tell from the way they brace against the lariat whether the cowboy caught the heifer or the heifer coquetted with the cowboy.

CANAVAN, THE MAN WHO HAD HIS WAY

The writer who should unfold the exact processes by which females accomplish this primeval mystery would come by a very pretty bit of physiological-biological psychology and would make Darwin squeeze closer to Laplace to make room for him. It is as old as Madame Dinosaurus and as new as the fresh egg that shall disclose an eventual pullet. But the males are still wondering—when they are enough aware even to wonder.

So Canavan thought himself more than ever Canavanny when he led Mrs. Cadbury, *née* Newnes, to the altar, though, in fact, he was not Canavanning at all.

Before the honeymoon had waned a quarter Canavan had found himself a little bit in awe of his new wife—as he had been of the plush patent rocker which had been his first purchase in the way of luxury long, long ago. The new Mrs. Canavan knew by intuition which fork to use, and what the French names meant on the bill of fare, and whether champagnes were really worth while, and all that sort of thing, in which no amount of will-power and courage is of the least assistance.

Canavan had never dared reveal to her just how humble had been his start in life. And she could never have guessed what he was in no hurry to tell. He concealed the truth, not from any shame of it, for he was prouder of the length of his rise than of anything else, but because he felt that he would lose authority over her. The truth would be but a weapon in her hands, a loaded shillelah to crack him over the sconce with when he raised his head in pride.

Marriages should perhaps be performed in laboratories rather than in churches and mayors' offices, for they are like putting together two complex compounds to form a third compound of whose properties no man can know a jot in advance.

215

LONG EVER AGO

The Cadbury-Canavan wedding was the usual surprise. Two explosives had been mingled and the result was inanity.

Mrs. Cadbury had married Canavan because she had tired of milksop conventionality and thought that a giant of masterful uncertainty and uncouth power would be an interesting thing about the house. It was for the same reason, no doubt, that Venus married the blacksmith.

Canavan had married Mrs. Cadbury because it seemed to be the final crowning garland of his climb. To conquer the woman whose horses had ground him to the asphalt had seemed a bit of poetic justice too beautiful to let slip. A definite design is as important to a career as to any other work of art.

But the result of the Canavan wedding was dull and stupid disappointment for both. The ex-Mrs. Cadbury had taken on a husband who was shy and constrained in her presence, and less assertive than Cadbury had ever been. Canavan had attached himself to a bundle of nerves. He was overawed by her inheritance of knowledges and usages which he felt himself unable ever to acquire. In her presence he felt like an overgrown lout come late to school and stood beside a precocious little girl who was skimming the fourth reader while he was plodding the primer.

The yacht had seemed a refuge from the public, which had been duly startled by the anomalous wedding and watched the strange pair with frank curiosity. But the yacht only emphasized the incompatibility of the couple.

And so, this morning early, they were abroad upon the deck of the snowy yacht before the sailors had polished the planks. Bitter unrest gadflied both of them.

Canavan had been driven to the last resort of Plutarch

for nepenthe, and had found new discontent. He was about deciding that he would go back to New York, and build up a name that should make him biographable.

It was then he heard the woman's voice over his shoulder. He shrank within himself and hid Plutarch away. As he would have said, "she caught him with the goods on him." He knew how she would laugh at the conjunction of Canavan and a classic. If she could know what he was thinking she would have hysterics, he was sure. Here he was, en route to conquer the world, and not yet unafraid of his wife. He was no longer Canavan at all, at all. He was again the foregone street-cleaner, henpecked at home and boss-berated at his groveling, shoveling job.

And so when his mismated wife, the queen to whom he was only an appendix, an inferior, a prince consort, caught him staring at his cap and asked, "What on earth are you staring at my dear?" some bitter devil led him to abase himself still further in her sight, and say:

"I was comparin' it with the cap I used to wear."

"And what kind of a cap was that?"

"It had D. S. C. on it," he growled.

"If it's a conundrum I give it up. What does D. S. C. mean?" she said, mechanically, gazing with idle interest at an attendant seagull that was pacing the yacht.

"It stands for Department of Street Cleaning," he said.

Her yawn ended with a gasp. "You don't mean that you ever—"

"Oh yes, I did. See those lads shining the deck? Well, I used to holystone Fifth Avenue. It was there that you ran over me."

"I ran over you?" she exclaimed, in a bewildered horror.

He tried for a sickly joke. "Yes, it was the first time you ran across me. I had several escapes from your horses, and your coachman used to see how close he could come to me. Finally he scored a bull's-eye. You and Cadbury were riding together, as usual. I caught sight of you before the hoofs began to do a clog on me. They took me home in the ambulance. I could show you the scar one of the horseshoes left on my shoulder."

She had swayed and dropped into a deck chair, and she gazed at him as at some fascinatingly loathsome reptile.

"Do you mean to tell me that you used to be one of those street-cleaners—one of those unspeakable scavengers?"

"That's what I'm after telling you," he confessed, shrinking from the blinding flash of her bitter eyes.

"And you—you dared to marry me!—to— Oh, this is too hideous to believe."

"What matters it what I was?" he pleaded. "You said you loved me, you said you admired me, Beatrice." He put out a trembling, pleading, clutching hand.

She shuddered away.

"Don't you dare touch me! Don't you dare lay your horrible hands on me, you—you thing!"

He looked from her to his hand. His hand was his history. He saw it pushing the scraper, he saw it wielding the coarse brush, he saw it lathered with soap and cleansed, he saw it sliding for his hat in the timid, old way, he saw it torn and scarred with rough stones, he saw it grasping the red flag—the red flag of authority! There was salvation in the thought.

He remembered with a deep, swift breath of recovery how that hand had gone from the staff of the flag to learn new powers. He clenched it now into a fist—it was still a big fist. He could not but remember the way it had quelled Honoria's tyranny. He had often paled with shame at the thought of such unmanly use of strength, and yet, afterward—afterward Honoria had strangely changed for the better—she had become a wife to him instead of a household boss; she had loved him and not despised him.

He remembered how he had thumped the Newnes horses with the nub of the red flag. And now was he to let the Newnes girl trample him down again? Not so long as his name was Canavan.

He rose and confronted the patrician beauty shrinking from him, not in wholesome fear, but in haughty contempt. He reached for her roughly. She gave a little smothered shriek:

"If you touch me I'll jump overboard."

He answered: "If you move I'll throw you overboard. You're going to sit right there and hear me out. You have the truth of it. I was a street-cleaner and I did my work well. But I was afraid of everybody on earth, afraid of my wife, my boss, afraid of the motors, the horses, the people who walked by, the police, everybody, everything. One day your horses ran me down. It was no thanks to you that I wasn't killed entirely. But I lived, and I got a new job with a blasting gang.

"One day they gave me the red flag to hold. Your carriage came along, and your coachman wanted to drive over me again. I held him up. You stuck your pretty face out and talked to me as you did just now. I wasn't afraid of you then any more than I am now. I made you stand fast till the blast was over. Then I went on up in the world till I got to where I saved your husband from the penitentiary.

"The stripes would have looked no better on him than my white wings looked on me. When I saved him I saved you from being the wife of a convict. Then your husband and you made friends with me. You used me and amused

219

yourselves with me. I was good enough for you to show off to your crowd. When Cadbury died you thought I was good enough to marry. And marry me you did.

"I'm none of your divorcin' kind. Once married, married till death, is my creed. And yours, too, now. And let me tell you once for all, Mrs. Beatrice Newnes Cadbury Canavan, that you are my wife, and my wife you stay!

"Whether I was a street-cleaner once, and whether I become a street-cleaner again is my business, not yours. Your job is being Mrs. Canavan, and you can't resign.

"I hold the red flag on you, and the ground under your feet is full of dynamite."

She looked up at him and saw a face full of command, a face that bespoke a soul of dynamite.

Wherever he came from, whithersoever he was bound, he was power personified. He was the Canavan she had expected to marry. He was Petruchio, and she was the Shrew proud of her tameness. To the infinite surprise of herself and of Canavan, she found herself groping his way with a prayerful hand, and she heard herself pleading, "Forgive me, Danny; I didn't know what I was saying."

The little hand was lost in his fist like a white bird in a nest. There was much to think, but nothing to speak, till Canavan, seeing a steward bowing in the companionway, spoke with his old authority:

"We'll go in to lunch."

And he ate with the first fork he found to hand, without waiting to watch her choice.

VIII

THE AFTER-HONOR

I

THIS was before they were married, of course. It amused Mrs. Cadbury to talk to Mr. Daniel Canavan in what she supposed to be an imitation of his Irish dialect. And it amused him to butter the brogue thick on his own speech because it amused her, but more because it was a remembrant luxury on his tongue. It filled the roof of his throat with youth to make words as he had made them when he was the young Gael that left the peat-heaps of Erin for the gold-bearing bushes of Broadway. Time had worn away his Irish, but it was easy to resume it when it suited his whim.

Mr. Canavan was widowed these five years of the red-headed, gray-eyed bog-trotter he had brought with him from Ireland, her that had prospered in their poverty and languished when politics began to make a rich man of him. Mrs. Cadbury had lost her husband six months back, and her costume was belatedly following her heart into half-mourning. Widower and widow—and philandering!

This day she had lured Canavan to the Ritz-Carlton for lunch and she was just after asking him:

"Where are you after going to-morrow, you wearer of the grane?"

He winced indulgently. "Your grammar is that bad it gives me the toothache in me ears. Anny Irishman that said 'grane' for 'green' would be a Dutchman, and how can I tell what I'll be after doing till I'm after doing it?"

"You're not answering my question."

"Well, if it is that you must know, to-morrow is visitors' day at Sing Sing, so I'll be going up to see one of me friends in the pinitintiary."

"Not so loud, for Heaven's sake! The waiter will hear you!"

"Is it a waiter you fear most? Rich and poor are exactly alike, they're so different. The poor are afraid the police will hear them; and the rich, the waiters. I'm thinking that if I had a gang of butlers and feetmen drawing their pay off me, it's little I'd care what they thought of me. And of all things to be afraid of—a waiter! And him scared to death for fear he'll lave the mate fall on you. But perhaps the word pinitintiary hurts you because you can't forget how close your late laminted come to joining the lodge!"

"That's pretty low of you, Mr. Canavan!"

"Not so low as you think, maybe. For I'm one of thim that believes there's manny a fine lad wearin' stripes— only they don't wear stripes now. Annyhow, some of the best friends I have, and min I admire, too, are doing their bit up the river."

"Ugh! How can you say that!"

Mrs. Cadbury could never outgrow the feeling that Canavan was a kind of gorgeous dragon, something cold and sinister and floundering, yet fascinating and potent, something from his own bogs. She had but the vaguest idea what a bog might be.

And she was as curiously wonderful to him, as fragilely

exquisite, as helplessly royal, as the chained princesses must have been to the dragons that desired them.

Each was an unfailing novelty to the other. He had known no woman like her, and he was as unlike the men of her acquaintance as different specimens of the same genus could well be.

Her husband had inherited a superhuman fortune which left him a violent idler, a weakling in everything except polo. Almost anybody could "ride off" Rodman Cadbury from any important effort outside the game, but when he sat like a huge clothes-pin on his cat-like pony he feared no hardship, no desperation of endeavor, no risk. After breaking most of his bones, he had finally broken his neck in a practice match. He had been genuinely mourned by his team-mates; for the lack of him lost them the tournament of that year with the visiting Englishmen.

None of the newspapers failed to include in his obituary mention that Cadbury had narrowly escaped criminal prosecution for consenting to certain financial manipulations that fell into sudden obloquy a few years before. That was about the only old-fashioned thing Rodman Cadbury had ever been guilty of. None of the newspapers had mentioned that it was Daniel Canavan who had saved Cadbury, for that was one of the few things none of the newspapers knew. Canavan had shunted off the prosecution as invisibly and by as complex a leverage as a man in a switch-tower sidetracking a distant freight-train.

Cadbury had had a way of dropping people who had been useful, for gratitude was a painful emotion to him. But his wife had gone on cultivating Canavan, though hardly so much from gratitude as from curiosity. Then, too, he had that innate gentlemanliness which distinguishes almost all Irishmen, for their talk of kings is not

entirely fiction. He was afraid of no man. He was no
snob and he would not truckle. Such a man usually suc-
ceeds in the highest society, if he chooses to frequent it.
For about all that the upper circles demand of anybody
is to be interesting; to have money enough to go along
with the procession; to be a little different, but not too
much so; to have self-respect; and not to care a damn
what common people think.

So Mrs. Cadbury had made a sort of pet of Canavan.
Where other women of her stratum affected musicians
and artists, exotic noblemen, or Pekingese, she toted a
politician about. To-day she had ventured with him
into the Ritz-Carlton for luncheon, and he had rewarded
her with bland allusions to his friendships among convicts.
Seeing her dismay, he was moved to seriousness, and he
stooped to an uncharacteristic effort at justifying himself:

"There's as much luck in jail as in harse-races, Mrs.
Cadbury," he said. "And it's a matter of honor, too."

"Honor among thieves?" she sniffed.

"Sure there's honor among thieves," he beamed.
"There's honor iverywhere, of wan kind or another.
There's a million kinds of honor, all told, but there's wan
kind of honor that few people seem to reco'nize. Everybody is always tahkin' about the kind of honor that keeps
a man out of tim'tation, but nobody seems to re'lize
that there's another kind of honor that tries to save the
pieces—a kind of *post-mortim* honor."

"That sounds profound," she said, lifting her brows with
a sarcasm which he smothered under a sort of gigantic
condescension.

"Let me see if I can explain it the way you'll understand
it. I have it. It's like ahtomobiling. Everybody that
drives a cair lahng enough is sure to run over somebody
some day. The before-honor is a matter of being ahful

careful going round carners and zippin' through crowded streets with kids bouncin' off the kerbs like popcorn from the top of a stove. Some of these cheffures scoot through Fit' Avenyeh like they was areoplaning the Milky Way and nobody in sight. Others go careful till they hit the country; then they let fly.

"Sure the finest moderen examples I've iver seen of a perfect trust in God is the way some of these motor-lads shoots round a shairp turn in a road.

"But careful or not careful, wan time or another, you're sure to boomp somebody with the cowcatcher, or some absent-minded person will look at you comin' and walk right into you.

"And now it is that the second kind of honor comes in. Once you've scored your first knockdown, what do you do?

"It used to be the fashion—till they passed a lah against it—not that lahs does much good—but, annyhow, the quick get-away used to be the fashionable thing. The man behind the radiator would back off till he cleared the human obsthruction and then he'd jam on full speed ahead and try to kick up enough dust to hide the tail number.

"It's haird to blame people for runnin' away in such cases. They niver mint to swat the victim. They had no special wish for to have their headlights dinted or their limonsine spatthered with red. If they stop to apologize they're li'ble to be manhandled be a mob; they're sure to be taken to the station-house and to get some ahful pitchers in the papers.

"And there—as handy as may be—is the little lever that 'll jump them out of trouble at a speed of about a million miles a minyute. Why should they wait? They don't.

"But there's some—not manny, but some—who says

225

to themselves: 'It was the old lady's own fahlt; she just
naturally jumped off the wahk into the wheel. But there
she lays. She's hurted bad. First, I'll get her to the
horsepital, then I'll give me real name to the officer and
take me medicine as it comes and sell the car.'

"They're the kind I lift me hat to. Of course they
oughtn't to have hit the lady—but—annyhow, they stand
fasht. They have nothing to gain, everything to lose.
But they stand fasht.

"Blame them as you will for the accident, it seems to
me there's a rebate comin' to them for standin' fasht.
It's true of other crimes than motoring. The same thing
holds. Once the deed is done, there's the divil to pay.
Some folks repudiates even that debt. But I honor the
man that pays his bills to the Old Nick.

"It is some of those last that are in the pinitintiaries
to-day. Not all, mind you. I'm not throwin' anny bo'-
quets at convicks. There's a lot of thugs in Sing Sing
I wouldn't vote for for President, even if the Hall sup-
ported them. I wouldn't trust everybody in a jail—anny
more than I'd trust everybody in a church.

"But manny's the man Up There doin' time, who
might have done worse than he done, might have been
more of a coward or a brute blagyard than he was,
might have dragged other people into the muck with
him.

"That's one of the raisons they've taken the stripes
off them in Sing Sing. It's a grand place, Sing Sing.
Was you never there?"

Mrs. Cadbury gave him one look of condensed concen-
trated reproof.

Canavan smiled as at an impudent infant.

"The first time I wint up I says to the warden, 'Warden,' I says, 'they tell me you've got a fairly gamy lot

of ex-citizens here. Is it so? You ought to know them. How is it?'

"The warden—a nice quite felly he is, too—he says to me, 'Mr. Canavan,' he says, 'I've got the wans that got caught,' he says. 'They's plinty here that's as good as the average outside. There's plinty outside that's worse than the worst here. All over the country, cashiers is tappin' the tills to play the races or buy their sweethearts something. Some of 'em has luck—the horse wins and they put it back in time, and nobody the wiser. The rest of them come up here and board with me.'

"That's the warden's own word for it, and it's true. Everywhere in the worruld there's people doing funny tricks in business and not gettin' exposed. There's burglaries goin' on this minyute in this town that nobody will ever be laid off for. There's millionaires this minyute doin' fancy finance that would get them a transfer from their clubs to the State boarding-house if the searchlight fell on them at just the right time.

"It's on'y exthraordinary good luck that keeps some of us out, and it's on'y exthraordinary bad luck that puts some of us in. But now and thin, wan of us goes in for raisons of honor. It was that way with the young felly I'm visitin' to-morrow."

"He is a young fellow, then?" Mrs. Cadbury caught him up with an unconscious quickening of interest that did not escape Canavan. Again he absolved her with a smile.

"You women are funny things. You ahlways must have your haroes young whatever, mustn't you? Age is what you hate and fear most. Yet it is a fine thing for a man to grow old—whin he doesn't overdo it. It would never succeed in a novel, but there's haroes in reel life that's bald-headed—and I've even known fat min to be brave.

"But, annyhow—this lad is still young, and good-looking, too. I'll introduce him to you when they let him out."

"No, thanks," snapped Mrs. Cadbury.

"Oh, you should be proud to know him!" said Canavan. "He's the most honorable thief I iver sah. If it wasn't for his high sinse of honor he'd be a free man to-day."

"His honor got him into the pinitin—the penitentiary?" she gasped.

"Sure! They sintinced him for it."

"How? Why?"

"Let's pay the waiter and move ahn. He's lookin' as if he wanted to rint our table to somebody else. I ahlways hate to keep a waiter waitin'. Their poor feet get so sore. Did you ever notice a waiter's feet? He may look like ahl the dooks of England in the face and he may wear his dress soot like an illusthration, but if you wish for to onmask him, look at his feet. A waiter's idea of heaven is to set in a kitchen with his shoes off and his feet on a chair."

II

Mrs. Cadbury was averagely human, but to sit in the Ritz-Carlton and hear a disquisition on waiters' feet was a mite too trying. She was glad to get out into the open air, and she was nerving herself to give Canavan a little lesson in the A-B-C of manners, when she found that he had forgotten her to shake hands with the big footman.

She turned with a gasp of horror to find the footman looking down into Canavan's outstretched palm, and blushing as he brought his saluting hand from the vizor of his cap. The man was afraid to look at Mrs. Cadbury. He could fairly sniff the brimstone she was thinking. But

228

THE AFTER-HONOR

Canavan was clapping him on the shoulder and giving him blarney.

"If it isn't McNulty! And lookin' like the admiral of the Irish navy. And how's the old woman who bore ye to the glory of the sod? Tell her there's a box of the turf comin' to me anny day now, and I'll sind her the fillin' of a flower-pot."

Then Canavan waved Mrs. Cadbury in and clambered in after her. In place of being abject with the apology she was determined to exact, he was florid with pride.

"That lad McNulty is the fine lad for you. Talk about your haroes! He's the haroest of thim all. Besides being Irish, which makes him a fighter, McNulty is a born soldier, built for airtistic bloodshed. Wasn't he a sergeant in the airmy in the Philippines before he was twenty —and some day a lootinant as sure as I'm not English.

"But what should come to him, just as he's re-enlishtin', but a letter from his old mudther sayin' how she was lonelying for 'um, now that his father was kilt in the railroad yairds, and his yoonger brudther, a fireman, boornt blind savin' about siventy-five hystherical Polish Jewesses from a fire-trap in a shirt-facthry? And what does he do but refuse to re-enlist and come home to be near the two of thim? And ahl the job he can get at all is openin' carriage doors for dudes and dudettes, and salutin' overfed plutocrats—him that was not long since salutin' his superior officer and sayin', 'Captain, if you'll lind me the loan of four min I'll shwim this river and enfilade the pants off thim haythin that hasn't anny on!'— excuse the language but it was his, and not mint for ladies —and didn't he do it, too? Five of thim cla'ned out a trinch that held up a rigimint for two days."

Mrs. Cadbury was moved to exclaim, "What a hero!"

"Hero's the word, only he's more of a hero now than

thin, for it comes natural to the Irish to fight, but it takes the blood sweat of a martyr for wan to be a footman. But McNulty does it, and takes the scorn of people who ought to be shinin' his shoes for 'um. And ahl for the sake of lettin' his old mudther smoke her pipe with him evenings.

"That's the kind of haro-work that gets a man no headlines in the papers, and no chapthers in the histhry books, but it's fine work, fine work it is—whedther it lades a man to bein' a door-opener or to bein' a convick."

Mrs. Cadbury felt a stir in the dust of a little-used room in her heart. Canavan's earnestness and volubility thrilled her beyond idle curiosity, and she was like a little girl pleading for a goblin story when she said:

"You were going to tell me about your friend in the penitentiary." The word came more simply now. "Was he a hero like Mr. McNulty? You said it was his honor that got him there."

"Oh yes. McNulty knocked him out of my head. He was a— But here we are at your home."

"Let's take one turn round the Park while you tell me— if you don't mind."

"'If you don't mind,' said the angel to the poor sinner as she led him off to heaven in a chariot!"

Mrs. Cadbury flushed with pleasure at the Irish of this, and gave the driver instructions; then leaned back and nodded a "go on" to Canavan. He took from a waist-coat pocket a cigar about the size and shade of a chocolate éclair, and without troubling to ask permission pinched off one end and lighted the other.

Somehow she liked his assumption of authority, and she admired his careless ease as he snapped the match with a finger-nail and shielded it from the gusty wind in the hollow of one hand.

THE AFTER-HONOR

"That's wonderful!" she cried. "My poor husband would have had to stop the car and use up a box of matches before he could get a light in such a breeze—and usually I had to open an umbrella. Where do you Irishmen learn the knack?"

"I learned in a ditch," he said, and she felt jolted again; but he mused blandly on. "Three or four matches in a hatband had to keep the clay stub goin' all day. It's funny how much a man can do when he's got to. That's the strongest wakeness of the rich; there's so manny things they haven't got to do. But I was goin' to tell you about O'Meara—Dermot O'Meara. He's no such man as McNulty, mind you. O'Meara has as little fight in him as a man could have and be pure Irish. And he was sure that.

"His father's from my county, but his mother is from Kilbeggan in West Meath. His father was ahlways as honest as the day is lahng—and the day is plinty lahng to a day laborer. Maybe he was honest because he niver sah annything to swipe; all the money that iver come nare him was in the envelope they shlipped him through the windy of the pay-shanty.

"But the boy Dermot, he always had a liking for the cash. A newsboy at six—saved his money too—soon had other boys workin' for him—ran a boot-blackin' business bechune extras. By the time he was twelluv he was a depositor in a savings-bank. Later he was goin' to night school. He had his soul set on the bankin' business, and be the time he was twinty-wan he was assistant paying-teller in a Hairlem branch. He'd paid a bondin' company to insure his honesty, and he was shovin' money out through the gratin' like it was lettuce for a rabbit.

"His father took a day off just to stand outside and watch him at it. The old man called a policeman over

231

to show him, and said: 'Whist, Coogan, that's me own bye there. You'd think it was clods of mud he was jugglin', but it's boondles of boodle. He has the backache nights, from shovelin' the gold coins out the way. He learned shovelin' from me. As soon as he's practised the thrade of money a little betther, he's goin' to build a bank of his own. I'm to have the cellar to dig. He wants a good cellar.'

"And it looked as if the lad would get his wish. The president of the bank told me himself the boy had a big future. He promised me he'd give him his chance. But, oh, Joseph and Mary, what a gulluf there is bechune the future a man's goin' to have and the future that becomes his past!

"Here's me, that niver did annything but see how far I could twisht the lah without breakin' it, ahlways pushin' meself forward and wahking around what I couldn't wahk over, and here I am lollin' in a motor with the most beautiful lady in the worruld at me side—and she payin' for the gasolene.

"And there's Dermot O'Meara, who was ahlways thinkin' of somebody else, always afraid he wouldn't do the rightest of two right things, always frettin' over the honorable coorse—and there he is sleepin' in a steel cell at night and wearin' the livery of shame be day, whilst his wife and childer blush to be known be his name—and at that, it was for their sakes he come to his misery.

"The Lord love ye if it wasn't for fear of bein' blashphemious, I'd say that this earth is governed worse than New York itself!"

III

Mrs. Cadbury was amazed to find the bluff and burly Canavan in a state of such cynic philosophy. Somehow, after the curious fashion of woman's interest in man, it endeared him to her to find him capable of helplessness and despair. The commonplace life he described was so strange to her that she feared to interrupt his unusual flow of talk. She merely urged him on with another query:

"His wife and children sent him to the penitentiary, you say?"

"Them and his father and mudther—but it was the wife that stairted it. I'm after telling you how young he was to be where he was. Well, he was a good lad, and she was a good girl, and nayther of thim thinkin' of marryin' for years to come. But they wint one holiday on a chowdther-party gave be a ward politician, and through losing their way and wan thing and anudther, they miss the boat and can't get home till next day.

"There was no evil done excipt by the lahng tongues of the neighbors, but Dermot he was that worried he could think of only wan answer to the shcandal, so he marries the girl. She's a nice girl and manes well, but she has the fatal habit of presintin' him with a bye or a girl as fasht as—the lahs of nature—excuse me, but—well, annyhow, befoor the time for Dermot to be thinkin' of taking a wife at all, he's the father of a family of three, and he's pulling down the magnificent salary of eighteen a week.

"There's a flat to furnish on the instalamint plan, and docthors and druggists and groceries and the like, till he's drove narely wild for to stretch the money out. And the worst about greenbacks is that they're not printed on rubber. You can break thim, but you cannot stretch them.

"And all the while that Dermot O'Meara is counting the pinnies at home, at the bank he spinds his days shufflin' hundred-dollar bills like they was pinochle cairds. By and by throuble begins to gather round him like the Old Horny was testin' him out.

"His wife cooks with wan hand and dandles a baby with the other, and wan day she blisthers her cookin' airm at the gas-stove that bad that he has to have a woman in to get his dinner and do the wash—not to mintion another baby comin'. Typhoid fever lays up wan of the flock for three months, and when they're shut of that the ipidimic of infantile parolysis lays holt of anudther wan and there's a horrible battle to save it from bein' a cripple for life.

"Dermot slips behind in his rint, his furniture instala-mint is overdue two months, and his premium on his life insurance has two days' grace only, and he's borried to the hilt on his policy. He feels like a lonely Roosian surrounded be a pack of hungry wolluvs. And ivery day he's payin' out thousands of dollars to annybody who pushes a check at him. But the money begins to slide through his hands kind of reluctant. That old felly Tantalus had nothin' on O'Meara."

Mrs. Cadbury was harrowed by the picture. "It's a crime," she broke in, "not to pay those poor bank clerks more money. No wonder they go wrong so often."

Canavan was immune to illusions. He sighed. "If they had a million dollars a week, would it make thim honest?"

"They ought at least to have enough to live on," Mrs. Cadbury insisted, stoutly.

"How much is that? How much is enough?" said Canavan. "Whin I was takin' ahl of a dollar and a half a day for tin hours' grubbin' in a nice cool sewer, we had just barely enough, me and Honoria and the baby we had thin—God rest the sweet souls of thim. And we owed nobody—a good raison, too, for nobody would trust us for a pint of beer. A few years later I was hauling in me twenty-five thousand dollars a year—no matter how—and at that I wasn't sleepin' nights for wondherin' how I'd pay off the fifty thousand dollars I owed."

He shook his head dismally. "No, Mrs. Cadbury, if it's going to make human bein's honest you are, I'm thinkin' you'll have to poultice something besides the pocket-book.

"But, annyhow, it's ivery man for his own problim, and poor O'Meara's problim had his head shwimmin'. He borried some money off some loan sharks to tide him over and they tided him under. The time came whin he wanted fifty dollars, and wanted it bad, and eighteen dollars was comin' in—and the loan sharks was howling for that. Where was he goin' to get it?"

"I wish he had come to me," sighed Mrs. Cadbury. Canavan laughed at the fantastic regret, but he could not help reaching out to squeeze her hand.

"There's plinty more lads in his shoes this day if you're lookin' for thim, and could find thim, and they you. Or if you could invint a way to bring together those that want help and those that want to help, you'd go a lahng way toward savin' the worruld. But, annyhow, no angel like you strolled Dermot's way; or, if she did she came up to his windy, drew out a satchel full of cash to pay a dressmaker or a milliner, and passed on. She prob'ly never saw the sad eyes behind the bar like a hungry fox in a cage. And Dermot wint on pushin' out the money that would have mint salvation to him and he niver dr'amed of touchin' it for himself. The only way he could think of to invest eighteen dollars and make one hundred and fifty dollars was on the ponies.

"He had niver seen a harse-race except in the movin'-

pitcher theaters, but nare where he lived was a thick-dured house with a sad-looking man always standin' nare the steps. Somebody told Dermot he was the lookout for a pool-room.

"Young O'Meara had walked by ivery day for years. Wan day he passed it and wint back, and passed it again. So he did until the lookout begun to grow unaisy, think-ing he was a detectuff. The last time Dermot passed, he didn't. He wint in.

"Whether it was because of what they call beginner's luck, or because they sah he was a good come-on to en-courage, they let him win. He wint home with the one hundred and fifty dollars and told his wife a grand little lie about how he got it. That night in his prayers he asked God's blessin' on that pool-room, and he breathed deep for days.

"It wasn't manny weeks, though, till the doctor took him outside in the hall and told him to get his wife and babies to the mountains or he'd be sorry. It was the mountains or Woodlawn. Dermot wint back to the pool-room—put up his eighteen dollars and lost it.

"But he narely won, and a slinkin' tout gave him a tip that couldn't fail, on a race to be run in N' Orlins next day: a dark harse named the Mudhen because he could shwim home when it rained.

"Dermot wint home with legs and head wabblin'. He was dead droonk on misery. He had to rest three times on the stairs to his flat. He was that sick and afraid he wanted to run home to his mudther and cry in her lap. Outside of his own dure he was a wake, sick, dish-thressful lad; the minyute he stepped through the dure he was the head of a family. The kids howled: 'Papa's home! Papa's home!' like they was sayin': 'Clang, clang! Here comes the firemin. We're saved! Ring down the curtain.' His wife turned her big eyes his way and flopped on his neck, and he re'lized that he didn't have time for to be sick or to give up. He drew a stiff upper lip. Us Irish has a large upper lip for the purpose. Sure, it's lots of exercise we've had at endurin' since Brian Boroihme passed out and the English passed in.

"To hear Dermot O'Meara talk to his flock that night, you'd 'a' thought he had just been adopted by John D. and Andrew K. and presinted with the Soob-Threasury.

"He laid awake that night and figured it all out. He worked over his duty like a bookkeeper who can't strike his trile-balance. He told me all about it whin it was too late for me to do annything—for he was tried by a joodge I had no control of whativer. That's wan throuble with these reform joodges that shlips in sometimes. They won't listen to advice.

"And there was Dermot the trusted empl'yee of a bank. It would be dishonorable to look twice at anny of the bank's money. But there he was, the trusted father of a family. It would be dishonorable to lave the childer starve or grow up wakelings, and his wife to die for lack of a little mountain air.

"'What kind of a man,' he says to himself, 'would he be to desert the helpless wans the Lord had sint him and to murdher thim just from lacking courage enough to pick up a little money where it was layin' round by the barl?'

"He told me he remimbered something from the Good Book, 'Thou shalt not muzzle the ox that threads out the grain!' or somethin' like that. There he was in the bank tramplin' on money like it was corn-shucks, and yet he felt sure that if he picked up a few bills and asked the president for them he'd be fired. Maybe he wouldn't have been, but, annyhow, he was afraid to risk it.

LONG EVER AGO

"So there was a grand battle of honor against honor, and may the best honor win. And it did, accordin' to his lights. He said to himself, 'I'd rather be a t-thief and branded than murdher me own holy kin. I'd rather bear the reproach of all mankind than look into the eyes of me own babies and refuse thim what I have but to put out me hand to get for thim.' He figured that honor begins where charity does—at home.

"And with that same he fell asleep like a child.

IV

"The next afternoon, at closin' time, whin Dermot is carryin' the bank's money from his cage be the double arrum-load like it was kindlin'-wood, and pilin' it up in cords inside the safe, he just flicked off a couple of fifties and vest-pocketed them unbeknownst to anny one.

"He makes thracks for the pool-room and gets wan of his fifties down just in time for the evint at N' Orlins. And it's rainin' in N' Orlins, and what does he do but make a tin-to-wan killin' on the Mudhen. The tout was so surprised he had barely strength to claim half for his commission and hike for a box of headache powdthers. And Dermot flew for home and told his wife he had found a liberal friend to make a loan, and they spint half the night packin' the thrunks.

"The next marnin' airly he took her and the babies to the train and kissed thim ahl good-by with trimblin' lips. And now he was left alone in New York and ahl he had for coompany was a bad case of ulcerated conscience. He was havin' about the laste fun out of crime that iver man had, for he had no wickedness in 'um.

"He had none of the makin's of a politician or a crook. He spint nothin' on clothes or liquor or ladies or jools.

THE AFTER-HONOR

He didn't even go to see the harse-races he bet on. He celebrated his luck, whin he had it, be payin' instalamints on the furniture and on a doctor's bill and his accident policy. He hated debt that bad, he paid off all he could. He overpaid, laving himself no margin for future throuble.

"His letters from his wife was small coomfort. He found that the expinses of the mountain hotel was more than he expected they would be, and he expected they would be. The sick did not get well by anny miracles. O'Meara could see only wan way to pay those bills and pay back what he had borried unbeknownst from the bank—and that was to borry some more, make anudther invistmint in the pool-room, and make a killin' big enough to pay off iverything.

"But it was himself he was killin'. He couldn't seem to win, so he borried more. He got to takin' the bank's money so fast he had to figure out a way to double-cross the double intry. Maniacs are clever to a point, and Dermot was goin' crazy. He devised a shcheme that worked temporary. But he was gettin' into deeper and deeper wather.

"That's wan of the raisons, I'm thinkin', why the moral lahs is made so sthrick. The honesty of a man is like the purity of a woman; and the moral lah is like the rope that holds a skiff to the dock. Once you onloosen that, there's no tellin' where it's goin' to drift.

v

"All this time Dermot O'Gara has been so worried over his wife and kids, he's well-nigh forgot he has parents of his own. But he's so ashamed of so manny things, this is just wan more drop in the bucket. And thin one day,

239

a Friday it was, his father and mudther sind for him to dinner.

"The whole family, includin' four other childer, day laborers and servant-gerls, are envyin' Dermot for his aisy life. They gathers round the table, and whin the dinner's over—they had a dispinsation from the priest so that they could have mate that dinner and the priest himself was there, and not overfond of fish himself—whin they've passed from ice-crame to beer, the old man tries to make a speech and the old woman has to finish it for 'um. She explains that this is a grand surprise party, for this very day she and the old man have paid off the last cint of the mortgage and they own their own home clear and free.

"It's hairdly more than a shack in a back yaird, according to your ideas, Mrs. Cadbury, but it's theirs and it's a palace to them, and they have no more rint to pay, nor interest. They can live there in pace and quite the rest of their days—so long as the old woman's back don't fail her at the washtoob and the old man can lift a pick and lave it fall.

"The childer is surprised to find that the old folks has had anny money they might have borried, but it's too late now to lay hold of it, so there's grand hilarity in the O'Meara tribe that night, and the old couple is idiotic with pride in their home.

"Finally the old woman grows garrulious wit' pride and other things, and she cackles, 'We're all proud of the roof that shelters us, and Mary be praised for it, but it's a prouder day that none of our childher is in disgrace and that wan of thim—I needn't say which—wan of thim is in a bank, trusted and respected be the rich and the powerful.'

"And Father O'Brine adds a few words tellin' how

proud he was for to have Dermot in his parish, and hadn't he married yoong and raised childer and been a credit to the Church and the nation, and were there more like him it would be well and betther.

"And the old man O'Meara is so overcoom wit' prosperity and beer that he thries to take Dermot on his lap and kiss him like he was a babby again. And such laughter and cacklin' from the rest as you'd think it was a wake.

"It was haird sleddin' for Dermot, that dinner. The more he blushed and begged off the more they praised his modesty. He had a wild wish for to tell them then and there, for his secret was fair sweatin' through the pores of him, but he thought it would be murderous crool to spoil the hilarity of the old people with such a blasht as that on the wan glorious night of their haird lives.

"So he told them he had to be goin' and he wint—straight for the river.

"But on the brink he paused. He could ind his own troubles there, but he'd lave behind him poverty and disgrace for the others to fight, and he not there for them to lane on. So he wint away from the comfortable-lookin' river and crawled back to his lonely flat with no wife or chicks to cheer him and only the creakin' furniture lookin' unpaid instalamints at him. He found there a letter from his wife—she was comin' to her time and she was wearyin' for him to hold her hand and— Well, he did a dishonorable selfish thing for once—he just laid down on his bed and cried like a gerl.

"The next morning, a Sathurda, he was half a minyute late to the bank and he found ivery wan in a flurry. A tip had come that a State bank-examiner was arrivin' Moonda marnin' to surprise them. Everybody was set to work cl'anin' up for inspection.

"And now Dermot O'Meara knew he was like a man in
a burnin' ship. He could stay aboard and be cooked, or
step off and be dhrowned.

"The president and cashier of the bank and the whole
foorce worked late that Sathurda afther the dures was
closed, but alahng about four on the clock the house-
cl'anin' is done and iverybody rehearsed to look surprised
whin the inspecthor turns up Moonda marnin'.

"The laste excited mimber of the whole crew was Dermot O'Meara. He'd had ahl the excitement in him wore
out in the pasht few months. But whin he takes the
lasht boondle of lahng green into the safe he passes a
nate packudge of bills into his inside pocket. There's a
label round thim with a lahng pin into it, and it's marked
$2,000. He might have taken tin thousand while he
was at it, but his sinse of honor to the bank held him
back.

"It made a perceptible boolge in his right side, but
iverybody was in that haste to be off, nobody noticed
it. Dermot had sint his soot-case to the station in the
marnin', and now he took a street-cair to the New York
Cintheral and stepped aboard the five-o'clock ixpress.

"He was knockin' at his wife's dure in the hotel the
next marnin' befoor she was up. She was scared to see
him, but the childer attackted him as if they was a band
of Indians, and nightgowns was flyin' through the air
like the week's wash in a high win'.

"As soon as iver he'd disentangled himself from tne
childer he sint thim off to breakfast and tould his wife
he had asked for a vacation so as to be with her and hould
her hand like she wrote him for to do. But since he was
tired of people and n'ise, would she mind lavin' the hotel

for a smaller wan in the woods, where he could have a bit
of fishin' to rest his nerves?

"If she suspicioned annything, she was afraid to pay
attintion to it just thin, and he managed to get his flock
away from the hotel and vanish into the wilderness,
lavin' no clue whativer. He'd been plannin' it and he
pulled it off as nate as if he was old Settin' Bull slippin'
his squaws and all through a cordon of the United States
Airmy.

"It woud take a bookmaker to tell how he moved
from place to place like a hunted animal with his pack,
but he managed it. He wasn't missed at the bank till
Moonda noon, and thin a note arrived sayin' he was
called away be sudden sickness. The hue and cry wasn't
raised till a Win'sda.

"Whin the baby was born, it was in the North Woods
of Canady. A few days later the proud father took his
wife out into the forest and tould her the whole thing.
It was a sad day for her, but he persuaded her that his
motives was all honorable and for the sake of his family,
however they boomped against the moral codes of the
lah. And she believed him. Sure, hadn't she proof of
it in the miserable, forlorn, pale-faced scrawn he was?

"So now a woman's wit was added to the man's and
they moved farther north to a new mining-camp and
changed their name and taught the childer a new game
of pretindin' to belahng to the family of McCann.

"Dermot tried for to make a killin' in the mines, for
the fever was in his blood; the millionaire microbes filled
his system, and he dramed of payin' the bank back and
clanin' the slate for a new start. But fate was against
him. It was surprisin' how manny people wanted to know
his past histhry, and the childer kept forgettin' the pairts
he had learned them.

"Wan day O'Meara heard that there was a stranger in camp makin' inquiries about him, and he knew his hour had coom. He knew that thim banks niver let up on a man, and he had another sarious tahk with his poor wife. He put into her hands ahl that was left of his two thousand except a hundred for himself, and that night he stroock out across the mountains to another railroad.

"He didn't dare lave his wife know his whereabouts. Faith, he hardly knew them himself. His ups and downs was ahl downs, and in three months or so he turned up in a horsepital in San Francisco in a delirium of typhoid. He got his sacrits off his chist at last and the trained nurse, who was sweet on a plain-clothes man, passed thim alahng. She figured that the rewaird would make a nice nest-egg for to be married on. And whin Dermot O'Meara came out of his thrance it was to find a copper for a nurse.

"They took him back to New York as soon as he was able for the journey, and he tould me it was a joy to have an ind to the game of hide-and-seek, with him ahlways It."

VII

Canavan paused to light a fresh cigar and Mrs. Cadbury sighed.

"So that was the end of your honorable gentleman's problems."

"The end?" said Canavan. "It was only the front end of his throubles. That's what I'm afther sayin'. People seem to think that honor is a matther of a few decisions here and there. Honor is like breathin'. You're usin' it ahl day long.

"No sooner was poor Dermot safely in cold storudge than he was approached by the surety company that had

244

gone his bond. They had been scoutin' round to find some way of savin' themselves from makin' up what Dermot had appropriated.

"Somehow they had learned that old man O'Meara had a family home up at 999 East 999t' Street, or wheriver it was. They had brought pressure to bear on the ancient couple, and their hearts were that broke and their pride that blashted, they'd have pawned their souls for the lad.

"So down to the Tombs prison comes the agent of the bonding company, that oily with smiles the rain would have run off him. 'It's ahl right, Mr. O'Meara,' he says, 'it's ahl right! Your throubles are over and done. Your father and your mudther have nobly agreed to martgage their home for the two thousand dollars. The bank has consinted to accept resthitution and shtop prosecution, and you'll go free.'"

At this point Mrs. Cadbury wanted to applaud, like an East Side mind at a melodrama. "How splendid!" she cried. "Those poor people often have the noblest motives, haven't they? Think of that old couple sacrificing themselves so gloriously for their son."

Canavan looked at her as if a child had spoken at a political caucus. He smiled dolefully.

"'Think of that old couple,' you say. That's what Dermot O'Meara thought of. And it was haird thinkin'. On wan side was freedom for himself, another chance to win back, and the soci'ty of his wife and his childer. On the other side was the prison, the losin' of his years, and losin' of his vote—that's a big thing to an Irishman, losin' his vote. He had his mouth open to say 'Glory be!' whin he remembered his father and mudther. He remembered the dinner they gave, the pride they took in the house they had bought for to shelter their white hairs. He saw the sthruggle they'd make to pay the interest and to pay off the martgage, and the sure black day whin they would be foreclosed, turned adrift with broken backs, broken lives, and the big terror in their old gray souls.

"He wanted to take the money; he wanted to chance the future; he wanted to believe that he'd win out big yet. But exparience had learned him that such things happen oftener in fairy stories than in rale life, and somethin' inside of him said 'No!' Somethin' took him be the throat like a parolysis. He could not consint. When he shook his head the agent turned scairlet with rage and called him a fool and a scoundrel, but he shook his head.

"Dermot begged the agent to lave him free till he could work and pay back what he had lifted from the bank. But the man laughed at him. He threatened him with the full limit of the lah if he didn't consint to the martgage. But O'Meara said 'No'! The agent sint for Mrs. O'Meara and she begged the lad to take anny-thing from annybody rather than go into the dark volley of livin' death. But he said 'No.'

"It was his sinse of honor, of coorse, and naught else that made him do it. It was love of his wife and his childer that had drove him to the airly crimes. A man of less honor of wan kind and more honor of the usual would have left his family to sicken and starve from the first, but Dermot couldn't do that. And he couldn't lave his old folks buy him out of the deep hole with the price of their own last pinny.

"Dermot's wife turned against him and called him a baste with a hairt of stone. But Dermot said 'No.' The agent called him ivery name he could lay tongue to, but Dermot said 'No.' The bank pushed the prosecution and Dermot got the limit. It was a shatthered man they took up to Sing Sing, and they jammed him in with crooks that had broken into houses, broken skulls, stolen for the love of luxury and for the scorn of dacincy. There's no drawin' of fine lines in Sing Sing.

"But me—well, somehow I've always felt that I'd rather have been Dermot O'Meara goin' to jail than some min goin' to Congress. I'd have held me head higher."

Mrs. Cadbury, the exquisite and the inconsequential, the dandled pet of luxury who had never in her life known the remotest approach to moneylessness, stared at Canavan and studied him. In him she seemed to study the whole of that foreign world of his where people do incessant battle on the steep edge of the ravine of pauperdom, where the solid ground is just a few inches from the direst want.

She felt that her own life had been a mere tinsel flippancy. She was a doll at the side of this man, this tragic, life-bruised man, uncouth but acquainted with realities. She was Helen of Troy on the walls, and the amusing politician was a Hector home from the wars, victorious himself, but saddened with the memory of companions who had been crushed and trampled under in the tumult.

Her life seemed to have been but a gliding about in artificial pleasances like the Park, through whose smooth roads her automobile was smoothly sweeping. Outside, she knew, were the hard streets where millions were waging the struggle for life.

She was pondering aloud:

"I know the Governor very well. I'm to be at a dinner with him next week. I wonder if I paid back what the poor fellow stole—borrowed; and if I guaranteed to see to his future—I wonder if the Governor wouldn't—"

247

"God love you for a—" Canavan began.

Just then the car shot through a curving glade and a tattered little boy playing ball with a friend leaped backward into the road to catch a wild throw. He leaped into the front wheel and was borne down, spun round, butted hideously along the gravel, and then—the wheel rose and thumped as it passed across the little sack of bones.

Before the frantic chauffeur could bring the car to a stop the rear wheels, too, had risen and thumped.

Canavan had been smitten aghast by the suddenness of the disaster. He was used to quick action in a crisis, but here he was a passenger, far from wheel or brake. He was abjectly helpless. He saw Mrs. Cadbury glance back, then forward. No one was in sight except the terrified playmate fleeing in the distance. The road was clear. Mrs. Cadbury bent forward to call to the chauffeur.

"François, quick—quick!" Her frantic eyes caught Canavan's dumb stare. She finished her sentence: "Quick—let me out! I must go to the child!"

Canavan wrenched the door open as she flitted past and tottered down the steps. Before he could swing to the ground she was kneeling in the dust with the dusty little wreck of childhood in her lap. She was staggering to her feet and tripping on her own skirts when Canavan took the limp form from her arms.

They got back in the car and now it was full speed for the nearest hospital, past staring crowds that saw a disheveled beauty with a lavish hat askew, and mopping with a lace handkerchief the dust from a ghastly white ragamuffin.

At the hospital it was hard to say, from the looks of them, which had been rolled in the dust, Mrs. Cadbury or the child she carried. Perhaps some extra attentions were paid to the real victim when it was learned that the great Mrs. Cadbury stood sponsor for him. Reporters somehow seemed to spring out of the ground, and a photographer set up his terrifying tripod to catch her as she came forth from the hospital.

She had made the doctors learn from the child his home address as soon as they brought him back to the agony of consciousness, and she was off again in her motor.

"I must find his mother and break the news to her and bring her here in the car," she was chattering to Canavan.

Throughout the last half-hour Canavan had felt useless and awkward. And even now he could only stare in unusual homage. But he was too sincerely impressed for blarney. The best he could manage to hand her was a peculiarly Canavannish posy:

"There's mateerial in you, Mrs. Cadbury. I'll have you educated yet so that you'll be a credit to me wan of these fine days."

IX

THE BITTERNESS OF SWEETS

LEAN little Mollie Finneran had just lost her job. It was not much of a job, but she was even less of a success at it.

It was not for lack of ambition on the part of her father and mother. They had wasted as little time on her education as the truant officer had permitted. They had not pampered her; they had not weakened her with luxuries and rich foods. In fact, they had almost trained her to the ideal point of getting along on nothing at all. But the best they could secure for her in the way of employment was this job as cash-girl. She got three dollars a week, and didn't get it. Her parents got it.

She was required to carry home the entire three dollars. From this she received a modest dole for car fare —one way—and for lunch. By the latter part of the week, as it usually befell, her father or mother had spent the balance at the liquor-store, and Sliver omitted the midday meal. But when Sliver could afford a luncheon it was usually taken at the ice-cream-soda fountain, where a mess of syrupy aniline dye, a pledget of adulterated ice-cream and a froth of imitation carbonic bribed her palate and left her insides in a state of nausea that proved a splendid antidote to appetite. She was almost incredibly thin, and was called "Sliver" for reasons all too manifest.

THE BITTERNESS OF SWEETS

But Sliver was not a success as a cash-girl. If she had had food oftener, or had not been placed ironically in a parish of tinware bounded on one side by a delicatessen department and on the other by a candy counter, she might have had more soul to give to her business. The thoughts of youth are long, long thoughts, and Sliver thought how long it was between meals.

Sometimes the mirage of things to eat would so fascinate her that she became a wax figure of meditation, deaf to the loud tappings of pencils on showcases and the reiterated wails of "Messenger! Mess'njah! Messunjurrr!"

For weeks the saleswomen scolded her, and the aisle-managers yanked her by the ear out of her dreams. Then the slack season arrived and they asked for her resignation—offered her her portfolio.

She accepted her exile with fine pride. Her language was not so graceful as Rosalind's "Banished! What's banished, but set free?" But its spirit was the same.

"I'm toined down, am I?" she sneered. "Well, it's a bum joint, anyway, and used up too much of me time."

She accepted the pay-envelope with disdain, and promised to give it to the poor.

She made a good exit, but once outside she felt as crushed as if the building had fallen over on her.

She wondered what her family would do now without her three dollars, and how she should kill time in the miserable streets or in the miserabler top floor back. She feared a beating, many beatings. She resolved not to go home at all.

Even as she planned revolt her feet, like a team of old horses, turned aside at a bakery window where she always paused as before a roadside altar. If only she had some money of her very own! If only she could squander even a dime on doughnuts! She felt that she could do desperate deeds for a cream-puff. What wouldn't she do for money enough to evoke that musical cry: "Brown the wheats! Draw one!"

A young reporter hurrying down the ugly street paused to gaze at her. He had written verses in college and he still poetized everything, to the great wear and tear of blue pencils at the copy-desk. So now he saw a prophetic wistfulness in Sliver's attitude, and in her overgrown eyes the darkling of a love-dawn.

As he made off on his errand he stopped short again, for he noted that the girl was observed by an elderly man whose swart and villainous mien was struck across with a black mustache and buried in a perfidious fur overcoat. This evident scoundrel halted and stared at the girl with approval.

But the swart knave moved on without speaking and the reporter went his way, too, looking back and wondering what dreams of love they were that must be thrilling the shabby little, thin little, quaint little creature poised in reverie before the baker's window. And so he passed out of Sliver's life. But the swart man came back.

The reporter had thought that Sliver was musing upon love. The swart man had thought she stared enviously at the lithograph in the window. This pictured "Carl Bruni's Flying Swallows," a sextet of girls appearing in a cheap vaudeville theater near at hand.

But Sliver was meditating neither love nor lithograph. She was musing on a little squad of éclairs well polished with counterfeit chocolate, and a golden beach of Apfelkuchen made out of dried apples, and a dark mountain of mock gingerbread, an Alp of frosted cake composed of eggs, and a pseudo-pumpkin pie as large and ruddy as a harvest moon.

THE BITTERNESS OF SWEETS

At the heart of each of us at least one little mouse gnaws and gnaws and hardly ever rests. With some it is remorse, with others ambition, or love, or jealousy, or avarice, or grief. With Mollie Finneran it was hunger.

Sliver had always been hungry. Never once in her life had she had enough to eat. As far back as she could remember Sliver had known famine and nothing else.

Wild thoughts of buying three dollars' worth of partnership in the bakery shop went like Roman candles through her brain. But she knew that she would take the money home, and if she met the usual abuse for being late, the usual suspicions that she had never justified, and the ruthless punishment for losing her job, she would accept these also as part of the weather.

She bent a farewell look on the blissful vision of food, and she wept a little because life was so bitter and cake so sweet, and she could not have any cake.

It was at this crisis in her soul that the swart man returned upon his steps and, drawing close to where she pined before the baker's window, murmured to her with a foreign accent. And as everybody who can read knows, a foreign accent is a proof of a villainous disposition.

"Say, keed, you wanna make beeg money, huh?"

Sliver's self-respect was militant at once. She whirled on the stranger with a fierce snap:

"Beat it, you big boob, or I'll holler for the bulls."

Sliver was virtuous almost to the point of viciousness.

The old villain backed away with haste, and the storm of rage left Sliver's heart almost as quickly. Young as she was, she was used to such encounters. She accepted them as rain or soot. Bad as her home was, unguarded as she was from the evils that crowded about her, she had walked thus far through the world without contamination.

She resumed her contemplation of the baker's Para-

,dise. She wept with craving. A sniffling sob was cut in half by a sudden remembrance of the words "big money." Big money meant big meals. Perhaps the voice had been from heaven instead of the other place. Some angel may have offered her big money, and she had answered with insult!

Then, as if by a miracle, she seemed to have wished the angel back. Over her sob-shaken shoulder came that dulcet voice again:

"Dawn't git mad, keed; but dawn't you wanna make da beeg money queeck?"

Sliver turned and studied the angel. He wore little glossy shoes and a fur-lined overcoat and a shabby silk hat. This was plainly no angel; and if he were a devil, Sliver felt that she could exorcise him with one swift kick on the shins or an elbow drive in his stomach. And she could always bite and scratch. Reassured, she mocked him with skeptical contempt.

"Ah, go ahn! Whaddaya mean—beeg money queeck?"

The Italian took courage; he pointed with a much-ringed hand at the lithograph in the window.

"See dat pitture, huh? 'Bruni's Flyeen Svallows,' huh? I am Bruni!"

"Ah, go ahn!" said Sliver, masking her awe.

"Sure, I am Bruni. I invent dose svallows, and bring to America from Eetaly, yas! Ve play now at deesa t'eater right here, huh? You have not see my svallows, huh? You come see now."

Sliver's heart sank. So it was only a scheme to get her money. This old scoundrel was a runner-in, a bally-hoo, for the five-ten-and-fifteen-cent palace where worn-out vaudeville acts and tattered films were alternated.

Sliver sneered at the old man and shook off the hand that seized her arm with urgence.

254

THE BITTERNESS OF SWEETS

"Ah, go ahn! You said I could make big money."

"Sure! One of my svallows she is get seeck; she cannot maka de jomp to Patersona. I most get a new svallow. I offer you de job."

"Ah, go— What would I have to do?"

"Awnly to fly—fly in de air."

"Ah, go ahn! I can't fly. I never loined to fly."

Mr. Bruni laughed with indulgent patience. Sliver came back to the main issue. "You was talkin' big money. How much do you slip your swallers?"

"Six—"

He was going to say "sixteen." She thought he was about to say "six," and her heart leaped with joy. He slyly fell to "twelve," not knowing that he had doubled the sum in her eyes and quadrupled her latest wage. Twelve dollars a week! Was he offering her as much a week for floating in the air as she had earned in a month for lugging her feet along the department store Marathon?

"Twelve dollars," she sneered. "Twelve nothin'. Ah, go ahn!" Mr. Bruni nodded violently. Sliver would have fainted, but she had never learned that, either.

Mr. Bruni, seeing that she was wavering, pressed his cause.

"You come see my svallows now—right here, huh?"

Sliver had no money except the three greasy bills which were impatiently awaited at home. She hesitated, then spoke with hauteur:

"I got no small change."

Bruni laughed. "It cost you not wan penny. I pass you in."

It is believed that no layman exists so rich as not to be elated at the thought of entering a theater on a pass. To Sliver it was just a little more flattering than if St. Peter had invited her to walk into heaven without penance.

255

LONG EVER AGO

She found herself in a cave of gloom at whose farther end a Niagara of pictures was cascading. She felt the little hand of the old man take her arm. It was like grasping a rolled-up umbrella.

After a thousand feet of cowboy adventure had reeled past the fascinated eyes of Sliver, a melancholy youth set out a placard announcing the "Engagement Extraordinary of the World Famous Bruni's Swallows, by Carl Bruni." The pianist chopped the piano with the vigor due to an engagement extraordinary, and the tarnished old curtain went up with importance, disclosing six young girls, all of a size, all slim and sprightly, all clad in feathers, with the heads of birds for caps, with wings for sleeves and swallow tails for trains.

They sang and danced, and to Sliver they were a choir of seraphim. Suddenly at the end of their dance they rose straight in the air, with their wings outspread and their pink legs and slippered feet far back.

Sliver rose with them in exultation as if one of Mr. Bruni's wires were already affixed to her belt. She stood rapt till a harsh voice from the rear growled, "Down in front!" Then she dropped to her seat, but her soul went on rising and falling, swooping and soaring, with the enchanted birds.

Sliver felt that heaven had fairly broken open about her head. She was to sing and dance and fly and get a million dollars a week for it. It was like being paid to see Coney Island.

Mr. Bruni had brought the original swallows to this country from Italy a score of years before and made a profound sensation in a spectacular production. The charter swallows had long since outgrown their fledgling days. Mr. Bruni himself had been in his time a Harlequin; famous, for a Harlequin, and thin and lithe as his own lath sword. He had since taken the shape of an old fat hen and acquired as motherly a disposition.

As swallow after swallow took flight from age or over-development he had recruited others. Gradually, as the novelty had worn off the idea and the costumes, he had lapsed slowly from a Broadway feature to a roadway feature, from a one-night-stand sensation to vaudeville on "the big time," thence to "the family time," "the big small time," "the opposition" big time and small time. Now he was on the wee small time and his glittering spectacle was sandwiched between moving pictures.

Another year would see him—where? But to Sliver the swallows were now what they had been to Broadway twenty years before. To her the obsolescent little man was a great manager, the tiny fire-trap theater was a temple of wonders. To be one of these swallows! To flit through such scenes! Then fairy stories did come true!

When the curtain fell on the birds, all lyrical and afloat in the air, Sliver beat her palms raw in applause.

In the lobby of the theater Bruni said:

"Vell, you like my svallows—huh?"

"Great, Mr. Bruni," said Sliver with the manner of a expert; "they're simpully great."

"You like to be one—huh?"

"I'm goin' to be one," said Sliver.

Mr. Bruni, like many another villainous-looking man, had a matronly soul. He said: "Your mawther geeves her consent—huh?"

"Me ma?" said Sliver. "Sure she will." She knew that her mother would refuse—less because she feared for Sliver than because she feared for the pay envelope. But Sliver was determined that nothing should stop her from realizing this opportunity. It was so inconceivably beautiful that she said:

"Say, why did you pick me out for this when so many goils are so much classier?"

She wondered why he had not selected Sarar Boinhardt, or Mord Adams, or Juliar Marler for the vacant position.

Mr. Bruni was too gracious a gentleman to confess that he chose Sliver because she was a sliver, and because she was at hand and looked cheap. He explained that he had an eye for genius and could tell a born swallow the moment he saw one.

He was so paternal that Sliver broached the question of expenses. She confessed that she was a little short of money just now. He volunteered to be security for her board for the first week and to furnish her costume. He added that he would also pay her railroad fares—which struck her as mighty generous.

She ran home to bid her mother farewell. She found the flat empty; she judged from the signs of struggle that her parents had had another argument. The flat-iron had left another dent in the wall and its nose was covered with plaster. A neighbor informed Sliver that her father and mother had left the house for a ride in the picnic wagon the city kept at their disposal. The neighbor guessed that they would doubtless "get the Island for another thirty." So Sliver did not leave the three dollars, but merely a little note:

· dear ma i bin fired at the store but i got anothre Jobe in nu jearsie wil rite soon yoor loveinge doughtre

Then she sped to the theater and asked for Mr. Bruni. She was referred to the stage door. This was too glorious. She found Mr. Bruni and he led her up an iron stairway to a tenement of dressing-rooms and introduced her to his flock. The swallows sat about in their feathers and their unmitigated make-up. Some were mending their plumage, one was reading a book, one was sewing at a child's clothing, and one was industriously masticating gum.

At Mr. Bruni s request the gum-chewer, who was about to leave the troupe, permitted Sliver to try on her costume. An extra pair of tights was found and Mr. Bruni withdrew while Sliver made the change behind a chair.

With her arms bare and her shanks in hose a world too wide, she was unimaginably thin. She was such a pauper in flesh that Mr. Bruni, recalled to inspect her, felt sorry for her. He rebuked with a glare the ridicule in the eyes of the other swallows, and told Sliver that she looked very nice. He wondered what the gallery boys would say of his sixth swallow, and he dreaded the comments of the house-managers; but he was still more afraid of rejecting this pitiful little soul that had paid such reverence to him and his achievement.

When she had doffed her splendor, Sliver was permitted to sit in the wings and watch the swallows do their supper turn to an almost empty house. It astounded her to see the mechanism at work and to realize that the lightly flitting swallows were raised and lowered on wires and pulleys controlled by stage-hands in overalls. Such romance in front of the scene, such realism back of it! But she was bewitched at the miracle of it all. "Yestiddy a cash-goil; to-morra a boid!"

She slept that night in the deserted flat, and the next morning she was awake at the first streak of soiled daybreak that pierced the dirty window. She leaped from her slumber and pirouetted and danced, took flying leaps from the edge of the bed and from the table, and practised aviation till the neighbors thought her father and mother must have escaped from the law and resumed their debates.

Sliver heated as much water as the clothes-boiler would hold and bathed in it, and made the neatest toilet she could. She borrowed an old telescope bag from a wealthy neighbor and packed what little wardrobe she possessed.

She reached the theater before the night watchman was awake. The hours she must survive before Mr. Bruni arrived seemed unendurable. That little mouse, forgotten in her excitement, began to gnaw at her stomach, and she realized that she had had no breakfast.

She went to the nearest of Mr. Childs's lunch-rooms and tried to look professional. She wondered what lady actors "et in rest'runts." She ordered a breakfast of such variety and substance that the waiter grinned as he punched hole after hole in her ticket, and finally commented:

"Say, kiddo, are you just eatin' your last Thanksgivin' dinner, or are you doin' this on a bet?"

Sliver answered him with quiet dignity:

"Ah, go on, you big stiff, or I'll bounce one of these cups off your bean."

He knew those cups and he went on.

But when Sliver came to pay for the feast she trembled, not with repletion, but with terror, at the inroad on her funds. The theat'ical life was a norful expensuv thing.

She hastened back to the theater and wheedled the stage-door man into admitting her to the dressing-room so that she might be ready when Mr. Bruni came. She flung off her scant and material rags and donned her ethereal pinions; also her terrifying pink tights. When Mr. Bruni finally arrived and knocked at the door she felt gusts of fright sweeping across her skin. She was ashamed to go out before him. But no one was present save Mr. Bruni and the youth who had hoisted the swallow she was to supersede. This youth Mr. Bruni introduced as his "asseestant, Ned Krook."

Mr. Krug looked Sliver over brazenly and snickered. She flared with modesty at his gaze and with wrath at his smile, but she said nothing. Mr. Bruni laid off his hat and his fur coat and his other coat and taught Sliver the dance steps. It needed all her reverence for him to keep down her amusement at his appearance as he flung his barrel-like body this way or that, and kicked up his short, fat, almost kneeless legs. She was a trial to his temper, for she had no tradition, instinct, or training in the dance, and he had no breath or agility.

After roughing out the steps Mr. Bruni took up the flying program.

As Ned Krug was buckling the harness on Sliver he murmured: "You two was cert'n'y some scream; fat old gander tryin' to learn a squab to dance a toikey-trot. But you're all right, girlie; you and me's a sketch. We'll have swell times togedder, won't we?"

"Yes, we won't we!" was Sliver's only answer.

Krug liked her haughty manner. He mumbled: "Sure we will. I'm batty about you and you'll find me a regular feller."

He kept his hands about her waist longer than seemed necessary and Sliver gave him a smack in the face. It was so loud that Mr. Bruni, at the opposite side of the stage, turned to see if a pulley had broken. Sliver opened her mouth to demand:

"Say, Mr. Bruni, how much of this guy's noive have I gotta stand for?"

But she feared to be dismissed at once, and she was not used to calling for help in her perils. So she said nothing.

LONG EVER AGO

She went up kicking and swirling. She was out of Krug's reach, but more than ever in his power. He gave her one or two sickening lurches to emphasize this fact and she was frightened beyond screaming. But she was even more afraid of being returned to her old life.

In time she learned to swim in the air, to keep her equilibrium, and to take a superlative joy in the new element she had gained. So Bruni told her the time and the train for the morrow's journey and left her to put off her celestial raiment and get back to her dingy self.

When she came down from the dressing-room she found Krug waiting for her. She made her nails ready for a cat-like defense, but, to her stupefaction, he lifted his hat to her! It was the first time she had ever received this tribute and it was overwhelming. And he said in his most sugary tones:

"You cert'n'y slipped one over on me. Me nob is buzzin' yet. But I like a girl's got some fight in her. And you're light as a fedder, too. Gee! you're a pipe to lift. Dey's a lot o' tips I can give you dat 'll help some. Supposin' you and me was to have dinner togedder. You must be ready for de eats after all de work you done."

Sliver was prepared to dislike Mr. Krug, but before such gallantry who would not relent? And how tactful it was of him to mention food. She was heroine enough to refuse his "Ah, come ahn," once, twice, thrice, but that was her limit.

So she went with him to a restaurant a little less clean and a little more expensive than the dairy lunches that had marked her highest social arrival heretofore. Mr. Krug, as host, majestically went down the line: oysters, soup, steak, fried potatoes, and pie. He urged Sliver to join him in a pitcher of beer, but she would not be persuaded. There had been too much beer in her environs. She had carried too many pails of it up too many stairs.

But oysters—these were almost her first, and they were as large as small hot-water bags. Each one of them was a problem. But she solved them all. She solved the soup, together with two slices of bread that she broke up in it, following Mr. Krug's example. She ate the steak with the eager fangs of a young animal, and hurried the potatoes down in single file. Of the pie she left not a crumb, and she drained two cups of coffee.

Even Mr. Krug admired her triumph. He said:

"Girlie, you're the goods when it comes to the knife-and-fork dance. Dey won't make no hash out of what you leave."

She winced a little at this and flashed back:

"If you don't like my style you ain't gotta pay for it. I got the price of the check right here."

Krug was startled. "Gee! but you're the hair-trigger kid! Why, I love to see you wallop a plate. Dat other broad dat's leavin' de show used to turn up her nose at everything I bought her."

"Oh," said Sliver, cannily, "you think you're trainin' me to take her place on the wire and off, do you? Well, you better change cars; we don't use them kind of transfers on this line."

She said it with such an ominous glare that Krug was thrown into a panic. He was still young enough to think that he knew womankind. But Sliver was not yet a woman. She was a famished child.

What she had learned of love in the streets and in her family history had not emphasized its attractions. She was not ready for love, and still had a child's disgust for its symptoms. Whatever the future might develop her into, Sliver had no further interests now than food, success, and sleep. She had had the first, to-morrow promised the second, and she was desperately ready for the third.

She shook off Krug's further hospitality and went home alone. Her heavy feet could hardly lift her unusual weight up the long stairs. Her last strength went in the task of wresting off her shoes and folding up her pitiful finery. Her soul was asleep before her lean hands had finished drawing the quilt about her thin and ropy little throat.

The journey to New Jersey was the beginning of an era of travel. New Jersey, in the eyes of Sliver, had always been a foreign country. She gave herself a last good breakfast in New York that she might have pleasant memories of America.

From the station at Paterson she and the other swallows lugged their heavy suit-cases to a boarding-house that was accounted the worst even in Paterson. After an hour in the theater to test the tackle and rehearse the music cues, the swallows flew boarding-houseward for an early luncheon.

The others, who had known better days, though not always, made dismal faces at the food served by Mrs. Ablowitz. They called it "somepum fierce." But Sliver was fiercer still, and she first flattered and then dismayed Mrs. Ablowitz by her voracity. A rate for the week had been agreed on, and Sliver determined to eat till she was enjoined.

That week was the birth of a new Sliver. She had food, food, food—three foods a day, and a snack of supper at a fascinating lunch-wagon after the evening's work was over.

And such work! Such a thing to call work—to dress in pink tights and feathers and a wig of dangling curls, to use powder freely, set a rose of rouge in each cheek, incarnadine and enlarge the wan lips, and blacken the eyelashes desperately! And then to sing songs and dance, and finally to flash into the air on unseen wires, to beat the wings in ecstasy, to curvet and caracole, to hover above the heads of the admiring people and know the beatitude of birds! And, strangest of all, to be paid for this—to be paid twelve dollars a week for it, with feathers and railroad fares thrown in!

At her first matinée Sliver forgot most of her words, and the rest stuck in her parched throat. She could not keep step with the dancers, and when she was hoisted into the air she lost her balance and hung head down, kicking and sprawling till she was lowered.

This convulsed the small audience so completely that the house-manager begged Bruni to keep it in. The old man was insulted at the suggestion. His birds were artistes, not clowns. He expended so much temper on the manager that he had no wrath left for Sliver. But he explained to her that the sacrilege must not occur again and ordered Krug to give her a special rehearsal. On this account she could hardly refuse Krug's invitation to supper after the show. She was as hungry at eleven-thirty as she had been before dinner, and as Krug watched her his admiration was tempered with anxiety.

On the way home he carelessly slipped his arm about her waist, and withdrew it promptly minus four or five small pieces excavated by her ready nails. He was so startled that he apologized. The next evening he was permitted to feed her only on condition that he quit what she called his "damnonsense."

This was the basest ingratitude in his eyes, and the supper series ended. Lacking his support, she paid for her own suppers. In the mornings she bought herself beakers of ice-cream soda, nut sundæs with maple syrup spread over, and boxes of "chorklut pep'munts."

At the end of the week she found that her wealth was not so elastic as her appetite. She had no money to pay the small bill for her laundry when the stage-door man brought it. She had nothing to pawn and she was forced to borrow from another swallow against pay-day.

She did not dare buy herself a supper that night. She smiled invitingly at Krug, but he was nursing a grudge and did not take the hint. She lay awake while the mouse gnawed as of old.

The fourth week found the swallows nested in Red Bank. The lonely Krug, watching the infuriatingly elusive Sliver, was startled to realize how pretty she was. He had understood the secret of the curves in her nether members; they had been stitched in, with results that might have bewildered an anatomist. But those pipe-stem bare arms of hers had grown actually round and full. Those dangerous elbow-spikes were blunter.

His experienced arms tested her weight when the signal came to hoist. Yes, she was heavier. And so was his heart. He approached her again with a supper invitation. She accepted graciously with a round-cheeked smile that made him gasp. Her appetite was undiminished.

On the way home he said:

"Say, girlie, you're not so skinny as you was, are you?"

"So the other goils was tellin' me," she said. "Yestiddy I hadda let out me skoit at the waist, and to-night I left off me plumpers."

"You're sure one armful now," he said, and made bold to prove it. She gave him her elbow in the solar plexus, and when he began breathing again he realized that she had not improved so much as he thought.

Sliver grew prettier as she grew plumper and Krug began to feel an awe of her, as if a little tight-clenched bud were blooming into a young rose before him. He began to plead humbly for her affection; he talked of the joy of marriage. Two of the swallows were married and one had left a child at her mother's. But Sliver laughed him to scorn. She was as fleet and airy-minded as a swallow when the mating season is farthest away.

Krug grew more lorn as she grew more luscious in his sight. But he grew tiresome to her. His compliments bored her. She was getting them from all sides. She was overhearing people in the audience refer to her as "that pretty one on the left." She knew that she was growing beautiful, because the other swallows were more and more unpleasant to her. Life was one long festival; her appetite grew almost lyrical. She kept candy in her make-up box and in her bedroom.

And so she romped across the weeks without a thought of trouble in her world. Then one evening she heard two men in a stage box discussing the swallows. She heard herself referred to as "the fat one on the left." She mistrusted her ears.

She gulped her supper in haste and hurried to her room to study herself in the mirror. The concave of her cheeks was convex now. Beneath her little pointed chin she had the hint of a second one. Her throat was full, her shoulders soft and padded. She had difficulty in unhooking her dress. Her arms were roly-poly; there was a swaddle of fat at her hips; her thighs were arched and her calves bulged.

Sliver felt a knife of terror in her heart. She resolved that she needed more exercise. After breakfast she took a long walk. She tired quickly and her breath was gone so soon that she had to pause for an ice-cream soda. She invested a penny in a weighing-machine. Her ninety pounds were one hundred and fifteen! The traditional limit of weight for a swallow was one hundred pounds.

That night she noted that the other swallows were kinder to her than for a week past. This was alarming. Krug resumed his old insolence and patronage. This was convincing.

He invited her to supper, and somehow she dared not refuse. When he asked her what she wanted he said:

"Go easy on the heavy stuff, girlie. Take it from me, it's easier putting on weight than pushin' it off."

She ate heavily to prove that he could not coerce her with his advice. As they walked to her boarding-house his arm slid round her waist and she had a hard fight to tear it away.

"Stop it," she gasped, breathlessly. "I hate it, and I hate you."

"That goes double, then, girlie," he answered, truculently. "I guess I won't trouble you long."

"You mean you're goin' to quit the show?" she said, all too hopefully.

"Me! it ain't me!" he laughed. "You ain't de first swaller dat's been crowded out because she weighed in too heavy. I've saw more 'n a dozen of yous livin' skeletons swell out into fat ladies and den blow. I been doin' overtime h'istin' you, and sayin' nuttin' to nobuddy. But it don't get me nowhere, and I'm goin' to lay down. It's me duty to me boss to wise him up to de strain you're puttin' on his tackle. O' course, if you was pals wit' me, I might go troo wit' it, but—well, sleep on it, kiddo, and gimme your answer to-morra. A woid to de wise is officious."

Sliver slept on it that night, but she slept ill. Her brain was a paddock of nightmares; one of her recurrent torments was a vision of herself as a fat woman in a museum, a billowy, pillowy freak. She woke again and again in cold sweats of horror.

She fell to work on all the exercises she could remember from the newspaper accounts of how to get thin. She bent stiff-kneed and touched the floor with the tips of her fingers till she grew dizzy and fell to the floor. Then, being there, she rolled herself along the carpet like a barrel till the people in the room below were wakened and alarmed and ran up to knock at the door and ask if she were having a fight or a fit.

She refused her breakfast and fled from the house, where the aroma of waffles seemed to have claws to clutch at her and hale her back. She walked and ran, sinking down to rest on packing-cases or other sidewalk obstructions. She walked and walked till her feet outached her heart.

Her pain and her fatigue were almost unendurable. But quite unendurable was the thought of going back to the life she had left; back to grime and tenements and brawling parents, and three dollars a week and somebody else to spend it.

She frightened herself away from bakers' windows by the remembrance of her past. She achieved the heroism of a lunchless noon. She wore through the matinée with no sustenance but the juice of a lemon, and the very thought of it tied her into a knot.

After the matinée she did not go back to the boarding-house. She told her fellow-swallows that she "had a date out." Krug heard of it and jealousy tormented him as hunger tormented Sliver. He vowed to temporize no longer. He searched for her, but his wanderings did not come across hers, and he found no chance to speak to her alone.

When she got back to the stage door her feet were

heavy, but her head was light. Outside a cigar-store, near the alley leading to the stage door, there stood a weighing-machine. Sliver did not know that these whimsical devices vary not only from one another, but from themselves also. All she knew was that the same solemn dial that yesterday registered her weight as one hundred and fifteen pounds, now, after a night and day of fasting and pilgrimage, proclaimed her weight at one hundred and seventeen.

She crept down the black alley of despair, and her knees were hardly able to hoist her to her dressing-room; her fingers hardly managed to doff her street clothes and don her plumage. She toppled down the stairs just in time for her turn and she was so pale that Krug forbore to trouble her as he snapped the hook on her belt.

The curtain rose and the piano roared and the swallows began to sing and dance. Sliver strove to do her part, but the floor writhed and the walls wiggled and the audience eddied. She heard the other swallows upbraiding her. She felt that the audience was laughing at her, suspecting her sobriety. To be accused of that! Her desperate little mind fought with the mutinous, unpaid, and unfed troops of her nerves and fought in vain.

The audience was openly ridiculing her, and a few women were whooping and rocking with laughter. Bruni was charging back from the front of the house, when the audience suddenly hushed its noise. Sliver collapsed; her joints gave way one by one from her ankles up, and she lay outspread on the stage, a pitiful, broken-winged bird.

The other swallows stared, then moved to her aid. But just at that moment the cue arrived for their flight. The men at the wires had seen nothing of what had happened and they bent to their task. The advancing swallows felt themselves dragged backward irresistibly, then up they went into the air.

And Sliver was lifted too. Still aswoon and all limp, she was gathered up like a clay figure and carried high, hanging doubled downward from the waist, her head against her knees and her hands flapping against her feet.

The stage-manager rang the curtain down just as Bruni reached the scene. He was horrified at the interruption to his sacred rites, but his heart melted at the sight of Sliver. Always a showman first, he ordered the rest of his flock to stand by to continue, and, taking Sliver in his arms as she was lowered to the stage, unhooked the wire from her belt. Her weight amazed him and he staggered under it to the wings, groaning:

"*Per l'amor di Dio!* my svallow is a goose!"

He turned her over to Krug, who rushed to his assistance; then he made haste to the footlights to explain to the audience that the svallow was all right to-morrow and the leddies and jontlamen need not be alarmett. He backed off into the curtain wire and bowed himself slowly through a narrow crevice. The curtain went up and the Engagement Extraordinary went on.

Sliver woke to see Krug staring down at her with more tenderness than she had thought him capable of. She expected no consideration at all from Mr. Bruni, whose show she had spoiled. But he was all aflutter and proffered her a flask of brandy.

Sliver pushed it away. She was afraid of liquor and she dreaded the thought of its effect on her wits after her prolonged starvation. Bruni did not urge the point, but advised her to go home as soon as she could change her clothes.

She made haste to get away from the theater before the other swallows came off the stage to bombard her with questions. As she undressed and redressed, her hunger came back over her in gusts of emotional intensity. She could have gnawed the soap. The rabbit's foot in her make-up box tempted her.

She darted down the stairs and out of the stage door as the swallows hopped from the stage. Krug caught up with her and took her well-filled sleeve. He suspected the cause of her distress; his first word was an irresistible plea:

"Looky year, kiddo, what you need ain't no medicine or no booze. Plain food and lots of it is what you want. Am I hep?"

"Yep," she sighed. And he steered her into a restaurant over whose door hung one electric word, a gleaming imperative "E A T."

And she ate. Between the exorbitant demands of her irate stomach and the tactful insinuations of her extravagant suitor her wisdom had the minority vote.

Krug did not seek to lure Sliver with cocktails or liqueurs. He did not hint at that ultimate East Side prodigality known as "opening wine." He did not offer jewels or fine clothes or a life of ease.

He offered her a life of work and plenty of food. He plied her with subtle soup, with fat pork chops and fried potatoes, with more of the same, with glasses of half and half (half milk and half cream), with jellies and with comfits, and finally for a climax he set before her that last word in fatteners, apple pie with ice-cream on it.

And she fell for it. He murmured to her gallantly that he didn't mind how heavy she got. He'd put on a double wire if necessary and a block and tackle big enough to hoist a safe. If on'y she'd treat him white, he'd go into de bakery business.

But Sliver wanted to be a swallow. A little later she

could cut down her commissary, but food was as much of a heavenly novelty to her starved body as the art life was to her starved soul. She promised to be good to Krug if he would be good to her.

There was a moon leering down at them as they left the restaurant; a well-fed moon like a méringue in the sky. A sense of luxurious well-being filled Sliver's heart and she thought kindly even of Krug—until they reached a heavily timbered street, where the walk led through a subway of gloom. And there he took his bargain into his arms and crushed her against him with gorilla violence, and pressed back her head and took the kiss she had promised him. And more than one, with increasing ferocity.

Until she smothered and fought him and wrenched away and took four strips of skin from his nose with her finger-nails and beat him on the mouth till it bled.

As she ran she heard him sputtering and calling into the dark: "I'll get you for this! You'll see! I'll get you!"

Sliver did not stop running till she reached her boarding-house and locked herself up in her room. There she broke down in a storm of tears.

She felt no remorse for her broken pledge; it was good to dupe the devil; there could be no perjury with the prince of evil. She vowed that she would not belong to Krug though his master himself came down the chimney breathing fire. Rather than that, she would leave the flock. Rather than belong to a man whose touch she hated she would go back to the freedom of her old life. Whatever its faults, it left her free at least. Plainly she was not meant to be a swallow. The others ate and ate and ate and grew only the thinner for it. But if she touched so much as a pudding it went straight to her cheeks. Heaven evidently meant her to be fat and she would yield to Heaven.

In this grim resolve she fell asleep and dreamed herself a hungry cash-girl again.

When she woke up the cash-girl fled, but the hunger remained. She was the first one in the dining-room and she ate as if she were condemned to execution and this her final breakfast upon earth.

She left the house for exercise and passed a billboard where the flight of Bruni's birds was lithographed with more imagination than skill. But this critic was no better than the artist and Sliver felt a great sorrow in her heart at giving up her wings.

Grief depressed her so utterly that she sought surcease in the only stimulant that gave her respite. She entered a bakery and bought lavishly. She came forth carrying a large paper sack bulging with kickshaws.

She hurried home like a robber with a bag of swag. As she ran up the steps of the boarding-house and darted through the door she collided with Mr. Bruni. At the sight of him she was overcome with guilt and shame and remorse. She flung herself into his arms and embraced as much of him as she could encompass.

Amazed by the onslaught and the outburst, he led her into the empty parlor, settled her in a chair, sat down by her, and asked:

"Leetla keed, you are seeck? You have bad news from home? Huh?"

"It's meself I've bad news from," Sliver whimpered, and with that beginning told him all; poured out the little history of her saccharine past; showed how the baleful habit of food had fastened its tentacles upon her, till now she was lost beyond redemption. She confessed that the cause of her swoon was a useless effort to starve herself into shape. But she said never a word of Krug, his influence, her compact with him or his threat against her. She turned in a soppy resignation punctured with sobs.

Poor, fat, old Bruni, who had a smile for almost everything, did not smile at this tragedy; he did not make fun of Sliver or minimize her torment. He had gone through the same conflict, and lost. There was no excuse she could have given that could have made so straight for his heart. He took Sliver's dimpled hand into the cushions of his and spoke with as much sincerity as if he were consoling and counseling a repentant Magdalene.

"Leetla keed, you have right to cry, for now your life commence-a to hoort. You are goeen each day to make-a de beeg fight. When I am yong like you, I am slim and gracefool like-a de greyhound dog. I am de fines' dancer in all Eetaly. I do not say it. I know it. Averybody know it. Ask anybody, 'Who is fines' dancer in Eetaly?' He say, 'Carlo Bruni.' So! I am reech and proud and I begin to eat. I drink not moch—a leetla Chianti, maybe; but I eat, and eateen kills more people as drinkeen. I dance, but I puff. I say, 'I am not well. I most eat more.' I eat. I grow soft. I grow fat. I say, 'To-morra I begeen to stop to eat so moch.' But what a man will not do to-day he cannot do to-morra. Bineby, you ask anybody, 'Who is fines' dancer in Eetaly?' He say, 'Carlo Bruni was.' Bineby I stop to eat. It is too late. I get fat jost de same. And bineby Mr. Bruni stop to dance. He manage other people to dadce. Now I do not eat moch, but I do not dance at all.

"And now you, you poor leetla keed, now your time comes. If you dawn't stop now, to-day, and never begeen again, you become fat like me, old Bruni. You will not be happy. You will not be pretty. You will be fat old lady before you are yong woman.

"If you geeve up to eat, you can become great arteeste. At feerst you are not pretty, you have no grace. I am sorry I take you for a Bruni Svallow! But you learn and bineby I say, 'I choose good when I choose dat gerl.' And bineby, if you take care of yourself, I make a great dancer of you, you make beeg money—not twelve dollars a week, but twelve hundred dollars a week.

"To be an arteeste is better as to eat too moch, eh? And to dance is greatest art of all—musica, dramma, scultura, poesia—all in one. If you eat and grown to be fat you shall be also unhappy jost de same. If you are arteeste you shall be unhappy, you shall soffer, but you shall be arteeste. You are not goeen to love your dinner more as your art, huh? No! You are goeen to be brave leetla keed, and bineby leetla keed is great arteeste, huh?"

She nodded her head so violently that she shook tears from her lashes to the fat hand he laid on her fat cheek. And so he left her, put on his perfidious fur overcoat, twisted his wicked mustaches, and went his way.

Sliver took the bag of cream-puffs and éclairs and gingerbread into the back yard and threw it into the ash-barrel. It was like tearing her heart out and flinging it away.

On her way to the theater she remembered Krug's threat, and it frightened her. Then she felt reassured because she had forestalled him by confessing the truth to her adored Bruni. She felt more comforted when she saw Krug smile as she passed him in the wings.

It was so dark that she saw only the whites of his eyes and his teeth. She did not see the swollen lip nor the four lines across the bridge of his nose. These had taken a deal of explaining to the rest of the crew. They had laughed at his contradicting stories. But they had not seen him as he set a little file to gnawing at the wire that lifted Sliver into the air. Half through he filed it, where it would rub across the pulley. And then he waited his time.

Sliver put on her swallow-clothes again with a joy as of coming home. The buttons were tight and the hooks pulled fiercely at the eyes, but she felt sure that she could gradually starve off enough surplus to make her worthy of her glorious career. Even Krug was cowed and all was well.

She danced and sang like a forgiven prodigal, and when the cue came to soar aloft she pressed sorrow back beneath her with wings as joyous as a skylark's. Even the other swallows felt the lilt of her ecstasy.

And then, at the height of her climb, she felt a queer little jolt in the wire, a tiny slipping, and then—she was no longer upheld, no longer a bird, just a helpless body, falling, falling—

The audience caught a scream of terror, a vision of tumbling feathers, a thud, a motionless heap, a panic among the swallows still in the air, a panic in the very curtain that ran down its wires with a shriek, a hubbub back of the canvas, a pale man who stepped forward to say, "Is there a doctor in the house?"

One man rose in his place and, edging through the crowd, was motioned round behind a stage box.

Then the piano began to clatter, the curtain went up, and a comedian in green whiskers and a comedian who wore his hat down over his ears and said, "Oi! Oi!" dashed out and began a duel of wits.

Bruni's fat heart had almost stopped in his fat breast when he saw his swallow drop from the sky. He reached the stage in an ague of terror. He found Sliver once more unconscious and bruised, but her heart still beat under his trembling hand.

LONG EVER AGO

The stage-manager, furious at the second mishap, was ordering the swallows "to get back in two," howling into the flies to send the front drop down, and shouting in the wings for the next team that played "in one" to jump in. It was not their turn, but at all costs the audience must be kept at ease.

Bruni never dreamed of questioning this generalship. He dragged Sliver up-stage as the drop flapped into place. When the doctor arrived they talked in whispers, while the comedians on the other side worked like Trojans to coerce the audience into laughter and forgetfulness.

The doctor hoped that no bones were fractured. "She's pretty well padded," he said. Her flesh was at once the cause of her disaster and its remedy. A closer search showed that one of her arms was snapped, and the ambulance was called.

Krug heard the gong of the hospital wagon; he saw the still form carried forth feet first. He felt himself a murderer. When Bruni came back to demand the cause of the accident he could not enact the jaunty scene he had rehearsed for himself. He gulped and choked and mumbled the words:

"I knew it was comin'. I been warnin' her she was eatin' too much. She's 'way over de limit, and—"

"You knew eet comes," stormed Bruni. "Den w'y do you not tell me—huh?"

"How do I know de wire wouldn't hold?"

"De wire would hold two of her unless— Give-a me de wire."

Bruni did not wait to have it brought. He sought it himself and examined the broken edges. As he dragged them into the glow of a brilliant box-light he glanced up at Krug, and Krug cleared his throat and shifted to the other foot. Bruni studied the wire keenly; the polished

278

bevel the file had made was as distinct in one half of the wire as the ragged tear in the other.

Bruni thought hard a long moment. Then he called to one of his other assistants:

"Giorgio, run get me a police-a-man, queeck!"

Krug beat Giorgio to the door. He never came back.

Bruni thought that this was best. It saved the swallows a scandal and Bruni eighteen dollars of unpaid salary.

When Sliver came back from the place where she had gone she was in a white hotel of many beds in one room—a hotel filled with the guests of pain.

She suffered agonies at the surgeon's hands, but her soul had anguishes all its own. She was afraid to see old Bruni, but when he came he was so overjoyed at his diplomacy, his financial coup, and the safety of his new daughter in art, that he had only words of comfort.

She was so weak that her secret feud with Krug escaped her close little heart.

"Krug said he'd get me—and he did. Not the way he wanted me at foist. But he got me good and plenty. It was me own fault, though, for toinin' meself into a machinery-buster."

"Dawn't you believe you boosta da machine of Bruni. Krug is de machinery-booster. He is a—a traduttore, but he make no more de trooble for you, leetla keed."

Sliver was overjoyed to have this remorse removed. But she had others. "All the same, I busted your show, and I busted me arm, and you'll never wanta see me again."

Bruni shook his black curls and smiled. "Carlo Bruni is notta de man for leave a svallow veet a brokena ving. Ve play five svallows till you come back."

Sliver squeezed his fat hand in one of hers and chuckled. "I was in another horsepital once. They don't feed you

very good in horsepitals. When I get outa here I'll be
a Sliver for sure. And I'll keep meself so slim they'll
have to use opery-glasses to see me. From now on I'm
strong for you and me art."

He took her at her word. And when she was well she
kept it, with the lofty self-denial of a priestess at an altar.

Now and then on her way to and from the theater the
Tempter calls her eyes to the windows of candy-shops,
or the heaped-up treasures of the confectioner's; or a land-
lady in his employ urges her to try her pie. But thus
far she has fought back Chef Lucifer so well that she is
almost again the Sliver she was when Bruni, who is so
proud of her now, found her weeping before a pastry-
shop because she could not buy.

Sometimes still the struggle with her besetting vice of
luxury is so fierce that she pauses over against a baker's
window to defy the demon and prove her strength. And
the battle brings tears to her eyes again because she
could buy and must not.

Myriads of women have wept seas of tears because life
is so filled with bitterness. Sliver is weeping a little private lake of her own because it is so full of sweets.

X

IMMORTAL YOUTH

SLIPSHOD and sloven, lugging a pail of suds and trailing a listless mop, the scrubwoman dragged her dawdling feet up from the basement into the main hall of the art-gallery. Here the masterpieces of sculpture stood clustered like an enchanted forest of marble and marvelous trees. But the matter-of-fact attendant in uniform had nothing more poetic to say than:

"Are you Mrs. Flannery?"

She nodded as if her identity were as unimportant to the world as it was to her. The man jerked a thumb over his shoulder.

"Go up them stairs at the far end of the hall and toin to the right till you come to the noo gallery. Ask for Mr. Kelton. He's waitin' for you."

She nodded drearily, as if Mr. Kelton were as unimportant as everything else, and wandered on. She wasted no glance at the marble or plaster classics. But they, in their petrified moods, seemed to regard her with studious interest.

Niobe and her daughters checked their grief, and Laocoön and his sons paused among the writhing serpents till she and her indifference should be out of sight of their anguish. The Apollo Belvedere alone attitudinized, even for her, as if hoping that she would share his approval of himself. The horned Moses gathered his beard aside,

and the Day and Night of Michelangelo seemed to raise
themselves heavily in protest at the intrusion of such a
workaday character in their mighty counsels. Cleopatra,
with asp on bosom, glowered at her. The Venus of Medici
simpered, caressing her own milky flesh; the Melos alone
ignored her, busied with ambrosial thoughts. The Marble
Faun mused over her with his eternal smothered chuckle;
and all the snowy populace seemed to say: "How did
she get into Olympus? What can she know of passion
or romance, of tragedy or idyl—that sloppy old scrubwoman?"

The draped statues poised their eloquent wrinkles in
amazement at the remarkable ugliness of the chaos that
served Mrs. Flannery for costume. The elaborately coiffed
goddesses seemed to stand astonished at Mrs. Flannery's
hair, with its sparse and tightly drawn skein yanked back
to a small knob, resembling a crab-apple with a skewer
in it. These stone people could hardly have known that
the one lock brushed low over Mrs. Flannery's left forehead was meant to conceal a scar which the late Mr.
Flannery had raised there as his chief claim on her memory.

Mrs. Flannery moved on her way like realism snub-
bing romance. If she had had any thought of the statuary
at all, it might have been, "Better a live scrubwoman than
a dead goddess."

But she was not thinking of gods or goddesses, Mrs.
Flannery. She was thinking of how heavy her pail was;
how tired the plaited muscles of her broad back were;
how the rusty hinges of her knees would grate when she
had to kneel at her orisons to the demigod of cleanliness.

The heroic stairway she clambered had no interest for
her, except its length. Once it was climbed and her breath
regained, she turned to the right and trailed her swish-
ing mop through sun-flooded galleries of paintings. But

her face stayed empty of expression until she reached the new room in the new wing. Here the canvases, bronzes, all the works of art, were hidden under sheets of cheese-cloth and tarpaulin. The ceiling, with its arabesques and its frieze, was trowel-fresh or mold-damp, but the floor was a litter of plaster-spatter, lath-splinter, and the general débris of decoration.

Mrs. Flannery opened her eyes here. Here was her business and her demesne. She was important to this room and it to her.

She found a man loafing about, waiting for her to keep the tryst.

"Is this Mr. Kelton?" she asked.

"Is this Mrs. Flannery?" he answered.

"Looks like it's the both of us," she said, with an almost smile that was remarkably pleasant for so dull a face. With awakened professional pride she brushed the vagrant lock back over Michael Flannery his mark and surveyed her territory.

"The plashterers didn't do a t'ing to this floor, did they?" she said. "They on'y made a pig-pin out of it, that's all."

"That's all," echoed Mr. Kelton. "It will look better when you get through with it. First you must clean up this mess on the floor; then swab everything with a damp cloth; then you can take the coverings off the statues and pictures. And for Heaven's sake be careful! Don't stick that mop of yours through any of the Old Masters, and don't knock any fingers or toes or noses off the statuary. It was probably one of you women who robbed the Medici of her fingers and the Hermes of his right arm."

Mrs. Flannery's pride was touched. She bristled professionally. "What do ye t'ink I am, a hypopottimoose? Sure and this ain't the first airt-gallery I've set foot in.

LONG EVER AGO

Wasn't I an old hand in stoodios before you was out of short pants?"

"Was you—were you?" said Mr. Kelton, absently, as he peered under one of the cloths at a hidden Ter Borch.

"Sure was I," said Mrs. Flannery, and began to get down on all-fours with the circumstance of a kneeling camel.

When this descent was negotiated, she looked up as a quadruped and demanded:

"Usedn't I to be a model in me young days?"

"Used you?" came from the muffled curator.

"That I used. In thim days I had a shape, too. They was artists, and good ones at that, who said me figger was divine. They said it would drive you crazy."

Kelton peered out at her and dared not answer:

"It does still, Mrs. Flannery."

Mrs. Flannery set to scraping the dirt in heaps and began to think aloud:

"Yis, sor, in thim days me shape was in great demand. I was almost iv'rything beautiful and glorious. Wan week I was a nymp', the next week I was a sylp'—or whativer the divil it was, I dunno. Annyhow, it was wan of thim ladies that don't wear anny"—she looked about cautiously, then lowered her voice to a confidence— "Whisper!—ladies that don't wear anny clothes to brag about, but is great on grace—disgrace, I'd call it nowadays. But in thim days—oh, the Lord love ye!—I usedn't to think anny more of posin' than I do now of rollin' up me sleeves. Some days I was a society lady, and then a queen, and what not. Why, I was a Gibson girrul before this Gibson felly would lave go of his bottle."

"You don't tell me?" came from somewhere under cover.

"Sure, it's me that's tellin' ye. Wanst they was a pome

284

wrote about me. Honesttogawd! Let's see how it wint."
She sat up on her haunches awkwardly as a Newfoundland dog. "This is the way of it, as I was after tryin'
to remimber it the other day.

> "Oh, laughter-lovin' Venus of the—the mien Hibernian,
> I toast your beauty in a beaker of Fa-Falernian.

"Whatever it is, 'Falernian,' I dunno; only I think it
wasn't ice-cream sody.

> "I pour loibation to the passion of yer wishtful face,
> The curve of ivvery ivory limb
> Hairmonious in a heavenly hymn
> To Grecian drames of beauty, Grecian gods of grace.

"That's the way it began; the rest of it I fergit.
'Ivvery ivory limb!' Can you see me now, wit' me legs
tied into bow-knots from rheumatics? Oh, wirra, wirra!"
She fell back on all-fours and went on with her work,
chattering too garrulously to notice that her audience had
quietly vanished.

"Wanst I was after recitin' it to me old man. And
Flannery says, 'Aw, shut up and fergit it.' A fine soul
for poetry had Flannery—the dirty loafer, sleepin' off his
drunks when he wasn't out collectin' 'em! Oh, it's sorra
the day I ever took up wit' the likes of him, me that
wanst had artists and handsome young gintlemen writin'
pomes to me."

She sat up again in her Newfoundland posture. Seeing that she was alone, she laughed with the gift of self-
derision that had saved her from despair all her life; then
she went back to polishing the floor, eventually drifting
into snatches of an old song of ribald tendencies:

> "Oh, the priest of the parish in his caravan
> Kim over the mountains to marry Susanne.

LONG EVER AGO

Oh, the priest of the parish in his caravan
Kim over the mountains to marry Susanne.

"There was McDermott and Patrick and a couple o' score more,
Wit' their long spades and pitchforks to ride the bride home.
And you're welkim all, heartily welkim,
Gramichree welkim, ivvery wan.

"Whin the bride she was dressed she was comely and fair,
And as nate round the waisht as a two-year-old mare;
Her body was dressed wit' blue trimmin's around,
And her hat was a castor that cost her a crown.
And you're welkim all, heartily welkim,
Gramichree welkim, ivvery wan."

And so she sang and swept, scrubbed and clattered,
till the litter was removed. Then she began on the floor,
working from the outside in smaller and smaller circles.

After a time Kelton returned with a man whose wealth
was as evident as his years. His prosperity was in such
contrast with the curator's careless attire that he looked
almost dapper.

"This is the room, Mr. Harbeson, or rather it will be,"
said Kelton, "when the woman here gets through with it."

Kelton's manner was markedly deferential. Mr. Harbeson accepted this as a matter of course and custom.
He glanced about with an interest hardly more than polite.

Kelton went on: "Under that canvas is a handsome
onyx tablet explaining that this is the Catherine Weldon
Harbeson memorial gallery."

"Indeed?" was Harbeson's entire comment.

After a somewhat irksome silence Kelton ventured:

"It was a beautiful idea for a memorial to your wife, sir."

Harbeson smiled drearily. "I wonder if poor Catherine would think so. She wasn't much on art, Catherine. Hardly thought it proper, I'm afraid."

286

IMMORTAL YOUTH

"You don't say!" Kelton exclaimed, with a soft pedal on his amazement. "I'm sure she would like this gallery, though. It will be the gem of the whole museum."

"Not really!"

"Indeed it will, sir. And do you know I think it is a pity that more rich men don't follow your example and spend their money in this way. They have millions for endowing colleges, scientific schools, manual-training schools, athletic fields, hospitals, charities, but they overlook the religion of the beautiful."

Harbeson turned a gray and quizzical eye on the enthusiast.

"The beautiful?—Mr. Kelton! The religion of the beautiful?—in America? Really, Kelton, my boy, you get strange ideas in this quiet old gallery. You might as well be marooned."

"To be marooned in such a Paradise—that's not so bad."

"Paradise, eh? You actually enjoy living here?"

"It is the world to me, sir—a dead world, perhaps, but a beautiful one. Of course, you think I'm crazy."

Harbeson's eyes seemed to warm a trifle. "Yes, I suppose you are." Then he added, "I used to be crazy, too." Kelton turned a surprised look on him as he went on: "Mad as a hatter, or, worse yet, mad as a sculptor. When I was a boy I was insane over beauty, especially plastic beauty; and say what you will, Kelton, of your paintings and poems, your plays, music, romance—the one, pure, absolute, final art is sculpture."

"I agree with you," murmured Kelton, motioning him out of the path of Mrs. Flannery's ruthless flail.

But Harbeson was incandescent with his thought. He went on regardless of the encroaching menace, regardless even of his usual discretion in enthusiasm, unwontedly extravagant of rhetoric:

LONG EVER AGO

"It's the flesh, my boy—the flesh! not the skin only and the complexion, not the eyes and the expression merely, but the muscles beneath the clothes, the bones beneath the muscles, the marrow inside the bones, the soul inside the marrow—all that marvelous living fabric of strength, suppleness, grace! None of your daubs on a flat canvas, none of your ink-slinging descriptions out of the dictionary, but the flesh, the flesh!—not described, but realized! presented, round, full, flexible, projected into three dimensions—no, into four dimensions, for the fourth is soul. Why, nobody but a sculptor begins to know what real beauty is."

"Too bad you gave up art, sir," Kelton observed.

"How the devil did you find that out, eh?" Harbeson exclaimed. "I thought it was a secret of my youth. Yes, I was an artist once—long ago—longer than I like to remember. I came on from the West. Do you know, I had never seen real art then, and I was rather prudish, I suppose. I wanted to make statues of generals and horses and cowboys—everything exact. I thought mainly of the finish of the buttons, the tassels on the chairs, every hair on the chaps of the cowboys. The finer the detail the greater the art, I thought. Then I came East. I wandered into this very museum. It was like being cremated and born again. When I saw that multitude of Greek statues I was so shocked I could hardly stand up. They hit me hard as simply naked and indecent—the shameless monuments of a foul-minded race.

"But before I left the museum I had a new soul, I was revolutionized. I began to see the enormous difference between being stark naked and divinely nude. The whole world was new. I looked at men and women with a pair of eyes from which the scales had fallen—or been put on again, as in Eden. I saw the forms through the

288

clothes—saw the people themselves within their clothes—
with neither pruriency nor prudery, but with artistic and
critical appreciation of human architecture—architecture
that breathes and moves and feels."

To Mrs. Flannery the rhapsodist was only a pair of
feet much in the way. She flickered her mop nearer and
nearer, with more and more professional authority, until
Kelton, fearing a catastrophe, took Mr. Harbeson by the
arm and led him to a safer spot. But he could not lead
Harbeson's mind from its old pasture:

"I was poor then, Kelton, poor as the devil. Lived
on coffee and rolls, mostly—with now and then a mad
debauch at a forty-cent table d'hôte, wine included—at
least they called it wine."

"I didn't know you had ever been poor, sir," said
Kelton, feeling suddenly more at ease in the presence of
this Mæcenas.

"Huh!—poor? I should say I was! And I didn't like
it. I used to say, 'If I could only get leisure in some
way, so as to do the things I want to do, instead of the
ghastly old things that will sell'—only they didn't sell.
Just a few years ago some people tried to get me to endow
a poor starving sculptor, a genius in embryo. I said,
'I'll give him ten dollars a week, provided nobody else
gives him any more.' They thought I was a miser and
a brute, and got a sentimental woman to set him up in
comfort. What's the result? He hasn't done anything
worth while since. I'd have saved him for art; but he
was ruined—just as I was—by a sentimental woman."

"A sentimental woman ruined you, sir!"

"Yes. And this gallery is her monument. Bless her
heart, her intentions were good. But you know where
good intentions are used for asphalt. There's a vast difference, my boy, between sentimental and being temper-

amental. You see, I was living on artistic ideals and ambition, with a little stale bread. Along came Miss Catherine Weldon and asked me to make a marble bust of her. She offered me a hair-raising price. Later I learned that it was a charitable ruse.

"The woman tempted me, and I fell. The sittings were numerous and—well, eventually I found that I had somehow dared to propose to her, and she had somehow dared to accept me. Her wealthy parents raised the usual row, and, as usual, hastened the marriage. My wife fitted me up a gorgeous studio and bought me a frock-coat and a tall hat, and I began to talk about art instead of digging at it. I began to dabble in theories instead of clay. In due time the studio made an excellent nursery for the children."

"Too bad! Ts! Ts! Ts!" clicked Kelton, in sympathetic reproof.

"Don't think I am so beneath contempt as to be slandering my poor dead wife. She was a noble woman—and I revere her; but—well, she wasn't an artist. That is not a criticism, Kelton; it is a description. She was very uneasy when I had a model. A model was to her simply a shameless creature on parade. Besides, she didn't like to have the children grow up in—the presence of unclad statuary."

"Mrs. Harbeson was from New England, I believe, sir," Kelton murmured, hardly meaning to be satirical.

"Very much from New England," assented Harbeson; then came to himself with a start. He felt alarmed and ashamed, as one who realizes that he has been blabbing in his sleep.

"I don't know why I should have poured all this into your ears, Kelton, except that artists have a craze for publishing their secret feelings. Please forget it. I have tried to live down my artistic past and atone for it by taking care of Mrs. Harbeson's property. After a little practice the business game fascinated me. It's an art, too, of a sort. I began to make a little money of my own—I caught the knack. And now I am a respectable citizen, safe, sane, and stupid—instead of a crazy artist."

But he could not pose as a Philistine in this room. He broke out again with the frenzy of an artist before an understanding listener:

"Once, though, it was my idea of heaven just to chisel the splinters of stone from the prisoner rising to me—rising to me from the marble! Nobody who hasn't been crazy can imagine the joy of taking a lump of shapeless, clammy mud and with a few sweeps of the thumb rounding it into the throat of a goddess—or the breathing bosom of a woman—or the eyelids of a sleeping beauty."

His hands were in the air, giving action to his thought as if they were sentient beings.

"It's playing the Creator in a small way, sculpture is," he said. "But I'm a fallen angel now, Kelton. My fingers are so stiff that I can hardly hold the coupon scissors. The other day I was in a fellow's studio, and I took up a piece of clay to make a head of it. Ugh! I couldn't make it look like anything but a mud pie. There was a time, though! There was a time!"

And he lapsed into a luxury of remembrance. Kelton seemed to be hesitating over a message, and finally he said:

"You've led up very neatly to the surprise I had in store for you, Mr. Harbeson."

"Surprise?"

"Yes. A few days ago we received a number of paintings and statues willed to us by James Farwell."

"Oh yes, old Farwell. I knew him well."

"Among the statuary was—what do you suppose, sir?"

"I'm no good at conundrums, Kelton."

"A statue of yours, sir."

"Of me?"

"By you."

"No!"

"Yes."

"Really! Wh-what was the name of it?"

"There was nothing on it except '*Harbeson sculpsit.*'"

"The one Latin word I used to know! Well, well, *Harbeson sculpsit!* I used to expect to scratch that on something that would defy the ages."

"I rather think you did, sir. This statue of yours is a pretty good bit."

"You don't say so! What did it represent?"

"A crouching nymph, sir."

"Oh, I remember. It was the one ideal thing that I ever really finished. Mrs. Harbeson hated it because it was so scantily draped and because—I believe there was a certain amount of gossip at the time about the model who posed for it. So I gave it to Farwell for a wedding present. That was ages ago. Lord! but she was a beauty, the model! Her name was—er—what was her name? Let me see! I'm afraid it's gone from me for the moment. But I'd know her if I met her anywhere. She was a beauty. She was ignorant and illiterate, but her flesh was divine. She had a good heart, too—a wild, loving, laughing way. What was her name? It's hideous to grow old—and forget. And to think I could forget her name, of all!"

His memory was in such a desperate wrestle with itself that Kelton intervened.

"Would you care to see the statue, sir?"

"Care? Would a mother care to see a long-lost child?"

IMMORTAL YOUTH

"It's right here, sir. I put it in this room as a surprise to you."

Kelton went to a shapeless heap of canvas over a pedestal in the center of the gallery. He reached out to lift the muffler, but Harbeson checked him.

"Wait a minute, man. I feel as if I were about to see the dead brought back to life. What if I shouldn't like it now? What if it should rob me of my one illusion— that I spoiled a great sculptor to make a third-rate capitalist? Wait a minute, please. I—I think I'll just sit down."

He sank on a leather-covered bench. He was shaking from head to foot.

"So she's under that cloth, eh? Just a minute, if you don't mind. Ah, now!"

Kelton whipped the canvas away and unveiled a little wonder-work of dreaming marble, a nymph that crouched on a tuffet of moss and smiled an eerie smile.

Kelton looked at the sculptor with fatherly amusement and found him struck motionless. He was all eyes.

"Not half bad, eh?" queried Kelton.

"Not half bad?" Harbeson echoed. "Why, man, it's —it's wonderful. It's great!" He moved toward it as if it had him under a spell. He walked round and round it with religious awe, murmuring, "And did I—did these hands—really carve that?.'

"It has your name on it, sir."

Harbeson paused. Nothing could express him but Doctor Johnson's phrase, "My God! what a genius I was then!"

He was filled with an afflation of pride, the inalienable rapture of a creator seeing that his work was good.

"I remember it now—so well," he murmured. "My teacher gave me that block of marble. It was an odd shape. He couldn't use it. But I seemed to see that

293

little nymph crouching inside it, calling to me, 'Let me out! Let me out!'

"As I saw her in my vision she resembled a certain model, who only posed draped. I remember I had a terrible time persuading her to pose for this. But I succeeded. I hardly stopped to eat or sleep. The model fell into the mood, understood, and was tireless. She was a heroine in her way. She actually collaborated with me. Her body was as necessary there as my vision. And to think that I can't remember her name! It's shameful. It's dishonest! What becomes of the old models, anyway, Kelton?"

"Where are the snows of yesteryear?"

"That's true. Where are they? But if they had their rights they'd not be forgotten, these models. Their names ought to be carved on the statues alongside the sculptors'. As well omit an actress's name from a playbill. And now even I can't remember her name."

Kelton looked at him with an amiable, condescending smile.

"So you are a little surprised?" he said.

"Surprised? I'm thunderstruck! You can't realize what you've done for me!"

He wrung the curator's hand so heartily that Kelton winced. Then a silence ensued, Harbeson staring at the statue, Kelton feeling very much out of place. The sculptor, the statue, and he were three—a crowd.

"If you'll excuse me, sir, I'm needed in the office. I'll leave you alone with her."

Harbeson absently assented. "Thank you, Kelton. I won't detain you."

When Kelton was gone Harbeson remained leaning on the pedestal, gloating over every plane, every profile, musing on every muscle and tendon. His very hands remembered their former paths and he modeled the enveloping air with a kind of sensuousness.

He was too deeply engaged to notice that Mrs. Flannery was still in the room. He did not hear the swish of her brush, nor her heavy breathing, as she agonized about at her penitential trade. Finally, with such a rush of affection as the father of the prodigal felt when he saw his boy on the hills, Harbeson bent forward and kissed the home-come statue on the bewitching mouth. The lips of stone seemed to warm and respond, as if her soul came back to his. He bent his head on his hands and wept, the dry-eyed, silent grief of a man who has forgotten how to cry.

There Mrs. Flannery found him when she made the last circuit. As she worked round the base of the pedestal she was confronted by the same troublesome pair of feet. She rapped the tiles warningly, with no effect. Coughed. No effect.

"Excuse me, sor," she said. "I say, excuse me, sor, but I—I've got to finish this job."

No answer. She tapped Harbeson's foot with the edge of her scrubbing-brush. He looked down in a daze.

"Good heavens! Where did you come from?"

"Sure, and ain't I workin' here the lasht half-hour? Would you excuse me just for wan minyute?"

Reluctantly Harbeson moved away, went into the embrasure of a window, and gazed out, not at what he saw, but at what he dimly recalled.

Mrs. Flannery polished to a radiance the last inch of floor. Then she sat back on her heels with a sigh of relief, rubbing her weary back. She noted a fleck of plaster on the pedestal before her, scraped it with her finger-nail, dabbed it with a damp cloth, decided that the whole pedestal needed attention. Beginning at the base, she worked her way round and round it, with her customary spiral progress. She was crooning again:

"And you're welkim all, heartily welkim—

"O Mother o' God! it's you! O Mother o' God, it's you!"

Her wild cry startled Harbeson out of his reverie. He whirled round to see the scrubwoman, in frantic agitation, caressing his statue and wailing like a keener at a wake.

Harbeson turned to her.

"What's the matter?"

"It's meself that's there," she shrilled. "It's me! That's the ghost of me when I was a colleen." Then she forgot him as she clutched the little shoulders of the nymph. "Oh, you heart's child, you! Oh, my dairlin' that you are! It's too cold here for the likes of you." She whipped off her apron and covered the chill marble.

"Don't do that!" snapped Harbeson, as much out of his head as she, and he snatched the cloth away.

The woman struggled for it. "It's me, I tell you. I posed for that. I wint hoongry and cold while the artist sculped it. Lord love him, he was that poor."

Harbeson stared at her in angry incredulity.

"You posed for that? You! Who are you?"

"Mrs. Michael Flannery."

"That wasn't her name. You can't fool me."

"I'm Peggy O'Donnell that was."

Harbeson's face lighted up as the name rekindled his memory. "That's her name. But you—you're not Peggy."

He forgot even to conceal his contempt; but she met it with unresisting meekness.

"No, but I used to be. Now I'm only old Mrs. Flannery, the scrub. But I was like this once, and he told me it didn't do me justice, at that. He loved me, he did. And now look at me!"

The contrast was sublimely ridiculous, unendurable. Harbeson would not have it.

"Don't you dare to tell me you're Peggy O'Donnell!"

"The divil fly away wit' you, what would you know of it?"

"I am the man that carved this statue!" Harbeson answered, with the pomposity of achievement.

Now it was Mrs. Flannery's turn to scoff.

"You—you an artist? A prim, old, pinched-up spalpeen like you, an artist? Why, he had long hair wit' curls—they were always droppin' over his eyes; and he wore a dirty old velvet coat, and a string tie that looked like he slept in it. And he had a young, smilin' way— and the two eyes of him! You him? Why— But listen, now; if you're the man you can tell me how it all came about."

Harbeson was too much unnerved to resent the insinuation. He ransacked his memory.

"Well, Peggy O'Donnell was the daughter of a scrubwoman. Peggy was a beauty. I asked her to pose for me. But she'd only blush and say, 'No.' Finally she consented just to wear a low-necked gown."

"For the bust of a society leddy," Peggy interrupted.

"Who was too busy to pose every day," Harbeson added.

"And he married her afterward," said Mrs. Flannery, darkly.

But Harbeson did not hear, in the onrush of his thoughts. "My teacher gave me a block of marble. I saw a statue in it. I made Peggy see it. She got excited, too. So I put off finishing the bust of the rich woman—though I needed the money."

"He did need it," said Peggy, stubbornly clinging to the third person.

"And I asked Peggy to pose for the statue. But she wouldn't. I implored her. But she wouldn't."

"Irish colleens is wild things, but they have clane hearts."

"I told her it was for the cause of art and beauty, but she wouldn't pose."

"That I wouldn't."

"Then I begged her for the sake of my ambition. And she cried a little. But she wouldn't. And then I said, 'For the love of me, Peggy, will you?'"

"And I did. For the love of—of him."

"I remember now how scared she was, how she hid and begged me not to make her pose; but finally she came out from the screen, hiding her eyes and drawing her hair about her. And she was like—all the beauty in the world, like music for the eyes. And she blushed so hard."

"I'm blushin' now to think of it," said Mrs. Flannery, in a voice too low for him to hear.

"But I told her there was no reason for her to blush. It was the noblest use a woman could make of the beauty God gave her. And then I began the statue."

"Go on; you're remimberin' it right. But are you remimberin' annything of the money?"

"The money? Oh yes, Peggy wouldn't take it. And there was mighty little left. And that gave out, and I had a hard scramble for food."

"It was hungry we used to go in thim days. But what did we care? We was young, the both of us."

"And it grew cold, too. And I couldn't keep up a

good fire. But Peggy insisted on posing. And the last day— But if you're Peggy, you'll remember."

He stopped short, defiantly—and Mrs. Flannery caught the torch from his hand and ran on:

"You—he was finishin' it, workin' like one gone mad. And he forgot the time—forgot me—forgot the cold. And I waited there, unwillin' to spake a word to wake him, and I grew colder and colder. Faith, I turned blue! And I shivered so he would have noticed it, only it grew darker and darker. It was that that he noticed first— the darkness. He worked till he couldn't see; and thin he yells—I can hear him now: 'Peggy, it's finished! it's finished! we're immortal, you and me!' and thin—if you're the man, you'll not be after forgettin' that."

Harbeson took up the relay. "All the answer I got was a little sigh. I ran to Peggy—and she had fainted away. I wrapped her up in some costumes and blankets. Then I kissed her, and we were both sort of crying and laughing at the same time."

"Yes, and thin?—and thin?"

The scrubwoman's face was illumined as if she stood in a sunset. But Harbeson did not see her; he went on:

"And then I ran out and borrowed some money of a friend, and Peggy and I blew ourselves to—"

"A table dee hote! wit' wine!"

"That's right. We were young and we were crazy, and we loved each other. What else mattered?"

Blinded with the far focus of his eyes, he saw only the mirage of Peggy, and his groping fingers caught the gnarled knuckles of Mrs. Flannery in a clutch of rapture. The scrubwoman's ancientness fell from her and her dusty heartstrings jangled like an old harpsichord. But when her eyes opened she looked down at her corded

299

forearms. She was wrenched back from the clouds and she groaned.

"For the love of Heaven, mind what you're doin'! If annybody should see us what would they say of you? Oh, and I was almost thinkin' I was back in thim days, and whin I wake up—look at me!"

Harbeson's mood was too tender to acknowledge her crudities. He smiled at her gently and answered:

"But look at me! I think I've drifted farther away than you have, Peggy darlint."

"That's what he—what you used to call me," she murmured, with a strange radiance among her features. Harbeson felt the glow of this Indian summer, and he groaned aloud.

"If I could only have sold that statue I should have put your beauty into a hundred masterpieces, Peggy. Why would nobody look at my work? And I got poorer and poorer. And that rich woman came back to have the bust finished, and—and I married her, Peggy."

"It's well I know that. Didn't I go away and throw meself in the river the same night."

"No! No!" he cried with a tremor of dread. "What a dog I was! I never dreamed of that."

"Don't fret over it now," Peggy smiled, all motherly. "Sure and I didn't drown—more's the pity. Somebody fished me out and brought me back to life. I come nearer goin' to jail than to heaven, for the attimpt at suicidin'. But the judge gave me a solemn tahk and let me go whin I promised not to try it again. But I couldn't stand the sight of a stoodio anny more. I hated the word artist—thin. I went back to me own kind—coal-heavers and the like of that. It was thin I met Flannery."

"And he married you?"

"Yis."

"It was like Venus being married to Vulcan."

"Venus! Humph! It wasn't long that I was a Venus after I took to supportin' Flannery. He bate the Venus blood out o' me."

"He beat you! He dared to beat Peggy O'Donnell!" Harbeson gasped, unable to believe.

Peggy laughed. She raised the lock of hair and showed the scar.

"Not with his fists only," she said.

"Where is he? I could kill him for that!"

"You'll have to kill the dead, then. Sure and whisky got to him before you, only a short time ago."

"And he left you nothing?"

"Nothing but a little more room and a chance to spind me own earnin's."

Harbeson's head drooped under a load of shame as he realized what his own neglect had meant to the goddess of his youth. He felt guilty of a crueler crime against her than anything Flannery had done.

As he sat bent with the weight of remorse Mrs. Flannery studied him. The incense of remembered dreams faded from her mind. Harbeson became once more the capitalist; she once more was Mrs. Flannery.

"I've loafed long enough," she said, briskly, picking up her scepter, the mop. "I must get on wit' me scrubbin'. Good-by to you, sor."

Harbeson reached out and caught her arm impulsively.

"You'll never scrub again, Peggy—never! It's pretty late in the day for me to try to make up to you for all you've lost, but I'll do my best. You shall have everything now that you ought to have had then. I couldn't buy it for you then, but I can now. And I'm going to see that you never want for anything more, Peggy O'Donnell."

LONG EVER AGO

She looked at him with bewilderment. Her eyelids clenched tightly, but big tears welled through them.

"I shall never want for annything more, did you say? Oh, sorra the day! Can you get me back me youth, and the beauty I'm after losin' so long ago? Can you?"

He drew her to the pedestal where the little nymph crouched in her ambrosial perfections. He said:

"They're here, Peggy—your beauty—my love—our youth. We three were all young together, and now you and I are—what we are, Peggy. But she'll be smiling just like this when we are dust in our graves. Art is immortal youth, Peggy, and eternal love. I'm going to carve your name here alongside of mine. And when this old city falls in ruins they'll carry our little nymph to some new city, and she shall be young and slender and smiling and beautiful—for our sakes, Peggy darlint, for ever and ever and ever. Amen!"

This was a trifle abstruse for Peggy, but she had her own joy of the thought, for she said:

"I had no childer by Flannery, exceptin' two poor little sickly waifs that died in their cradles—praise be! I'd kind o' like to think that this is our child—yours and mine—and will live long after us—always young, always like me whin I was Peggy O'Donnell—and beautiful—and you loved me."

THE END

www.ingramcontent.com/pod-product-compliance
Lightning Source LLC
Chambersburg PA
CBHW021953010726
47494CB00003B/721